Martha Grimes lives in Washington DC and visits England regularly to research her internationally best-selling Richard Jury novels, all of which are available from Headline and have been widely praised:

'Notable for its . . . authenticity and for the cast of delightful eccentric characters' *Publishers Weekly*

'A good puzzler' *Manchester Evening News*

'Grimes is gifted at exploring the private, sometimes horrifying yet utterly mundane thoughts of ordinary people' *San Francisco Chronicle*

'Martha Grimes is a real find' *Evening Standard*

D1407419

Also by Martha Grimes and available from Headline

The Horse You Came In On
The Dirty Duck
Jerusalem Inn
I am the Only Running Footman
The Five Bells and Bladebone
Help the Poor Struggler
The Deer Leap
The Old Fox Deceiv'd
The Anodyne Necklace
The Old Silent
The Man With a Load of Mischief
The Old Contemptibles
The End of the Pier
Hotel Paradise
Rainbow's End
The Case Has Altered
The Train Now Departing
Biting The Moon

The
Lamorna
Wink

A Richard Jury Novel

Martha Grimes

HEADLINE

First published in hardback in 1999
by HEADLINE BOOK PUBLISHING

First published in paperback in 2000
by HEADLINE BOOK PUBLISHING

10 9 8 7 6 5 4 3 2

ISBN 0 7472 6841 X

Typeset by Avon Dataset Ltd, Bidford-on-Avon, Warks

Printed and bound in Great Britain by
Clays Ltd, St Ives plc

HEADLINE BOOK PUBLISHING
A division of the Hodder Headline Group
338 Euston Road
London NW1 3BH

www.headline.co.uk
www.hodderheadline.com

To my cousins, Joanna and Ellen Jane,
and in memory of George and Miles

Oh!
My name is John Wellington Wells,
I'm a dealer in magic and spells,
In blessings and curses,
And ever-filled purses,
In prophecies, witches, and knells.

—Gilbert & Sullivan,
The Sorcerer

Contents

Part I

Do You Remember?

1

Still wearing his cabby's cap – he ought to put it in his act, this cap, because it looked so unlike what a magician would wear – Johnny was sitting at the gaming table palming cards. He brought the Queen of Hearts to the top of the deck again and again, as if it were marching right up there of its own volition.

It was dead simple; it always astounded him that people couldn't suss it out. Magic was kind of like murder or like a murder mystery: distract, dissuade – that was the way. Put a clue here and at the same time call attention to something quite different over there. The way a magician uses his hands. Keep looking at one hand and so will your audience. This leaves the other hand free and offstage.

He shut his eyes and leaned his elbows on the gaming table. Except for the trunk that sat in the window alcove behind him, the gaming table was the most interesting piece of furniture in the cottage. His Aunt Chris had inherited it, along with a few other pieces, from her own aunt's estate. It was fascinating; it gave the place that 'Vegas look', Chris was fond of pointing out. The table was large and round and covered in green baize. All around it were small drawers in which you could keep cards, chips, or whatever.

Johnny began to polish the slick card, *la carte glissée*. He liked the sound of it. *La carte glissée*. He stuck it back in the deck, pressed the deck with his thumb, and felt the break. Then he fanned out the cards and looked for the break. There was the slick card. A handy card for different tricks.

Chris looked a lot like his mother. They looked alike, but they weren't alike. His mother had taken off years ago to nowhere. His father was dead.

This is the way life is, thought Johnny, slipping the King of Clubs to the top. Life is violent reversals in a nanosecond.

Turn your head, and you've lost it.

Blink, and it's past you.

Wink, it's gone.

2

'Just bring me a pot of poison,' said the elegant man, replacing the Woodbine Tearoom menu carefully between the salt cellar and the sugar bowl.

Johnny's face was straight as he wrote it down. 'For one?'

The elegant man nodded. 'And a pot of China tea for me. Oh, yes, and be sure to bring a plate of scones.' Melrose checked his watch. 'She probably got lost.'

Johnny wrote down *China tea, scones*. 'One China tea, one poison, one scones.'

'Might as well make that two cream teas. Since we're in Cornwall, we can't pass that up, can we? And better make sure the pastry plate's always within arm's reach.'

Johnny wrote down the order, nodded. 'I'll hold up on the scones; wouldn't want them to get cold. Until your friend gets here, I mean.'

'Uh-huh. The poison's for her.'

'She must be a real treat.'

In the act of polishing up his specs, the elegant man gave him a long look. (A long green look, Johnny would

say, if he ever had to describe it. Some eyes he had.)
    'Oh, she is.'

The Real Treat came quickly through the door of the
Woodbine Tearoom with the wind and the rain at her
back, pushing, pushing, as if the weather bore her a
personal grudge.

    The Real Treat removed her cape, shook it to displace
the raindrops from her person to someone else, and
succeeded, a goodly number of them landing on Melrose
Plant's face.

    Then the Real Treat sat herself down and waited for
Melrose to put the tea in motion.

    Melrose was relieved of thinking up conversational
gambits because the lad (the quipster) was back, as fast
as if he'd arrived by skateboard. Melrose was grateful.
Although he did wonder, who is this boy? Tallish, dark,
quite handsome, mid-teens maybe? Probably had to peel
the girls off; they'd stick like limpets. Confident air –
that was certain. He wore the white apron without
appearing to feel silly. God, most boys his age wouldn't
be caught dead waiting tables in a tearoom, much less in
an apron.

    'Madam?' He gave Agatha a quick survey: bird's-nest
grey hair, brown wool suit, ankles like small tree stumps.
'The gentleman suggested separate pots, the full cream
tea; that's scones and cakes, double cream, and jam.'

    Agatha brightened. 'Why two pots, Melrose?'

    Melrose shrugged, unwilling to solve the little
problem.

    The boy answered. 'He thought you might want a

different kind of tea. Instead of black tea, an oolong perhaps?'

This lad, thought Melrose, spends a lot of time in fantasyland. He wished he could accompany him now that Agatha was here, but youth has wings and age is shackled. How she had found out he was coming to Cornwall, who had spilled the beans, Melrose was still trying to work out. At least she didn't know his *reason* for coming here.

He had seen the property advertised for rent in *Country Life* and had, on the spot, rung the estate agent Aspry and Aspry and made an appointment with a Mrs Laburnum to see the house in three days. He had booked his first-class seat on the Great Western from Paddington, London, and felt mightily pleased with himself that he'd acted on impulse for once. 'Something I seldom do,' he had said (smugly) to Marshall Trueblood as they sat drinking in Long Piddleton's favourite pub – that is, in Long Piddleton's only pub – the Jack and Hammer.

'You?' Trueblood inhaled his drink and started coughing. When he stopped he said, 'That's *always* what you do. You hardly do anything that *isn't* impulsive.'

Melrose sat back, surprised. 'Impulsive? Me?'

'Well, for God's sake, it wasn't *I* who suggested going to Venice that time when Viv-Viv had set the wedding date for marrying Dracula.'

'Oh, for heaven's sake, that's totally different, *totally*. That's just – you know, like joking around. I'm talking about doing something suddenly, such as packing up and going to Ethiopia. Something one does with hardly a moment's thought.'

'How much thought did you give to telling Vivian that Richard Jury was getting married and she'd better hotfoot it back home? All of ten seconds, if memory serves me.'

'Wait a minute, wait a minute. That was your story; you invented it.'

'No, I didn't. Well, maybe I did. All right, then. How about the time you—'

Melrose leaned across the table and clamped his hand around Trueblood's Armani tie and tugged. 'Marshall, what's the point of this? What?'

'Nothing. There is no point.'

Melrose flicked the tie back against Trueblood's pale yellow shirt. He looked, as always, sartorially perfect, a rainbow of rosy tints and amber shades.

'Except of course to point out you're totally impetuous. The only reason you think of yourself as one who carefully plans his moves and maps things out beforehand is because you hardly ever do anything anyway – what, what? – there are the times you've helped out Superintendent R.J. Talk about impetuous! Ha ha! Whenever Jury beckons, you're off like a teenager on skates.' Trueblood shot his hand out and made *whoosh*-ing noises. Then he asked, 'Where is Jury, anyhow?'

'In Ireland.'

'North? South? Where?'

'Northern Ireland.'

'God, why?'

'He was sent there on a case.'

'Oh, how shabby.'

Melrose frowned, thinking. 'What were we talking about? I mean before . . . Oh, yes. Cornwall.' Melrose took out a small notebook, black and spiral-bound at the top, the kind Jury carried. He leafed through some pages. 'Bletchley. It's near Mousehole. Ever heard of it?'

'No. And can't imagine why I'd want to. Nor can I call up a picture of you there, either. You are not at all Cornish.'

'How would you know? You've never set foot in that county in your life. How do you know what is and what isn't Cornish?'

'Well, for one thing, they're completely unimpulsive. You wouldn't last a week – *ow!*'

Back in the Woodbine Tearoom, Agatha asked, 'What's wrong with you, Melrose? You look a sight.'

Whatever that meant. He smiled and stirred his tea, dropping another lump of sugar into it, and thought of the dreadful train ride he'd just taken from London. He had been looking forward to it; he enjoyed the anonymity of a train – no one knowing who you are, where you're going, anything.

Well, he could stuff the anonymity back in his sock drawer. No chance of that.

Melrose had not climbed aboard a train in some time. The first thing he asked of the conductor was the location of the dining car. The conductor had said, oh, no, sir, no dining cars any more. But someone'll be

9

round in a minute with sandwiches and tea. Thank you, sir.

One illusion shattered. No lolling about over your brandy and coffee and a cigar at a white-clothed table any more. And the old compartments, where if one was lucky one might be the only passenger or, luckier, would meet a mysterious assortment of others. The outer aisle, where one could lean against the railing and watch the green countryside flash by. Sometimes he thought the only reason trains had been invented was for films. *Murder on the Orient Express*. It would be fabulous to be here in this insular, sinister, almost claustrophobic atmosphere when a murder was committed.

Or just observe those two youngish gentlemen, leaning towards one another, quietly talking. Scheming. *Strangers on a Train*. They could be exchanging murders.

Or that old grey-ringleted lady he had passed, knitting, he would soon see on a stretcher being borne from the train at a stop up the track—

The Lady Vanishes!

These days he was always waxing nostalgic – old films, old songs, old photographs. In this Hitchcockian reverie he did not see her coming, did not register her presence until he heard, 'What on earth are you looking so squinty-eyed for, Melrose?'

He was yanked thus from his reverie with such a vengeance, he dropped his paper and his mouth fell open and the hairs on the back of his neck stood up. 'Agatha!'

Throw Momma From the Train!

★ ★ ★

If ever there was an antidote to nostalgia, it had just burst through the door of the Woodbine Tearoom.

It put him in mind of another old film he had seen on late-night TV called *The Uninvited*, the 'uninvited' being a ghost who hurled back doors, laughed and sang, and presented its unseeable self to the horrified young heroine.

Unfortunately, his ghost was seeable.

For the last thirty-six hours she had accompanied him in his hired car round the bottom of the Cornwall coast. He had kept putting off the estate agent who was to show him the property, waiting for Agatha to find some entertainment other than himself that would keep her busy for half a day. He certainly did not want her around when he viewed the house, casting her accursed shadow over it. To say nothing of her endless carping. *You won't want this, Melrose. Look at that thatch; you'll be needing a whole new roof. Whatever would you do with all this rocky land? No, Melrose, it won't suit.* Et cetera, et cetera.

Fortunately, the young lad's arrival with the tea broke into these morbid reflections. The boy held up one pot, asking, 'Regular tea?' and Melrose smiled as he tapped his own place mat. The waiter set the other by Agatha's hand. Then he brought the tiered cake plate from the window embrasure and set that on their table also.

Melrose watched him stop at a neighbouring table, say something, move to another table and another. The Woodbine was small, but it was crowded. He worked the room as smoothly as any politician.

In a few moments, leaving Agatha to the scones and

double cream, Melrose rose and walked over to the cash register where the lad was ringing up bills. (He appeared to be both the serving end and the business end of this place.)

The lad smiled broadly. 'Tea okay?'

'Fine. I just wondered, do you have any free time during the day? I'm asking because I need someone to do a bit of work for me. Wouldn't take more than, say, three hours.' He held up a fifty-pound note he'd pulled from his wallet.

'For that I'd take a dive off Beachy Head.'

'It will be neither that heady an experience nor that dangerous. The lady I'm with, and don't look at the table for I fear she reads minds, is also my aunt and sticks to me like superglue. I need to be rid of her for a few hours, and as you seem extremely resourceful, I thought you—'

'Could take her off your hands.' The boy shrugged, smiled. 'I could do. When?'

Melrose handed him the fifty. 'Well, say in an hour or so?'

'Done.' Holding up the note, he added, 'You trust me with this?'

'Why not? You brought the poison.'

3

The car was a newly minted silver Jaguar with oxblood-red leather seats. These people probably had to impress their clients with proof of the agency's solvency. Esther Laburnum was the agent for this particular property, named Seabourne.

Melrose had seen the picture in *Country Life* as he was flipping past articles on gardening and on the country's 'Living National Treasures', artisans who continued in outlandishly arcane avocations such as thimble-chasing or making rock gardens for doll's houses. Then there was an article on the hunt and its grave importance to the country. The print practically bled entitlement.

The properties shown usually took up a page apiece and as often as not failed to give the asking price; instead, the copy indicated the property's price would be given 'upon application'. This bit of showmanship Melrose imagined was from the 'if-you-have-to-ask' school. Melrose didn't. He'd torn the page from the magazine and gone to the telephone.

That had been several days ago, and he was pleased

with himself for undertaking to see the real thing. He discovered now, as he stood looking at it, that the picture of Seabourne hadn't done it justice. But, then, it would be quite impossible to capture the atmosphere, the slight menace, the rather edgy romanticism that the place stirred in him. He told himself he was being overimaginative. It did no good.

Architecturally, the house wasn't especially imposing. It was Georgian, built of grey stone that worked as a kind of camouflage, making it fade into the land and woods around it. It sat on a cliff, a craggy rock-strewn promontory above the sea. It had been this setting that particularly appealed to him, as it surely would to anyone with an ounce of romance in him. The whole prospect – house, woods, rocks, sea – looked drained of colour, which added to the romance. If a grim-faced chatelaine in black to her ankles had opened the heavy oak door, it would have added even more. Melrose was fully prepared to be swept away.

But it was Esther Laburnum of Aspry and Aspry who swept back the double doors to the largest of the reception rooms (there were three) with a flourish, saying, 'There!' in a pleased-as-punch tone suggesting she had just worked some sleight of hand and had called up a fully furnished room, right down to the pictures on the wall.

Three of the walls were papered in a serene grey and the fourth, with a fireplace at its centre, was given over to shelves for books and niches in which were displayed various pieces of sculpture: Etruscan heads, marble busts. A mahogany sideboard, flanked by walnut armchairs, sat beneath a portrait of an undistinguished old man with a churlish look that said he'd sooner be anywhere at all other than sitting for his portrait. The hound at his feet sported a similar look.

Except for the sculpture, nothing else suggested any interest in the exotic; the room was as English as English could be. Chairs and sofa were covered in linen and chintz, patterns of bluebells and roses or intertwining ivy and hollyhocks. One of the chairs was drawn up to a kidney-shaped writing table with marquetry inlay. Against one wall between long windows was a campaign chest, a fine example of its kind.

'Isn't it lovely?' trumpeted Esther Laburnum. She was a large woman with a boisterous voice, the sort that carries through a restaurant and condemns the other diners to hearing its business.

The room looked so lived-in, thought Melrose. It was as if the occupants, hearing the approach of Mrs Laburnum's Jaguar, had decided to run and hide.

'Is the rest of the house this comfortably furnished?' When she assured him it was, Melrose said, 'But the owners have left so many of their personal belongings behind.' He nodded towards the portraits and pictures.

Esther Laburnum agreed but said the house was on the market when she'd joined Aspry and Aspry. It had been on the market for some time now, and she hadn't known the owners. She was new to the area. 'In any event, the owners are apparently open to letting it or selling it or some combination of both. I mean, you might want to rent it for a while to see how you got on.'

They walked from the living room to the dining room,

in which stood a twin-pedestal dining-room table and two sideboards opposite each other on facing walls. If he pulled out drawers and opened cabinet doors, he was sure he would find silver, napkins, china.

From there they went to the study. Floor-to-ceiling bookshelves lined three walls. In front of one a refectory table of English oak stood upon a carpet that Melrose thought he recognized as Turkestan (a payoff of those countless hours spent being taught antiques by Marshall Trueblood). Against the fourth wall sat a large desk, its top covered with the tools of writing: notepaper, envelopes, journals.

It was a smallish and clearly much-used room. One could almost sense the impress of bodies against the armchairs. With the fireplace alight, especially on a day such as this one (rain-lashed, wind-lashed, he thought in melodramatic terms), he felt snug and safe. Melrose walked around checking the many leather-bound or gaudily jacketed newer books; it was quite a library, one appealing to diverse tastes. One end of the refectory table held half a dozen small silver-framed pictures.

'Are these the family?' he asked her, picking up first one and then another.

'I expect so. Would you look at that mantelpiece! What carving!'

Melrose followed his own line of thought. 'I don't understand why people would go off and leave behind such personal things. One ordinarily tucks them safely away in a locked cupboard or trunk or some such place. One doesn't leave them out.' He sounded quarrelsome, as if such behaviour shouldn't be condoned.

Mrs Laburnum answered with no more than an uninterested 'Um', leaving Melrose to peruse this little hoard of pictures and pursue his little mystery. There were four or five people represented here, all informally caught on film. The core group appeared to consist of a fortyish couple, very handsome; an elderly man who looked like the one in the portrait – yes, there was a trace of that squinty look; a pretty little girl of perhaps six or seven; and a little boy, probably a year or so younger, shown with his father on a sailing boat. Several other pictures had been taken aboard this boat. Melrose wondered how well off they were; judging by this house and the size of the boat, very. One or the other of these four was in the other photos with relations and friends. The grandparents seemed to be represented wholly by the old man.

Rarely did Melrose envy other people, for at home he was surrounded by friends more or less like him – unmarried, childless, unattached, really – and if anyone in his circle was to be envied it was he himself, with his manor house, his land, his money. What struck him about the family in these snapshots was that they seemed so hugely happy. Even the old man finally dropped the bad-humoured look. Their smiles were not the camera's but their own. Melrose envied them no end.

'Lovely little family, aren't they?'

He had forgotten Esther Laburnum in his absorption in the pictures.

'So sad about the children. I believe they drowned.'

'Drowned?' Melrose took this awful news almost as he would a personal loss.

'It was all extremely sad. It happened – oh, four years ago. What must have made it worse for them – the parents – was that they were out when it happened. I wasn't here then.' She had already told him this a couple of times. It was as if she were trying to dissociate herself from the house and its owners. 'Would you like to see the upstairs now?'

He told her he would. Yet he hated leaving the father and mother to the hellish knowledge that they hadn't been around to save their children. Obediently, Melrose followed Esther Laburnum (in whom he detected now an impatience to get the house 'viewed' and out of here).

There were five bedrooms, none of which Melrose lingered in, but just glanced around standing at the door. He saw some more framed photographs in the master bedroom and would have liked to have a look at them, but with the agent at his heels like a terrier, he didn't.

One room facing the sea intrigued him. It was entirely empty except for a grand piano. Sheet music sat on the piano stand and lay on the floor, as if a breeze had drifted it there. Yet he detected no draughts; indeed, the house was amazingly tight, given its age and size.

'I *believe* he was a musician; I *believe* he wrote music.'

Melrose heard the emphasis on 'believe', as if she didn't want to take the responsibility for supplying incorrect data. He walked over to look at the music on the piano stand. He agreed with her. 'This looks newly composed – was, I mean, before they left.' Melrose played no instrument, but he could read music and could pick out tunes with one finger. He sat down at the piano and did so, painstakingly. It ended right in the middle of a bar on the second page. It was as if the composer had been temporarily called away.

'I don't want to hurry you, Mr Plant. But I daresay you do want to have a look outside at the grounds.'

What he really wanted was for her to go away and leave him here, trying to pick out this music and to hear a whole orchestra supplying the background in his head.

He rose and followed her.

The day was uneven, uncertain. Intermittently, rain stopped and started, becoming more gauzy and misty as the afternoon wore on. Each time it stopped, weak sunlight tossed a veil of light across the gravel, barred by the density of the woodland. The light would have to be stronger to see through those branches.

Melrose was drawn by the rasp of the water and stood on the rocky promontory looking down at the sharp collapse of water spewing against stone. A stairway had been fashioned from the cliff and led down to the sea. Light glimmered on the wet stones. Melrose stood there looking and feeling as if he was getting down to the bedrock of existence. Unbidden, a few lines of poetry came to him about a woman looking out to sea: *Ever stood she, prospect impressed.* Who had written it? Hardy? Perhaps he'd find the poem in Seabourne's library. He was pulled from this reflection by a voice fluting at his elbow.

'There are steps going down to the sea. Right down there, see?'

Melrose turned away from the stark display, which

had suited his mood far more than the voice of Esther Laburnum. 'Yes, I saw them.'

'You have to be careful on them. The rocks are slippery.'

'I hadn't intended to go down there.' He picked up a thin stone and pitched it over, as people will do when they come upon water. He wondered why and picked up another.

'They must have slipped; that's what I heard.'

His pitching arm froze and he looked at her. 'Who slipped?'

'Didn't I tell you? The children. They found them down there.' She sighed. 'Isn't it terrible? Can you imagine such a thing?'

'I cannot. No.' He stood on the edge of the cliff and tried to. He tried to fathom the grief of the mother and father. Having no children, he found it difficult; still, he could imagine himself receiving such news about a friend – say Vivian, say Richard Jury – and imagine trying to live in a world where they no longer were. Even though all of this was indeed his imagining, he was surprised that the sense of loss could cause him pain. But it did. 'How old were they when this happened?'

'I'm not sure.'

Nor did she seem moved to guess. Esther Laburnum, who at the beginning of their voyage round this house had been talkative enough to be annoying, seemed to have decided to clam up completely. Melrose sighed. That was always the way of it: people holding forth until you could have swooned in boredom and then stitching their lips shut when it came to something so fascinating it could hold a deaf man in thrall. Well, perhaps she thought the tragic accidents would jeopardize a sale. Or perhaps her silence was owing to her growing desire to leave and show others round other properties.

'Was that why the owners left?'

'It might have been.'

Blood out of a stone. Melrose wanted to shake her. 'How long has the house been empty?'

'Four years, about.' She had her day-planner open, consulting something. 'No, I'm wrong. Somebody rented the place about two years ago. Decorators, they called themselves.'

Esther Laburnum sniffed and Melrose smiled and turned his attention back to the sea. Standing there, looking down, he could have slipped into a fugue state. It was too much, wasn't it? The house, the sea, the rocks, the stairs, the boy, the girl. Too much. He disliked the thought, but he couldn't help it: the place was irresistible. Had he not already been set on taking it, at least renting it, the story of the family would have hooked him for certain. He looked back at the house again, grey and windswept, and thought he'd been right before: it was like a film set. The girl in the white dress could come rushing out across the grass straight to the cliff's edge. Ah, it was all too film perfect.

They stood, staring down at the rocks. Or at least he stared; a glance in the agent's direction showed him she was looking at her watch. There was always a clock or a watch. Melrose wanted to see the inside again, the photographs, the portraits. He suggested they return to the house.

As if on cue, the sky darkened; the rain, which had stopped, now began to drizzle. Given the house, Melrose wondered if it should be seen in any weather but wind and rain.

'*Melrose!*'

If anyone could drag one from the haunts of memory and romance, it was that voice. He turned to see Agatha timorously making her way towards him. He had better get away from the cliff's edge before she got any closer. But she had stopped; he, naturally, was to breach the gap; she would walk no further; if he wanted to speak to her, *he* must take the lead. Well, of course, he didn't want to speak to her, but he moved forward in spite of that, being a gentleman.

'Melrose!' she called again, as if they were on opposite ends of King's Cross station.

The car she had come in was Cornwall Cabs, driven – much to his surprise – by the same lad who had served them in the tearoom. Melrose wondered how many times the boy changed hats in a day. Right now the one he wore was a cap pushed back slightly at a jaunty angle. He was leaning against the car, and when he looked at Melrose, he smiled ruefully and gave a dramatic shrug. *What could I do, mate?*

Agatha demanded, 'Melrose, what on earth do you think you're doing?'

He didn't bother asking how she knew he was here. All roads led to Rome except for hers, which led to Melrose. Maybe she'd planted some sort of electronic bug on him so she could track his movements. Melrose introduced Agatha to Esther Laburnum, who was put to the task of answering Agatha's questions. The agent told Melrose she had an appointment in Bletchley and had to leave. She handed over one of her cards. Then the two women, of nearly the same age, moved down the gravel, talking all the while.

It surprised Melrose that she'd leave without securing his signature on a lease or other document, given his clear interest in the place.

Agatha turned and started back to where Melrose stood with her driver. The lad stood up straight and pulled his cap down, snapped it down, really, in the manner of a chauffeur presenting himself to his employer.

'You pop up everywhere.' Melrose smiled at the boy. 'Your finding me was, I take it, part of your act?'

The lad opened his mouth to answer, but Agatha did it for him. 'What are you talking about? I told him you'd driven off with someone in a car belonging to an estate agency – who else would be driving people around in a Jaguar but an estate agent? I stopped in at the agency and asked where their agent – Esther there – was headed.'

'I see,' said Melrose. 'It was part of *your* act. Richard Jury could use a good profiler.'

'What is this place? Why are you here?'

He let her question rest on bated breath as he manufactured an answer. He said, 'It's a family seat, Agatha. Haven't I ever mentioned it? Pure chance led me to it.'

'Fate, like.'

Melrose looked at the driver in surprise.

Agatha said, 'Family seat? What family? Whose family?'

'Mine, obviously. It's a branch Uncle Robert probably declined to mention, given we were never proud of the Ushers.' Melrose dug his hands into his trouser pockets and gazed back, over his shoulder, at the great grey pile of stone. 'Imagine my surprise to see the place was up for sale.'

Agatha twitched her light coat further up on her shoulders. 'You're making it up. Well, you can stay for all I care. Esther has offered to drive me back to Bletchley.'

A first-name basis already. That was quick, even for Agatha.

Forgetting the lad who'd driven her here (probably assuming Melrose would pay for her ride), she turned and walked towards the agent's car.

'Apparently,' said Melrose, 'we're exchanging rides.'

The boy smiled broadly. 'Okay with me.'

'I don't know your name. Mine's Melrose Plant.'

The boy put out his hand. 'Johnny Wells. Are you ready to leave?'

As the Jaguar shot down the drive, Esther Laburnum put her arm out of the driver's side window and waved to Melrose, who waved back. Agatha, naturally, made no sign.

'I'd like to have another quick look round, unaccompanied.'

Johnny smiled. 'Can't say as I blame you. Take your time.'

'And I'll certainly pay you for yours.'

'It's okay. I'll sit in the car and read. Never seem to get enough reading time.'

Melrose walked back up the steps prepared to savour the house. He had not seen the kitchen, so he walked to the rear, through a butler's pantry, with wine racks still stocked with Madeira and port. The kitchen was very large, very gloomy, and yet very habitable. Like the rest of the house, it bore signs of recent habitation. Cooking utensils lay on the island in the centre of the room and a large pot sat on the stove.

He had seen the study but not the library proper. He felt the place was really getting to him, seeping into his bones. If he were to turn a corner now he wouldn't be surprised to come face to face with a portrait of a hauntingly beautiful woman who had either died or disappeared, the face in the misty light. Laura. He was close to holding his breath as he entered the library. There he came face to face with a painting of chickens.

Chickens? It hung above the fireplace, a large watercolour of a farmyard and chicken coops and a rooster striding amongst them. Whoever had hung that was in no danger from the face in a misty light. He sighed, not knowing whether he was sad or glad.

The room that really fascinated him was the one on the floor above, the empty one with the piano. As he climbed the stairs he wondered if the house had been used as a set for that film. He walked over to the long bank of windows, looked down at the water smoothing over the rocks, foaming up, receding, and moving in again. He mouthed a line or two of poetry. He would have liked to speak of its 'melancholy, long, withdrawing roar', only Andrew Marvell beat him to it.

He pictured himself here alone, reeling off cascades of notes up and down the keyboard, swaying to the music. He couldn't play the piano. But he could take lessons. That sounded a worthwhile project. How long would it take to learn? It would be worth it to drown out Agatha. He left the room and walked back downstairs and into the living room, the first room Esther Laburnum had shown him. Passing the portrait of the old man, he wondered if he was the patriarch of this family but couldn't quite match him up with them. The others were so smilingly beautiful. He picked up the silver-framed photograph, saddened again by the terrible fate of the children.

The double door opened suddenly. He reeled.

The Uninvited!

No, merely his cabby, saying, 'I'm really sorry to interrupt you. It's just that Shirley – she's the dispatcher – is on about needing the cab to go to Mousehole.' Apologetically, he held out his arms and shrugged.

'Oh, quite all right. I'm finished. Let's go.'

As they drove away, Melrose turned for one last glimpse of the house. 'It's quite a place. I'm thinking of renting it. Tell me, who's the old man in the portrait? He doesn't seem to go with the rest of it.'

'That's Morris Bletchley.'

Melrose was surprised. 'Bletchley? His family is related to the village somehow?'

'I guess there have been Bletchleys here forever.

Funny, as he's American himself. He's the chicken king.'

'The what?'

'Haven't you ever eaten in Chick'nKing? They're all over. It's a chain.'

Melrose thought for a moment. 'I think I've seen them along some of the A roads. You mean Seabourne belongs to him? Mr Chick'nKing himself?' Melrose was a trifle disappointed. Chickens. How unromantic. 'Now I see the reason for that chicken painting.'

'Never saw that, but it sounds about right.' Johnny negotiated a blind turn on the hedge-lined narrow road.

Melrose sighed. 'Well, I suppose it'll keep me from getting soppy. Chickens. Good lord!'

'You don't strike me as the soppy type at all.'

Melrose felt obscurely flattered. He started to take out his cigarette case, but stopped. 'Mind if I smoke?'

'Not me. Long as you give me one. I know it's hell for my lungs, but . . .'

Melrose passed the case and Johnny took one, still with his eyes on the road. Melrose lit both cigarettes and sat back, comfortably watching the dense woods pass by. 'Tell me, how many jobs do you have?'

'Oh, three, I suppose. Four, if you count the magic.'

Puzzled, Melrose said, 'I'd be glad to count it. What do you mean?'

'I'm an amateur magician, that's all. I really love it. My Uncle Charlie used to be a professional. Now he has a magic shop in Penzance. Every once in a while I do an act up at the Hall. That's a kind of hospice-nursing-home place. I'm not bad.'

'I believe it.'

'The other jobs, they're only part-time. We're winding down now from the tourist season.'

'Well, how else could you handle them except part-time? And what do you do in the jobless off-season months? Tutor at Oxford?'

Johnny laughed. 'Not likely. Next term I'm hoping for a grant. Scholarship. It's why I work so much. To pay for whatever the scholarship doesn't cover.'

'What about your family?'

'There's only my Aunt Chris. Chris Wells. She owns that tearoom, you know, the Woodbine. Oh, and there's Charlie, my uncle, but I don't see him much. Chris is partners with Brenda.'

'Brenda?'

'Brenda Friel. She's tops. Her daughter used to baby-sit me.'

'Baby-sit *you*? You sure it wasn't the other way round?'

Johnny laughed, then said more soberly, 'It was years ago. Ramona died when she was only – what? – twenty-two or twenty-three? It was really sad, that. She was pregnant, too.' He reddened slightly at this passing along of gossip. 'Chris told me. Brenda, well, you can imagine. But Brenda and Chris, they're a good team. Chris works harder than anyone I know.'

Except you, Melrose wanted to add.

'I know she'd pay my way through university; she'd pay the whole thing. Only I can't keep taking from her. A fellow's got to stand on his own two feet, right?'

'Which you appear to do admirably.'

'She's really pretty, too,' Johnny said, following his

own line of thought. 'Not very old, either . . . your age, maybe.'

Melrose turned his head towards his window, not wanting the boy to see him smile.

Johnny went on, enumerating his aunt's virtues: amiable, wonderful cook, patience of a saint.

Melrose had never known a person of this age to pay such compliments to a member of the family. It was not that he doubted the virtues of the aunt – after all, someone had provided an excellent role model for this lad – it was the boy's playing Cupid. Melrose was flattered. He did not think Johnny recommended just any unmarried stranger for his aunt.

'It'll be nice if you rent Seabourne. We could all get together, maybe.' Johnny looked at Melrose almost imploringly. 'Have some chicken, maybe.'

They both laughed.

Remember the chickens, Melrose thought, the next time I start going broodingly romantic. Do you remember—

But remember was not a good word to turn oneself away from romantic lunacy.

Remember was a goad, a bully, and a trap.

4

The Drowned Man was a typical country pub, but tipping its hat towards inn, since they let out rooms. It was pleasantly dark and quiet – perhaps a little too much of both, as an inn or pub or hotel calls for a bit of bustle, and it was clear Mr Pfinn, when he had finally appeared to assign Melrose a room, was not the bustling type. Slope-shouldered, wispy-haired, small, and wiry, he had seemed to resent Melrose's taking him up on the offer made by the sign outside: ROOMS TO LET. It was as if Melrose had burst into a cherished private home, ignoring the black wreath on the door. It was a sad and solemn pub. Over the two days he'd been there, Melrose saw no other people about, but there *were* dogs. They had all come to an inner doorway to watch Melrose check in and make his way unassisted up the darkling stairs.

There were five of them, and they liked coming to the door of the lounge bar when Melrose was there. They stood and stared. This appeared to be their chief form of amusement, a bit of cabaret that Melrose supplied. He tried to ignore them, but it is almost impossible not to succumb to a dedicated stare; one simply has to look up. The dogs did not come to the doorway together, but separately. He had identified a caramel-coloured Labrador, an Alsatian, a sheepdog, and two huskies. They came one by one as if each were handing back information to the next in a kind of relay. It was disconcerting.

He had broached this topic of the dogs' odd behaviour to Mr Pfinn. No joy there. Mr Pfinn was, for a publican, strangely taciturn. He was a moper, disliking equally every topic introduced, including the weather reports. Small talk, around Mr Pfinn, was nearly microscopic.

Melrose sat debating where he would have dinner and decided here was probably as good as anywhere. Last night he'd tried Bletchley's other pub, the Die Is Cast. Wondering at this penchant for names of ill omen, he remarked on it to the pub regulars but raised no smiles. So he bought a round of drinks and still raised no smiles. Melrose thought of himself as a fair raconteur and a fairly generous one. His ego really took a beating in the Die Is Cast. There was also a café called the Poor Soul up the street in the opposite direction, but seeing on the menu in the window that 'fish fingers' figured prominently among the selections, he decided against it. Bletchley might be 'village *noir*', destined to become a turning point in Britain's representation in films.

Agatha had rung and left a message that she was dining with Esther Laburnum. He would be dining alone. Oh, happiness! Agatha had put up at a bed and breakfast called Lemon Cottage, which was owned by one Miss Hyacinth Rose, who was quick to tell them she was processing milk into clotted cream and pointed out the pans all round the house sitting atop radiators. This was the real way of making the Cornish clotted cream that tourists went so daft over.

Mrs Laburnum would probably come away from the meal with a quite different view of (the profligate, the irresponsible, the dandified) Lord Ardry from that which she had formed earlier of (the easy-going, well-heeled, thoughtful) Melrose Plant. Indeed, given the dramatic difference between Ardry and Plant, he might have been the Scarlet Pimpernel. There was nothing, though, that Agatha could say that would put Esther Laburnum off letting Seabourne to him; he had the money to pay the rent all at once, if she chose. Also, given the house had been standing there for four years or more, she would probably simply like to get it off her hands.

Throughout these warm and pleasant ruminations before the fire, where licks of flame were turning the grey logs black, the Pfinn dogs had now come to join not Melrose but themselves, one by one to flop down on the hearth like big beanbags, snoring or whinnying in the grip of some dream. Why was it that dogs could fall asleep in five seconds? Mr Pfinn could start a kennel. Another husky or two and there'd be enough of them to run the Iditarod. He enjoyed that image, picturing himself in a fur-lined hooded parka, yelling *mush* as the dog sledge knifed its way across some frozen tundra.

He yawned. Time for the Drowned Man's dining room. He hoped there was a decent bottle of wine. Lord knows there would have to be a decent piece of fish. He polished off the excellent malt and hove himself up from the wing chair. The dogs did not mark his exit except for the quarrelsome sheepdog, who bared her teeth and growled half-heartedly and put her head down again.

'I don't believe it!' exclaimed Melrose.

'Mr Plant,' said Johnny Wells, filling up his water glass, setting the jug down, and whisking both menu and tasselled wine list from under his arm.

'Do you ever stop in this job-crazed life you lead?'

'Not much custom this time of year.' Johnny extended his arm out over the dining room. 'As you can see.'

'Yes. Still.' Melrose studied the menu. Not bad, really.

'The special tonight's the cod with cucumber sauce or apricot *confite*. That's kind of emulsified apricots.'

'I prefer the word *confite*, thanks.' He was going over the wine list with some care. 'This is extensive, I must say. Here's a Côtes-du-Rhône '85, here's a Côtes-du-Lubéron '86, here's a Bourgueil from Domaine des Raquières.' Melrose looked at Johnny over the top of his gold-rimmed glasses. 'Tell me another.'

'What about the Puligny-Montrachet?' Johnny dusted the table a bit, whisking imaginary crumbs.

'Yes, well, that's certainly another!' He closed the list. 'Do you have a nice little Bordeaux? In a bottle, I mean?'

'That's doable. But depends on what you're having, doesn't it?'

'What would you recommend?'

'The cod, hands down.'

'Since that's the only thing you've mentioned, I believe I'll have it.'

'Righto. And a white Bordeaux?'

'Whatever.'

Johnny left for the kitchen. He was back within five minutes with bread and the bottle of wine. And an elaborate corkscrew which he seemed to enjoy working. He got the cork out, poured a bit into Melrose's glass.

Melrose pronounced it excellent – of its kind – and asked, 'Listen, in addition to the chicken king, what do you know about the Bletchley family? Incidentally, is this village named after them?'

'Could be. Way back in time immemorial, there was a Bletchley gave the place its name. Maybe they're descendants, I don't know.' Slapping the napkin over his arm, Johnny said, 'I heard it's a bit of a strange family.'

'All families are strange until they're something else. I was thinking of the children.'

'Oh, aye. That was awful. I wasn't here when it happened; I was away at school. The house has been empty since that. I mean, the parents moved back to London or Penzance or somewhere. There was a spell when a couple of men moved in, always spoken of as "the Decorators", wink wink, nod nod, you know. Gay, I guess. They were quite nice. They did things to the house – decorating, I mean. Moved out suddenly.' Johnny frowned.

Melrose did not ask why. It's written in the script. Somebody always moves out suddenly.

Johnny shook his head. 'That's all I know. I'll get your starter.'

'Did I order one?'

'You'll want it. It's avocado baked with Roquefort. Outstanding.'

'I'll take your word. As in all things.'

Melrose sat looking out over the empty room at the dozen white-clothed tables, each with its small vase of white cyclamen. He turned his spoon over absently, thinking about that house. He would be insane to buy it. If not structurally unsound, it must still have a lot of problems – with the heat or the water supply or the electricity. And there was that eerie atmosphere . . .

. . . which he himself was fabricating, as he'd been doing ever since walking into the place. No, it was not sinister, not macabre. His trouble was that he was bored at Ardry End, and this was Cornwall, this was Daphne du Maurier territory, Manderley-in-flames country.

Johnny brought his starter and then whizzed off again as Melrose was entertaining thoughts of hauntings. Could any serious spirit choose to haunt the house of Chick'nKing? He wondered how chickens were dispatched around here. Tell them they were going for a weekend to Brixton-on-Sea and slam the door of the crate down?

He was beginning to feel sorry for the chickens. Were it not for this divine avocado and Roquefort dish, he'd be unable to eat. If he started identifying with doomed fowl he would be setting his feet straight on the road to vegetarianism. He would have to send back his cod! He hit his head with the heel of his palm, trying to dislodge these morbid thoughts. A little compassion is fine; too much and you wind up calling a dish of peas or potatoes 'veggies'. He could end up carrying a sign in front of poor Jurvis the Butcher's shop. Nobody would boycott Jurvis ('What? Give up my Sunday joint? You must be mad!').

'Something wrong, sir?'

Johnny stood with his dinner, steam rising from the fish and from the divided dish of cabbage, new potatoes, peas.

'No, no. Just trying to get water out of my ear.' He took another swipe at his head as Johnny set down his plate. It looked delicious, the pearl-white flesh just done enough to make it segment. The sauce was in a cup on the side.

Melrose picked up his fork and the conversation they'd been having. 'What about this, John, if they're heirs to the Chick'nKing fortune, why even bother with selling or renting? They'd hardly need the money.'

Johnny thought about this as he filled Melrose's glass again. 'Maybe that's why the fortune got to be one in the first place.'

'I don't follow you.'

'Mr Bletchley might have been a man who understood money. Might be, I mean. How's the cod?'

The cod was silky-smooth and so fresh-tasting it might have leapt from the water and into the pan. 'Excellent. My compliments to your chef.' He saw the smile begin on Johnny's lips, one that lent itself to only one interpretation. 'Don't tell me, please. You've already shamed the entire working world into silence.'

'Only when we've just one or two. Mr Pfinn, he doesn't want to call in the real chef unless there's several customers, which there isn't very often in the autumn and winter. I don't do any cooking in the summer, only when it slackens off like this. I learned from years of watching Chris cook. She's sublime. Really.'

'Chris?'

'You know, my aunt who I told you about.'

'Oh, yes. She owns the tearoom.'

'Along with Brenda Friel. Chris'll be doing the baking right now for tomorrow. About three times a week she makes meringues and scones and things. When I finish here I'll go home, give her a hand.'

'I hope *I'm* not holding you up!' Though Melrose doubted there would be very many things or people that could hold up Johnny Wells. He would find his way out of or around them.

'No, not at all.' Johnny checked his watch. 'There'll be a bit of a floor show in just a few minutes.'

'Need I ask who—'

'I'm a magician, remember?' He sighed. 'I don't have enough time to practise, though. You know where I've always wanted to go? Las Vegas, Nevada. *There's* a place for magic! Siegfried and Roy, ever heard of them?'

'Does sound familiar.'

'I reckon with a name like John Wells, I can't miss.'

Melrose frowned. 'I don't follow.'

'Here you are, such an educated gent, and you're saying you never heard of John Wellington Wells?' Johnny started singing.

> '*My name is John Wellington Wells,*
> *I'm a dealer in magic and spells,*
> *In blessings and curses,*
> *And ever-filled purses,*
> *In prophecies, witches, and knells.*
> *If anyone anything lacks,*

> *He'll find it all ready in stacks,*
> *If he'll only look in*
> *On the resident Djinn,*
> *Number seventy, Simmery Axe!'*

Johnny finished off with a flourish of the white napkin draped over his arm.

'It's showmanship, magic. It's all showmanship.'

5

He called out 'Chris!' as he always did when he got in. There was no 'In here!' called back from the kitchen.

Johnny walked across the small front parlour. The cluttered Tudor cottage was still warm from a fire that had recently gone out. The kitchen was warmer yet. On the long white enamel table and the top of the cooker were trays of freshly baked biscuits and scones. The oven door was open, and another tray of meringues sat inside the oven. Lightweight and sweet, they vanished quickly and magically on the tongue. A bit too sweet for him.

Johnny looked around for some sign of his aunt and found an apron tossed across the back of a chair. He recalled that meringues took an hour to bake and then another hour to cool down. Chris did this by turning the oven off and leaving the meringues inside. The oven was cool but not cold.

Right now it was a quarter to ten. That meant she had probably been here until nine o'clock, maybe even later. That meant she'd just left.

But for where? Nothing was open now except the

pubs, and she didn't often go to them, and never, as far as he knew, on baking night. What she did was to go upstairs, get in bed, and read. She loved to read. She loved routine. *It's just another word for 'ritual' and ritual's always a comfort.* She was right; it was a comfort knowing you were expected at certain places at certain times. That people depended upon you. He could have guessed at Chris's movements on any given day and more than likely been right. It was a comfort, he thought, that she was like that, always right where you expected her to be, a person you could hang on to.

Johnny tried to emulate her in this way. If he didn't appear at the Woodbine exactly at 10 a.m. or at 3 p.m., the old ladies would complain. The girls who served there were a bit scatterbrained and couldn't seem to get in the spirit of afternoon tea at the Woodbine.

It was another ritual that Johnny understood. Chris had once said, 'See, it isn't just food and drink; it's more like regeneration. I'm not sure how it works, but I've seen these customers come in out of sorts and grumpy and leave renewed in some way.'

Although he was sure she wasn't upstairs (he would have heard her), still, he had to check. He went up the narrow, dark, piecrust staircase to the bedrooms above. There were three. His bedroom and her bedroom had a view of Mounts Bay. Although the door was open a crack, he still knocked. Perhaps she was in bed, sick. But he knew she wasn't. The mind tossed up all sorts of flotsam for one to cling to before it started to sink.

He looked at her dressing table with its three-sided mirror, hoping something – spilled powder, open lipstick tube, uncapped cologne – would give him a clue as to where she'd gone, what she was doing. But it was as neat as always.

He sat down in a rocker that faced the window that faced the square. Beneath the moon, the grass was silvery, the square luminous. He tried to think of emergencies. Maybe she'd cut herself and had to go looking for a doctor. Up to Bletchley Hall, maybe. There was always a doctor on the premises there, or so he thought. Or maybe something had happened to one of her 'ladies', as she called them, one of the old people she volunteered to help at Bletchley Hall. An emergency, that must be it. Or maybe his alcoholic Uncle Charlie from Penzance had called her for help. He'd done it before.

Ridiculous. Chris hadn't gone on a trip, for God's sake. Not without leaving him a note.

'Ah, dear, I hope she's not sick, sweetheart,' said Brenda, over the phone. 'Shall I call the Hall? Could she have—?'

Johnny had already done it. And the pubs; he'd called them too.

'How about the newsagent's?' said Brenda.

'Compton's? It's half ten, Brenda. Anyway, why would she go there at this hour?'

'For cigarettes?'

'No. She stopped smoking.'

Brenda sighed. 'Sweetheart, I know for a fact she's sneaked round there a couple of times.'

Johnny had to laugh. Chris's vanishing had not settled

41

on him fully yet. It hadn't reached the point of hardening into fact. It was still fiction, a vaguely alarming story that would of course resolve itself into just that: a story. 'Come on, Brenda. Can you really see Chris sneaking round?'

'Well . . . no, I expect not. But I know you think she's always fine. I mean that she's got no problems. But she does. Same as us.' She said this without a trace of sarcasm, said it with a kind of sadness.

'You're not helping, Brenda.'

'I'm not, am I? What about your Uncle Charlie? Maybe he got tossed in the nick again and she went to rescue him.'

'Without telling me? She wouldn't do that.'

Brenda sighed. 'I just can't think of anything. Would you like me to come round, sweetheart? Keep you company? We could worry together that way.'

He would like it, actually. But saying that made him feel impossibly childish. What he liked about Brenda was that she didn't dismiss other people's sadness, anxiety, or fear with banal sentiments like, 'You'll see; it's nothing to worry about.' So he told Brenda no, he'd be all right by himself. Which he wouldn't.

'Well, you needn't come in the morning if you don't want to, sweetheart.'

'It's okay, Brenda. I'll be okay. Thanks.'

In the way of the suddenly awakened, he thought, things must have changed; they can't be the way they were when I went to sleep. But the conviction that they were, were exactly the same, stole over him as he lay stiffly in bed, still in last night's clothes. He lay there not so much seeing as feeling the morning light, feeling the sea fret pressing against his window.

He rose and padded shoeless to Chris's room. Nothing had changed, as he knew it wouldn't have. He went downstairs, careful on the treacherous steps, and into the kitchen to put on the kettle. Meringues and scones still gave the impression that the person who had put them there would be back at any minute. He filled the kettle, plugged it in. *A cup of tea, a cup of tea, a cup of tea.* As if it were a mantra (and it very nearly was), he repeated the words over and over under his breath.

There was a phone on the wall over the kitchen table, so he sat down and unhooked the receiver to call Charlie. It really was the last thing he could think of.

'John-o! How are you?'

Even if it was only Charlie, his obvious delight in hearing from him made Johnny feel a little better. 'Fine. Listen, Chris doesn't happen to be there?'

Yes, yes she is. Right here; I'll just put her on. Johnny didn't realize how intense was his wish to hear these words until he heard the others.

'No, I haven't seen Chris since that last time she bailed me out.' Charlie's tone changed then, became more urgent. 'Why? What's going on, Johnny?'

'She isn't here. She's cleared off and forgot to tell me where to.' Johnny tried to laugh, but it was more of a choke.

'That's bloody awful. Did you try that place she does volunteer work? I seem to remember once the old lady

43

she was carting back home having some kind of fit and Chris staying overnight. You remember that?'

Johnny did, now. 'I did ring them up, but they hadn't seen her.'

Charlie seemed to hesitate. 'What about the police?'

It was something Johnny had hoped no one would suggest.

'Here, that's PC Evans. Not someone you'd want to have to bet your last fiver on, Charlie. Thanks, though.'

'Sure. And let me know, okay? Seriously. I can be there in an hour and a half if you want me.'

'Yeah. Okay. Thanks again.'

He hung up. As far back as he could remember, he'd never heard Charlie talk seriously and sober.

6

The following morning, Melrose sat in the Woodbine Tearoom at ten thirty, *sans* Agatha, who didn't show. She and Esther must have been on the razzle last night.

He drank his tea and watched John Wells move from table to table. The boy's face, which was by nature pale – handsomely, Byronically pale – seemed to be whiter this morning. His manner was certainly subdued. Melrose watched him move between and around tables – all of which were occupied – with none of yesterday's ebullience, move in a lurching, almost drunken fashion as if he were a little boat pitching in choppy waters. When he stopped, he seemed to be staring at nothing, but then at what (Melrose realized) was something: the door. He looked as if he was waiting for someone to walk through it.

Melrose motioned him over to his table. 'When do you finish up here, Johnny?'

'Soon. 'Bout an hour.'

'Could I talk to you? Could you come across to the Drowned Man?' The pub was directly across the street.

Johnny scraped the hair back from his forehead. 'Sure.' He sighed.

Melrose thought it was almost a sigh of relief.

'Morning, Mr Pfinn,' said Melrose cheerily, as he walked into the saloon bar sometime later. 'Beautiful day, isn't it?'

'Easy for you to say,' retorted Mr Pfinn, as he continued wiping the pint glass in his hand.

Easy for him? It was as if Melrose the tourist, the just-passing-through person, could revel in this fine day and then depart, leaving Mr Pfinn to be plagued by the rest of September. Mr Pfinn did not ask Melrose what he wanted but merely looked at him from under his hedgerow of eyebrow.

Melrose sat down on a bar stool. 'Half a pint of Old Peculier if you have it.'

'Bottled.'

'Fine.'

Mr Pfinn slapped the bar towel over his shoulder and plucked out the bottle from a shelf beneath the beer pulls. Morosely opened it, morosely poured.

'I expect there's a big change in custom, summer to winter, isn't there?'

'Depends.'

Most things do, thought Melrose. 'On what?'

'Why, on the weather, man.'

Melrose thought that was what he'd just said.

Mr Pfinn saw fit for once to elaborate. 'Too many tourists.'

Melrose always marvelled at the ability of inn- and

shopkeepers to bite the hand that fed them. He excused himself and took his half-pint to a corner table, darker even than the bar. Wavering lights pooled on surfaces; slowly turning shadows gathered in corners. Nothing moved but the publican's hand wiping the glassware. They could all be under water.

Half an hour passed in this way, during which time a few regulars entered and sat at the bar, all of them turning to eyeball Melrose. Johnny Wells came in from an Indian summer brightness to the cold shades and shadows of the Drowned Man.

He looked done in, thought Melrose, as he waved Johnny over.

'Obviously, something's gone wrong for you. What is it?'

'It's my aunt.'

Melrose waited.

'I don't know where she is.' He shrugged. The gesture didn't do much to minimize his trouble. He told Melrose about the previous night. 'Something's happened to her, I know it.' Johnny looked everywhere but at Melrose, as if seeing concern in another's face mirroring his own would be too much for him. He'd break down.

'Not necessarily. From the way you describe it, it sounds more like *she* happened *to* something.'

'What do you mean?'

'That she apparently left under her own steam, for one thing. You say there was no sign of anyone else's being there. It might not be your Uncle Charlie's emergency, but that doesn't mean it wasn't somebody's.'

'She'd've called.'

'Hard to believe but there still are places and people that don't have phones or fax machines or even e-mail.'

'Well—'

'As well as you know her, you can't know everything about her.'

'I've lived with her most of my life,' Johnny protested.

Maybe that was what rankled: that his aunt might know someone who was more important than Johnny.

Then he looked up, his expression changed. 'She wasn't at Bletchley Hall either. Or at least that's what the nurse said. I'm not sure she even asked around.'

'Bletchley Hall. Just what is that?'

'It's a sort of hospice-nursing home the other side of the village. Chris helped out there with things like transport, giving rides to her ladies, as she called the ones she dealt with. And other things. Still, that doesn't explain why she didn't call.'

'Ring the place again, then. Mr Pfinn' – Melrose raised his voice – 'have you a telephone in here?'

As if he were taking up a challenge, Pfinn pulled a black telephone out from under the counter and brought it over to the table. 'That'll be a pound to use it; that's besides the call itself.'

Melrose put a five-pound note on the table and moved the phone over to Johnny.

Johnny talked to a different person this time. She hadn't seen his aunt for several days. Johnny asked her to check with some of the others to make sure. Yes. Thanks.

'How about the police? Have you talked to them?'

Johnny nodded. 'They can't do anything, or won't do

anything, until more time's gone by.'

'You mean the Devon and Cornwall police have to wait for twenty-four—' Melrose stopped. Of course. He pulled the telephone closer.

Divisional Commander Macalvie, according to the police constable who'd answered the phone at Exeter head-quarters, wasn't in his office but he'd see if he could find him. In another minute, the constable was back.

'He's gone to Cornwall.'

'*Cornwall?*'

The constable reminded him this *was* the Devon and Cornwall Constabulary.

Melrose ignored the sarcasm. 'Where in Cornwall?'

The constable didn't know. Sorry.

'Is there any way he can be reached?'

The constable's irritation was obvious. Of course he could be reached. But not by the public.

'Could you get a message to him? It's rather important.'

Yes, that could be done.

Melrose gave him the message.

7

Brian Macalvie was not there to take Melrose's call because he was at that moment on a public footpath that stretched between Mousehole and Lamorna Cove, a path that made its rocky way along the cliffs above Mounts Bay and the Atlantic. One would find, if taking this two-mile walk, that the sea air acts as a restorative unequalled in other parts of England, untainted and unpolluted air that results in a pleasant light-headedness.

But the sea air had not served as tonic or restorative for the woman who lay on the footpath. One could not, however, blame location or light-headedness for her death, as she'd been shot twice in the chest with a 22-calibre semi-automatic pistol. There was not much damage done to the chest area. The precise calibre of the bullets had not been discovered, of course, before the police surgeon and firearms expert had been given a chance to examine the body.

The chance was hard to come by.

'Are we stopping here all day, then?' asked Gilly Thwaite. She was the scene-of-crimes expert and the first one permitted the opportunity to examine both the body and the scene. The first one, that is, after Commander Macalvie. Until he gave her the go-ahead, she couldn't even set up her camera equipment or take pictures with the hand-held. It was as if a camera flash would contaminate the scene.

It was extremely rare that any of his investigative 'team' got smart with Brian Macalvie, who had eyes of a near-unholy cerulean blue, a hot blue that could strip you with a look. Maçalvie was famous for his long and inflexible silences when first viewing a body and its context, its *mise-en-scène*. No one was permitted to get close enough to examine anything at the crime scene until he was done with looking. No one in the CID could look the way Macalvie could look. Macalvie seemed to get lost in looking. Until he had seen everything seeable, no one was supposed even to breathe on the crime scene.

They had all been standing first on one foot, then the other, for nearly fifteen minutes while (Gilly Thwaite had said) 'the whole damned scene erodes'. This had earned her another long blue look.

The medical expert, a local doctor from Penzance and not officially with the Devon and Cornwall Constabulary, had been one of those waiting in silence for Brian Macalvie to finish looking, and it irked him no end. He'd objected more than once to being kept here, an objection that fell on deaf ears. Macalvie was now kneeling near the body. The woman was in early middle age and quite pretty, though in a rather hard way that bespoke the backlash of too much makeup over too many years. Same thing for the hair, the bright gold of a crayon. She was wearing a designer suit, now darkly stained, and an expensive watch, but no other jewellery. Near her right hand lay a piece of black plastic that looked like the corner of something. Macalvie took out one of the small plastic bags he carried around and dropped the plastic into it.

The good doctor was chirruping away about his whole surgery full of patients, it being Monday, his busiest day of the week, people having caught the flu or broken bones falling out of boats over the weekend. Weekends were disaster areas in Penzance, he said.

Macalvie couldn't care less about Penzance weekends or the doctor's heavy schedule.

This place on the public footpath was not far beyond Lamorna Cove and perhaps a hundred feet from the nearest house. They knew this because they'd had to leave their cars in its parking area. Two men had been dispatched to go back and have a look round.

'We don't have a warrant.'

'So look around the outside.'

These two were back and telling Macalvie that the place was unoccupied. No sign of life. They could make out that the fireplace in the living room hadn't been used in a while and no wood was stacked there. In a place as cold as this one in late September, one would expect to see fireplaces in use.

'Okay, Gilly. Go ahead.'

They might have been playing at statues till then, for everyone seemed to want to move arms and shake out legs as if numbed. Gilly started moving around the body with her camera.

'When she's through, it's all yours, doctor,' Macalvie said. 'Then yours, Fleming.' He gave the forensics man a punch on the arm. 'I'm sure you'll turn up something.'

'Maybe, guv,' said Fleming. 'But not whatever it was you stuck in that Baggie.'

Macalvie could inspire terror in incompetents (of which the Devon and Cornwall police had more than their share, he was fond of pointing out). Fleming wasn't one of them. Neither was Gilly Thwaite, though he could still have her wishing sometimes that she'd never joined the force. The good ones, the crack technicians, Macalvie kept by him. He smiled ruefully at Fleming and handed over the Baggie. 'Sorry,' he said.

He watched Gilly as she moved in for the close-up shots. He wished the victim could tell him something with a look. But the faces of the dead wear no expression, no matter whether they're looking down the barrel of a gun or at a charging bull. Except in the case of a spasm, which freezes the victim in instant rigor mortis, the expression on the face gives nothing away.

Death is the great expression leveller.

8

Melrose was coming to the bottom of his third Old Peculier while sitting at the bar of the Drowned Man. There had been a very brief debate with Mr Pfinn as to whether he had any more, an argument hardly supported by the fact he had half a case of the stuff on a shelf beneath the bar. Melrose hated this whole business and what it was doing to this seventeen-year-old boy, whose entire family consisted only of an afterthought of an uncle in Penzance and this dearly loved aunt, Chris. And now she was gone.

How had he become embroiled in this boy's life, a boy he had known for only a day?

As if time mattered. Melrose had always believed you could meet and fall in love with a woman in the time it took to put out your hand and say hello.

It disturbed him that he could reach that point immediately where Johnny had landed: abandoned and betrayed. Not that his aunt had abandoned the lad, of course not. No more had his own mother abandoned Melrose; of course she hadn't. Nor his father. But Melrose still loathed public schools and the British penchant for sending children away to them.

There was Harrow. What he remembered most about Harrow was the midnight vigil. He could never get to sleep before then. He'd lie in a narrow bed, crying soundlessly. He hadn't dared make any noise or he'd wake up his roommate – what had been his name? He could not understand this reaction to public school – or, rather, to leaving home. About as independent as a baby penguin, he'd been.

Harrow wasn't the first time, either. Before that, when he was eight, there'd been a boarding school in France. Why in God's name had they packed him off to the South of France? It still made him blush to remember how he held on to his mother that day in Paris – her hand, her skirt, cool skin, warm wool. And his father's embarrassment: 'For heaven's sake, lad, be a man! Get a grip on yourself! Soldier on, lad!' And despite the fact his father would say it, Melrose was trying to do just that: get a grip. So hard was he trying that the voice at his elbow gave him such a start he nearly fell off the stool.

'Plant!'

'Commander Macalvie! My lord, how are you?'

'Me? I'm fine. You don't look so hot, though. Where's your sidekick?'

He meant Richard Jury. 'In Northern Ireland. Side-kicking.'

'Christ, how'd he wind up there?'

'I don't know. CID matter, some kind of inquiry connected with something in London.'

'Wiggins go with him? If he didn't, I could use him here.'

Macalvie's partiality for Wiggins had always mystified Melrose, as it mystified Richard Jury.

Pfinn came down the bar, drawn perhaps by Macalvie's static electricity, the copper hair, the cobalt-blue eyes. Pfinn asked him what he'd have. If anything. Pfinn always managed to make it sound like an imposition.

Macalvie asked for lager. 'So what's this emergency?'

'A woman's missing from here, from Bletchley.' Melrose told him the details. 'It hasn't been your requisite twenty-four hours.'

As he'd been talking, the expression on Macalvie's face changed.

'What's she look like?'

'I don't—' It was only then that Melrose realized her looks had never come up, not around him at any rate. Brown hair? Possibly. No, he did recall Johnny saying she was around his age.

'I can never tell what your age *is*, Plant. You still won't eat your peas.'

'Very funny. I honestly don't remember Johnny's describing what she looked like, except to say she's pretty.' Melrose paused. 'Why does that look on your face bother me? Why, incidentally, are you in Cornwall? I don't expect you're sightseeing.'

Macalvie cleared his throat. 'Where is this boy?'

'Working at one of his several jobs.' Melrose consulted his watch. 'It's probably the cab at this hour . . . or else he'll be getting the dining room ready here.' Melrose called to Pfinn, asked him if Johnny had come yet. No, he hadn't. Not for another hour, most likely.

Melrose asked again. 'So what are you doing in Cornwall?'

'Having a dekko at a body found not far from here. You know Lamorna Cove? It's about five miles away.'

'A body. Male or female?'

'Female. We haven't ID'd her yet.'

There was a silence before Melrose asked, 'How long has she been dead?'

Macalvie took his lager, handed over some money, drank off a third, and said, 'Not that long. No more than twelve, sixteen hours. Pathologist has to do a post-mortem, of course.'

'Well.' Melrose's stomach turned over. That really was the sensation.

'The nephew must have a picture of her.'

'I'm sure he does.'

'Well, I'd rather see that before I show him mine.'

'Yours?' Melrose said, his tone anxious.

'Can you get hold of him?'

'I'll try his house, and if he's not there I'll call the cab dispatcher. There're all of three cars to dispatch.' He turned to Mr Pfinn and asked for the telephone and Johnny's telephone number.

Giving out employees' telephone numbers was not something he did. The same telephone ceremony was repeated as had been that morning. It would cost him a pound.

'No, it won't,' said Macalvie, riveting the man with his eyes, then producing his identification. 'And we'll have that number, thanks.'

9

Johnny heard the telephone as he was coming up the path to the cottage. He fairly flew through the door and snatched it up as the last ring echoed in the air.

Hell! He slammed the receiver down. The phone had become Janus-faced; on the one hand it might be Chris; on the other hand, bad news *about* Chris.

He did not know, for all his worry, how he'd been able to go about his daily routine of the caff, the cab, the pub in such a humour as to be – or at least make things appear to be – perfectly normal. To keep it down, the anxiety, the fear. 'Deny' as Uncle Charlie was always saying. Deny, deny, deny. But this wasn't denial; if it had been he wouldn't be anxious or fearful.

He sank down into a chair at the gaming table and let his gaze wander around from the mantelpiece to the bookshelves to Chris's favourite armchair covered in blue cotton with a design of white phlox. The background had once been blue. It had gone through so many washings and been exposed to sunlight long enough that it was hard to make out the flower pattern. He supposed you could drain the colour from anything over time – the aquamarine from the ocean, the blue from the sky—

Shut it! Johnny ordered himself. This was self-pity and it kept a person from thinking. He yanked one of the small drawers in the table open and got out his cards. He riffled them several times, liking the feel of the rush of the edges against his thumb. He cut the deck twice, pulled out a nine of diamonds, made it look as if he were putting it atop one of the thirds, when he wasn't. He stacked the three parts together, shuffled, shuffled again. *Voilà!* He pulled out the nine of diamonds.

A basic little trick anybody should be able to see. Surprising how little people did see.

He left the cards on the table and started an aimless circuit of the living room. Looked at the fire screen, the books, the basket full of magazines and another of embroidery which Chris scarcely touched, so busy was she. He stopped at a glass-fronted étagère full of cups and saucers ('A Present from Lyme', 'A Memory of Bexhill-on-Sea') and bisque figurines and tiny animals and was taken by the number of places they'd been. Nothing elaborate – no Paris or Venice or anywhere – just little seaside resorts here in England. He stopped at the trunk in the window alcove and ran his hand across the top. Opened it, looked inside. He had to do a lot of work to perfect this illusion.

The rain came and made the day dark and the room darker. He had been in here in half shadow and hadn't turned on any lights. He stood looking out of the window of this cottage that now seemed sorrowful, the objects in it wasted, as if Chris's absence had deprived them of purpose or usefulness.

He turned on a silk-fringed lamp, which cast its buttery glow on part of the room. He stopped at the fireplace and looked at the snapshots and three larger framed photos on the mantelpiece. One of Chris and Charlie, one of Chris and him, one of her and his mother. She looked like his mother and his mother had been beautiful. This was a photographer's posed shot, which was not as alive as the others; these formal posed shots never were. He studied the picture of the two of them, the two sisters. He knew he thought of Chris as a mother; he couldn't help it. So this was like losing his mother all over again.

Johnny rested his head on his arms for a moment, then marshalled what energy he had left and plucked up his peaked cap. He liked to wear it in the cab. Shirley had asked him to take an extra shift this evening because Sheldon was sick. 'Read: hangover,' she'd said.

'Read: I can't, Shirley. Sorry. But I'm going to Penzance.'

Shirley was all right about it; she knew something had happened to Chris.

He put the cap on, looked in the mirror over the mantel, softly sang:

> *'My name is John Wellington Wells,*
> *I'm a dealer in magic and spells'*

But for once it didn't cheer him. He grabbed up his jacket and was out the door.

He was getting into the cab when the telephone rang again, but this time he didn't hear it.

10

'Who else could ID her, then?' asked Macalvie, gulping at his beer as if it were the last one he expected to see for a long time.

'If it's Chris Wells, a number of people. Almost anyone in the village.' Seeing Macalvie about to move to question Pfinn, Melrose shook his head. 'I shouldn't start with him. He'll set your feet on the wrong path if he can. If there's such a thing in your police lexicon as an anti-witness, it's him. Let's go across to the Woodbine. Chris Wells owns it, along with another woman, Brenda something. She could identify her partner.' Melrose looked again at the photo. Whoever she was, she had been good-looking. He wished he'd listened more closely to Johnny's description of his aunt. No, he didn't; he didn't want to be the person who said, yes, that's Chris Wells. He didn't want to be the despised messenger.

Macalvie drained the rest of his beer, set down the empty pint, and regarded it as intensely as he might've regarded a fresh clue. He did everything intensely. He had those blue eyes that turned their surroundings dull and drab and burned away any extraneous matter in

Macalvie's line of vision. Melrose wouldn't relish being
the suspect he interviewed. In the half minute since
Melrose had spoken, Macalvie had leaned straight-
armed against the bar, staring at whatever scene was
unfolding in his mind. If Melrose had ever wondered
what aspect of his job – if any – Brian Macalvie disliked,
showing a police photo to the victim's friends or relations
was clearly it. Melrose was relieved this particular
relation was not around.

'Let's go,' said Macalvie, moving away from the bar
and digging a cigarette from a pack in his shirt pocket.
He still smoked an unfashionable pack and a half a day.
Melrose took out his own case, glad he could share the
sin.

Brenda Friel was such a sweet-tempered woman that
not even the presence of the Devon and Cornwall police
in her kitchen disturbed her. The two men took up
whatever room was left over from an island of butcher's
block table and her big Aga cooker. She was not
concerned about the scones and biscuits she'd just
removed from the oven, only about Johnny Wells.
Thinking that Chris was the reason the police were here
in the Woodbine, she said she was glad they had come
straightaway.

Brenda pushed a lock of brown hair from her forehead
with the back of her hand as Macalvie told her about
the dead woman in Lamorna Cove. Her face grew very
still, that petrified stillness one adopts when terrible
news threatens to topple your world and any movement
will bring it on.

As Macalvie produced the picture, she closed her eyes, then opened them and expelled a long breath. 'No.' She all but whispered it. 'No, that's not Chris.' Relief nearly overwhelmed her, and she staggered back and leaned against the table, upon which rested the scones and biscuits, giving off a gingery aroma that, in its suggestion of the homey and ordinary, seemed to mock them, faced with possible tragedy.

Melrose let out his own breath, surprised he'd been holding it. Chris and Johnny Wells must call up powerful emotions in people. 'That's another thing,' said Melrose, speaking his thoughts. 'Where's her nephew? We've been trying to get in touch with him. He doesn't answer his phone. I know he works at various jobs, but—'

'I think he's gone to Penzance. A relation there just might know something. This is the first time Johnny's ever asked for time off. He's so dependable. Like a rock.' She tore a couple of small plastic bags off a roll; then, holding them, she said, 'That woman, she doesn't look much like Lamorna Cove—' Brenda stopped, then, frowning, said, 'Let me see that photo again, will you, sweetheart?'

Macalvie assumed he was the sweetheart here and again produced the picture.

'I can tell you who it looks like: a woman that lived in Lamorna Cove as a girl. Her name was Sadie May. She worked here awhile. But she married since, anyway. Name's Sada Colthorp, her married name. Believe it or not, that girl married into the aristocracy. I think she married an earl or viscount or one of those.'

The smile she gave Melrose acknowledged him as

'one of those'. Though the smile, he noted, was a trifle ambiguous.

'Did you ask round at the Wink? The pub there? It's probably their one topic of conversation now.' When Macalvie nodded, she went on, 'I expect they didn't recognize her grown up. Of course, that doesn't mean they'd talk to the police about it. People can be so close-mouthed, can't they?'

'They can, yes,' said Macalvie. 'How is it you yourself recognized her?'

'Because she came back.' She looked slightly surprised, as if the police should have known this. 'It was about four or five years ago she came to Bletchley. For old time's sake, perhaps. She worked for us fifteen, twenty years ago, it must be. Ramona, my daughter, was just a little thing then.' Brenda smiled at the memory. 'I never knew Sadie that well, but Chris did. None of us ever liked her that much.' Brenda shrugged.

'And what?' asked Macalvie.

Her eyes widened. They were a pale, swimming blue. 'I'm sorry?'

'None of you liked her that much. I feel an *and* or a *but* hanging on the end of that comment.'

She shook her head. 'Nothing, except Chris really disliked her.' Then, possibly to turn Macalvie's attention to the photo and away from the person in it, she asked to see the picture a third time. She appeared to have no qualms about looking at a corpse, as long as it wasn't her business partner. She stood with the biscuits in one hand and the picture in the other. 'Nothing ever happens around here, and Lamorna's only five miles away, and nothing ever happens there either. But now a woman is missing from here and another found murdered there. I was sure when you handed me that photo it would be Chris I'd see.'

'Thank the lord it isn't,' Melrose, who'd said nothing thus far, put in.

'Your daughter, she'd be in her twenties now? Maybe she could tell us—'

It was, Melrose thought, like peeling a layer of light from her face. The words seemed to have stunned her. 'Ramona's dead.'

'I'm sorry,' said Macalvie. 'She must have been young.'

'Twenty-two. It was leukemia. She'd been ill a long time before we even knew what was wrong with her.' Brenda stopped and took a deep breath. 'She was seven months pregnant, too.' Here, Brenda cast Macalvie a reproachful look, as if to say, the police might not be able to stop women from getting murdered and disappearing, but couldn't they have done something about a dying young mother-to-be?

'I'm sorry,' Macalvie said again and clearly felt it wasn't adequate. 'Really sorry.'

Brenda shook her head, then she handed each of them one of the little plastic bags. 'Ginger. They're the favourite.'

They were still warm. Melrose right away took a bite out of his. He saw Macalvie looking at his bag, curiously, as if anything given him must be a bribe. Then he shot Brenda a smile straight through the heart. 'Thanks. And if you think of anything . . .' He handed her a card. 'You'll let me know.'

'I will, yes. But what about Chris, sweetheart? This Lamorna business doesn't tell us a thing about where she is.'

'No, but it damned sure tells us where she isn't.'

11

Now you see it. The white sign lettered in marine blue was nailed above the door to Charlie's magic shop in Penzance. Johnny really liked Charlie, which Chris said was to his credit, given that they were so different. But he wondered if they really were, the way they both loved magic and illusion. The place always fascinated Johnny, even now, when his feelings were at such a low ebb.

The place had been advertised as being a 'flat with sea views', but the sea view was there only if you craned your neck and got smack up against the window, turned your head sideways, and looked through trees; that way you could see a small slice of the sea.

Charlie had much of Chris's manner, even if he didn't have much of her character. Lean on her and she would never let you down. Try leaning on Charlie and you'd hit the ground. He wasn't very dependable; he was a raging alcoholic and because of this Chris 'cut him some slack'. ('Poor Charlie. He can't help it; we've got to cut him some slack, love.') Yet most people would feel exactly the opposite, heaping on Charlie's head recriminations and reckonings.

They just didn't understand addiction, Chris would say. Neither did Johnny, really. He wondered how it would *feel* to be an addict, hung up on booze or crack or heroin. The closest Johnny had ever got to heroin was Lou Reed's song.

Charlie had shown Johnny a few new tricks – lord, but he was fast with his hands. After he'd put the cards up, he reached under the counter and pulled out a gun. Johnny staggered back.

'Oh, hell, John-o, it's not real. Just part of an act a friend of mine's putting together. Looks authentic, doesn't it?' He slapped it down on the counter and said, 'You know what Chekhov said, "If you put a gun on a table in Act One, it better go off in Act Three." '

Johnny picked it up. 'I'm glad this one won't.'

'Lousy play, then. Come on.'

They'd closed the shop and gone along to the Lamb, where they were now sitting, Johnny drinking ginger ale, Charlie a club soda. Johnny wondered how difficult it was for Charlie to be so close to booze and yet not drink it. Charlie never drank around Johnny, anyway. It shows his regard for you, Chris had always said. Charlie did not know any more about Chris now than he had earlier. But he could understand Johnny's need to talk to him; he and Chris were the only family left. He asked Johnny if he'd notified the police.

'Yes. But it'll be twenty-four hours before they'll do anything.'

'That's to eliminate all the unhappy husbands or wives who've left out of choice.' Charlie was helping sort through the various options and the only alternatives.

'Okay, she either left under her own steam or was taken.'

'It could be a combination, couldn't it? I mean, she could have thought she was leaving on her own when really she was tricked into leaving. Like maybe somebody called up and said I was in hospital, something like that. And on her way she's abducted.'

'Uh-huh.'

Johnny sighed. 'That's pretty melodramatic, I suppose.'

'Melodrama happens. She didn't leave you a note, you said, but remember Tess.' Charlie read a lot of books and spoke of the characters in them as if he and they were on intimate terms. When the name didn't register with Johnny, he said, 'Hardy's Tess, Tess of the D'Urbervilles. The whole tragedy could have been averted if the note from her boyfriend that he'd shoved under the door hadn't gone under the rug. She never saw it. Are you sure she *didn't* leave you a message? Did you check under the rug?'

'No.' Johnny smiled. 'There aren't any rugs near the doors.'

'I meant that metaphorically. Could she have left a message *anywhere* you might not have come across it? Could she have told someone to make sure they told you? That sort of thing.'

Johnny nodded. 'But if she had, they'd have told me.'

'Okay, let's take it from another angle. Forget about the note.' When Johnny opened his mouth to object – Chris would *never* have done such a thing, left without letting him know – Charlie held up his hand. 'I'm just thinking out loud, running down possibilities. Say someone out of the past comes to the door, convinces her that she has to go with him immediately. Now, I can't think of anything in her past that might warrant such an extreme action, but you—'

Johnny shook his head.

'Don't be so quick to dismiss it. Chrissie's had a tough life, tougher than she probably ever told you about.' Charlie had shifted his position; he sat sideways facing the bar, one leg crossed over the other at the ankle.

Johnny watched him. 'If you want a drink, Charlie, go ahead; don't mind me.'

Charlie smiled. 'Thanks, but I'm testing my will.'

'Chris says it's nothing to do with willpower. That's a mistake most people make about . . .' He shrugged.

Charlie was looking at the bar, shaking his head in a wondering way. 'That's Chrissie.'

And in a way it did sum her up; that really *was* Chrissie, who never rushed to judgement, never condemned out of hand, had an open mind and a great sense of fair play.

But she wasn't soft, hadn't that sticky sweet manner that one might expect to find in such a person. Chris could be sardonic and ironic, so that some people thought her too edgy. What a mistaken impression! What she had in abundance was patience. Like the way she treated Charlie. No, you could tell Chris anything and not be misunderstood or judged or told not to feel that way.

'What do you mean Chris had a tough life? Tough, how?'

'She had to put up with a lot. After her mother died, it pretty much fell to Chris to take charge, she being the oldest. I suppose, though, there's some good that comes of that kind of responsibility. Once you undertake it, you don't forget it.' Charlie stared glumly into his glass.

There was a silence as Johnny thought Charlie must have been mourning the loss of a pint. After all, he depended on it, as alcoholics say, 'like a friend, a best friend'. It was perfectly possible Charlie missed beer and whisky as much as Johnny missed Chris. He said, 'She hadn't been gone long; I mean, she'd only just taken things out of the oven.'

Johnny's tone was so dejected that Charlie reached across the table and put a hand on the boy's arm. 'This sounds like hollow comfort, but I bet when we know what happened, after she comes back, we'll be amazed we didn't see it.'

'It's like she just – vanished. As if there'd been some sleight of hand, a huge trick played,' Johnny said.

Charlie smiled. 'Sleight of hand's our stock-in-trade. Given what's going on, you'd better have this.' He pulled the fake gun from his pocket and put it down on the table.

'I thought you said a friend needed it for his act.'

'I've got another.' Charlie flashed a smile. 'Forget Chekhov.'

12

He had crossed the t's and dotted the i's on the lease. He had handed over a wad of money (in the form of a draft on his bank) and received the keys in return.

Melrose was again at the house he was free to inhabit for the next three months, happily without the estate agent following him about or Agatha erupting on his horizon. Tomorrow he would take back the hired car, jump aboard the train to London, go from there to Northamptonshire, collect his Bentley and some clothes, and return and live here for three months, or longer, or less.

How fortunate he was to be rich. He only partly agreed with that glib saying that money can't buy happiness. It certainly made misery a lot more bearable. Money was at the moment freedom to live here, or to live there, or to take a lease for three months and leave after only one.

But that did not answer the question, why was he using his freedom in this way? He had wandered into the large living room and was standing now before one of the long windows looking out over the weedy garden.

He wondered if he was coming up against a midlife crisis and this move was the first sign of it. No, he decided, midlife crises were not an option with him; he was too sanguine. He was simply overpowered by the melodramatic quality of this house and its situation. He certainly was given to regard himself in more melo-dramatic terms. It was quite fun, really, to picture himself standing on a shelf of rock, looking out over the swell of the waves folding over the rocks: *Ever stood she, prospect impressed.* He couldn't get those lines out of his head.

He turned from the window in this smaller reception room and looked at the sheeted furniture, at its ghostly glimmer in what was fast becoming dusk. He moved over to an armchair, took hold of a corner of the sheet, flicked it off like a matador provoking a bull. He then went about removing the sheets from sofas and chairs, wondering where people put the laundry. At home, Ruthven and Martha took care of such things, made them disappear from sight (Melrose's, at least) as if a party of elves had been at work while the house slept. Could he make it on his own? Perhaps he should advertise for a housekeeper. Yes, it would be good to have a housekeeper, not so much to keep house as to bring him up to speed on gossip. Although he would not have wanted anyone like Agatha's char, Mrs Oilings, he thought he could strike a happy medium between capable housekeeper and capable gossip.

He wondered where he should dump the sheets. He considered putting the kettle on (so nice to have all of this equipment provided) but decided to take a long, long walk round the house before tea. It rather delighted him, too, that he could do his own tea and drink it in the living room or library with no other company than portraits and pictures of those absent.

He found himself trying to absorb what traces there were here of the lives of the Bletchleys. Maybe it was because the family depicted in those snapshots had been so beautiful – before the double tragedy – that he wished in some way he could join them.

Melrose's memory of his own father was fitful, fluid and vague. He had not been terribly fond of him, nor had he greatly respected him. His feelings were all for his mother. The seventh Earl of Caverness had spent most of his time riding to hounds and only occasionally taking his seat in the House of Lords – with, as far as Melrose knew, no particular effect on the country or himself. He remembered a distant man, if not an absolutely cold one; Melrose had wondered, when he was old enough to wonder such things, how his mother, a very warm and loving woman, a woman who had these qualities in abundance, could be happy with him.

She had not been; she had been happy, but not with her husband. And knowing this had weighed Melrose down. He didn't really know why.

Nicholas Grey. Melrose had deliberately distorted the image of Nicholas Grey, again without understanding exactly why. Even knowing who and what he was, Melrose still at times hated the man, saw him as an interloper in the Belgravia house. Would it have been easier to accept his mother's affair if Grey had been a seducer, a rotter, and a layabout? And his mother a woman caught in his spell? Or was it simply that the real

Nicholas Grey was none of these things but was instead the sort of man it would be difficult to live up to?

He had seen Grey several times in the Belgravia house, which Melrose had since sold. He had sold the house for that reason – it was where Nicholas Grey had come. The sale had taken place a few years after the solicitor had handed over a letter that his mother had directed be given to Melrose long enough after her death to give him time to get over the worst of it. His mother had been dead for five years when the lawyer had given him the letter. And he hadn't got over it.

He returned to that letter time and again, reading it so often he had worn down the fold so the two parts barely hung together. Nicholas Grey was Irish (the letter said), and it was that which one could say killed him. He had died in Armagh in a skirmish with the IRA. He had himself at one time when he was younger been a member of it, until he finally couldn't put up with what he felt were random and arbitrary assassinations. Grey had been a hothead but not an anarchist. He was a man sublimely caught up in his cause and had the reputation of being a brilliant strategist, a matchless orator, and an inspiration to the men under him. Grey had disliked the aristocracy, not in theory but in fact; he had hated it for what it had become.

What Lady Marjorie, his mother, had done was to trade a fairly amiable and undemanding man born to wealth and leisure for one whom it would be very hard for Melrose, his son, to live up to, a father who had stamped Melrose with a nearly impossible romanticism for which he could find little or no outlet.

He thought she had been wrong to tell him, and yet her motives, if clouded, had been good ones. His mind, he hoped, was large enough to allow for this. His own motives he felt were equally cloudy. He told himself that in relinquishing the title of eighth Earl of Caverness he was squaring things with his nominal father, the seventh earl. But he suspected that what he was really doing was squaring things with Nicholas Grey, though he couldn't say why.

He wondered if it was his vanity, rather than his heart, that had been bruised.

He would much rather weigh in as the real Melrose Plant than as the bogus Earl of Caverness.

13

She had said:

I make no apology for my behaviour (which might strike you as arrogant and selfish), except insofar as you're being made unhappy; I did not want you to read this until some years after my death – when you would be over the worst of it . . . There is so much of Nicholas in you, your looks, your moods, that it haunts me.

She was not telling him '*to unburden myself and thereby place a heavier burden on you*' but to fill in what she saw as a tremendous distance between what he, Melrose, really was and what he had to think he was, '*a gentleman, an aristocrat without a past –*' Melrose still wondered what she meant here—

and an uncertain future, the Earls of Caverness having been unremarkable in their lives and legacies. They were perhaps what people think of when they think of the aristocracy. You do not fit this mould and never will, I think.

Even as a child you showed no interest in aristocratic trappings. You wanted to be a 'plain old fellow' (your words) and go to the local comprehensive school. Your father, of course, wouldn't hear of it; he was, he said, 'scandalized' by the very notion.

Once you went missing for a whole day and we found you in Sidbury on a picket line demanding more government subsidies for the farmers. You carried a sign you had made yourself. Every word in it was misspelled except for 'the,' 'and', and 'HELL'. Your father was mortified.

I asked him if it was because of the spelling.

Melrose laughed. He always did, here.

You were always 'organizing'. You organized the servants, the dogs, your friends, my clothes. The servants you said could all have a better time of it if they were on strike. More money, more time off. (Ruthven told me and with a straight face that there was something in what you said. It was one of the few times Ruthven tried to be witty.)

I don't know what you told the dogs, but I did see you outside by the hydrangea bush, lecturing them. Their behaviour, however, remained pretty much the same.

You organized your school friends, and all of you marched into the kitchen at school to complain about the sticky toffee pudding. You organized me, too: my luncheons, my Women's Reading Club, my days in London, my clothes.

*You always seemed to see a world of possibilities,
things that needed changing, the sort of thing the
aristocracy wanted to keep at bay. Change made us
anxious and uncomfortable. 'We've got to get organized,
Mum. We've got to get organized.'*

It could still catch him unawares, this letter, the con-
creteness of it, which made him live these scenes over
again, or the sense of loss, washing across him like those
waves at the bottom of the cliff. The letter answered
some questions but opened up others: why hadn't she
divorced her husband or, at least, gone off with Nicholas
Grey? He remembered her as a very independent
woman. Had she been stopped by her husband's threat
to keep Melrose? She had left these important issues
unexamined.

Or perhaps she hadn't. Perhaps she felt that the
'important issues' were exactly what she had written:
Nicholas's idealism, the sticky toffee pud, the dogs being
lectured, the sign with the misspelled words.

He must have been very important to her, even more
than Nicholas Grey had been.

Melrose had all but forgotten the drab landscape at
which he'd been looking; he had certainly forgotten the
bunched sheets, but they were now doing service as a
handkerchief he could wipe his eyes on.

Remember, remember.

Here he was, a gloomy person in an empty house
looking out on grey cliffs and sea, wondering what he
was doing here . . .

Just trying to get organized, Mum.

14

He took the pile of sheets into the big kitchen (getting closer, surely, to some meaningful laundry-disposal system). He deposited the sheets by a door that led down to some underworld he had no intention of venturing into unless Dante were with him. He would have made a hopeless detective, if a cellar could cause him such trepidation.

Turning to the making of tea, he took an old tin kettle from a shelf above the cooker, filled it, and set it over the gas flame. He watched it. Would a watched kettle ever boil? He decided not to subject it to this particular laboratory study and turned again to the shelves. Crockery abounded; he saw three teapots of various sizes. Cups ranged from stout white to slender floral ones. From a small market in the town he had purchased the bare necessities (tea, milk, sugar, butter) and from the Woodbine Tearoom had bought several spiced buns.

When the kettle boiled, he poured water over the tea leaves and then arranged everything on a metal tray that he carried into the book-lined study. The view from its window was similar to the one above in the piano room (as he had christened it). It looked out over the broad-shouldered rock, the edge of the cliff, but had not that feeling of suspension above the rocks. If one were given to vertigo, the view from the piano room might present difficulties.

Melrose sipped his tea and ate his bun in perfect peace. How wonderful! Solitude even at Ardry End was hard to come by. Perhaps he was fit for the life of a hermit. Give up all his worldly possessions and live in a hut on a shelf of rock and watch the sunrise every morning. Up before the sun! What a dreadful idea; he shuddered.

He thought of the Bletchleys. He could empathize with them and their painful memories; what had happened in this house was too painful for them to continue here. And yet . . . memories could never be eradicated. Was it even possible that they gathered force from having been torn from a place one no longer came to?

He regretted selling the Belgravia house. He saw that gesture now for what it was: an act of revenge or, worse, spite. Punishing his mother and Nicholas Grey. His memories of Nicholas Grey were even more abundant or, at least, more finely wrought because now they couldn't be diffused.

Melrose tried not to think of *this* Nicholas Grey – of heroism and courage and self-denial – preferring instead to picture him as the snake in the Eden grass, the betrayer of his father and seducer of his mother.

The trouble was, he could not love his father much because he always drew back from Melrose. This did not happen because his father knew the boy was not his son; Lady Marjorie would never have admitted this. Had his father known, she would have had to pay a high price; there would literally have been hell to pay. He would not have divorced her, no. That would have rewarded her behaviour, for she could then have gone immediately to Grey.

What he realized now was that he had renounced the titles not because it was the honourable thing to do but because he hadn't wanted them. It would have been nice to believe that he felt like an impostor, unfair to the Caverness line and especially unfair to his father. He would have preferred to believe he was doing the honourable thing, only it wasn't so. He just wanted to be rid of the Earl of Caverness and be, as his mother had written, 'a plain old fellow'.

15

Melrose was seated at his regular table in the Drowned Man's dining room, trying to stare down the dogs in the doorway, when Johnny Wells slapped through the swinging door of the kitchen with a jug of water and a basket of bread.

'Ah!' exclaimed Melrose. 'We've looked for you at your various places of employment. That is to say, the Devon and Cornwall police looked.'

Johnny took a step back, wide-eyed. He still held the jug of water, slices of lemon floating on top like pale flowers. 'Me? Why?'

'I'm glad you were gone. The police were called to a place – Lamorna Cove, you know it?' Johnny nodded, waiting. 'A woman – *not* your aunt; *not*, I repeat, your Aunt Chris – was found dead, murdered. I was, as I said, extremely glad you weren't here to be asked to look at the police photos taken at the scene.' Melrose went on to describe what Brenda Friel had said.

'Christ! I'm glad I wasn't here too.' He filled Melrose's water glass and handed him the tasselled wine list. 'I was in Penzance. My uncle lives there, and I thought he might know something.' Johnny shrugged. 'He didn't. I didn't expect him to. I'd already rung him up once. I suppose I just wanted someone to worry along with me. And you – *you're* leaving, Mr Pfinn says.'

There was that note of accusation in his tone over Melrose's hurried – and irresponsible? – return to Northamptonshire. He was flattered to be included in those people Johnny chose to worry along with him, and said, 'But I'll be back in no time, within the next few days, as soon as I can pack up a few clothes and my car. I've rented Seabourne for three months.'

At this Johnny looked relieved. 'Good. I'll look for you, then.'

'I'll be coming here on a fairly regular basis for dinner. I'm not much of a cook.' Melrose felt abashed at the truth of this and looked down at his napkin. Was he much of *anything* when it came to looking out for himself? He removed a card from his silver card case and wrote his telephone number on the back and held it out to Johnny. 'If you hear anything about your aunt, give me a ring, will you? I'd truly like to know.'

'I will.' Johnny studied the card.

'This detective, Commander Macalvie, is very, very smart. If anyone can get a lead on your aunt, he can.'

'But isn't his time going to be taken up by this murder in Lamorna Cove?'

Before Melrose could respond, Pfinn stuck his head round the swinging door to the kitchen and motioned to Johnny.

'He doesn't like me being friendly with guests. Do you know what you want?'

'Certainly. Same as last night. The cod and a salad.'

'Wine?'

Melrose opened the list, ran a practised eye down the page (doubting that the Drowned Man could really be host to all of these wines), said, 'The Puligny-Montrachet.'

'Right. Is your friend going with you?'

Friend? What friend? Oh, God – Agatha. Having been Agatha-free for the last twenty-four hours, he had managed to forget her. 'You mean my aunt? Yes, I expect so, unless she's joined the staff of Aspry and Aspry.'

Johnny laughed – not loud, not long – but a laugh nonetheless, before he left to get Melrose's wine.

Melrose sighed. He did not fancy another railway experience with her. But then he brightened at the thought that he would be free of Agatha for three months!

16

Except he wouldn't be.

Melrose could not absorb what she was saying. It was such freakish bad luck that he went blank. This was in the Woodbine the following day where morning coffee was the excuse for collective gossip. The talk was, of course, about Chris Wells's sudden leave-taking. They avoided words such as 'disappear' and 'vanish', feeling them too weighted with dread. 'Up and gone' or 'left without a word' – these were the phrases used, and they were bad enough.

The news had spread quickly; Chris Wells's leaving was the most dramatic thing that had ever happened in Bletchley. Combine that with the murder in Lamorna Cove, and they had enough to talk about for months. The village was aghast – pleasurably so, as Melrose inferred from the buzz going on around him, talk as rich and spicy as the gingerbread and tea cakes.

Not, however, at the table where Melrose sat with Agatha, since death and disappearance took a back seat to anything befalling his aunt. She was saying, 'The flat is quite a nice one and being let on a month-to-month lease, so it should suit me quite well.'

Melrose made no comment. His mouth felt as if it had just got a shot of morphine. But his lack of commentary didn't bother Agatha.

'Anyway, it's only a month, as I'm not sure how I'd take to the sea air, and besides I have much too much business to take care of in Long Pidd to permit me to stay away longer. I'm not like you; you've nothing whatever to keep you from stopping here. And I think it would be good for me to learn a trade. Esther is an excellent agent and will teach me the ropes.'

That what he had said jokingly to Johnny last night about Agatha and estate agents was coming even partly true made him want to laugh himself sick. Agatha, who couldn't sell cod to a cat – Agatha, selling property?

'Since Mr Jenks closed his Long Piddleton branch of the agency in Sidbury, there's been a real gap in the Long Pidd offerings.' Jenks was the estate agent who had once had an office in Long Piddleton. 'That building has been up for rent for ages.'

'That building, if you remember, is next door to Marshall Trueblood.'

As much as she loathed Marshall Trueblood, this announcement didn't appear to dent her enthusiasm. 'I needn't see him; I'll be working. And he spends half his day in the Jack and Hammer, so I shan't be troubled with him.'

Melrose swallowed the taste of hemlock and tried to reason. 'Agatha, *nothing* ever comes on the market in Long Piddleton. Why in God's name do you imagine Mr Jenks left?'

'Obviously, the man wasn't very good at his job. There's the Man With a Load of Mischief, for one example.'

'That's been up for sale for donkey's years. You'll never sell that pub.'

Agatha ignored this. 'There's one of the almshouses. You know how popular listed properties are with Londoners. Long Pidd could do with some gentrification.'

'I also know Londoners would be living next to the Withersby lot. There's gentrification for you!' Mrs Withersby was the Jack and Hammer char and chief moocher.

'There's Vivian's place. She's getting married, or have you forgotten?'

Melrose heaved a sigh deep enough to bring him out of a coma. 'No, I haven't forgotten. But you have, apparently. Vivian's been about to get married for years. She's not going to marry the count; surely that's obvious. She had the cottage listed once several years ago when she must have been a little closer to marriage than she is now. Maybe she just likes an excuse to keep going to Venice.'

'This is just like you, Melrose. The glass is always half empty to you!'

For once, she was right. If he wanted to look at Agatha's being in Bletchley for a month, he should remember it was only a month. And in Long Piddleton, instead of her turning up at Ardry End, she would be turning up at her workplace. *That* would certainly be a boon. Even if she tried to get him to buy the Man With a Load of Mischief, and she probably would.

So the glass – praise be – was half full!

'All I need to do now is return to Long Pidd and gather together a few things. Then we can motor back to Cornwall together.' She jammed up a tea cake and added a dollop of clotted cream.

The glass was half empty once more.

17

'Property? An estate agent? Ouch!' Marshall Trueblood was so enthralled by Melrose's Cornwall story he hadn't noticed his pink Sobranie burning down to his fingers. He dropped the stub in an ashtray. He pulled the dark green handkerchief from its pocket and rubbed at his finger. Trueblood's colours changed with the seasons. Today, he looked molten: dusky-gold French-cuffed shirt, russet-hued silk wool jacket, pine-green tie speckled with fiery little leaves. He looked like autumn in flames.

'She probably just caught a London train,' said Diane Demorney. Then, as if this comment were too much exertion, she yawned. If a yawn could be called 'elegant', Diane's was.

Melrose's look was puzzled. 'Who, Agatha?' Agatha-as-agent had been the last thing under discussion.

'No, this boy's beloved *auntie*. Haven't you been following your own story?'

'To London? What makes you think that?'

Diane looked at Melrose wide-eyed. 'To shop, of course. To buy clothes. You can't buy clothes in *Cornwall*, for heaven's sake.' This reminded Diane of her own, apparently, for she looked down at her white suit. Her clothes were the antithesis of Trueblood's. She always dressed in some combination of white and black. This further set off the contrast between her pearly skin and jet-black hair, which looked carved more than cut. The clothes were extremely expensive. So was the skin. So was the hair.

Diane's gestures were elegance personified, thought Melrose. If only her brain would follow suit.

She said, 'You're making a mountain out of a molehole, Melrose.'

'Molehill,' said Melrose.

'Anyway, I'll bet there are a hundred perfectly easy explanations for all this.'

'None of your hundred reasons will work because she didn't tell her nephew she was leaving.'

Diane took a leisurely sip of her martini. 'Good lord, can you imagine *me* alerting a *nephew*?'

'No, but I can imagine me alerting the Vice Squad,' said Trueblood.

Diane rinsed the olive in her martini and studied it as if checking its marinade status. 'How frightfully unfunny, Marshall. My *point* is that the aunt would be sure to tell him – well, that's *his* story.'

Frowning, Melrose asked, 'Meaning?'

She cocked her head and raised a satiny eyebrow. 'Well, for heaven's sake. Meaning it's the nephew who's telling you this. It's he who says she'd never leave without letting him know. How can he be so sure?'

Melrose sat back, a mite surprised. There were times

when Diane demonstrated a sort of nuanced thinking. Anyway, it was hard to look at her in the same light after her heroics in saving his life. For her, bored heroics, but heroics nonetheless.

'Perhaps she went to London to shop; perhaps she went to Paris with a lover.' Diane tended to measure others' intentions or actions against her own.

'This lad, John, is very responsible, very reliable, and—'

'Very intense,' Diane finished for him. 'Too much so for his own good, it sounds like.'

The door to the Jack and Hammer was blown open by wind and the entrance of Vivian Rivington. Without saying hello, without removing her coat or sitting down, she said, 'Melrose. I just met Agatha in the street and she says you're going back to Cornwall.' As she said this she sat down, still with her coat on.

'For a few months, yes, that's right.'

'*Months?*' Vivian stared at him as if the body snatchers had come and carted off the real Melrose Plant and put this thing of caprice in his place. 'You can't be serious!'

Diane said, 'Ridiculous, isn't it? There's no reasoning with him when he gets like this.'

'Like what? I don't "get like" anything.'

Diane went on, 'I've told him his stars are not up to it.'

'You make it sound as if they're too decrepit to go with me to Cornwall.'

Diane was still entertaining readers of the Sidbury paper with her astrology column, largely because she knew nothing about astrology and was therefore free to invent. 'You know what I mean.' Diane ate her olive.

'No, I don't, Diane. *Nobody* understands what you mean in that column. "Get a life" is hardly using the stars to predict—'

Vivian fairly shouted, 'But you *can't* go to Cornwall!'

They all looked at her and her deeply blushing face.

Surprised by this outburst, Melrose said, 'I can't?'

Now Vivian was momentarily tongue-tied. Finally she said, 'Because Franco is coming here and we're getting married!' Having apparently frightened herself with her own outburst, she looked round the table to see if their various expressions confirmed the fact she'd said it.

No one spoke. Even the normally unflappable Diane looked at Vivian open-mouthed.

When they did speak, it was all at once.

'Count Dracula—'

'Good God! When did this—?'

'If you're going to London for your gown—'

Trueblood lit a jade-green Sobranie and said, 'Tell me, Viv-Viv, when was all this decided?'

'Ah . . . not long ago.'

Melrose said, 'How soon is this to be? When is Count Drac—' Vivian's look at him was as blood-curdling as anything Count Dracula could scare up. 'I mean, when is Giopinno arriving? Dear God, this is something!' exclaimed Melrose.

'He's coming in . . . a few days. Maybe a week . . .' She studied her hands.

'Ah,' said Trueblood. 'And exactly when does this wedding take place?' He smiled, wolfishly.

Vivian looked at him with suspicion and reflected.

Her blushes were replaced by a kind of death's-head grey. 'The exact date hasn't been set yet. But it'll be either this month or next. September or October,' she added, in case they hadn't got their months in order.

Do you remember another September . . .? Whatever the words, the song played sadly in Melrose's head, all humour fleeing him in an instant. He said, 'But of course I'll return for the wedding. Cornwall isn't halfway round the world.'

'Return?' She said it dejectedly, as if it was as rueful a word as 'remember'. '*Return?* I would think you wouldn't even *go*.' Vivian regarded Melrose sadly. 'It's the last you may see of me single.'

'Yes, well . . .' Melrose hardly knew how to respond to this.

Vivian rose. She had still not removed her camel-hair coat, the caramel colour blending beautifully with the browns and deep reds of her autumnal hair.

'I'm certainly thunderstruck,' said Diane, in a thoroughly unthunderstruck tone. Still, it must be so, for she'd forgotten her glass, which sat empty before her; even the olive had gone. Thunderstruck, indeed.

'Well, I've got to go and . . . do things.' Vivian turned and walked out of the pub. Her expression was not a happy one.

'Well. *Well*,' said Melrose. 'I'd say this calls for another round.'

'It has done for the last ten minutes,' said Diane, blowing thin columns of smoke through her nostrils.

Melrose called to Dick Scroggs, still reading the Sidbury paper – his favourite was the astrology column

– and made a circular gesture with his hand indicating drinks for all.

Scroggs looked at him as if Melrose were calling on him to work out a message in semaphore.

'It never occurred to me Vivian would actually do it,' said Melrose, morosely.

Trueblood said, 'Uh-huh.'

'Marry that smarmy Italian? After all this time? Not only that, but to do it *here*! That's a turn-up for the books!'

Diane said, 'I expect she'll have to live in Venice where she won't understand a *word*. They speak Italian there.'

'It's their second language,' said Trueblood. 'Do you mean you actually believe that story?'

Melrose and Diane stared at him.

'She was making it up.'

'She wouldn't do that,' Melrose said uncertainly.

Trueblood shook his head at his friends' gullibility. 'Listen, old bean, if she were really going to marry Dracula, we'd have heard long before this. She would have wanted plenty of time to think up excuses not to do it. She'd also want to allow us plenty of time to work out a plan to prevent her.'

'Excuses?' Diane looked at Trueblood in disbelief. 'Why would she need excuses? Good lord, it's easier just to divorce someone than to think up reasons for doing it. I should know; I've done it often enough. Dick!' She called over to Scroggs. 'Are we ever going to get our drinks here?'

Melrose said, 'I still don't get it. Why would Vivian make it all up?'

Impatient with Melrose's obtuseness, Trueblood said, 'It's obvious. She wants to keep you here.'

'A wedding in a few weeks would hardly keep me here for three months.'

'Oh, don't be such a twit, Melrose,' said Diane. 'There's nothing rational in all of this – thank you,' she said to Dick Scroggs, who was setting fresh drinks before them.

When Dick left, Trueblood said, 'Go on. Tell us more about this Cornwall murder.'

'There's no more to tell. Someone in Bletchley thought she recognized her. I don't think the victim will be hard to trace.'

'What was she wearing?' Trust Diane to sweep away the extraneous and go directly to the heart of the matter.

'I don't know. Macalvie didn't tell me. But in the police photos it looked like a suit, amber or ecru, maybe – God help me! I'm getting as bad as you, Diane.'

'Who is he, anyway? Macalvie, I mean,' asked Trueblood. 'I think he called here, to the pub once, looking for Jury.'

'He's very high up in the Devon and Cornwall police. Jury's known him for years. They worked cases together. Or as much together as one can ever get with Mr Macalvie. He's brilliant, though.'

'Speaking of Richard Jury . . .' said Trueblood.

'He's in Northern Ireland.'

Diane looked absolutely scandalized, as if they were watching the Pope kiss a pig. '*God*, Melrose! What is he doing *there*?'

'I don't know the particulars. New Scotland Yard

hasn't ever put me on a need-to-know footing.'

'Did Sergeant Wiggins go with him?'

'No. Macalvie's trying to get in touch with him, though.'

'I knew it,' said Diane. 'I warned him.'

Melrose frowned. 'Wiggins?'

'No, no. Richard Jury.'

'His horoscope playing up again, is it?'

'His Venus is in a peculiar position in relation to Mars.' She tapped the ash from her cigarette into the metal tray.

'Whose side is he on?' asked Trueblood. 'The IRA? The Loyalists? Catholics? Protestants? Irish? English?'

'The side of the dead, I imagine. He's not helping the RUC, it's just that something happened there that's connected with something in London. At least, I think.'

Diane was still worrying over the fashion sense of the dead-and-gone in Cornwall. 'You don't know if it was a designer suit she wore, then?'

'What? You mean the unfortunate victim in Lamorna?'

'Yes. If it was, you know, a Lacroix, it would certainly narrow the field.'

'Narrow it to where? London? Paris? Rome?'

Diane's patience was being tried. 'Not only there. There are some quite fashionable shops in Edinburgh. And the Home Counties. One would have to broaden the base a bit.'

Melrose shook his head. 'Whatever the base is, you're way off it, love.'

'Actually, old sweat, she isn't,' said Trueblood.

'Are we breaking now for an Armani commercial?'

'If the woman was wearing Ferre or perhaps Sonia

Rykiel, the garment could almost certainly be traced. You know, through the place where she bought it; or, if someone else bought it, then through that person.'

Melrose hated it when Diane made a sensible suggestion.

'I wouldn't mind knowing someone who'd buy me Ferre,' she said, and returned to the matter of Chris Wells. 'Now, she sounds Cornwall through and through; what's in her wardrobe is probably cardigans and plaid things and Barbour knockoffs from Marks and Sparks. Anyway, the question of her outfit doesn't really apply, does it? Are you sure she didn't just go off on her own?'

'No,' said Melrose. 'I'm fairly sure she didn't. From what I've heard about her, she isn't a capricious person.'

'Then you think she was abducted? Or lured away somehow?'

Melrose nodded.

Diane sipped her martini, tapped her cigarette into the ashtray, and said, 'I expect one has to make *some* sort of arrangement.'

'Surrey,' said Macalvie. He had called Ardry End to tell him that they'd ID'd the dead woman. She was Sada Colthorp, former wife of Rodney Colthorp, Viscount Mead. He lived in Surrey. 'For God's sake, that's only a hop, skip, and jump from Northamptonshire.'

'I don't know how you hopped, skipped, and jumped as a lad – if you ever were; you were probably just a little policeman – but my hopping and skipping did not cover a hundred miles. That's how far Surrey is from here.'

'Don't be ridiculous. It's hardly fifty.'

Melrose knew he'd do whatever Macalvie asked him to, but it was more fun arguing about it first. Besides, he felt he deserved to let Macalvie know how much he was being put out. 'Anyway, you said you'd already talked to Colthorp when he came to identify the body. So what good would it do for *me* to talk to him?' He knew the answer to that, too. For the same reason Jury was always asking him to step into the role of eighth earl.

'Because aristocrats have that in common – the aristocracy.'

'I stopped being one years ago. I've forgotten how.'

'Oh, come on. It's like riding a bike. You never forget.'

Melrose sighed. 'I would if people let me.'

'Colthorp collects cars. Vintage cars. That's why you want to see him.'

'I do?'

'Sure. That old Bentley of yours. Isn't that an antique by now?'

'It may not be, but I am. Let me get this straight: it's because I, too, have an interest in vintage automobiles that I want to see this Viscount Mead – what's his name?'

'Rodney. Rodney Colthorp.'

'Right. It's really his cars I'm interested in, and he'd be damned interested in my Bentley. Do you realize I know absolutely nothing about cars, including mine?' Knowing Macalvie couldn't care less, Melrose sighed and got out his pen. 'So, which part of Surrey?'

As Macalvie told him, Melrose had the happy thought that if Surrey was not close to Northamptonshire, it was certainly close to London and, therefore, to Bethnal Green. He smiled.

18

'Lord Ardry.' Viscount Mead put out his hand and looked at Melrose with an enthusiasm that was flattering. He had answered the door himself, which testified to his being long on humility or short of cash. Staff did not include a full-time door opener, or, if it did, Rodney Colthorp had given the man a good deal of elbow room. Ruthven would be scandalized.

Viscount Mead couldn't resist looking past Melrose at the latter's Bentley, one of the prewar models, or at least Melrose believed it was. It had been in the family for ages. He wondered if this man was astute enough to tell that Melrose – and his Bentley – were flying false colours. But all Rodney Colthorp said was, 'What a beautiful car,' as he pulled at his grey moustache, a nervous, contemplative gesture. Then, as if he had forgotten Melrose was there, said, 'Oh, sorry to keep you standing on my doorstep. Come in, come in.'

Doorstep was not the word Melrose would have chosen to describe the area at the top of the two dozen marble steps he had ascended to reach the door. The

house was on a much grander scale than was Ardry
End, which it resembled.

Perhaps more glorious than the house was the
expansive garden and lawn at the back, dotted here and
there with sculptures, a gazebo, and a folly or two. It
stretched as far as the eye could see. It was both
windswept and sheltered by internal hedges, with broad
brick paths and gate piers. There were bold tall grasses
backed by young pines, box hedges, and long vistas that
drew the eye to the steeple of a church somewhere. One
path between low walls made its convoluted way,
vanishing somewhere in the distance.

'Is that path there for walkers?'

'No. It's my butterfly corridor. I'm trying to keep
species from disappearing completely and help them
migrate. The Adonis blue is one. It's simply beautiful.'

Rodney Colthorp said this while they were comfortably seated in one of the several drawing rooms, this
one furnished more informally than the larger room
they'd passed, whose furnishings were dark, heavy, and
priceless.

Melrose drank Viscount Mead's hundred-year-old
Scotch and felt expansive.

Colthorp leaned his head back on his chair and sent
both words and pipe smoke towards the ceiling. In a
sort of meditation on the merits of aristocracy, he said,
'Of course, you know this as well as I . . . but there are
certain rituals, silly as they might seem to others, which
should be retained or the whole damned boiling will go
down. I know a lot of it seems like claptrap: the hunt, for
instance. We do get a lot of these hunt saboteurs

knocking about, being damned rude. I don't ride myself, but I can understand the appeal of it. What I fail to understand is why the great hue and cry of these animal liberationists doesn't concentrate on the real horrors of experimentation and slaughterhouses. I can only think the—' The cell phone, whose resting place must have slipped Colthorp's mind, was finally rescued from a spot between cushion and arm of the armchair. He excused himself and pulled up the wobbly antenna. The call was not to his liking, apparently, for he began it with a huge sigh, followed by a series of grunts, growing more and more impatient over the thirty seconds or so of the caller's comments. 'No. No, Dennis, I've told you time and again I do not want to speculate, certainly not in a diamond mine in South Africa.' He shook his head, as if the caller could see how much he didn't want shares in a diamond mine, and shoved down the antenna, his expression registering extreme impatience.

Melrose smiled. 'Your investment banker?' He wondered what such people did, actually.

'No. My son. He's the youngest, he's twenty-two. He's always on to me about the market. Day trading, futures, selling short, selling long – I haven't the least idea what the boy's talking about. He himself does quite well by it, has done for years. But that doesn't mean I'd be as lucky. Now. Where did you say you were from?'

'My home's in a village near Northampton, but at the moment I'm renting a house in Cornwall. Place called Bletchley.' Melrose waited while the name hit home. It took five seconds. Colthorp stopped in the act of tamping down his pipe.

'But that's where Sada – you know about the woman who was murdered near Lamorna Cove?'

'Yes, yes indeed. Quite a stir that's causing.'

'Police from Devon and Cornwall have been here, and I've had to fly to Penzance to identify the body.'

Melrose feigned surprise. 'Police here? Why? Did you know her?'

'I was married to her.'

Melrose managed to look appropriately shocked.

Colthorp went on, 'Poor girl. Sada wasn't a very substantial person. I don't mean anything was wrong with her mind; rather, she had so little substance. Marrying her was – well, the purest folly. Looking back, and I've done a deal of that, I can't remember why I thought it a good idea at the time.'

'Who can? Not I, certainly. Hindsight would save us all, wouldn't it?' Melrose smiled sympathetically and held back from asking questions about Sada. On the contrary, he turned the conversation away from her before Colthorp began to wonder exactly why Melrose was here. 'I'd love to see your cars.' Once around the grounds, as it were, Melrose was sure he could find occasion to reintroduce the subject of the dead wife into the conversation. Colthorp certainly seemed willing to talk about her.

'Yes, of course,' said Colthorp. 'That's what you came for, after all. We'll go out to the garage. Sorry I rattled on.'

'Not at all,' Melrose was quick to put in. 'How could you not speak of it, after all?'

Colthorp rose, set down his glass. 'A bad business.'

He shook his head. 'A very bad business. Sada might have been troublesome, but lord knows she didn't ever deserve this.'

Troublesome. Melrose made a note of that.

From the house they walked across the circular drive to a ten-car garage, although *garage* seemed the wrong word to describe such an elegant building, with its high windows gathering the late-afternoon sun and dashing it across the highly polished bonnets of the cars sitting inside. Melrose knew nothing about cars, other than how to drive them. He was, though, fairly certain that the first of them was one of the old Fords, a Model T, its black metal polished to within an inch of its life. This at least he could identify.

'Ah, yes. The old Tin Lizzie. They drove it to the top of Pike's Peak, if you can believe it. Those others' – Colthorp's gesture took in the next two cars – 'there you've got an Overland Touring Car and a 1912 Cadillac Touring Car. Something, aren't they?'

Melrose fussed over them, hardly knowing what the fuss – which consisted of mumbled words of praise, peering inside, and noting the appointments – was about. He commented on the myriad once-felt-to-be 'luxuries' of the cars, the turquoise and blue varnishes, the wonderful scent of old cracked leather, the big wheels, the running boards. 'Marvellous, marvellous.'

They moved on to a cherry-red Lamborghini. 'That's Dennis's. And that one further along, there' – Dennis's father pointed out a black Porsche – 'it's the latest model, one of their XK-Eights, quite a fabulous car. Fabulous price, too.'

Melrose bet he was looking at something in the neighbourhood of £75,000. Fabulous indeed.

Colthorp went on, 'He's young; he goes for that slick continental stuff. Myself, I much prefer the more substantial ones, the touring cars, that kind of thing, or that Wolseley further along.' He nodded towards a dark green car, its body of a graceful roundness that had long since fled the automobile scene. 'It was Dennis who put me onto the Cadillac, courtesy of an American friend of his, 'bout – oh, ten or eleven years ago.'

Melrose calculated: if Dennis was twenty-two today, that would have made him twelve ten years ago. He could not help commenting on this.

Viscount Mead laughed. 'Oh, the friend himself wasn't a child. No, no, he was a grown man. But Dennis knew him, right enough. Dennis always has had a lot of unlikely friends – for a boy, that is. A boy back then, I mean.' Colthorp chewed at the grey moustache and seemed to be ruminating on this point, as if he was wondering about Dennis's unlikely friends. But what he said was, 'He never liked Sada, though.'

That didn't surprise Melrose, not with inheritances and changing of wills in the bargain. He ventured a guess here, trying to keep it as tasteful as possible. 'I expect that's true of most children when a new stepmother comes along.'

'Loss of love and money, you mean? Oh, Dennis is quite sure of my love, and' – here he made a noise both of amusement and dismissal – 'he doesn't care a fig for my money.'

Melrose thought this rather disingenuous, considering the Lamborghini sitting there. 'He has expensive tastes, though.'

'Mmm? Oh, I didn't say he hadn't. It's *his* money bought that and the Porsche.' Colthorp chuckled. 'For all I know, Dennis has more than I. He invests. Or did I tell you? That's what the phone call earlier was about. No, Dennis didn't trust Sada, didn't trust the old friends out of her past who came here. Sleazy film folk, a few of them. When I met Sada, she was doing the occasional bit part in bad films. Might even have been a pornographic film or two, Dennis found out. One friend was a film producer who came here several times. Funny chap. What was his name? Bolt, I think. Bit of a wide boy, that one. Untrustworthy, bad influence. Good car, though. Dennis tried to buy it. Jaguar – mmm, can't recall the model. Sporty little car, two-seater, I think.' He meditated on this for a moment and then got back to his ex-wife. 'Sada had been down on her luck, as they say, when we met.' He sighed. 'She wasn't all that interested in cars, for some reason.'

Melrose smiled. 'Hardly a suitable companion, then.'

Colthorp laughed. 'Time we nipped over to that car of yours for a good look. Hack through the underbrush and lead the way!'

If there was a way to lead – considering the exquisitely kept lawns and gardens – Melrose led it. He hated the Bentley's intervening on mention of the 'troublesome' Sada. But as Colthorp seemed really to want to talk about her, the subject would come up again.

When he came abreast of the old Bentley, Viscount Mead shook his head as if words couldn't cover the subject. For once, Melrose was glad that Ruthven (or Momaday, when the spirit moved his groundsman) kept the car polished to mirror brightness.

Colthorp walked twice round it before settling into staring at the car, tweeded arms folded across his chest. As Melrose had done earlier, Colthorp uttered appreciative words; unlike Melrose, they could be understood. 'Where did you ever get it?'

'My father did, actually. It was the year before he died. He rather liked cars himself.' He remembered it now, the way his father had really been smitten with the car, how he had been like a teenager with his first ride. This was one of Melrose's few fond memories. 'He really did love this one.'

'And no wonder. Well, if you ever want to sell up, you know who to call.'

This might have sounded a little vulgar, had Colthorp not been so intensely drawn to the old car.

Now he rubbed his hands and said, 'We're due for a drink, I'd say.'

They retraced their steps to the house. Overhead, the whirring buzz of a helicopter stirred the eucalyptus and tall grasses. Colthorp looked up, muttered, 'Bloody noisy old thing.'

Melrose had not thought the house that near to Heathrow.

Whisky in hand, they settled back into the same seats they had left, and Colthorp picked up the thread of the conversation about Sada. 'We separated – oh, five years ago; she managed to go through the money I settled on her and in a year she was back, wanting more. I expect I should have told the police about that, but you know, it slips my mind most of the time. She actually threatened to sell the story to the tabloids. About me and . . . well, never mind, it's not all that juicy a story. I must say, it made me queasy in my stomach to think she'd do something like that. Dennis threw her out with a "publish-and-be-damned" attitude. He's quite forthright, Dennis is.'

Melrose smiled. 'Sounds it. But her trying to blackmail you, that must have been extremely painful.'

'It was, it was,' answered Colthorp, tossing back the rest of his whisky and rising to get another. When he motioned to Melrose's glass, Melrose raised his and shook his head.

'So she was on, you might say, her last legs?'

Colthorp sat himself, dug into the cushions at his back, and said, 'Dennis put a private detective on her.'

Here was a treat! How he wished the omnipresent yet absent Dennis were with them now.

'Found out that most of those films were not just bad B films, but bad *pornographic* B films. Not that that's something the Dirty Squad might cut you a look for, but she had form on a number of counts. Sada, it's funny to think, was more impressed by her social standing when we were married than she was by the money. She adored being Lady Mead and being given place to when we entered somebody's dining room. Funny how the frills and furbelows of aristocratic doings are lusted after by those who want to bring it down. Not that Sada wanted to, oh, no. It fitted her to a "T" even if she didn't fit it. No, Sada would have viewed the prospect of that bill abolishing hereditary peers with a lot more indignation than I do.'

This was interrupted by the cell phone's *brring* again, insistent as an insect. Again, Viscount Mead scooped it up from underneath the cushions, answered, listened, and sighed. 'No. *No.* I do not want shares in a racehorse. Where he came in at Newmarket on Saturday doesn't interest me in the least . . . Dennis, for God's sake, do not keep bothering me with your fly-by-night silver mines and horses and all the rest. Anyway, I've company here, goodbye.'

Colthorp was about to sign off when he brought the phone back to his mouth and said, 'And for God's sake, get that helicopter out of my butterfly corridor!'

19

He had never known the sun to glare in London, but in this early evening it did, as if trying to deliver the knockout punch to the encroaching dusk. Coming out of it and into the museum evoked in Melrose a feeling of being submerged, dark and cool.

He had been once before to the Museum of Childhood when he'd come months ago to take Bea to dinner. That little restaurant – what was it? Perhaps she'd like to eat there again. Dotrice, that was it, the name of the restaurant. French, very classy, and she'd ordered steak and *frites* and talked about her 'blue period'. Not her feelings but her painting. He had been surprised to discover just how good she was when he'd seen her paintings hanging on a wall of a Mayfair gallery.

Beatrice Slocum, he was told by a kindly elderly lady in rimless glasses, had gone out to the chemist's but would be soon back. Melrose had the impression that this woman was someone who would be especially good with children. Indeed, she reminded him of a nurse he'd had as a small child . . .

There, he was doing it again, remembering. And he

110

seemed prepared to be reminded of anything by anyone these days. He wondered if this lady truly was like his nurse, Miss Prescott. *Nurses to their graves have gone . . .* He gave his head a sharp little shake, almost afraid of himself and his penchant for nostalgia. It had to stop.

Melrose concentrated on the displays. The doll's houses were the first thing one saw upon entering. He'd thought before how charming they were, the bits of furniture reflecting the taste of a particular time, the tiny appointments, the little figures going about their business of housekeeping. The child in the photographs, the Bletchleys' dead daughter, would have loved this. Quickly he banished that thought from his mind and walked up to the second level.

Here were the trains and games. Watching the long train move sluggishly round a track was a grave-looking boy of perhaps seven or eight. Melrose almost saw in his back the shape of the boy who'd been here over a year ago when he'd visited it. Nostalgia reinforced by déjà vu, that's all he needed. He was simply too suggestible.

But, no, this was a different boy, watching as the train stopped between green fields, one with a cow cropping the grass, the other with a couple of horses, taking their ease at this ambiguous hour.

The boy exclaimed, 'Hey! It's s'posed t'stop at the station' – (pronounced by him '*stye*-tion'). 'So wot's wrong wi' it? I put in twenty p, me. Twenty p oney got it 'alfway round.'

Perhaps he thought Melrose a member of the museum staff. Or did children merely turn to the nearest grown-up to demand recompense for their losses?

Melrose said, 'Let's get it going again, then,' as he slotted a 20p coin into the slot. The train stuttered to a fresh beginning and started up. They watched it in silence, snaking its way past the little station, past crossings and through tunnels, and finally giving out again beside the field with the one cow.

'It ain't supposed t'stop there, mister.' He threw Melrose a baleful glance, as if things had been jolly good before the coming of this adult.

'Well, it ain't my fault, is it? Come on, let's see the peep shows.'

The boy sighed. A peep show was a poor second to a train ride, but it was a free poor second, so the boy followed Melrose.

They were side by side and with their heads lowered, looking through the peepholes at the intricate interiors of the boxes, when Melrose heard a voice behind him.

'Oughtn't to be showing that child the peep shows, it might give him ideas.'

Melrose turned. 'Bea!' he exclaimed. She looked to him, at the moment, quite beautiful. The hair that had been dyed an awful aubergine purple when he'd first seen it was its own self again, browny-gold and warm like buttered toast. There was something of solace in it.

The boy, seeing what must have appeared to him an especially boring interlude between two adults, walked away, back over to the train.

Melrose saw the boy's back was turned and, in one of the few ungallant acts of his life, took Bea by the shoulders, pushed her back against the row of boxes, and kissed her unmercifully. She did not protest.

Not until the fun was over, that is. When he finally set her free, she was all indignation. 'Never would've thought it. Fancy you!'

'Which you do, I hope.'

'Never mind. Fancy doing that in a public place, and you an earl!'

'I'm not. And why do I find your outrage unconvincing?'

She shrugged. 'Because you're so pleased with yourself, I expect.'

He denied this, but she disregarded his denial as she walked away. Turning and seeing he still stood there, she said, impatiently, 'Well, come on. I'm off.'

Melrose followed. 'Where to?'

'Home. I've got some steak and potatoes fritz.'

Melrose was entranced. Home. 'Not fritz, it's *frites*.'

Bea ran down the wide stairs. 'Don't know why you bother with me, someone clever as you.'

Melrose smiled. He knew why.

'Home' was a roomy flat up three flights of stairs. No lift. He would gladly have driven a Tin Lizzie up Pike's Peak had Beatrice Slocum's flat been at the top of it. Once inside, she flicked on the light and he flicked it off.

'There you go ag—'

He kissed her. It was a very long and lush kiss, and she joined in, after scant resistance.

'So,' he said, separating only long enough to say it, 'where're the potatoes *frites*?'

'In the bedroom.'

'Mm.'

This time she kissed him. 'With the steak.'

Her arms were still wrapped around him and her chin on his shoulder when he said, 'Do you ever think of marriage?'

'Me? Sure. A lot.' She rolled away and looked up at the ceiling, sighing. 'We're not good marriage material, us.'

He turned to look at her. 'No, I expect "us" aren't, not if you look at us like bolts of cloth to be cut and stitched.' After another moment's reflection, he said, 'I'm pretty rich.'

'Uh-huh.' Peacefully, she yawned.

Melrose turned to look at her as she yawned again and did something blubbery with her lips. 'You look like a fish.'

'Ta very much. That'll really get your proposal up and running.'

'Who said I was proposing?'

Bea spread her hand to catch a beam of moonlight. 'What are you trying to sell, then, if not yourself?'

Melrose reached up and took her hand and kept it. 'I'm doing an inventory.'

'Of what?' She yawned, loudly.

'Myself, my things.'

'Sure.'

'It's true. I try to do one every year. It's quite extensive. For instance, down in my wine cellar, I have a whole case of a Premier Cru from Puligny-Montrachet. And that's just for starters.'

She lay in silence, turning this over. She said, 'Down in my basement cubicle I have a case of Malvern water, fifty cans of mixed nuts, and a giant cactus. Just for starters.'

He looked at her sideways, surreptitiously. She'd found some chewing gum – not, he hoped, a plug from under the end table. She was chewing raucously: *crack crack crack*. 'I could never marry a woman who did that in my ear all day.'

'Good thing, 'cause I could never marry a man who's so snobby.'

This brought Melrose up and resting on his arm. 'A snob. *Me?*'

'Um.'

'Well, I'm not.' He fell back on the bed again. 'Haven't we strayed from the point?'

'We? You're the one who strayed; I was just listening to you go down your wine list. You should've been one of them blokes like at Dotrice's.'

'The sommelier? Thanks. Anyway, we were talking about marriage – in a general, very hypothetical way.'

She did not reply. Her eyes were closed.

'Are you asleep?'

'No, but I'm considering it.'

She was just trying to irritate him. 'What are you thinking?'

'About this painting I'm stuck on.'

Not terribly complimentary that here he was *maybe* proposing and all she thought about was work, work, work. However, he'd humour her. 'Exactly what are you stuck on?'

'The mouth. It's a portrait.'

'Who of?'

'A friend. Just a bloke I know. But I know a lot of blokes. Friends like, you know.'

This friendly bloke-ness irritated him, as he knew the bloke himself would.

'Come on, get up' – she was sitting up herself now, pulling at his hand – 'and I'll show you.'

'I don't *want* to get up.'

'Suit yourself.' She was out of bed and putting on a man's white shirt that she kept on a hook behind the door as if she was used to wearing it. Melrose frowned. Given the size, the shirt must belong to a very big man. Now she was out of the door.

'Hell,' he said to himself and fell back against the pillow. He heard her rummaging around in the living room. *Crash, Clang.* Bloody hell. Was she so enmeshed in her art she couldn't leave it behind for one night?

Then she was back lugging a large painting, which he was quite prepared to dislike. She turned it round for him to see and his mouth opened in astonishment. 'My God. It's me.' He could scarcely believe it.

'Clever of you to recognize it.' She was chewing gum again and trying not to smile.

In the painting he was seated in a leather wing chair, but leaning forward a little as if talking to an invisible companion. The viewer might have been that companion. The eyes were a gritty green that stonewalled any attempt to glamorize him, just as she'd kept the firelight from sparking his hair.

'My God, Bea, how on earth did you do this without me?'

'I guess I wasn't.'
'Wasn't what?'
'Without you.' She grinned and chewed. *Crack*.

Part II

A Dealer in Magic and Spells

20

ISLINGTON

On her way downstairs from her flat, Carole-anne Palutski heard the telephone ring in Superintendent Jury's flat and quickly took the chain from around her neck where his key was warm from her skin (as the Super said, 'That key could defrost the stubbornest lock'). She unlocked the door. By the time she got across the room, the ringing stopped. Hell, she thought. Hell. Her spirits had lifted momentarily, thinking it could be him calling. Whoever it was didn't leave a message. She had bought this answering machine second-hand for a couple of quid. The Super hated answering machines, which she said was really strange for a policeman, as police lived by emergencies and what if there was one? What if she got arrested (wrongfully, of course) and only got to make the one phone call? He said he didn't think there was much chance the answering machine would go along to the nick and bail her out. 'Ha ha, always joking, aren't you?' she'd said. 'An answering machine's a way you can call and leave messages. You

121

know, for me or Mrs W.' Well, he actually had called and
left messages, four for her and two for Mrs W. He told
Mrs W he really missed her chicken soup. He told
Carole-anne he really missed her fortune-telling and
wondered if this Irish lass he presently had his arm
around was in the cards.

Ha ha, she thought, winding the tape back and
listening again to his last message and wondering again
what the background noise was, all that loud yelling and
what sounded like exploded glass. Was it bombs going
off? Or just a room full of loud people breaking windows
in their drunken, loutish ways?

He hated e-mail, too. He'd said, 'There was always
that bit of suspense after you wrote a letter, thinking
about the other person reading it and wondering when
and what he'd answer. And the self-righteous feeling of,
there, that's done. Proud of yourself because you'd finally
written that letter. But now? You send e-mail; before you
can even think or feel those things, the answer's back,
no thinking between yours and theirs. It's all too fast;
everything's immediate, now now now.'

He didn't think she listened to him. Well, she did.
Now she went to the calendar tacked up on the wall and
took it down and filled in another square. She wrote in
all sorts of things she and the Super had done, like
going down the pub or to the Nine-One-Nine to listen
to Stan or seeing some film or other. Again, she
wondered why he'd got the calendar. It was put out by
some farming association and she couldn't see how the
Super would have been on their mailing list. Each month
had a picture of a farm animal. September's was a cow,

with its head turned to face the camera, looking squarely at her as if it knew she was filling the squares in with false information.

He'd been gone for nearly a month. September was filling up with all the entries she'd made. Wouldn't he be surprised to see how busy he'd been? She looked back at August. Nothing, blank squares all. It was the same for July and June. Why did he have a calendar, if there was never anything on it? Her own calendar was so heaped up with entries she had to write along the sides.

Yet she thought it was strange that his July and August looked full, and when she pictured her own calendar in her mind it looked empty. Carole-anne wondered if there were people who, when they weren't there, made you wonder if *you* were. Made you wonder if you were real. When they weren't there to tell a person she looked like a Key West sunset, did she look like anything at all?

Holding the calendar, trying to think of something to write in for today (how many times could they go to the Angel?) she went over to the phonograph. It was the only one she'd seen and it fascinated her. She had tapes and CDs (the whole world is miniaturized, he'd said), but he had actual records. He had 'September in the Rain'. She put it on and lifted the arm over the record.

For a hard surface, she put the calendar against the window and wrote in *Ireland, Rain*.

Into the square for the last day of September she wrote *Home again*.

Down in what was referred to as the 'garden flat' but was really a basement, Mrs Wassermann sat in her favourite overstuffed chair, hands folded. There had been a few days she had even spent in bed, but she forced herself up and dressed at a decent hour, mustering what self-regard she had.

For three weeks now, except the times when Carole-anne had insisted, she had not been out of the flat, not on her own. The world beyond the door could be pitiless, unless you were protected by amulet, charm, or spell. It was the way she'd been years ago, just sitting and looking out of her low window upon the feet of passersby. She'd been this way until Mr Jury had fitted the door with extra locks, 'Locks not even a bunch of drunken Irish rebels could kick through.'

The trouble was, he wasn't here. Oh, she'd not minded when he'd gone out of London other times, for he'd only been away a few days at a time. But this time it had been nearly a month. And he'd gone to Ireland – *Northern* Ireland, which, as everyone knew, was still a dangerous place to be. He should've been back by now.

Mrs Wassermann sighed and propped her head on her hand, her elbow on the arm of the chair, and watched feet walk by her window.

VICTORIA STREET

Detective Sergeant Alfred Wiggins sat at his desk in New Scotland Yard and looked dejectedly over at the other desk, behind which no one sat. He had lined up his usual anodynes: nose drops, eyedrops, black biscuits, Bromo Seltzer, apricot juice, a few herbs, and Fisherman's Friends. He looked at all of them without spirit, without interest, without needfulness. He did not feel headachy, croupy, nauseated, muscle-sore, or feverish. That was the trouble; he missed his ailments. He needed them, usually.

One would think it would be a relief, this failure of need. But it wasn't. It had always been a bit of a lark, mixing up the apricot juice with a tablet of Bromo Seltzer (that cure-all he had found when they'd gone to Baltimore), maybe with a little rue; or tossing back a few pills with the afternoon tea, which he would drink with a black biscuit or two. When he knew Superintendent Jury – his guv'nor – was going to Northern Ireland, Wiggins had made him up a travel packet of small vials with precise 'indications' (Wiggins fell quite easily into pharmaceutical jargon).

He had been gone for nearly a month now. When Mr Jury was sitting over there at the other desk, hands behind his head, watching one or another procedure of Wiggins's mixing potions, commenting on the vanity of it all, joking, Wiggins felt it was worth it. But now he felt more like the tree fallen in the forest with no one around to hear.

Was he, then, there?

As if to test out his there-ness, the phone by his hand rang.

Richard Jury! he hoped against hope. But it wasn't; it was Brian Macalvie.

The next best thing. Wiggins smiled.

Fiona Clingmore sat at her desk, looking at her sponge bag, her Cucumber QuikFix facial, the new mascara wand and eyeliner, sighed, and with her forearm swept them into her desk drawer. Hardly seemed worth it these days.

But to put a good face on it, when Alfred Wiggins came into the office, she picked up her shell comb and ran it through her hair, before using it as an anchor to hold it on one side. She said to Wiggins, looking at the cat, Cyril, sitting and watching the door to the outside corridor, 'Cyril does that all the time. He thinks your guv'nor must be going to walk through it any moment now.'

'Maybe he needs the vet,' said Wiggins, having the urge to cheer things down. 'Maybe he's sick.'

Fiona waved a deprecating hand, sweeping away such a suggestion. 'Cyril's not like you. I'll tell you this, though. He' – and here she bent her head in the direction of the inside door to Chief Superintendent Racer's office – 'hardly knows what to do with himself with Mr Jury gone. Why, he can walk right past Cyril here without so much as a "bloody damn" or trying to kick him or setting those sardine traps. It's like all the starch's gone out of him. It's like when you don't get any sleep and then you don't have any dreams, so you go kind of queer all over. Kind of crazy, you know. That's him. When Mr Jury's not here it's like he' – she nodded again at Racer's office door – 'goes berserk; he doesn't have anyone to put a lid on him and so he keeps blowing off. You know, kind of like a pressure cooker exploding.' Fiona shook her head and sighed as she went about rubbing some cream into her cuticles.

* * *

For the cat Cyril, it was like imagining fish; he could look at the water until a darkness, a blotch, or a shadow in the riverbed slowly surfaced. Even if it wasn't a fish, even if it was only a bit of paper that had unhooked from a rock, or maybe it would be a jam tart or a Christmas cracker, a shoe or a shark.

But the shark was already there, wasn't he? On the other side of his office door, flapping and splashing, going at Cyril whenever he could, too stupid to be an imagined fish.

Cyril sat still as still water waiting for Him to come through the door. Any moment now. He always did sooner or later, but if Cyril stopped watching, He wouldn't. He'd get away like a fish's shadow. Cyril was sure if he put his whole being into watching, and not be distracted by sardines and fax machines, he could open the door and have Him come through it. Just like that.

Presto.

DUBLIN

The old priest wrapped his hands around his pint of Guinness as if it was a cross.

'What happened was they picked me up in the Shankill, kidnapped me you could say, if ordering a man t'get into a car at gunpoint is kidnapping. We drove a distance from Belfast. It's hard to say how far, for I scarcely recognized anything we passed, so dark it was. I've never seen a blacker night, dark as devil's dung. I think where we ended up was Ballykillen – that's north; I think we were near Craigavon.

'They talked the whole way, as if they were just a bunch of lads out for a night on the town. There were three of them, a three-man unit – IRA, of course. And then they told me why they'd picked me up; they needed a priest to administer last rites. I said to them, "You could surely have got a priest nearer to wherever it is yer taking me now, couldn't you?" He said, "Ye looked good to us, Father." I asked, "Who's sick to dying they had to scrape a priest off the streets?" They laughed harder. "It's an execution, Father. We're about to kill a man."

'I told them, no, I couldn't do this, watch a man be murdered.

' "But you won't have to watch, Father."

'Finally we stopped in front of this white cottage that in the pitch blackness looked like a moon against the sky. We went in. They'd taken a sledgehammer to the door, which I'd learned was just the IRA's way of knocking. In the parlour, or what was left of it, for they'd pretty much trashed it, sat a man tied to the chair he was in. I don't know if I ever saw a more pitiable sight than this fellow asking me to help him and knowing he was going to be executed. Every man there had a machine gun. I asked them what he'd done but they just waved the question away and told me to get on with it. I told this poor devil that only God could help him now and it was better to die absolved of his sins. Those words sounded so empty, what good were they to him? The four of these IRA boyos standing round with their guns. I did what they wanted. They took me back to the car and told me to wait.

'Why didn't I stay with him? They wouldn't've let me,

but still . . . I would've gone to the police, but if I said anything to the police – well, those killers and all the others would still execute victims, but without any priest to offer them absolution. And yet I think there must've been something I could have done. It was twelve years ago that happened. What do you think?'

'That you didn't have a choice, Father. Any more than if you'd been asked to tell something you'd heard in the confessional.'

The old priest was silent, looking at his beer. It had gone down in the pint by barely an inch with all his talking. He said, 'What are you here for? In Dublin, I mean.'

'Looking for someone.'

'Ah. Well, I reckon we all are. But can I buy you a pint before you have to go on looking?' The priest smiled.

So did Jury. Still, he rose, though he had no place he had to be and the search seemed hopeless.

'Some other time,' said Jury. 'Nice talking to you, Father.'

Part III

Blessings and Curses

21

He had driven back to Northamptonshire, packed up the Bentley, and made the long drive to Bletchley (*sans* Agatha, who had blessedly decided to remain in Long Piddleton a bit longer). Melrose kept his eye out for Chick'nKings along the A road, but saw only Little Chefs.

He parked the car in the garage, which sat some distance from the house and which might once have been a caretaker's cottage, although the size of the property did not seem to warrant an extra building.

Melrose had not brought much, only a couple of largish suitcases with clothes in one, books and CDs in the other, the CDs mostly Mozart and Lou Reed. He had not noticed a stereo system in the house, but he could always go to Penzance and buy one. Maybe he had skinhead inclinations, this love of loud brash music, but probably not, since it was all Lou Reed (or, of course, Mozart); he imagined the skinhead population was far less discriminating.

He lugged the suitcases through the door and set them down. He saw that in the room to the right, the drawing room, someone had started a thriving fire whose flames shot straight up the chimney and whose light thrust portentous shadows across the walls.

Who had done this, Esther Laburnum? He doubted it, but she had mentioned a caretaker or gardener; he seemed a more likely person. The fire was such a welcoming touch, a stranger attending to one's needs.

There was central heating; still, some of the rooms were so large, so cavernous, that the fire gave not only warmth and light but comfort. He took the suitcase of clothes upstairs and disposed of its contents in a chest of drawers in the careless manner that one might do when one hadn't a Ruthven around to stack perfectly ironed shirts and handerchiefs in drawers. Melrose did not think of himself as an aesthete, but he admired Ruthven's aestheticism. Ruthven (and his wife, Martha) established an order that went ticking along, hardly ever a beat missed. One got used to it; one got spoiled, too. Melrose dumped a dozen pairs of socks in one of the drawers where Ruthven would have tucked them in like babies in bassinets. Then he went back downstairs.

He commenced another wander through the house, allowing himself a much slower pace than last time. He went from drawing room to dining room, thence to the library and the study. Along the way, he once again studied each of the silver-framed photographs. He looked longest at the one of the Bletchley family gathered on the dock near the boat. They were a handsome group. The small sharp face of the elder Bletchley (Mr Chick'nKing) jutted out from under a brimmed cap that left it half in shadow. The face struck Melrose as shrewd. How happy the two children looked. Losing a child must bankrupt one emotionally. After that loss washed over one, would there be any feeling left at all? A little, perhaps; perhaps enough to be going on with. And in the Bletchley case, it was not just death but death cloaked in mystery. His thoughts went to places where wholesale wipeouts were a daily occurrence, an hourly anguish. It was unimaginable to the observer, whose mind could not possibly encompass the depths of sorrow into which a mother or father might sink.

He was overtaken, as he looked around, by a sense of the familiar. Initially, the house had reminded him of Ardry End; now, it did even more. It was not as large and hadn't as many rooms, but the feeling was the same. Was he one of those people who, upon venturing into something new, are actually reinventing something old? A person so attached to the past that whatever path he takes leads back to it, rather like fresh footsteps on a course of already trammelled ground?

He went from the study to the winding staircase and upward. These rooms he had scarcely glanced at. He looked in on each of five bedrooms gathered round the stairwell: two on each side and one at the front of the house. The bedroom at the front had its own bathroom; the two on each side shared bathrooms. He had stowed his belongings in the first bedroom to the left of the stairs because it gave the best view of the sea, a very dramatic view. Melodramatic, he should say; it depended on who was doing the looking. Thus far in his Cornwall experience, things seemed to be shaping up with melodrama to spare.

The bedrooms were fundamentally the same except for a variation in furnishings and colour. He had chosen one with a thick four-poster bed and worn leather easy chair, which he had pulled over to the window and set beside it a glass ashtray on a bronze stand. He designated this room as a smoking room.

The other bedrooms did not yield anything in particular in keeping with his mawkish mood, but upstairs as well as down he was struck by the rooms' readiness to receive visitors. Satin quilts and counterpanes; books on night tables. (By his own bed, volumes that leaned towards rigorous self-improvement: Emerson, Thoreau, and *The One-Minute Manager*, whose advice he was sure he should follow and equally sure that the lessons in the first two would shine in print but not in action. Really, these Americans could be so self-involved.)

In the piano room (which continued to fascinate) he was impressed anew by the sense that someone had left it just a moment ago. Bletchley – if it had been he who had last used it – might have only a few minutes ago inked in the notes on this score resting on the piano stand. Melrose wondered about him, wondered what the deaths of his children had done to his music. He wondered if the composing was a comfort. He stood by the casement windows and watched the sun going down. The tops of the clouds looked wet with light; the waves were edged in silver.

The position of the windows, the way they seemed to overhang the rocks so that one was looking directly down at the sea, made it, of course, impossible to see what was on the cliff directly beneath him. It had hidden the woman down there from his gaze until she moved to a spot where the side window, the west-facing window, revealed her.

Melrose was dumbstruck. He had been so much in the company of ghosts, or at least had entertained ghostly thoughts, that a human presence now seemed unreal. It had started to rain since he'd returned, and he found himself looking down through a rain like floating gauze at the crown of this stranger's light hair. She was wearing a fawn raincoat. He turned the fixture of the casement window, rolling it open. He called, 'Hello!'

The woman looked behind her, seeing nothing.

'Up here!' Melrose shouted.

Then she craned her head upward, one hand tented over her eyes.

Melrose recognized her as the woman in the photographs, the mother of the two drowned children.

22

'Please come in,' said Melrose, finding her still outside, waiting.

Stepping into the kitchen, she introduced herself as Karen Bletchley and added, 'I've been seeing Esther Laburnum about the house. You're Mr Plant.'

'I am indeed. Are you very wet? Let me have your coat.'

She thanked him as she removed her raincoat and afterwards ran her hands through her hair, shaking it a bit, getting out the raindrops. Her expression, which Melrose imagined she meant to make light and transparent, was instead grave and opaque. The smile she mustered was wintry. So were the eyes, their sadness seeming to spill over like tears, but she did not cry. She looked hurt enough to cry, though, as if Melrose had delivered a blow. The look seemed permanently stamped on her face.

He said, 'I'm just going to make some tea. You look as if you could do with a cup.'

'I certainly could. Thank you.'

'There's a fire in the study. Why don't you go in and I'll be along?'

It showed her acceptance of his place in the house – he was now the one living there – that she did not try to take over the tea preparation but was content to sit and wait. She was not a fusser.

He got the tray ready, using the good china, the cream-coloured Beleek that always struck him as too delicate to use, as vaporous as breath. When he entered the study, she was looking at the books, replacing one and taking out another.

'I hope you don't mind?'

'But of course not. They're your books.'

'Still.' The one she held she laid on the table as she sat down across from him.

The two easy chairs were drawn up to the small table as if sharing tea were their exclusive purpose. He raised the pot. 'Shall I be Mother?'

She laughed. 'By all means. I've always loved that expression. It's so antiquated.'

For a fraction of a moment, Melrose could have kicked himself, remembering that the word 'mother' would flood her with memories. But she seemed too sensible to go looking for unexploded bombs at her feet. Her eyes moved here and there, taking in the books and furnishings as if it were she rather than he who was the prospective tenant.

'Where have you been living since you left?' He offered her the plate of biscuits he had tumbled onto a plate from a fresh packet he'd bought.

She took one and bit down before she said, 'London.

We have a house there, too. And one in Majorca. But this house, this house . . .' She shook her head as her eyes focused on the framed photographs. She took up the one of the two children and herself. 'I expect Esther Laburnum told you . . .'

Melrose leaned towards her across the tea tray. He said, 'I'm terribly, terribly sorry. I have no children, so I won't say I can imagine how you feel. I can't imagine it. I can't imagine the well of sorrow this opens up in you, but it must be bottomless.'

Karen Bletchley looked at him, looked at him deeply, her grey eyes turned on him full force so there could be no mistaking that this was a person barely able to draw back from the precipice she had literally stood on an hour ago. That the feelings she had for her dead children would never, ever, be eased by the passage of time. She had been about to drink her tea, but the cup trembled too much and she replaced it in the saucer. Her hand seemed unable to let the teacup go, as if the very air had taken on a Beleek fragility and might crack if she moved.

She shook her head. 'But it's been four years, after all. I should—'

'No, you shouldn't, and no, it hasn't. It was only yesterday.'

She sat back then and picked up her cup with a firmer hand. She drank the tea, set the cup down again. 'Thanks for saying that. Truly, thanks. I seem to be surrounded by people who tell me either time will take care of the pain, or that I shouldn't dwell on it, or not to be morbid. Time does nothing, at least it hasn't up to now.'

'It doesn't apply. If you remember it just as clearly, why wouldn't you feel it just as much? It's hardly a comfort to be told you *shouldn't* feel it.' Melrose poured out more tea for both of them.

Accepting the fresh cup, Karen Bletchley settled now in the chair as if taking comfort in it and sipped the tea. After a long silence, she began the story. 'I don't know why Noah and Esmé went out. When I left sometime around eight o'clock, they were in bed, as usual. Mrs Hayter, our cook, sometimes took care of the children when we were gone, or we got a sitter in. Mrs Hayter was beside herself when I came back. Poor woman, she blamed herself for their leaving the house.' She fell silent, coughed, and went on. 'Mrs Hayter said she'd heard a noise, and that's what woke her up. She got into her dressing gown, found her torch, and went downstairs; her room's on the second floor. It's really more of a flat I fixed up for her so she'd have more privacy. She came down and there was no one here. She couldn't understand that and wondered if she'd dreamt the voices. She went to Noah's room, found he was gone, and then to Esmé's. She was gone too. The woman was in a panic, looking in every room up and down, until finally she went outside. At that point she said she was terrified, just terrified. Of course, she would be.

'The sea was very rough that night and there was a blowing rain, the sort where sounds get lost on the wind. She thought she heard crying but couldn't be sure and couldn't determine the direction the sound came from. The last place outside – the last place she wanted to look was over the cliff's edge. A combination of vertigo and fear kept her from it until she'd searched the grounds as well as she could. But she finally did, she said, and saw them. Down there in their dressing gowns, side by side, a little curled up even, as if they were in bed asleep. Waves washed over them; the tide had come in. They drowned. She knew they were dead. She knew it.'

Karen paused, shook her head. 'She was afraid we'd think she hadn't done everything she could in not going down the stone stairs, she said. But she couldn't, she was too terrified. Then she called the police; I came back first, and later Daniel. I can tell you this, though, I can tell you this.'

She had a way of saying things twice that had the effect of incantation, as if she might charm answers out of the dreadful night's events. Melrose leaned forward.

'The children meant almost as much to Mrs Hayter as they did to us. It would have taken colossal fear for her not to go down to them where they lay. Imagine her fright.' Karen stopped.

'And the police?' Melrose prompted.

'Were baffled. It's odd, you know, to see that look on the face of a policeman.' Here she turned from seeking images in the fire to look at Melrose again, and smiled a little. 'If the police hadn't arrived before we did, probably there'd be two more bodies fallen down those steps. I tried to get down but they wouldn't let me. That was just before the ambulance attendants brought the – brought the children up. It was hard manoeuvring the stretchers—' She stopped, took a sip of lukewarm tea. Then she said, 'There's something horrible about all of this.' When Melrose opened his mouth to comment, she shook her head. 'No, not just Noah and Esmé's deaths, but the circumstances, the reasons. They couldn't have fallen or been pushed from the top; there was no damage like that to their bodies. The police leaned towards its being an accident, yet they couldn't understand why two little children would go out voluntarily in their nightclothes to clamber down those stone stairs. It made no sense. The only thing I could imagine was their trying to get to the boat. We keep a small boat tied up down there to get us to the sailing boat, further out.

'This huge, unanswered question hangs over me. I can't stop wanting to know.' She sat back. She picked up the book she had taken from the shelves. *Poor Harry* was the title. 'Noah's favourite.'

She handed it across to Melrose as if it could help him understand or explain the whole dreadful business. As if at least he could contribute a modicum of wisdom, or a fresh vantage point, or a new answer. '*Poor Harry,*' he said, smiling and going through the pages, stopping to look at one or another of the illustrations, which pictured a round little boy in a variety of tight spots. He looked up. 'Harry was the scape goat for poor Noah?'

Her laugh was genuine; she appeared pleased that he'd got this much. 'A broken cup, a trampled rosebush, a torn place in a jacket sleeve. "It was poor Harry, Mum, that did it." Oh, yes, we were awash in poor Harry's escapades.'

Melrose smiled and handed back the book.

She went on, 'Daniel really couldn't stand living in this house afterwards. He didn't want these constant reminders of the children. He did try, but he had finally to leave. The London house was easier, not so many memories.'

Melrose nodded towards the displays of photographs. 'You left everything behind, even these pictures.'

She let her eyes wander over them again. 'I know. It's because – I wanted to keep the house as it was when they were here. I wanted it to be familiar to them.' She shrugged and looked away. 'I don't expect you believe in' – another shrug – 'ghosts, do you?' This was said in an offhand conversational manner. With her eyes trained on something past him – desk or window – she said, 'I'm just casting about. How about séances?'

When he laughed, she smiled. He said, 'You want me to believe in something of the paranormal.' Melrose drew in a little, turned thoughtful. 'It's odd, though. I could almost say, "Funny you should ask." When I first came into your house I was immediately put in mind of an old film which I must have seen on late-night television years ago – are you sure this house has never been used as a film set? No, I expect not; it's cheaper simply to use what's near to hand. Anyway, the winding staircase, the double doors to the living room, and the piano room – at least that's what I call it – are so much like a house in a film from the forties or fifties. *The Uninvited* is the name of it. It's perfectly sappy, the story and the *whoosh*-ing special effects; doors thrown open by unseen hands, a young lady named Stella with a dreadful British accent – the actress was American, I think – always on her uppers, hearing things, seeing things, things floating about rooms cold as ice. Anyway, I spent a few lovely moments wondering if the house was haunted and, if so'

– he shrugged – 'why so?' He smiled.

So did she. 'Nothing as far as I know has ever happened. Of course the place hasn't been lived in for years except by a couple of – decorators, I think it was.'

'Ah! The Decorators.'

She leaned back, looking comfortable now. 'Anyway, I'm glad you haven't a closed mind to this sort of thing.'

He raised his eyebrows. 'In case . . .?'

'In case, that's right.' She looked at the window. 'It's *dark*. My lord, I've been here ages.' She started to gather her things up.

'Where are you going?'

'Into the village. I'll stay overnight. I can get a room at the Drowned Man.'

Melrose said, 'I don't know that Mr Pfinn would thank you for requesting one.'

'I do remember he had the reputation of being a bit hard to get along with.'

'Why he wants a line of work that forces him to deal with the public, I can't imagine. Of course, he has five dogs to back him up in any negotiation with guests; still, the dogs are friendly enough. It's just that they're always with one; they strike me as being preternaturally interested in a guest's comings and goings. They attach themselves to one. Listen, why don't you stay here?'

'Here?' The suggestion seemed to take her breath away. It was also clear she was pleased by the invitation. 'This is very kind of you, but—'

'No, it's no trouble. It's also the most sensible thing to do, since I want to ask you about something, or tell you something, and I need time to talk about it. I don't know if there are sheets on the other beds, but there's plenty of linen – well, you know that. And that's the only chore. That and helping me cook dinner. I've brought a mountain of groceries in, things I really like – potato-y things – and fish.'

'Potato-y *things*? What did you find in the potato line that isn't potatoes?'

'Well, they're all potatoes, strictly speaking. Only different colours and different sizes. I love potatoes. I love mashed spuds, but one doesn't feel comfortable requesting them in Daphne's.'

She laughed. 'I see. We live very near Daphne's; we live right off Pont Street. When you come to London sometime, we'll be happy to have dinner there with you. I'll insist on mashed spuds.'

'With lumps in them.'

She laughed again. 'That might be more than Daphne can bear. But you must still have dinner with us. You'd like Daniel; he's awfully nice.'

'I'd like that,' said Melrose. 'Then it's agreed. You'll stay the night here and we'll divide up the cooking chores. The potatoes will be mine, so they'll have lumps. I don't like potatoes beaten to within an inch of their lives, as most people do. You can do the fish. I have Dover sole, and the fishmonger told me the very best way to cook it is to grill it with a little butter and salt and pepper and nothing else. He was determined on that point: *nothing* else.'

'I can manage that, certainly the nothing else part.'

'Now we come to the salad. I got a lot of salad stuff. I bought a wedge of Stilton and one of blue cheese with a thought to making blue cheese dressing.'

'You've really thought this through, haven't you?'

'Possibly I was expecting you. Now, I remember having a particular blue cheese dressing, probably in another life, for I only came across it once, which was thick and smooth as velvet, not the kind you get with the dribs and drabs of cheese in it; no, this was magnificently smooth. I have no idea what ingredients to use.'

'I do. I think I know just what you mean.'

'Good! Then why don't you check the beds and I'll go in the kitchen and put on a pot to boil.'

The kitchen had everything; it was the kitchen of a serious cook. Copper-bottomed pots and pans of every size hung on a rack suspended above the butcher's block; there was an exemplary and massive cooker and a refrigerator at a subzero temperature that would have satisfied Byrd and his men; there were tiers of herbs and spices.

Melrose dumped one bag of potatoes into a colander and turned on the water. He was not totally ignorant of food preparation techniques from his rare visits to his kitchen and Martha, his cook. He knew he was supposed to clean the potatoes, but he did wonder if he was supposed to cut out all the tiny eyes. They were not at all disfiguring. He thought, if I were a potato, would I prefer my eyes removed before boiling? No. Satisfied with that answer, he set about scrubbing them.

While he performed this lowly task, he thought about Karen Bletchley and the unceasing sadness that must have been her lot for these four years. While he was thinking this, she appeared in the kitchen doorway to say that she'd found the sheets and made the bed.

'Then that,' said Melrose, dropping a potato into the simmering water, 'calls for a drink.'

They sat down in the places they had occupied before, with whisky instead of tea, to continue the story.

Having lit cigarettes, she said, or started to say, 'What did you want—'

Melrose interrupted. 'You said there was something horrible in all this, apart from what happened to your children.'

'Well . . .' She seemed uncertain of going on. 'The children told me, perhaps a month or so before this happened – it was this time of year, in September – that more than once somebody would stop to talk to them. I mean somebody taking a walk in the woods. They loved to play out there.' She nodded to the wood to the left of the house. 'It was fun for playing hiding games, you know, and for fantasizing. This person, or persons, came upon them in the woods. A man, a "nice man", they said. And, once, a "nice lady".' Karen sipped her drink. 'I didn't always pay the strictest attention to what they said because they invented so much; Noah and Esmé were always pretending; they had a number of imaginary playmates. And tourists like to walk in those woods, too.'

Melrose was thoughtful. 'This Mrs Hayter. She's reliable?'

'I've never had reason to think she's not. Believe me, I asked myself that question many times. But why wouldn't she tell the truth?'

'Perhaps to make it appear that she wasn't here alone, that other people were involved. It could even have been you and your husband. The police must have questioned you pretty thoroughly. It's the parents who immediately come under suspicion.'

'That's dreadful.' She looked away, towards the window.

'Yes, but it happens all too often. Yesterday I read in the paper an account of a mother whose boyfriend didn't want her child around. The mother first fed the boy barbiturates to knock him out before she drowned him in the bathtub.'

In dismay, Karen shook her head. 'No.' She was silent for a moment, then said, 'You said you had something to tell me.'

'It's rather strange. Do you know a woman in the village named Chris Wells?'

'Chris? Of course. She owns the Woodbine tea place.'

'Her nephew—'

'Johnny?'

Melrose nodded. 'Says she's disappeared.'

'*What?*'

'He pretty much exhausted every place she might have gone and reason for going there.'

Karen shook her head again in disbelief. 'Did he try Bletchley Hall? Chris does a lot of volunteer work there. But when did this happen?'

'Before I went to Northamptonshire to collect my gear. So it's been over a week. Clearly, the boy's right: she's disappeared. And there's something else. Perhaps you've already heard about the murder in Lamorna Cove.'

'Murder?' She sat forward, eyes wide. 'My God, you mean Chris—?'

'No, no. A woman named Sada Colthorp.'

'Lamorna. I've been there; it's not much, just a few cottages and a pub and a little café operated for tourists. And a hotel, I think. Lamorna Cove's popular with tourists; it's quite lovely.'

'This Sada Colthorp was murdered at the same time Chris Wells disappeared.'

Karen looked at him. 'The police think there's some connection?'

'I don't know what they think.' He changed the subject. 'You mentioned Bletchley Hall. It's owned by your father-in-law?'

'Daniel's father.'

'The elder Mr Bletchley.'

'Morris, his name is. He seems to prefer Moe. He bought the place and donated it to the village, by way of a trust. He gave it his name, as he does everything. Except for Chick'nKing. I suppose even he couldn't see "Chick'nBletchley." He lives at the Hall. That does not mean he's dying. Far from it. Having told everyone he knows how to live, he's now telling them how to die.'

There seemed to be no rancour in her tone. Only amusement, a half-remembered smile.

Melrose smiled too. 'Domineering.'

'You've no idea. Can you imagine choosing to live there?' She made a sweeping gesture with her arm, taking in the whole room. 'This wonderful house is his. He could live here or anywhere. The man's a billionaire. That fast-food chain, I can't begin to estimate how much it's worth. And he's got a large investment in property. I can't comprehend it: living at Bletchley Hall among the dying.'

'Perhaps,' said Melrose, reflecting, 'he's overwhelmed by the fear of death.'

She'd been about to sip her whisky; her hand stopped in midair. 'Moe? He's not afraid of anything. And if he were of *that*, I'd think he'd steer clear of a hospice, to say the least.'

'Not necessarily. Someone with business genius might think he could master anything, including death, by meeting it head on. You know, to gain some sort of control. We don't think about death nearly enough. We run from it.'

She frowned. 'Isn't that rather morbid?'

Melrose was disappointed. The 'isn't-that-morbid response' was what he'd expect of a mind cluttered with clichés. It was also begging the question. 'No, it isn't.' Inwardly he sighed. No wonder he had problems with women if he was going to contradict them at every turn. Anyway, Karen Bletchley was a woman he shouldn't be considering as a 'problems-with-women' candidate. Melrose lit her cigarette, then returned to the subject of Lamorna Cove and Sada Colthorp. 'Does she sound at all familiar to you? Her maiden name was Sada May. Or Sadie, she seems to have called herself. I mean, you wouldn't have known her, would you?'

'I? Why should I have known her?'

The question had been innocent enough. Melrose thought she was being defensive. 'Only because she's from Lamorna, apparently.'

The silence now was not particularly companionable. She wore the look of one who, having accepted an invitation, was wondering how to renege on it. Melrose felt not so much uncomfortable as sad, the sadness attendant on something at best ephemeral, unnamed or unnameable, finally slipping away. A little too heartily, he slapped the arms of his chair and said as he rose, 'Time to get to the spuds. They'll be mush, but who cares, since they'll be mashed anyway.'

Her frozen look melted a bit as she said, 'The sole won't take long. By the time you get the lumps in the potatoes, it'll be done.'

It was a shot at the former easy exchange that didn't quite make it.

At dinner, they both pronounced the sole good enough to pass the inspection of the fishmonger and the potatoes properly lumpy and the wine exquisite. Bletchley had a wine cellar which Melrose hadn't known about until he apologized for the Beaujolais Nouveau which he claimed could hardly be considered 'nouveau'. Karen asked, why, if he didn't like it, had he bought it?

'Because the Oddbins fellow was so thick in his praise of it; I didn't want to seem to be doubting him.'

She laughed. 'Good lord, but you are a pushover. The fishmonger, the wine merchant.'

It was then she had told him about the wine cellar and invited him to choose his own. They went down together. He had found half a dozen bottles of Puligny-Montrachet, a Premier Cru, and his favourite Meursault. He commented upon her husband's excellent taste.

'More his father's. Though it's not necessarily his knowledge of wine. It's more Morris's insistence that if it costs a lot, it's good.'

Melrose was dusting off the bottle. 'It's true, though, isn't it? At least when it comes to wine.'

Her tone was a trifle acidic. 'You sound like someone Morris would like.'

'Oh? But then I must sound like someone you wouldn't.'

Having drunk a bottle and a half of the Montrachet between them, Melrose said, 'Who was the investigating officer when the . . . accident occurred?' He reproached himself for the coldness of the question.

Karen flinched, but she gave it some thought. 'I'm afraid I don't remember their names. I do remember, though, the high-ranking one was very . . . intense. A chief inspector or superintendent, he was. I remember his eyes. It wasn't just that they were very blue, they were a burning blue. I could almost see the tiny flame. I also remember he made me feel that his priorities were mine.'

'They were. You're talking about Commander Macalvie. Another thing about him: he never gives up.'

23

Brian Macalvie *breathed* police work. For him it was like the advertisements of carpenters and handymen: 'No job too small.' A divisional commander, Macalvie was one of the highest-ranking officers in Devon and Cornwall. Yet he would happily chase a speeding car and hand out a ticket.

He was demanding – how could he not be? – perhaps too much so, for the people under him often applied for transfers. As far as Melrose was concerned, if these lesser lights couldn't tell the difference between arrogance and commitment, maybe the CID was well shut of them.

Melrose was speaking to Macalvie now; he'd called him after Karen had left the next morning to report on his visit with Rodney Colthorp.

'Bolt. Simon Bolt. There was an investigation . . .' Macalvie paused, musing. 'Years back he lived in Lamorna. Which is where I am now. You'll be interested in the crime scene. Come along.'

Melrose was taken aback by this invitation. Although he had always got on with Macalvie, it was usually when Jury was on the case. Macalvie disliked amateurs, but then he disliked most professionals, too.

It must be instinct.

His earlier question still unanswered about the death of the Bletchley children, he asked it again: 'Couldn't they have been, say, drowned in their own bathwater and then *moved* to the rocks?'

'No.'

'How can you be sure?'

'The little kids were holding hands.' Macalvie hung up.

Johnny Wells sat in the kitchen of the Woodbine, taking some small comfort in the familiar aromas of baking scones and freshly brewed coffee, and taking comfort also in the familiar movements of Brenda Friel.

Brenda stopped her hard beating of a pastry dough that already shone in the light like satin and looked at him. 'Sweetheart, you ought not to worry so much. I know Chris will be back.'

How? he wanted to ask her. But she was only trying to lift his spirits, so he said nothing about Chris. Instead, he said, 'What about that murdered woman in Lamorna?'

Brenda's eyes widened. 'You aren't thinking that has anything to do with Chris?'

He sat studying the worn place on the vinyl floor and went back to sampling one of the Sweet Ladies. 'These are terrific; no wonder people like them. What's in the meringues?' He thought he should be generous enough to make Brenda feel her Sweet Ladies had got his mind off Chris.

She laughed. 'I don't give out my recipes, sweetheart. People have been trying to get this one out of me for years. The scones are done; you can take them right on the baking sheet as proof positive that they're fresh-made. You know how particular Morris Bletchley is.'

Johnny smiled for the first time that day, thinking about Moe Bletchley.

24

They bent to get under the tape that cordoned off this section of the footpath, then walked on wet leaves to the place where the body had been found. Macalvie hunkered down and looked with such intensity, the body might still be there.

'What are you looking for?'

Macalvie grunted. 'Rest of this.' He held up the fragment of black plastic he'd retrieved from his forensics man, Fleming, who'd exacted a promise from Macalvie that he return it.

'What is it?' Melrose turned it over and over.

'Probably a piece off the top of the plastic box that holds a tape. You know, video tapes.'

'Oh.' He waited for Macalvie to continue, but he didn't.

Macalvie stayed in this kneeling position, motionless, for what seemed a long time. The place didn't lend itself to measured time. All that could be heard was the low soughing of the waves below them and the slight rustle of the trees around them.

Macalvie rose and looked behind them in the

direction of the house where they'd left the car. A large front garden had been converted to hard standing to accommodate several cars.

'Who lives there?' asked Melrose.

'No one, now. Sada Colthorp's friend Simon Bolt used to. So there's a connection with our murdered lady. With some checking – well, say more of a lucky break I had running into a detective in London who works in the Vice Squad. He told me Bolt was in the filmmaking business. Producer, director, scriptwriter. He managed to do all of it because he wasn't making *Titanic*. Or anything else that might be shown in your local cinema. He made zip films: a lot of blood, S and M, that sort of stuff. His sideline was pornography – though it all sounds pornographic to me. They tried to get him on vice charges but couldn't make it stick. Anyway, that's who the house belonged to.' He frowned. Even Macalvie's frown was intense, as if more were stored in his expression than was common to a frown. He divested himself of what was superficial, shallow or oversimple. Everything not case-specific was burned away, and that included the suppression of his Scots accent and Glaswegian upbringing. He seemed to be getting down to cases and roots.

'This where the tape comes in?'

'Probably.'

Melrose looked at the trammelled ground where police had worked. What was it Rodney Colthorp had said about Bolt? *Bit of a wide boy, that one.*

25

The usual frisson of apprehension ran like a ripple through the crowd when Macalvie walked into the bar of the Lamorna Wink, time stopping for a second so the scene looked like a frieze rather than a room with flesh-and-blood people.

Melrose got the drinks. Some of Macalvie's fame had rubbed off on him, for the regulars watched him walk up to the bar and signal the barmaid. They had taken a table in the corner near the fireplace, though even the corner offered little escape from the inquisitive eyes of the customers. Macalvie, however, didn't appear to notice his celebrity as he went up to the jukebox, slotted in some coins, and punched up a tune. He was still wearing his coat even though the fire poured out heat as if it came from a pitcher.

One might suppose the man was always cold, as some people are. But Melrose felt as if Macalvie was instead always leaving. He was surprised by the deep anxiety this provoked in him, as if a support kept threatening to give way. In this respect, Macalvie was different from Richard Jury; Jury seemed cloaked in a sort of melancholy, yet always seemed to leave some of his comfort behind; when Macalvie left, consolation left with him. And it seemed to have something to do with that coat which he never took off.

Macalvie said, 'There was so much lying going on in that house, I didn't know who not to believe.' Arms crossed on the table and looking at his drink, he went on, 'We got there a few minutes after midnight, the ambulance before us. I told them not to take the bodies up before the pathologist and I looked at them. It was raining by this time and the steps were like glass, bloody slippery. The little kids were lying on their stomachs. The bodies didn't sink or get carried away because they got tangled up in the rope that anchored the boat. They were side by side, their faces turned towards each other as if they'd been talking; probably they had, before – well, whatever happened, happened. They were wearing cotton pyjamas, hers white, his blue, and flannel dressing gowns which would have been some protection against the cold but not much. Slippers, too. Two of them – the slippers – had been washed away by the choppy water. Their feet weren't any bigger than the palm of my hand.' His elbow propped on the table, he held up a hand for Melrose to judge. 'They were holding hands.'

He stopped at this image, which was clearly disconcerting, as if he had no choice but to re-enter the scene.

'So what had happened? Did they go down the stairs because they wanted to get into the boat? I didn't believe that. Why did they, then? They must've been told to go down the stairs. Or been told – something. A trick? A treasure? No one in that house had any idea of what they were up to.

'Karen Bletchley got back to the house half an hour after I got there. There'd been trouble getting hold of her, the housekeeper told me, because the people she was having dinner with in St Ives weren't on the telephone. Hard to believe, in this day and age, with that kind of money. But maybe that's what the well-heeled call roughing it. Daniel, the father, was purportedly in Penzance on business. He didn't get home until an hour later.'

'Purportedly?'

'When a man goes out at nine o'clock at night, it might be for a beer, but I have trouble thinking it's business. I also doubted it was business when he stalled on producing the name of this business associate. I assumed it was a woman but didn't want to make a point of it then. He was too cut up, remorseful, and – as the Irish say – destroyed. The sort of man who blames himself because he lacks hindsight.'

'But later?'

'Did I pursue this line of inquiry?' Macalvie smiled and took another swallow. 'Of course. Finally, he admitted it but refused to give the name of the woman. Bletchley's stubborn, believe me. Even when I threatened him with obstruction, he refused. Anyway, Dan Bletchley was away when he was needed and the man probably never will get over it. To be gone when you know you were desperately needed: I know what that's like. I felt sorry for him. All of his life he's going to hold himself responsible.'

They sat, whiskies in hand, the main source of light and heat coming from the fireplace. They had drawn as close as they could to it.

'Karen Bletchley was hysterical at first. It took two WPCs to hold her back from the clifftop, to keep her from going down those stone steps. I told the police surgeon to sedate her, just enough so I could talk to her.' He looked up when Melrose made a sound of disapproval. 'You think the police are heartless? Give somebody twenty-four hours to think things over, and you won't get a proper statement. Too much will be suppressed, not necessarily intentionally.'

Melrose said he was going to get refills. While he stood at the bar, waiting for the fresh drinks, he wondered if Karen Bletchley had told Macalvie the same things she'd told him.

'What did she tell you?' he asked when he'd returned to the table.

'After the initial questions had been answered about where she was' – Macalvie accepted his refilled glass from Melrose – 'she asked did I believe in evil spirits? In hauntings? In premonitory occurrences? "It's not what I believe, it's what you do," I said. She said there was something wrong at Seabourne – which I was only too willing to believe, given what had happened, but not that ghosts were responsible.' Macalvie paused for a drink of beer.

'She went on: "I thought at first I was simply too imaginative. Or reading into behaviour things that didn't exist. Furniture moved around in their schoolroom, for instance. When I asked them why they'd done it, they said, 'We didn't,' and tittered. Noah and Esmé are – were – very close." Then she said, "Every once in a while I'd see some new bit of clothing, like a handkerchief or a bracelet they claimed to have found in the woods. One day I was watching them and saw them talking to a strange man. At least I thought it was; I couldn't see very well into the trees. I was rather frightened. It all seemed so – menacing. And one day I saw a figure in dark clothes and dark hair across the pond further along. A woman was standing there. Were these people putting them up to their tricks? The children did silly little things, like putting a tiny tree frog in Mrs Hayter's apron pocket. The poor woman had a fit! But when I asked them, they just denied it and looked . . . sly. That's the only way I can describe it – sly. It was almost like a campaign to make us uncomfortable." '

Melrose studied his glass and thought about Karen Bletchley, there in the study, but did not interrupt.

'I asked what her husband's response was to all of this. She didn't answer for a moment, but finally said that Daniel brushed it aside as a series of childish pranks. "Good lord, Karen, a tree frog in someone's pocket and you think we're in the grip of evil spirits!"

'It's Daniel Bletchley's father, Morris Bletchley, who actually owns Seabourne. He went to live at the Hall – a kind of nursing home, which he also owns – not long after the death of the children. They were his grandchildren. At the time it happened he was living with them. He's used to controlling things. He's apparently a hell of a good businessman, given the success he has with that chicken franchise.

'I'm mentioning this only because now he was confronted with an action – and its horrible consequences – that was out of his control. He said the least of any of them and seemed to be affected most. At least more than his daughter-in-law – despite the hysterics. Anyway, that was my impression.'

The proprietress was calling time.

Macalvie said, 'You hardly ever hear that any more, do you, what with the new licensing laws.'

Melrose gathered up their empty glasses. 'Is it too late?'

'No, but I'm in the chair this round.'

Melrose made a face and took the glasses. The woman behind the bar pursed her lips but got the drinks. As he stood there, Melrose looked back at Macalvie and thought he looked stranded in the room now emptying.

He went back and set the drinks down. 'This case never closed for you, did it?'

Macalvie was lighting another cigarette. 'They don't, my cases.' He stared at the fire, smoked his cigarette.

'But this one especially. You've been reporting conversations verbatim. How could you do that after four years?'

'My notes. I've read through them so often, trying to work out what I missed, you could see light through the seams of the pages they're written on. That's why.'

Melrose thought of the letter his mother had written. 'Why do you think you missed something?'

Macalvie cut him a look. 'Because it hasn't been solved, so I must have.' Ash fell from the cigarette he wasn't attending to. He said then, 'Let me tell you

164

something. I was a policeman in Glasgow for several years, started out as a PC but wanted to be a detective. That was my great dream, to be a detective.' He looked over at Melrose. 'I bet you never thought I'd have a great dream, right?'

'You don't strike me as a dreamer.'

Macalvie smiled and went on, 'I got to be a DI pretty quickly, mostly because of a particular case I worked on. Quite a big case, it was. In a shootout, the suspect's daughter got caught in the crossfire. She was eleven or twelve. It wasn't my gun that did it but he thought it was and held me responsible because I was the one who'd been plaguing him all along.

'Anyway, I was transferred to Kirkcudbright. I guess to get the heat off. It was bad, the pressure. You can imagine there weren't a hell of a lot of murders in Kirkcudbright, which is a kind of artists' haven; artistic jealousy is about the top rung on their crime ladder.

'But I met someone. Maggie. She was a painter and a beautiful woman. I moved in with her. She had a daughter, Cassie, who was six years old. Maggie always used to tell me how much safer she felt with a copper in the house, how she could sleep easier. Then one night Cassie was taken right out of her bed and out of the house.'

'God, how awful!'

'We kept expecting a phone call, a ransom demand, something. But there was no word. Nothing for two weeks. Maggie was nearly crazy, forced into this limbo of not knowing. So was I.

'Then I got a message slipped into the newspaper we

had delivered. I was to go to an old cottage in the Fleet Valley. There was a map, a route I was to follow. Eventually I found the place. It was a derelict cottage, birds nesting in the thatch, windowpanes broken. The most intense silence; I've never known such silence. It smelled of death. I moved very slowly. I thought it was a trap. *Why* it might have been a trap, I had no idea. I found Cassie in the kitchen. She was propped up in a chair, shot in the chest. On the table was a piece of paper, and on it was written, *How does it feel?* And then I knew. The bastard had plenty of friends on the outside; this was payback for collaring him.

'There was a bowl of Weetabix in front of her, half eaten.' Macalvie paused, looked at Melrose. 'The body was warm, the milk still cold, fresh.' Out of electric-blue eyes, he stared at Melrose. 'See, they'd added that little detail, that coup-de-grâce, in case I hadn't suffered enough, making me think, if I'd only got there fifteen minutes earlier . . . But I couldn't have. They'd obviously monitored my trip. One of them probably called ahead to give my position.'

A flicker of pain brushed Macalvie's face. 'Fifteen minutes earlier I could have heard her voice, heard her cry. That was what I was supposed to think. The only consolation was she appeared not to have been mistreated.

'I called it in. Police, ambulance, they were there in under twenty minutes. While I waited I kept thinking, if I'd been smart I wouldn't have taken the route they gave me—'

'No. Then they wouldn't have gone through with it.

They'd have stepped up the anxiety even more and then put you through it again. I don't think there's a way to outwit a person whose only motive is to make you suffer.'

Macalvie sat back. 'That's why I never dropped this case. Those two kids—'

'I know.' Melrose thought how Brian Macalvie never talked about himself. And yet you always knew exactly where you were with him. You might not know where he came from, where he lived, who his mates and girlfriends were, but you knew his mental geography. You knew his territory.

Macalvie shook his head, drank the rest of his whisky as if preparing to go, but still sat looking at the floor, or his shoes or shadows. 'She felt so much safer with me in the house. Christ! Having me in the house was like having a ticking bomb there; I brought all that grief down on the poor girl's head.'

'What happened to her? Maggie?'

'I don't know. We broke up, of course, soon after the kidnapping. I begged her to stay. I thought I could help her, which was arrogant, I suppose but she wouldn't; of course she wouldn't. There was no way she could ever think it wasn't my fault.'

The proprietress, wiping glasses behind the bar, had been giving them hurtful looks for half an hour now. *The rest of the place is empty; there's just you two that's keeping me up.*

Macalvie looked her way, palmed his cigarettes back into his pocket, and said, 'Let's go.'

Outside they stood for a moment looking up at the stars and out over the water. Melrose said that not even the most vivid imagination would see such a bizarre murder here in Lamorna Cove.

'Not in Kirkcudbright either.'

26

Setting his electric wheelchair on a collision course with Matron, down at the end of the long gallery, Morris Bletchley released the brake and sped down a highway of oriental carpet.

Here she came, stomping towards him, looking less and less confident that she would win this game of chicken. She had a great ski slope of a bosom flying downhill from some stiff lace thingamabob at her throat. Her hair was in its usual punishing bun, stuck sharply with several silver-headed pins, pulling her scalp back to within an inch of its life.

Just pray your maker has gone to prepare one of those rooms always on offer, thought Morris Bletchley, arrowed straight at her. Why had he ever hired her? Probably for the same reason he kept her on: with the name MATRON pinned to her chest, she looked like she'd come from central casting. You just knew that's what a matron looked like. He'd had to put up with so many of those creatures when he was growing up, it satisfied his sense of the rightness of things that he should now be able to call the shots. There! She'd chickened out and was pressing her bosomy self flat against the wall. Moe stopped just short of her feet and asked innocently, 'You wanted to see me, Matron?'

'Mr Bletchley! I cannot put up with these ridiculous games you play.'

He loved the way she talked – such pomposity. 'But that's part of your job, to keep us old fools in line.'

'I wanted to see you about the Atkins woman. She's come, she's here, but she hasn't – or her family hasn't – her part of the fee. Which is small enough,' she added disapprovingly.

Moe Bletchley used a sliding scale; it was pretty much pay-what-you-can. Sometimes they couldn't. He subsidized the rest. The scale in Mrs Atkins's case had stopped sliding at ten per cent, which amounted to thirty pounds per day. Given it cost more like three hundred to provide rooms, medical care, full-time nurses, and gourmet food, thirty pounds was a drop in the bucket.

Well, it was Moe's bucket and he could have whatever he liked dropped in it. He cocked his head and said, 'So?'

She seemed astonished he should ask. 'How can we admit her when she hasn't fulfilled the terms of her contract?'

'Why didn't you tell her to sell her first-born grand-child?'

Matron drew herself up, tilting her breastplate even more. '*Mr* Bletchley! If you insist on bending the rules and relaxing standards, our job will become impossible.'

'I've been bending and relaxing for four years and you're still here, ain't you?'

She pressed the bridge of her nose, one of several mannerisms denoting victimization. She said, 'If you feel my services are no longer necessary—'

'Oh, but they are, they are! You are a formidable presence; you set an example!'

Still higher went the bosom, but this time with pride. 'I certainly *hope* to keep the younger and less seasoned staff on their toes.' She ventured a wintry smile. 'Now, if you care to come and speak with Mrs Atkins?'

Moe flapped his hand. 'I'll talk to her later. You show her where her room is. I'm off to visit Linus Vetch.' Moe removed his baseball cap, rubbed the top of his head, and slapped the cap back on. He gave a little wave and snapped the wheelchair into a ninety-degree turn.

Rules. Matron lived for them; they were her sound and substance. But it was pretty hard to apply 'rules' to the dying, much less enforce them. Heavy with anger and corsets, Matron turned on her heel and marched down the galleried hall.

Damn it all, thought Moe, wish we'd had her at Okinawa. Moe had served three years in the Second World War. In no hurry now, he rolled along on the deep blue and green oriental runner that not too long ago had been trod by Lord Bugger-all and his lady wife. They had sold up because they couldn't afford their stately home, then called Sheepshanks Hall, any longer. No wonder, when these British aristocrats (whom he disliked without exception) tossed money around like confetti, paying for big cars and horses and keeping a staff of fifty. They had been raised not to work but to lounge.

Moe was an American who'd spent the last part of his life in Britain. He'd peeled off all he wanted to in the States (millions) and come to see what was on offer in England (billions).

Moe had built up a fast-food chicken empire 'from scratch' (as he was fond of telling people, most of whom didn't get it, but then most people were pretty witless). He called this popular chain of eateries Chick'nKing. Franchises had sprouted all over England. He had even wanted to plant a few on the North Yorkshire moors and Dartmoor, but the idea had met with little enthusiasm from the council people and National Heritage. Moe wasn't long on aesthetics, except for the design and decor of his Chick'nKings. There he went to town; they were the brightest, boldest things on the horizon, painted in astonishingly brilliant colours. And he had broken the every-one-the-same commandment by having three different designs. It was his building planner – not quite an architect and a kid at heart – who loved to come up with fresh ideas for the shape of a new Chick'nKing. Some were egg-shaped, an enormous marine-blue egg, painted with bands of Easter-egg designs and standing on its fatter end. There were two dozen of these. Another group was designed to resemble a hen laying, or rather sitting on a nest. Then there was the newest line Moe had christened Chick'nTots, designed expressly for the kiddies. (As if the others weren't?) These were a huge hit with both children and parents. They were shaped like chicks and painted a buttercup yellow so bright you could see them half a mile away down the A30 to Truro. The Chick'nTots were popular with parents because there were small tables and chairs in a section set apart so the children could eat out from under the parental eye and even order from their own menus; it made no difference whether or not they could read since there were pictures of every dish. the kiddies' area was tended by a pretty Disney World-ish princess with a pink neon wand. She was there in case the kiddies started throwing food at each other. Peace would be restored immediately; it's amazing what a princess with a wand can do that mums and dads can't.

Another big difference between Moe's eateries and most others was the food. This had been brought about several years back. One of the Chick'nKings had run out of chips (tasteless but familiarly tasteless, which made the difference), and an employee named Patsy Rankin had just sliced some potatoes thinly, tossed them in the hot oil, and served up homemade chips the like of which had never been seen in any fast-food place. The customers loved them so much, sales of everything had leaped by over ten per cent. No one appreciated invent-iveness more than Moe Bletchley. Patsy Rankin was immediately transferred to the Birmingham head-quarters in charge of food innovation, a position created for her talents alone.

Chick'nKing had cost a fortune to get started but had already tripled that fortune for Moe Bletchley. The difference between his and others' fast-food emporiums was that the food was better and the buildings so whimsical they simply sucked people in.

Linus Vetch had been admitted six weeks before and was clearly rallying. The unusual thing about Bletchley

Hall was that the people who came here, all diagnosed with a terminal illness, did not all leave in a box. Actually, it was part hospice, part nursing home, and not a small part resort. Of course, no one could enjoy this last element if he wasn't deemed sick-to-dying. But some diagnosed as terminal got considerably better and left under their own head of steam – or perhaps to the disappointed expectations of their relatives who were then forced to return the elderly family member to his or her own hearth. This made Bletchley Hall a sort of miracle home and, consequently, a highly desirable last stop on the road to wherever. This rallying of seemingly hopeless cases mystified the doctors.

'What the hell's the big mystery?' said Moe. 'It was you fellas misdiagnosed these cases in the first place.'

'Mr Bletchley,' Dr Innes had said, 'Linus Vetch came in with oesophageal cancer. Hardly ever does a patient recover from that particular cancer. Linus Vetch has had radiation, chemo, a bone marrow transplant—'

'So? Maybe the voodoo finally kicked in. It happens.' Moe started humming.

This, of course, infuriated Dr Innes and no wonder: if a patient had terminal something, he should terminate.

'It makes me wonder,' Moe went on, 'why you fellas hate to see somebody get better.'

'That's absolute nonsense. I—'

Moe waved a thick-veined hand, meaning *shut up, man*. 'Thing's this: a fellow is diagnosed with a terminal disease. Then he doesn't die. Well, one of those premises is wrong. So it must be the first one. Unless of course you think we've got another Lourdes here and I'm the Virgin Mary.'

'Funny,' said Dr Innes. 'I never really suspected that.' He flounced off down the hallway in a manner that Moe was surprised hadn't raised Matron's suspicions.

Linus Vetch was propped up in his bed, looking wasted, true, but otherwise like a man on the mend. The poor fellow, in his seventies, had been through the hell of chemotherapy and a bone marrow transplant and still lived to talk about it. That he could talk was surprising, the radiation and chemo probably doing his vocal cords little more good than the cancer that had invaded his oesophagus a year ago.

Moe bumped into the lavishly appointed room and up to the bed, where Linus shot his hand up for a high five. They had taken to greeting this way ever since the once-dying man had been able to raise his arm. Moe had to admit it was amazing. He himself had never been sick (with anything other than contrariness) and he knew he had no conception of the physical pain Linus Vetch had been cursed with.

'So what's up, buddy?' Moe treated all patients – he preferred to call them 'guests' – as if they'd just stopped in for a pleasant weekend.

'Better today. Must be your cooking.'

'Brought you tonight's menu.' Moe believed looking forward to a fine meal could keep you going at least until you got it. Food was surprisingly soporific and comforting, and the meals here were cooked by two first-rate chefs Moe had lured away from two four-star restaurants.

175

Linus drew himself into more of a sitting posture and fumbled for his glasses. 'Where did I put the damned things? Always losing them.'

'Maybe they're in the drawer.' Moe nodded towards the bedside table. Linus always kept them there and always forgot that he did.

Linus found them and hooked them over his ears, as if for a better view of Morris Bletchley. Then he removed them and looked around the room.

He had the most searching look Moe had ever seen. Eyes that scanned the entire room, floor to ceiling, as if some sort of answer could be found in the William Morris-designed wallpaper, the Art Deco wall sconces, the beautiful wood floors, Kirman carpet, and high windows that looked out over the flower-bound stream.

Still, Moe wished he had the answer, or at least some answer to give Linus.

Linus said, 'What put you in that wheelchair?' He was always asking this. It was clear he was glad that Moe, although not dying, hadn't got off scot-free.

But Moe had. He could walk as well as the next man (as long as the next man wasn't Linus, who couldn't make it to the toilet without a steadying hand).

Moe slapped the wheelchair's arm. 'Life, Linus. Life put me here.'

27

When Emily Hayter answered her doorbell the following morning, she looked up at Melrose as if she'd been expecting to see someone else. As she opened the door, her small mouth seemed to form a word or words called back when she saw him. Her figure was hefty with age and too much of her own good baking. Melrose could smell some of it now, the spicy warmth of cloves and nutmeg that hung in the air.

He introduced himself, unnecessarily, for she clearly knew about him; had the disappearance of Chris Wells not superseded him, Melrose would be the most interesting thing in the village. Seabourne had stood untenanted for a number of years (except for the Decorators, who hadn't lasted long). Curiosity overcame inconvenience. She waved him in with the wooden paddle she was holding – he wondered what it was for – invited him to have a seat and a cup of coffee, and said the apricot bread was just cooling. Had it been timed for someone else's arrival?

Emily Hayter lived in a little street not much wider than an alleyway behind the village's main street where the Drowned Man and the Woodbine Tearoom sat. Her cottage was similar to her neighbours': a mansard roof sloping down to peephole windows and whitewashed clay. It stood in an overgrown garden. Indeed, the garden seemed to have trailed into the front room, for here where Melrose took a seat were weedy potted plants, ivy-bound, and papery, stricken buds and blossoms.

Yet Mrs Hayter struck Melrose as a woman of industry, so perhaps a lack of time was her problem. Coming in with a tray of coffee, she confirmed this. 'There just never seems to be time for things,' she said as she jammed the plunger down in her French press pot, which seemed to sigh in its downward descent in tune with Mrs Hayter's own huge sigh. 'You saw the state o' my garden, and in here too. You can see . . .' She waved the white napkins she'd brought in around the room as if they were flags of surrender, and poured the coffee. She did this with a grace that spoke of many years of pouring. The bread she now passed to Melrose looked delicious and was undoubtedly the source of the spiced air.

Once they'd settled back, she asked him how he was liking Seabourne. 'Very much. It's a beautiful place. A wonderful setting, too, up there overlooking the sea.' He added this, hoping it would cue her to speak of the children.

'Cold, though. Costs a fortune to heat those rooms.' Her glance swept over him, no doubt estimating the extent of his.

'I don't mind a nip in the air.' (Oh, yes, he did.) 'I'm used to it.' (Oh, no, he wasn't.)

Emily Hayter struck Melrose as a pump that would require some priming; she hadn't risen to the prospect overlooking the sea, so perhaps he should lead with more suggestions. 'The estate agent tells me the owner lives in the village. In a kind of nursing home and hospice?' He was sure she would be only too ready to talk about the eccentric Morris Bletchley.

'Oh, yes. Mr Morris started that. Used to be a stately home, and he took it over and calls it Bletchley Hall. I expect it's quite nice for those unfortunates so near . . .' She could not summon a cliché to make death more acceptable. 'Mr Morris, yes, he's a queer duck, that one.'

Melrose waited patiently to be told about Mr Bletchley's queer duck-ness while Mrs Hayter fed herself a morsel of apricot bread and washed it down with coffee.

'See, he owns the Hall so he can do as he wants. I expect it's generous of him to provide care like that, but as for me, I think you'd have to be a little batty to go live there, don't you? I mean, does a person want to be reminded of – you know – all the time? Yes, definitely a queer duck is Mr Morris.'

She did not go on, leaving Melrose to cast about for an opening to the tragedy of the Bletchley children. His eye fell on the rather bad examples of art hanging on her walls and then fixed on a print of a stormy J.M.W. Turner. He smiled, thinking of Bea. Turner was her favourite.

He said, 'That's a very nice Turner, there behind you.'

She looked round, as if it were someone else's Turner, and said, 'Morbid, I'd say. It was Mr Hayter liked that one. He died not two years ago.' It was as if death came to Mr Hayter because of the painting.

But Death and Turner did give Melrose an opening. 'Wasn't there an awful tragedy at Seabourne several years ago? Two children drowned, I believe.'

She was only too pleased to discuss it, which she did at length, as it gave her one more opportunity to exonerate herself. Her own account was exactly the same as Macalvie's. Winding it up, finally, she said, 'You see, sometimes they'd go down there to get on Mr Daniel's boat. You know, their father's. That's what the police thought, that they wanted to get to the boat.'

Not bothering to correct her on that score, Melrose said, 'But how could Bletchley get a boat in among those rocks?'

Emily Hayter was not at all interested in boatmanship and waved the question away. 'Well, he could, is all I know.' She had been interrupted by a nonsensical question and now would get back to her own report. 'Something woke me, something like a yell or a cry. I'm up on the second floor, so it's a distance. And I thought if some noise would reach up there, it must be pretty loud. So I put on my dressing gown and slippers and went downstairs. It was dark and I couldn't see down to the first floor; anyway, you can imagine I was alarmed. Then I stiffed myself up' – here she sat straighter, stiffing herself – 'got a torch, and –' She paused to select another slice of apricot bread.

'You went . . .'

'Straightaway to the children's rooms. When I saw they were out of bed, I got a worse fright than I'd got from the noise. I looked all through the house, calling them. Nothing. No one. Did I tell you the Bletchleys went off? Did I mention that?' She clearly disapproved.

'Then, you . . .'

'Well, I went outside, of course. There wasn't no one, nor did I hear anything. Only the sound of the sea. I must've been out there for a good twenty minutes, looking through the woods, and there was nothing. I didn't want to stay out, it being the middle of the night. I'll tell you something, sir.' Her voice dropped to a sibilant whisper. 'There's legends round these parts about that house—'

A legend. Oh, great. He must rush to inform Brian Macalvie. He pasted a smile on his face and hoped she'd get back to reality if he was patient.

'—that it's built on the graves of a family that was murdered in their sleep.' She leaned across the table, close enough for him to smell her nutmeggy breath. 'The place they say is haunted by the ghost of a governess named Marianna.'

There's always a governess, often named Marianna or some version of the name. Well, he needn't feel so superior. Who had been mooning about, hoping the imaginary Stella would turn up? He frowned, thinking again of Karen Bletchley's story: a woman on the other side of the pond.

'The poor girl fell in love with some pirate. He only wanted to rob the place blind, of course. He did and he left and she never saw him again.'

'Ah.' He was not sure what he was ah-ing about. 'And where did whoever saw it see this ghost?'

'On the cliff above those rocks.' Ever closer, she leaned towards Melrose, pulling her skirts more tightly down over her knees. 'They say she stands there always looking out to sea.'

Ever stood she, prospect impressed. There it was again, the line from Hardy. He felt the same unutterable loneliness wash over him, despite the warm cottage, the pleasant homely woman, the apricot bread . . .

He roused himself from the cloud that settled over him to hear her say, ' . . . and one of the Decorators—'

There they were again, those marvellous boys, the Decorators! They'd certainly left their imprint on Bletchley.

'He claimed he saw this ghost in the kitchen. But those two were – well, I can't imagine they were very dependable.'

It was clear what she thought of 'those two'. Melrose turned to another subject. 'Bletchley certainly has its share of bizarre and unhappy occurrences. This unfortunate woman who seems to have vanished – her nephew waited on me at the Drowned Man.'

She was nodding her head before he'd half finished. 'That'll be Chris Wells you're talking about. As you say, a strange thing to happen.'

'She owns the Woodbine Tearoom, doesn't she?'

'Her and Brenda Friel. Good workers, those two, and make no mistake, operating a business like that, that's hard work for not much return. I help out sometimes with my berry pies. They're real popular, my pies. If they go away, I go in and help out young John, Chris's nephew. I'd say a lot of kids could take a page from his book.'

Work was clearly the yardstick Emily Hayter used to take the measure of man. Melrose would rate perhaps half an inch. 'The lad is awfully upset.'

'And why not? Chris Wells is like a mother to him. His da died, and his own mother just went off when he was a little thing. Chris was her sister. I was thinking she might have gone to help that good-for-nothing relation of hers lives in Penzance.' She leaned nearer Melrose. 'It's the drink taken over with him. I've no patience with that kind of thing.'

'Good lord, Mrs Hayter, here I've been sitting over an hour and forgot why I came! I was wondering if you could spare me just a few hours every week to do some cooking. You've the reputation of being an excellent cook.' A little flattery never hurt.

He was right. If she hadn't before thought of herself as excellent, she did so now. 'Well, I did do a bit of everything. How much time were you thinking of?'

'Oh, just once a week.' He'd decided he really didn't want anyone at all, for he was enjoying knocking about on his own. But he needed some reason to call on her. 'I thought perhaps you could cook up a batch of food and freeze it and I could shove it in the oven or whatever when I needed it. You needn't bother with this week, as I'll be dining out a lot.'

They agreed on a time, and she took a notebook from behind a pillow on the couch (Melrose marvelled at this secreting of the notebook; were a number of villagers after her cooking and charring schedule?) and wrote something down with the pencil attached by a string to the notebook.

'There. I've put in seven a.m. the Thursday after next. So that's sorted!'

Not for Melrose, it wasn't. 'Could you make it a bit later? Say, ten?'

'Yes, I expect so.' She gave him a look that suggested she couldn't imagine what he'd be doing at 7 a.m. that her presence would interrupt. Out collecting fossils, perhaps? 'If you don't mind me saying it, sir, it wouldn't come amiss to have something done with the grounds. They're looking poorly.'

'Ah. Yes, you're right. Have you someone in mind?'

'It's Jason Slatterly used to be gardener, and very good he is.'

'Perhaps it was he who laid a fire for me the first day.'

'I'm sure it was. He does nice little things like that for people.' Here she blushed furiously and tried to cover it up by raising her teacup to hide her face.

Had Mrs Hayter romantic notions about Mr Slatterly? This appealed to Melrose, this never-say-die attitude towards romance. And in one who, though not precisely stout, had the solidly packed form of a fireplug, little dimension to waist, hips, and breasts. 'Tell me about him.'

'He was gardener for years when the Bletchleys lived there. The Decorators hired him back. But they wanted topiary designs. Mr Slatterly couldn't see his way to doing that and argued against it. But those Decorators would have their swans, wouldn't they? That's why the shrubbery on either side of the front door has that ragged look to it. The Decorators messed the place about for nearly a year and then went back to London, where they should have stayed if I'm any judge of things. This being Cornwall, we don't much care for the fancy ways of London.'

Melrose liked the way she made Cornwall sound like the Outer Hebrides. But then, Cornwall did rather think of itself as separate from the rest of England. And 'fancy' London was trickling to Cornwall more and more for their second homes, buying up decrepit fishermen's cottages or great piles of stone set atop craggy cliffs, like Seabourne.

'This Mr Slatterly, could you speak to him on my behalf?' My God, that was kingly enough.

She would be only too happy to do so.

He rose. 'Well, thank you so much, Mrs Hayter. And I'll be seeing you then in two weeks?'

'Yes, you will.'

'Fine.' Melrose let his gaze rest on the J.M.W. Turner, the original of which was in the Tate; had he looked at the painting in the Tate five minutes longer, it would have burnt a hole in his retina, the light was so glorious.

28

Morris Bletchley really interested Melrose.

Anyone who could buy up a stately home (small, but still stately enough), home for generations to viscounts, barons, and baronets, and turn it around into a combination hospice and nursing home was worthy of interest. Especially when the someone was an American who'd made his fortune in fast-food eateries.

On this particular golden September afternoon, Melrose stood gaping at the land beyond the high windows of the old Sheepshanks – now Bletchley – Hall. Formerly the ancestral home of Viscount Sheepshanks (or so the brochure told him), the grounds were simply magnificent, a blaze of marigolds and purple orchids blanketing much of the ground, but also arranged in knot gardens and parterres. The brochure had been given him by an overbearing, stout woman in a grey bombazine dress who had taken his request to see Mr Morris Bletchley, as she no doubt took all requests. Her face did not change its expression of being put-upon, as this seemed to be her lot in life. She had gone off to fetch Mr Bletchley, after directing Melrose to wait in this beautiful room in which he was standing, looking at an ornate fountain in which dolphins frolicked with bronze fish and cherubs; beyond this lay a gentle downward slope of lawn to the dip of a stream that bisected the land. Shallow steps led down to it, drifts of late-season grasses and clumps of spotted orchids grew along its banks. Dahlias, cyclamen, and purple clematis grew on the downward-sloping lawn. About the grounds were situated white benches on which now sat one youngish woman, no doubt one of the inhabitants of Bletchley Hall, all diagnosed as terminal, a diagnosis Melrose sincerely hoped was not acting itself out as he watched.

Sharing this room with him was an old woman who had probably got here under her own steam, given the silver-headed cane her hand was still closed around, but who was now peacefully sleeping.

The idea behind the hospice movement was that one could die at home, in familiar surroundings. So in this regard it wasn't a hospice; yet it was a happy combination of both hospice and nursing home – if 'happy' was the word. Melrose thought that if one had to die away from one's own home and kith and kin, one couldn't do better than Bletchley Hall. Or even given the choice between home and Hall, one might choose Bletchley. This was one of the times when he thanked God he had money. To be old and infirm was bad enough; to be old and infirm and poor was unthinkable. Deathbed scenes (he'd always thought) were grossly exaggerated in their display of filial devotion, the melodrama of relations gathered round the bed, weeping copiously, a battalion of black figures. More likely it was several hundred quid to the mortician and take her away. Or the family would all be out watching a cricket match or tucking into a set tea while Gran or Mum was expiring in an upstairs bed-room. No, the actuality of the moment of death leaned more towards the absence of loved ones than towards their presence.

But at Bletchley Hall, one could be certain of one's death being well-attended, the sheets white, the pillows plumped. Melrose could hardly wait for Sergeant Wiggins to see it. *There* was a man who could appreciate upscale care!

The room in which Melrose waited was not especially large, but the ceiling vaulting above his head was resplendent with elaborately carved mouldings; the room drank up sunlight as if pitchers of it were spilling across the huge oriental rug that shimmered like silk, and angels could have danced on the sunbeams. The old lady sitting in a big Jacobean chair that dwarfed her was so lit up she might have been called to a higher glory. Melrose hoped she slept. In a place like this, it did not pay to investigate.

The stout woman in grey returned to tell Melrose that Mr Bletchley was on his way and then crossed the room to raise her voice to the old lady: 'Mrs Fry! Mrs Fry! Time to wake up!'

Why? wondered Melrose. Surely Mrs Fry's caravan had reached a stage in its slow journey when it wasn't 'time' to do any bloody thing at all. Time for her had gone completely out of the window with the withdrawing light. Time was of no consequence.

And why was it necessary to yell at old people as if they were all deaf? A few more Mrs Frys and Melrose was rising to assist when the old lady twitched awake. How could she help but wake with that voice barking in her ear? Now it told her it was 'Time for your tea, dear.'

As the stout woman (labelled MATRON, she obviously functioned in some sort of managerial position) helped Mrs Fry up and out, an elderly man in a wheelchair buzzed in and up to Melrose and held out his hand.

'Morris Bletchley. People call me Moe. You wanted to see me? You wouldn't happen to have a fag, would you? As long as it's not that mentholated crap.' He gave Melrose a once-over, as if evaluating him for good-times possibilities. Melrose wished he'd stuck a flask in his back pocket.

'I do, yes.'

Moe Bletchley turned the chair and started towards the door with a 'follow me' wave. As Melrose followed, Bletchley said over his shoulder, 'Smoking room's this way. Got to be careful here. Emphysema, emphysema. Wouldn't want anyone with lung cancer watching me enjoying myself while I'm on the way to it.' Bletchley laughed, mostly through his nose. 'You too.'

Melrose thanked him for that emphysemiac blessing as the two made their way down a long gallery, Melrose walking as fast as he could to keep pace with the wheelchair, which might have run down more of the Bletchley Hall patients than emphysema ever would. The walls of this gallery once were hung with Sheepshank family portraits no doubt carted off by the viscount; Melrose deduced this because the paintings now hanging there, romantic ones of cottages and shepherds, drovers with sheep and sheepdogs, still lifes of pears and apples, did not fill up the vacated spaces and showed borders of fresher paint. Moe Bletchley whizzed through a shadowed dining room full of tapestry and velvet and a Waterford chandelier glowing as softly as stars on a summer's night. He snatched a menu from one of the tables. Menus, even! The food here must be as good as the coloured brochure pictured it.

At the far end of the dining room was a set of French windows curtained on the other side with something filmy, which Melrose's guide flung open, and they entered a room with glass on three sides, which had probably been added to the original structure. It appeared to be an orangery or sunroom. South-facing, the room was still lapping up remnants of the fractured light of the sun.

Morris Bletchley stopped his wheelchair, got out of it, stretched, and took one of the green wicker chairs. Motioning Melrose to sit down in another, he said, 'I don't need that thing' – he nodded towards the wheelchair – 'I just think it must be pretty discouraging if you're chained to a bed to have some old geezer waltz into your room on a pair of good working legs.'

From the sly glance Bletchley slid in his direction, Melrose decided this was only one reason for wheelchairing it around Bletchley Hall, and that the chair was also there for fun. Melrose smiled. This was not to say that Morris Bletchley was short on compassion or charitable thoughts; after all, he'd started this place, hadn't he?

And Bletchley was indeed a healthy-looking specimen, remarkably so if he was in his eighties. He was trim, with arms and legs that had not suffered too much bone and muscle loss; the only thing that hinted at old age were the cheeks, which turned cadaverous when he sucked in on the cigarette Melrose had given him and was now lighting. It was damned certain Morris Bletchley's mind hadn't suffered any ill effects of ageing.

Orangery, solarium, sunroom, whichever it was called, the long glass-enclosed room was filled with green plants – ivy, aspidistra, potted palms – and as the sunlight touched the leaves and vines with a high gloss, waves of green seemed to shimmer on the tiled floor and turn the green-painted wicker furniture greener. At one end of the room sat two old men playing chess. At the other end, Melrose was surprised to see a bank of slot machines.

'So! What can I do for you?'

'I've taken Seabourne for a few months. I wanted to meet you.'

'That'd make a change. Ordinarily the last person a tenant wants to meet is his landlord. Although I'm not really running the place any more. So, is there something wrong? Not enough heat or the pipes clanging? Get in touch with that estate agent person if you've got problems.'

'No, no. Nothing. The house is wonderful.'

'Good. So what's the real reason?'

'You mean—'

'That you came here.' Through pursed lips, Moe Bletchley exhaled a thread of smoke.

Melrose smiled. 'I met your daughter-in-law. She came to the house.'

A guttural sound, an *uh*, escaped Moe Bletchley's throat. 'What did she want? Karen?' His expression didn't change.

'I don't know, really, unless to revisit her old home.'

Moe uttered another noncommittal sound. 'She came without Danny.' It wasn't a question but a conclusion.

Melrose nodded. 'Your son? Yes. She was alone. She told me about the children.' He wanted to add some appropriate word of empathy but couldn't for the life of him think of one.

Here, Moe looked away and was silent for some moments. It was the stillness of his face in the green silence of the room that suggested to Melrose emotional upheaval.

Finally, the old man – who seemed to have grown visibly older in that silence – asked, 'So what did she tell you?'

Melrose gave him as exact an account as he could. Here was a case where the smallest of details could be important.

But Moe Bletchley looked at him as if Melrose were a news anchor, reporting yet another fatality. 'That's what she told you?'

Melrose frowned. 'Yes.'

Again, that guttural *uh*.

Somehow, the sound was more disturbing – dismissive, perhaps – than words. Melrose took out his cigarette case once again and passed it to Bletchley, whose own cigarette had burnt down to ash in his fingers. Moe looked finally from the length of ash into Melrose's eyes as if Melrose had worked some trick. Absently, he took another cigarette from the case but didn't put it in his mouth. He said, 'That detective fellow?'

'Commander Macalvie. He would have been a DCI then, probably.'

'Uh-huh. Sharp guy. He didn't believe her, you know. About the strangers in the wood, and the pond. Neither did I.'

Neither, thought Melrose, do I.

Moe Bletchley put the cigarette in his mouth then and took the lighter Melrose still had in his hand. The lighter clicked open and snapped shut. 'Why are we talking about this? Oh, yes. It apparently is the reason you came. Still, I ask why? Why are you so confounded interested?'

Sitting forward, Melrose said, 'Who in God's name *wouldn't* be, Mr Bletchley? It's one hell of a story. It's dreadful. But there's another reason: there's been a murder—'

'Over in Lamorna Cove. I know. News gets to me quick, son.' He kept clicking the Zippo's case. 'I know just about everything that goes on in this place.'

'Then . . .'

Moe looked back through narrowed eyes. 'No, I don't know the victim. A woman with a title, they said. So I can't help out. What I meant was, I know the people in Bletchley pretty well. Been living here for fifteen years. I'm an American, you know. I made a fortune over there with Chick'nKing; then I came over here and made another fortune. People love fast food. With *good* fast food – well, I figure you're doing everybody a favour.'

'That's very interesting, but I don't see the relevance.'

'I'm just making a point to you: I'm not stupid.'

Raising his eyebrows, Melrose said, 'I don't doubt it for a minute. Did I give you the impression I thought you were?'

Moe looked off towards the elderly pensioners still bent over their chess pieces. 'No. But it's generally the way the world views us.' He nodded towards the old men. 'Dithery, forgetful, besides not being good for anything in the world.'

'Mr Bletchley, I doubt very much anyone in his right mind could look at you that way.'

Moe answered, 'Oh, not here, maybe.'

'Not anywhere.' Melrose felt the old man had strong opinions about what had happened that he wasn't sharing. 'You don't get on with your daughter-in-law, do you?'

Moe raised his arm, hand clasped on the arm of the wicker chair as if he meant to lever himself out of it. But he didn't. After a moment, he asked, 'You married? No, I don't suppose so, or you'd be down here with the wife and kid. Not many men have the balls to go off on junkets by themselves.'

'No, I'm not married.'

'You're probably fortunate, then.'

'I take it you don't think your son is.'

He lowered his hand and picked up his cigarette, another gone to ash. 'No, he isn't.'

Melrose said nothing; he would certainly not tell Moe

Bletchley that he found Karen Bletchley charming. But had he, completely? There was that one instance when he felt the silence no longer companionable but hadn't known why the atmosphere had changed.

'You liked her, I'm sure.'

Melrose nodded.

'People do.'

Melrose considered. Speaking more to himself than his companion, he said, 'Why is she here?'

'Good question.' Moe shrugged, turned evasive. 'Oh, well, only Chick'nKing gets my unqualified endorsement.'

Melrose smiled. 'I'll have to try it.'

'None around here, I mean close by. Wanted to put one in Mousehole, but the city fathers said no. It's a cute little place; I can see why they wouldn't want a fast-food emporium in it. Thing is, people forget the huge revenues the chain generates and also the people it employs. They only think how it's an eyesore. I think it's pretty sporty myself. Chicken's sure friendly-looking enough. Anyway. There's one just outside of Truro, that's the closest. I have them make a delivery once a week. People here really look forward to it.'

'I can imagine.' Melrose thought for a moment. 'If you know the villagers, you know Chris Wells.'

He nodded. 'I do. Johnny – that's her nephew – has to make the pastry deliveries because Chris has disappeared. So what's happened? Why all these shenanigans? Why all this misery suddenly?' As he inhaled on his cigarette, he gave Melrose a suspicious look, as if this new arrival might be responsible.

Melrose got up to leave. But then he sat back down.
'Mr Bletchley—'

'Call me Moe, sonny.'

Melrose smiled. He loved that 'sonny'. 'You'll think
me rude, and you don't have to answer the question, but
– who gets this vast fortune of yours?'

Moe's expression changed, back to that particular
look of misery he'd worn earlier. 'That's okay, I don't
mind answering. Who gets it now is Danny, my son. And
of course a lot of bequests to charities and so forth.'

'You said *now*.'

'That's right. I had to rewrite my will, of course. Who
got it before was the kids.'

'The kids?'

'The kids.'

29

It was Marshall Trueblood *hello!*-ing him awake before it was Diane. Having reached blindly for the telephone, Melrose quickly convinced himself that this whole episode was part of his dream and the receiver was being pressed against his ear by invisible hands. He continued to lie in bed, eyes closed, feeling no responsibility at all for his end of this telephone conversation.

'– me that! You're doing it all *wrong, Diane!* Give—'

The dream figures appeared to be Diane Demorney and Marshall Trueblood, having some argument over – what? He rolled over and the receiver rolled with him, still held by faerie hands.

'– my hat! Come back with—'

Diane was clear as could be in his dream, wearing those black Raybans and that hat with its floppy brim so big you could see nothing but her mouth and chin.

'When you give me the phone! Then you—'

Screech!

Melrose turned back again. Good lord, that nearly woke him up.

'Melrose! Melrose!' yelled Diane. 'We know you're there, you said hello.'

'Hello,' he said. He heard himself snore, little ladders of breath sucked in, breathed out, snuffles like a pig rooting.

'Listen, old sweat, you've really got to get back here! Vivian's – what? Stop it! Stop!'

Here was the smooth-as-glass voice of Diane, as if she hadn't just let out a screech a moment ago. '*Melrose. He's here*! He's – give that back!' Tussle, rustle.

'Me, again, old bean. Look, we don't want to—'

'*Lord Ardry!*'

Melrose jolted in his bed. What voice from the past was this? What damned fool dream person? Scroggs, that was who!

'No, she don't look too good, sir, that's my—'

Who don't? Again the pig snuffle-snuffle breath catching at the back of his mouth.

'Good? Would *you* look good if someone was drinking *your* blood?'

Trueblood's voice. Melrose's dream self frowned mightily. He didn't like the sound of that, no. His dream self walked away.

A clatter, raised voices in the distance, the telephone receiver audibly wrenched from someone's grasp, Trueblood's voice gaining eminence. 'It's Giopinno, old sweat. Count Dracula. He's here. He's finally come. We're all wearing our wooden crosses and garlic!'

Snuffle snuffle, root root.

30

Melrose turned another page of the *Telegraph*, looking for the next instalment of the neighbourly feud over a parrot. It had really escalated while he was away.

Having arrived in Bletchley as safely and soundly as the Great Western Railway could manage; having deposited her luggage (steamer trunks, train cases, hatboxes, and the detritus from the *Titanic*), and having hooked up with her new friend, Esther Laburnum, Agatha now sat in the Woodbine over tea, asking Melrose if he was, finally, tired of this 'absurd foyer' he had made into Cornwall and that arctic-cold, barnlike Seabourne place.

She helped herself to a heart-shaped meringue.

'What about your own "foyer" into Cornwall? This county is surpassed only by Armagh in its lack of reverence for Queen and Country. Armagh, incidentally, is where Jury has made *his* "foyer," and I wish he'd come back.'

'What are you doing?' Agatha's eyes were slits.

'Doing? Helping myself to one of these delicious meringues, that's what. It's not the last on the cake plate, not to worry.'

'You know what I mean. You're mocking me, God knows why!' She was marmalading a scone with Chivers Thick Cut.

'God knows why is correct. *I* certainly don't.'

'Anyway, as I said, all Long Piddleton thinks you're dotty, coming to Cornwall to live in a big empty house, and you should go back.'

'It's really nice to hear I'm missed.' He knew she'd stomp all over *that*.

'Missed? I didn't say they missed you, only that you're being extremely irresponsible and foolish. Diane thinks' – and here she pulled a page of newspaper from a carryall dotted with mangy-looking cats – 'you're putting yourself in danger. Here.' She thrust it towards him.

'Quoting Diane, are we? Is this the same Diane you called *moon head*?' Melrose looked at the horoscope column, broadly outlined for him (in case he'd gone blind in Cornwall), and his own birth sign, Capricorn, also outlined and bearing only half a star before it. Diane wrote (if you could call it writing) the horoscope column for the Sidbury paper and of late had been apportioning certain numbers of stars, one through five, to each sign for that particular day. Five stars meant you could walk on water; four, a super day; and so on down the list. To get only half a star signified doom, the absolute worst day imaginable (except of course for the person who didn't get even a half, but there were none of those, not even for Melrose. Yet.)

BE CAREFUL!!! THE JOURNEY YOU HAVE EMBARKED UPON IS FRAUGHT WITH DANGER, HAVING ALREADY CARRIED

OUT ONE ABSURD PLAN, YOU ARE IN DANGER OF UNDER-
TAKING ANOTHER WHICH MIGHT SPELL THE END!

'So you see,' said Agatha.

'See what? You've always made fun of Diane's horoscopes, so why point to this as though it vied with the
Book of Revelation?'

'I'll say only this: don't be surprised if Trueblood and
the Demorney person turn up on your doorstep.'

This *did* interest him, for it made him think of last
night's dream. He crushed the paper in his lap. 'Why
would they do that, for heaven's sake?'

'Now you're interested! Well, it will do you no good at
all. I'm finished.' She did not mean with her tea, for she
turned to where Johnny was serving another table and
held up her hand, gently turning it back and forth like a
cheery hello from the Queen.

Melrose returned to his paper. 'Are you settled in at
Lemming Cottage?'

Her look was sharp. '*Lemon* Cottage, as I'm sure you
know.'

'True. I just had a blinding flash of all its guests
heading full throttle towards a cliff.'

'Very funny.'

'Just a little foyer into humour.'

'I should think you might take all of what's happening
more *seriously*.'

Melrose looked around the small room, where every
table was occupied. 'Take what seriously? Are *you* taking
anything seriously, except that Sweet Lady you're
washing down the scone with?'

What Agatha was shoving into her mouth was a Woodbine special, a wonderful confection of a long thin meringue holding a layer of dense chocolate, itself topped by a layer of chocolate mousse. The crispness of the shell was a counterpoint to the rich layers of chocolate. Melrose looked at the sheet from the Sidbury paper and wondered if he could start a food column.

Agatha pinched up the last morsel of meringue, saying it was quite tasty indeed. 'I should like the recipe for this.'

The wish being father to the thought, she set about getting it, hailing the overworked Megs to her side. She told her to see about the recipe for the Sweet Lady, to ask the cook for it.

Megs looked struck dumb as she shifted the small tray she was carrying. 'Well, Mum, I can't say. I can't say how it'd take her – Brenda, I mean.'

'I *know*,' said Agatha marshalling a tone one might use when speaking to the mentally challenged. 'That's why I say, *ask* the cook.'

But the girl was not yet ready to ask, not without giving a bit of the history of recipe requests. 'Just last Easter I think it was someone wanted her recipe for Bunnykens—'.

A recipe, Melrose reflected, he could easily do without.

'– and when Miss B wouldn't give it, this person got quite shirty. Not much later, another lady wanted to know how to make the meringues – Miss C's, that is, as they're different from Miss B's—'

Would they wander through the entire alphabet?

'– but she wouldn't give that out neither, nor would Miss C.' Megs shifted the tray again. 'Then someone wanted—'

Agatha interrupted. 'Good grief, girl! Get back to the kitchen! You can never tell when she might change her mind. She's clearly quixotic.'

The pronunciation of which word Melrose filed away to use later.

'Oh, *I* can tell.'

At this point, Melrose was about to pull up a chair and have Megs join them.

'I've been working here five years and Miss B's never given out a single recipe. There was even a *duke* in here once had the beef olives and you wouldn't believe the fuss he made when she said, and very nicely she said it, she was sorry but she never gave out her recipes. Especially not the meringues. Nor does Miss C.' Megs flushed, realizing that Miss C might never again have a chance to. But she soldiered on. 'They make them different, see; they put in secret ingredients. They don't even know each other's, so, you see, it'd hardly be like either Miss C or Miss B to give them out. There was one lady—'

Agatha flipped her hand at the girl, *off with you, off with you*, and Megs scooted away. Agatha returned her attention to the cake plate just as Johnny Wells pushed through the swinging door and met with the waitress going in from the dining room side. He was tying his apron, stopping at a table recently vacated, where he collected the plates and cups and stacked them on a tray. Paler than usual, thus more Byronic and handsomer.

Women would kill for that skin, that hair.

Johnny looked over at Melrose and, seeing Agatha returned, actually smiled broadly. He walked over to their table, taking one or two requests from the patrons as he went.

'Hello, John,' said Melrose. 'My aunt's put poor Megs up to trying to get a recipe from the prop—I mean, from Miss B.' *Proprietress* sounded too much as if there were but one, so Melrose had cut that word short.

Johnny laughed. 'Not a prayer, I'm afraid,' he said to Agatha.

To him she said, 'Never hurts to try. Dear boy, I'm sorry to hear about your aunt. What are the police doing? If anything, that is.'

Melrose's voice fell on her like a brick wall. 'On the contrary, they're doing quite a lot.' He cast a baleful look around the room that sent the curious back to their tea and Sweet Ladies. 'I know for a fact they're doing everything they can. You met Commander Macalvie; I don't think he's ever failed to solve a case.'

Agatha put in some welcome news. 'That doesn't mean the person's still alive once he's solved it.' She poked her nose in the teapot.

'Thank you, Agatha, for that cheerful note.'

'Oh, she'll turn up, never you mind,' said Agatha.

Johnny ignored this banal remark and said to Melrose, 'Trouble is, the police have enough on their plate without concentrating on a missing person who might not even be missing. There's the Lamorna Cove business.'

All the patrons were listening now, not even bothering with their tea. Wasn't this the biggest thing to hit

Bletchley since Moe turned their stately home into a hospice?

'But that's a good reason why they'd pay *more* attention to your aunt's disappearance.'

'Well . . . yes, I see what you mean.' He turned when another patron called to him, and left.

Melrose thought any bit of knowledge that might uncover the reasons for Chris Wells's disappearance would be welcome to Johnny, stuck as he must feel in this limbo. That brought to mind the little girl, Cassie, and her mother, Maggie, and how not knowing was virtual hell. But it was Macalvie who had had to endure the *real* hell. He was the one left with the bad news.

Policemen were always cast as the messengers who bring the bad news. Melrose couldn't imagine himself being able to fill this role. He wondered how Richard Jury stood it.

He supposed the answer was: Jury didn't.

31

That evening, while the sheepdog in the doorway replaced one of the huskies, Melrose found himself sharing the Drowned Man's saloon bar with two other guests, a woman in a brown suit who sat by the fire, reading as she drank her cocktail, and a man who looked to be in his mid-forties but could well be younger, age altered perhaps by serious drink, such as the ones in front of him on the bar: a shot glass of whisky and a pint of beer. The whisky was downed in one blink, a long gulp of the beer in another.

'Evening,' said Melrose, feeling very much a Bletchleyite compared to this inn guest who was passing through, although it wasn't much of an 'on-my-way-to' sort of village. It wasn't anywhere near a major artery. Since Melrose was ensconced in his own house now, he felt he was not flying under false colours to act as a resident. He added to his greeting, 'Are you getting on with the dogs?' – nodding towards the doorway into which all five were now crowded.

The man laughed and said, 'Looks like a line-up to me. Are we supposed to identify the guilty one?'

Melrose laughed too. 'My name's Melrose Plant.' He moved a couple of seats down the bar to hold out his hand.

'Charlie Esterhazey. Glad to meet you.'

'Do you live in Bletchley? I don't think I've seen you about.'

'No. Just visiting a relation. Johnny Wells. I think he works here.' This, thought Melrose, was the uncle Johnny had mentioned but never referred to again. Alcoholic, maybe, but a very engaging one. 'Then you're related to Chris Wells.'

Charlie turned to his pint of beer, drank what was left of it, and said in a melancholy tone, 'No, but I am to Johnny. It's terrible, what happened. Chris is such a great person.' He drank again. 'People are always leaving Johnny stranded. First his father died; then his mother took off; now this. I don't mean, of course, that Chris did it deliberately.'

Why not?

The question sprang to mind. Always before, it had been asked and answered, as if no one could possibly imagine Chris Wells leaving deliberately. It would have been an awfully hurried departure, a drop-of-the-hat departure . . . But why not? Everyone had called it an emergency, not really a 'deliberate' leaving; it could only be leaving in answer to some serious occurrence. This notion hadn't taken root because she hadn't informed Johnny – and it looked less and less as if she'd left willingly, since she still hadn't notified Johnny.

He felt he'd been sluggish in coming up with this alternative. And Brian Macalvie? A 'sluggish' Commander Macalvie was a contradiction in terms. Yet

207

since Chris Wells's disappearance had brought back to mind that old horror of Cassie's death and then the Bletchley children's, even Macalvie's usually clear and ordered mind could be clouded by what was on it.

'. . . a magician, good with cards, scarves, and pulling coins from behind your ear.'

Melrose had only half heard Charlie's talk. 'I'm sorry, what were you saying?'

'Johnny. I was talking about his love of magic. He's pretty good, actually. He's put on a few shows at Bletchley Hall. The tricks are standard, but he performs with such panache he makes them new.'

Melrose was deep in his own thoughts. 'Could she have?'

'I beg your pardon?'

'His aunt. Could she have gone off like that deliberately?'

'Well . . .' Charlie considered. 'I know the police wondered about an emergency, something that forced her to drop everything and leave.'

'No, I don't mean that. I mean "deliberately", as in "after deliberation". Just suppose she packed up and left without a word to anyone. But I'm talking in circles. That's what I'm asking you. Could she have done that?'

Charlie shook his head at the same time he made a sign to Mr Pfinn. He said, 'Completely out of the question. She's the most responsible person I've ever known. Dependable, reliable to a fault. So, my answer's no, she couldn't have. The only way I can picture her running off like that is if someone called and asked for help. Urgently. Me, for instance.' When Melrose gave him a considering look, Charlie smiled. 'No, I didn't call. I *am* the first one Johnny thought of, though, I mean as a walking emergency.'

Pfinn came along, reluctant as usual to dispense drink, and gave both of them a steely look as he said, 'You havin' dinner here, you two?'

'We two.' Eyebrows raised, Melrose looked to Charlie. 'Mr Esterhazey?' Charlie nodded, and Melrose said to Pfinn, 'Yes, we two are having dinner here.'

With no sign that he welcomed the news, Pfinn made a sound in his throat and walked away to speak to the woman in brown. It would appear that she, too, was to have dinner in the Drowned Man's dining room.

'Mr Esterhazey—'

'Please, just Charlie. Why be formal when we're sitting here getting drunk together?' He looked at the level of beer in Melrose's glass and said, 'Rather, *I'm* sitting here getting drunk together.' He helped himself to some peanuts in a dish, then tossed back the whisky and followed it with a cool drink of beer. 'These things are called boilermakers in the States.'

Melrose smiled. Charlie, alcoholic or not, was extremely beguiling. Perhaps because he was forthright. 'Chris Wells has come to your rescue, has she?'

'Oh, yes, more than once. Which makes me think that that night she came to someone else's.'

'But the someone wasn't who the someone said, or else something went wrong.'

Charlie was silent for a few moments, drinking and eating peanuts, before he finally asked, 'You think she's dead?'

The strain in his voice made it clear that this was an alternative he didn't want to consider.

Melrose was saved from replying by Mr Pfinn, who had come down the bar again to slap menus before them. 'Quicker if you order now. Got to take out the dogs.'

'*We* do?' Melrose looked over his shoulder at the five in the doorway in mock alarm.

'Course not. I mean me.'

'Very well.' Melrose looked briefly at the menu, which was all that was required, given there were only two choices: shepherd's pie and cod Angelique, whatever that was. 'I'll have the cod, minus the Angelique.'

Charlie said, 'I'll have the same and another whisky, if you don't mind.'

Pfinn minded. 'I'll bring it to you in the dining room.' A clear bribe, and he took away the shot glass.

The woman in the brown suit drained her cocktail and rose. She was apparently the only other diner. Melrose and Charlie pocketed their cigarettes and followed.

They took a table near the woman but not right next to her. Melrose thought tables in the same area would save Johnny from running all over the room. They said good evening to the woman in brown and she nodded and returned the greeting. She was a good-looking, rather regal woman who had once been beautiful but was now at that age – fifty-five or sixty, perhaps – to be called handsome. She seemed completely composed, not the sort to try and start up a conversation on the basis of a simple greeting.

They shook napkins across their laps as Johnny came

in from the kitchen, shouldering a tray holding salads, rolls, a water jug, and the shot glass now filled. He smiled a smile he seemed to have been working on as he passed – taking a moment to set down Charlie's whisky – and went to the woman by the window.

His smile a little more practised, he then bestowed it on Melrose and Charlie. 'Did you find everything you needed in the house?'

'I did indeed,' said Charlie.

'Thanks for coming. It's very kind of you,' said Johnny.

'No, no, not at all. I just want to help if I can.'

Johnny nodded and went towards the kitchen.

While they fiddled with their salads, Melrose said, 'You told me his mother went off and left him. Why?'

'Because she's worthless. His father – my brother – wasn't much better. I don't know how those two managed to find each other, but they did. How someone like Johnny could be born of that union, God knows. Really, the whole damned family makes you think you're living in a medieval court – Henry the Eighth or Elizabeth's, something like that. The intrigue, the backbiting, the deeds and misdeeds, the plots, the plans – there were no heroes. But then there was Chris. Like Johnny, she must've skipped that particular gene pool.'

'Do you know the Bletchleys?'

'People you're renting from? Not very well. I ran into the wife a couple of times in the Woodbine. Good-looking, I'll say that for her.' He picked a few sunflower seeds from his salad and added, 'Chris couldn't stand her.'

Melrose looked up. 'Really? Why?'

Charlie shrugged. 'The soul-searching eyes. Not her own eyes, yours.'

'That's a new one.'

'Yeah.' Charlie smiled.

For the first time Melrose realized he had the same ingenuous manner as Johnny Wells. 'What is it you do in Penzance, Charlie?'

'Magic.' He smiled at Melrose's questioning look. 'I guess that's where Johnny gets it. I have a little shop, called Now You See It.' He pulled a fresh deck of cards from his pocket. 'Here's a simple one: I shuffle the cards –' which he did. 'You pick one –' which Melrose did. 'Put it back in the deck.' Melrose did so. Charlie reshuffled. Then he fanned the cards out on the table, picked one, and held it up.

Melrose shook his head. He was sorry it hadn't worked. 'Not that, no.'

Charlie smiled. 'I know it isn't. It's under your glass. King of Clubs.'

That's where it was, too. 'How in hell did you do that?'

'Sorry.' Charlie shook his head, gathered up the cards, and shoved them back in his pocket. His eyes crinkled at Melrose over the top of his glass.

'Bloody amazing,' said Melrose.

'Uh-huh. The magic shop's the main job. I also take out boats. You know, tourists who want to see Penzance from away. The climate's great here and we get a million tourists. I take them out. I'm better with boats than I am with people.'

'Really?' Melrose gave him a long look.

32

A meeting ordained by the gods was how Melrose pictured the meeting between Sergeant Wiggins and Bletchley Hall. Imbued with the aura of death, death still missed being an actual fact.

Wiggins was talking about these 'homes for retired gentlefolk' as they drove towards Bletchley Hall in pale afternoon sunlight. 'There's of course your typical nursing home; it's small and gloomy and cramped, furnished with iron beds and the yellow light cast by forty-watt bulbs and old magazines. So old you can't even hold out for the May issue, no, sir, May's been and gone and if May didn't revive you, well, June's gone too.'

The rental car was a cheap model and ground its way up the shallow incline as if it was making for Everest's peak. It rattled, but no more than did Sergeant Wiggins, who could obviously speak at great length when a topic inspired him. (He must often have been muffled by Jury when they were on a case together.)

'– metal tray with scrambled eggs from a dry mix and weak coffee, a thimble of juice, thin toast—'

'Sounds like the B and B circuit, Sergeant Wiggins.'

Wiggins carried on. 'Would you even have your own room? Or have to share. Well, I'd hate that, I would. I'd think you could at least expect a little privacy when you're dying; it's a safe bet you won't get any *after*.'

Melrose wondered what sort of talkathon Wiggins thought he was bound for in the afterlife. If an imaginary nursing home could furnish him with this banquet of topics, what would imagining heaven do for him?

'Sergeant, you're a master of detail.'

Said Wiggins, 'They say the devil's in them.'

He certainly was in these, thought Melrose.

In the next five minutes, blessedly silent, they rounded the curve that gave them the first glimpse of Bletchley Hall. It was indeed an imposing facade, and Wiggins's surprise said he appreciated it. It left him – thank God – speechless.

They paused at the stone pillars that flanked the entrance. Ground into stone as if it had grown there was a brass plaque: BLETCHLEY HALL. The long driveway passed between low honey-coloured stone walls over which dripped lush vegetation. Behind the walls were gardens of orchids and beds of bright marigolds. In this temperate climate, even the occasional palm tree seemed at home.

Wiggins pointed one out. Surprised, he said, 'Palm trees, Mr Plant?'

'Well, you know what they call this part of Cornwall: Little Miami.'

'Surely not.'

'Just watch your back and your wallet.'

They stopped on the gravel between the marble steps

and the fountain, in which bronze fish, weathered into green, spewed up streams of water and cherubs frolicked, strangling the dolphins they rode. Even the gravel at their feet glittered like crushed diamonds. In the distance was the stream, the orchids, the tall grasses.

'My lord,' said Wiggins in a wondering way as he shut his car door. 'This must cost the *earth* to keep up.'

'I'm sure. Morris Bletchley *has* the earth. The unfortunate viscount and his lady didn't.'

The front door was open; during the day it might always have stood so to suggest either freedom of passage or a four-star hotel. Matron immediately came walking towards them. In her grey dress sprigged with tiny roses she looked like a tea cosy. Plant still didn't know her name, but as she seemed to enjoy being called 'Matron', that's how he introduced her.

Wiggins handed her one of his cards and the name seemed to freeze on her lips as she mouthed 'New Scotland Yard'. Nervously she ushered them in. Fumbling with her belt, she asked, 'What can I do for you?'

'I'd like to have a word with Mr Bletchley, if you could just fetch him?'

Matron nodded and weaved off as if struggling through deep water, dolphins, perhaps, and cherubs impeding her progress.

Melrose had detected a whiff of something mixed with her toilet water. A bit of gin in the *heure bleu*, perhaps? He wouldn't be a bit surprised to find Moe Bletchley had designated a cocktail hour in between dominoes and dinner. And why not, for God's sake? If you're at death's door what difference does it make if you go through it half potted? Melrose watched her walk the length of gorgeous Kirman carpet that led down the long gallery, off which were the dining and other communal rooms.

Wiggins was admiring the drawing room in which they waited, with its blue brocades and velvets, dark blue curtains and carpeting, and overhead a chandelier that, touched by the sun, showered confetti light across the rug.

They shared the room with two old women sitting in wing chairs who looked as if they'd just been caught in a spell and commanded neither to speak nor to move. They seemed – well, *stuck* there.

'Begging your pardon, gentlemen.'

The voice crept up behind them, and they turned to see a tidy-looking, dark-suited man of indeterminate years, who made one think of a funeral director.

'I'm Dr Jaynes. What is it you wanted?'

'To see Morris Bletchley.' Wiggins handed Dr Jaynes another of his cards.

'You're from Scotland Yard?'

'He is.' Melrose nodded towards Wiggins. 'I'm from Northamptonshire.'

Dr Jaynes seemed puzzled by this strange coupling of places. He said to Wiggins, 'You're here in an official capacity?'

My God, thought Melrose, if it was this hard to convince them of what a calling card clearly stated, how would you ever convince them you weren't dead yet?

'No, sir,' said Wiggins. 'I'd merely like to talk to

Mr Bletchley, as we told your matron.'

He still didn't seem convinced. Life at Bletchley Hall must really ride the rails of ritual if two strangers turning up created such a stir.

Dr Jaynes seemed at a loss. 'Of course, Mr Bletchley hasn't the time to see people unless they've an appointment.'

Melrose sighed. How was it he had missed the pleasure of Jaynes's company when he was here before? He told Jaynes he'd already talked to Morris Bletchley.

'I see, I see.' Jaynes was as tentative as one can get and still remain on the scene. 'Then I'll just have a word with Mr—'

But he could have saved his breath to cool his porridge, for here came Morris Bletchley at full tilt across the doorsill of the blue drawing room. He pulled up and braked. Melrose thought he saw sparks.

'Dr Jaynes, I'll see to these gentlemen. Hadn't you better get back to your patients?'

Dr Jaynes smiled grimly at Moe Bletchley and departed.

'What's going on?' Moe Bletchley fiddled with a lever on his wheelchair. 'I don't mean with *you* two, what's going on with my brakes? I nearly ran down Mrs Fry back there.' He chuckled. 'Could someone be trying to bump me off?'

Wiggins said, stepping into I'm-on-the-job mode, 'I don't think it would be efficient to use a wheelchair for that, sir.'

Morris Bletchley apparently got a real kick out of this pointing out of the obvious. 'And you're' – he looked at the card Matron must have turned over to him – 'Mr Wiggins, Scotland Yard, that right?'

'Yes, sir. *Detective Sergeant* Wiggins.'

Melrose knew this slight condescension would end smartly when Wiggins got a deeper whiff of this hospice-nursing home outfit.

'Well, Sergeant, I reckon I don't know any more about the Wells woman than I did when I talked to your cohort here.' He leaned his head in Plant's direction. 'Chris Wells helps us out, and she's damned good at it, too. Drove one or two of the guests to see their families, took 'em to hospital, that sort of thing. So I did have contact with her, but I didn't know anything about her family or friends. Come on, let's go in the drawing room – they won't mind,' he added, with a look at the old ladies.

Who hadn't, Melrose decided, moved an inch in any direction. Light wavered, shadows shifted in these blue environs, creating an underwater effect much lovelier than that of the Drowned Man. Melrose found it as good as a sedative and wasn't surprised that the old ladies had fallen asleep. He was having a hard time keeping his eyes open himself.

'Let's go out to the sunroom; I need a smoke and you can't do it in here. It would be hard on our emphysema patients.'

'And yourself,' Wiggins said sententiously.

Moe rose from his wheelchair and shoved it out into the hall. 'I need to stretch my legs. Come on.'

They sat around the same table. The two old chess players were absent, but an old woman at the other end of the sunroom was feeding coins into a slot machine with her face so close to the display she could have licked it.

'Are your patients here all wealthy?' asked Wiggins.

'No. Why? Are you supposed to be if you're dying?'

'Oh, no, it's just that this is clearly an expensive operation.'

'True. But I can afford it. If they were rich, why in hell wouldn't they just buy what they needed? Someplace in Arizona or the South of France, nurses round the clock, fancy equipment?' He grunted as he lit his cigarette, then remembered that Melrose smoked. 'Sorry. You?' He offered the crumpled pack around.

Melrose shook his head, turning away the cigarettes, not wanting to smoke under Wiggins's steely stare. As soon as they could get back onto the topics of murder and disappearance instead of emphysema and other illnesses, he would light up himself. It shouldn't take long. He said, 'But the South of France, that's not really what's wanted, or not all of what's wanted, is it?'

Both Moe and Wiggins raised a puzzled eyebrow. Wiggins said, 'I'm not sure I follow, sir.'

'If you're dying, you don't want to do it alone. If you have no family, or even an indifferent family, and few friends, you'd likely be shuttled off to hospital, cheerless and antiseptic. That's not a cheering picture, is it?'

'No, it isn't,' said Moe Bletchley.

As hospitals were high on Wiggins's list of places where he'd most like to settle down, he ignored the question and took from his inside pocket one of the pictures Macalvie had given him of the dead woman. 'Her name is Sada Colthorp. Did you know her?'

Moe frowned as he brought the picture close to his face and then held it arm's length away. He tried several different positions, as if moving it about would make it speak more tellingly of the woman shown. He shook his head. 'Got any other shots of this woman?'

Wiggins pulled out a morgue picture, a full-face shot. Bletchley put them side by side. 'She looks vaguely familiar. What did you say her name was?'

'Sada Colthorp. You might have known her as Sadie May. Her maiden name.'

Frowning, he shook his head. 'Nope. Neither name rings a bell with me.'

'She lived in Lamorna Cove as a girl.'

Moe shook his head again. 'Still doesn't ring a bell.'

At just that moment, from the dining room beyond and out onto the sunroom's tiled floor jolted Morris Bletchley's wheelchair, occupied by a young man with dark hair, probably in his early thirties. He was holding a big white box on his knees. 'Woodbine delivery!' He opened the big box to reveal iced doughnuts and several different kinds of pastry. Melrose's quick tally showed that there were at least twenty pieces of pastry and a dozen doughnuts.

'What the hell are you doing in my wheelchair, Tom? I keep telling you.' Moe peered into the box, more interested in the éclair he removed from it than the occupancy of his wheelchair. '*Damn*, these are good!'

'Brenda brought 'em. Did you know she used to live in Fulham? Right next door to Putney.'

'You told me. This is Tom—'

A clatter of coins interrupted Moe Bletchley's

introduction. It came from the direction of the slot machines. The old lady was jumping up and down, at least as well as her stick legs could manage.

Moe Bletchley looked her way. 'That damned machine pay off again? Have to fix it.' He grinned and finished his introduction. 'This is Tom Letts.'

Tom Letts's good looks seemed fragile. His skin was pale, like Johnny's. Unlike Johnny's it bore the terrible stamp of Kaposi's sarcoma.

AIDS. Melrose hadn't even thought of this as one of the several terminal illnesses that would be likely to turn up at Bletchley Hall.

Tom said he was pleased to meet them and looked around, as if one of them, but he wasn't sure which, had something to say that he had waited a long time to hear. He had one of the most ingenuous smiles Melrose had ever seen, and again he was reminded of Johnny Wells. They could have been brothers.

To Wiggins he said, 'You here about the murder in Lamorna?'

When Wiggins nodded and smiled, Melrose marvelled that the detective sergeant's response to Tom's disease was not to cut and run but one of kind regard. Wiggins, who claimed to be sought out by every springtime blade and blossom to test their pollen on, this same Wiggins could sit here and not turn a hair confronted by the ravaged body of a victim of AIDS.

'This woman.' He handed Tom the pictures, though Melrose was pretty sure Wiggins didn't expect him to recognize her. He really just wanted to include Tom.

The two old chess players had come in and were

seated in their same chairs, chessboard between them. The white box from the Woodbine now caught their attention and they began making their way towards it.

Moe leaned towards Melrose and Wiggins and whispered, 'Got to make allowances for these two. Their memories are shot to hell.'

Memories shot to hell proved no obstacle to Sergeant Wiggins.

'These are the Hooper brothers,' said Moe Bletchley. 'And that's Miss Livingston coming along. She'll make it eventually.'

Leaning on her cane and holding an antique mesh purse, heavy with coins, Miss Livingston made her slow way towards them, a look of grim determination stamped on her acorn face.

The two old gentlemen wasted no time on the strangers; they went immediately for the pastries. Hands started and hovered indecisively over the box.

Said one of the Hoopers, 'I'm having my usual, a . . . a . . .'

'Doughnut,' said Moe, almost absently, as if he was used to supplying the Hooper brother with information.

'Right!' Hooper's hand snapped down and plucked up one with chocolate icing.

'So am I!' exclaimed his brother. 'I'm having a' – he looked at what his brother had taken – 'I'm having one of those . . . one of those . . .'

Miss Livingston had reached them by now. 'Doughnut, you goddamned fool!' she yelled. 'Here, get your paws off.' And she parted them like Moses did the Red Sea. 'I want one o' them puffy things.' She reached nimbly into the box for a cream puff. 'Hel-*lo*, cutie!' she said to Melrose.

He lavished a smile upon her, rose, and pulled a chair round. Grey-haired Miss Livingston put Melrose in mind of a small bird of prey, with her little beaky nose, darting eyes, and fingers tough as pincers.

One of the Hoopers watched the chair being pulled round and then followed suit, dragging over a bentwood chair from against the wall. His brother did the same, and now all seven of them were gathered around the table, the new people turning owlish eyes on the original four who had been there.

The other Hooper asked gruffly, 'Why'd you want to see us, Colonel?'

'I think the cryptogram's been broken,' said Moe, eyeing a cream cake.

The Hoopers looked at one another. 'It *has*?'

'Both of you. You'd best go to Plan A before they come.'

The Hoopers stood up abruptly, one upsetting his chair. He picked it up, set it down with a thundering crack, and the two went back to their chess game, but not before Melrose heard one of them ask the other what Plan A was and saw the other shake his head, he didn't remember.

'Cryptogram?' asked Melrose.

Moe shrugged. 'Hell if I know. They're always rattling on about secret codes and being spies. Of course, they'll forget it before they're through the dining room, so it does no harm.'

Tom said, 'Still, it's like one thing they half remember

with any consistency.' He laughed.

'It's retrograde amnesia, something like that,' said Moe. 'It's not being able to remember something you heard not more than two minutes ago. They've both got Alzheimer's, but whether that's causing it, the doc doesn't know. Not surprising.'

Not caring a fig for the Hoopers' condition, little Miss Livingston's strong fingers clamped Melrose's forearm. 'Let's you and me go for a walk out there around the grounds. There's some spots only I know about, dearie. They'd never find us. Besides' – here she shook her beaded bag and set the coins jingling – 'I'm rich.'

Not at all tempted by this invitation, nevertheless Melrose gave her a darling smile and made a quick movement to free himself from her grip.

Probably used to Miss Livingston's little ways, Moe Bletchley ignored her and said, 'Tom here's been my chauffeur for years in London. He's such a good wheel man, there've been times I wished I could stick up a bank or a jeweller's, just so's I could zip out to the car with the swag, have Tom gun 'er up, and tear off on a chase.'

Moe said this with such obvious affection that Melrose could guess how an AIDS case had come to Bletchley Hall.

'How long have you been here, sir?' Wiggins asked Tom without (Melrose noted) shrinking back at all.

'Six months. But this is only since I got really bad.' He gestured towards his face and yet managed a smile.

After all, he'd been lucky to get into Bletchley Hall; so few were able to.

'How many patients do you have staying here?' asked Wiggins.

'Twelve. Twelve's the capacity; there're twelve bed-rooms besides the four for Matron, a nurse who's here full time, Jaynes, and me. The rest of the staff's not live-in. We have doctors, of course. One lives in St Buryan. Another lives near Penzance.' Moe Bletchley suggested Wiggins might like a tour of the place and Wiggins accepted with alacrity. Tom wheeled out with them.

Melrose excused himself from the tour, spent some five minutes disengaging himself from Miss Livingston and her pincerlike fingers and walked back inside.

33

He walked through the voluptuous green dining room. That crystal! That silver! He liked the idea that all this finery was laid on in case there was even one guest who could make it downstairs for dinner. Perhaps there was more hope of recovery in setting a good table than in administering a newly discovered drug.

He stopped before one table to look at the delicate arrangement of mauve orchids and cyclamen; touched the thin crystal of a wineglass, so delicate that a glassblower's breath might have sighed it into existence; lifted a knife as heavy as a vault or as weighty as memory.

For that's how he felt; memory really could weigh one down. Perhaps that's what had happened to the Hooper brothers. They'd had to remember, at last, too much, and decided nothing was preferable. Melrose walked on.

There was another drawing room across from the blue room, still occupied by the two old ladies, who seemed not to have moved a muscle. Should he call for help? No, the breath of one lifted the frill of the lace collar on her jabot. She at least was still breathing, which meant the other probably was also.

The drawing room across from the blue room that he now entered was somewhat narrower, longer, and done in the burgundy red of an old Bordeaux. This room was darker and – if it could be so described – deeper, as if it had been steeped in wine. The colours at Bletchley Hall, Melrose noticed, were exceptionally strong – none of your weak-kneed off-whites, ecrus, or pastels but colours that seemed to demand that one just hold on.

The red room didn't get much natural light, facing north as it did; it depended on lamps being lit and the logs burning in the fireplace, as a fire burned now. Because of this play of light and dark, Melrose hadn't immediately seen Tom, who sat by the hearth. His eyes were closed or almost closed, and he hadn't noticed Melrose come in either.

Melrose hung back, not wanting to disturb his doze.

He turned and was about to leave when Tom said, 'Hello. Come on in.' He was still in Moe Bletchley's wheelchair. Melrose walked to a wing chair in front of the fire.

Tom was holding a small sherry glass in his hand, which he raised. 'Want some?'

'I do, yes. Just point me to it.'

'Over there.' Tom indicated a table beside a window hung in a sea of dark-red curtains. Melrose found the sherry decanter in among other decanters – cut glass, probably Waterford, that shade called 'Waterford blue', a unique assimilation of blue and grey. This table was stocked with the best and most expensive whiskies, gins, and vodkas. 'I'm amazed,' he said, coming back with his sherry glass, Lalique, he thought, remembering Marshall Trueblood's lessons. The glass was shaped like a tulip just beginning to open.

'What's more amazing is how seldom we use it – the drink. It must be the idea that what's so readily available loses a lot of its power to tempt you. You'd think all of us would be driven to drink, wouldn't you?'

Melrose smiled. 'Maybe. Listen, why do you like that wheelchair so much?'

Tom smiled too. 'Because it's fancy, it's fun, and it gets his goat. You're living in Seabourne, aren't you?'

'I am, yes. At least for a little while.'

'It's haunted.'

Melrose laughed. 'You're not the first person to tell me that.'

'It is.'

'Come on, Tom. To tell the truth, the place does give me the feeling of – um, a film set. It really does. One expects to see spectral shapes forming at the top of the stairs. Anyway, I take it you've been in it?'

'I've stayed there.'

'You've known Morris Bletchley for some time?'

'Like he said, I was his chauffeur for years. Mostly in London. He had a terraced house in Putney, maybe still does, though he never leaves here much, now.' He turned his head to look out of the tall window and smiled as if the memory made him happy. 'That was just like him, living in Putney instead of Belgravia or some swank house in West One. It was a small house, too the Putney house. There was just me, a cook who came in daily, and an au pair for the children, who used to come and see him a lot. They really loved him.'

'His grandchildren?'

Tom nodded. 'Noah and Esmé. Nice kids. I used to drive them places: the zoo, films, Chick'nKings.' He flashed Melrose a smile. 'Of course.'

'I understand they drowned; it was a strange accident.'

'It was strange, all right. It was strange,' he repeated. Silence. Then he asked, 'Want some more sherry?'

'Yes. Thanks.'

Tom might have liked the wheelchair for reasons other than 'fun'. He rose slowly and, it appeared, painfully. It was a pain that hadn't seemed to bother him in the sunroom or hadn't registered, if it did. He continued talking as he poured and stoppered the decanter. 'Mr B was in London, in the Putney house. After he got the call he came to my room to tell me to warm up the car, that he wanted me to drive him to London airport.' Tom was standing in front of Melrose, handing him the refilled glass. 'I'll tell you, I've never seen Mr B look like that; *sunk*, he looked, as if he himself had drowned. I drove him to the airport; he keeps a Lear jet there, but he hardly ever uses it, only when he has to go to the Highlands or Paris or someplace. He really keeps it for his executives and employees. One of his girls who worked at the Watney C-K, her father had a heart attack, and Mr B got her to the airport and she was home in Edinburgh in an hour. He doesn't like the plane; he doesn't like ostentation; he's a plain man.'

Melrose laughed. 'There I disagree; he's much too complicated to be plain. Though I do admit he works at it.'

Tom nodded and turned the tulip-shaped glass in his fingers. 'Well, not plain, maybe, but generous. After a few years of this' – his hand swept over his body – 'when I got too sick to do anything, he brought me here. Most of the people here are ones he knew before. The Hoopers owned a bookstore in South Ken he was always going to. Miss Livingston was once his son's public school teacher.'

Afraid he'd got Tom off the subject of the grandchildren, Melrose said, 'And what happened that night he flew down here?'

'Of course, by the time he got to the house, it'd all been done; I mean, the police had come, and the ambulance had taken the bodies away. The man in charge, at least I guessed he was in charge, talked to Mr B for a long time. Then they all left.

'He told me it felt like the aftermath of battle, when you can't do anything but look at the bloody battlefield. His son's wife had got there first – I mean, after the cook, Mrs Hayter. Daniel, his son, arrived later; they'd had a hard time locating him, so it was a while after his wife got there. So Mr Bletchley, he had to get information from his daughter-in-law. Karen, her name is. And that really frustrated him.'

'Why's that?'

'Why? Because he doesn't like her. He always said she married Daniel for money. I guess it wouldn't be the first time. He was in a rage with both of them because they hadn't been at home when the kids got out of bed. I imagine Mrs Hayter came in for some sharp words too.' Tom sighed. 'It was too painful for him to live in the house after Noah and Esmé died. But at the same time, he couldn't stand to leave the village. It's the reason he bought this place. He didn't know exactly what he was going to do with it until he got the hospice idea – taking in only people who've been diagnosed as terminal. Strange thing for him to do, isn't it?'

'Not if you want the illusion that you're controlling death.' He'd said something like that to Karen Bletchley.

Tom moved the wheelchair closer to Melrose's wing chair. He leaned forward, in the manner of someone with important things to impart who doesn't want others to hear him. 'It's funny you'd put it that way, because not everyone leaves here in a coffin. Some of us actually get better. It hasn't happened too often, but it *has* happened several times. Cancer of the oesophagus, you can hardly ever win out over that. But a woman who had it went into remission and still keeps in touch. Then there's Linus Vetch, who should have been dead a year ago. He's still with us. There've been others – well, all of us are terminal; what a hell of a word – so when something like that happens it's like a bloody miracle. Don't think I'm talking about false hope. For me, it really *would* have to be a miracle.

'I don't think the comfort of this place comes from not having to die alone. I think it's because if you have to die, you want it to be in a place like this or someplace like a battlefield, where death's a fact, not a fantasy. Outside places like this and beyond wars and battlefields, death is more of a fantasy. People don't really believe it; they deny it at every turn.'

'*The Death of Ivan Ilyich*,' said Melrose.

'What do you mean?'

'Tolstoy's story. Ivan Ilyich is ill for a long time; he knows he's dying. But the doctors, his wife, and his children keep denying it.'

Tom said, 'That's what happens, isn't it? Here's the most terrifying experience you will ever have and you want to share how you feel and make others understand. But people won't let you. "Oh, stop talking like that; don't be morbid." Or "You'll see; you'll be up and around in no time." ' He stopped. Then he said, 'A lot of people have ended their days here in a way they could never have hoped for without Bletchley Hall. Every once in a while children or parents come to visit. Not often. Not mine.'

There was a silence while they grasped their sherry glasses. Melrose didn't know what to say that didn't sound banal.

Tom went on, 'Except for my sister, Honey. She's only seventeen and just three months ago got her driving licence – as she says, "to kill". The first drive she took was to come here from Dartmouth. That's a long way. I assumed Dad would give her a hard time about visiting, but he doesn't. I think maybe he and Mum are secretly glad Honey's got the guts to do it. And she keeps me from really hating them; she keeps reminding me that this is how they are. They don't know any other way to *be*. Honey. She's only seventeen and yet she knows that. It's something we don't realize about people. We do what we do because we don't know any other way to be.

'She takes me for rides. Sometimes Mr B goes with us. And a few times we've gone to Seabourne. You know what we do? We look for clues.' Tom smiled. 'He says something will turn up, that if we don't find it, somebody will.'

Looking at Melrose, Tom added, 'Maybe you're the somebody.'

34

An inductionist who never got around to tallying bits of string or footprints in zinnia beds, Sergeant Wiggins had never subscribed to T. S. Eliot's dictum about the rose and the typewriter, that if you could think of them in the same breath you might have the makings of a poet. Wiggins, who clearly hadn't the makings, could still think of the rose and the typewriter together. Contraries didn't bother him at all, nor did obverses, inverses, and converses. In Eliot's book, the rose and the typewriter were headed for a third encompassing emblem. But Wiggins's mind did not give birth; the rose and the typewriter remained discrete elements. They did not produce an objective correlative until a Macalvie or a Jury or (he gave himself credit for at least this much) a Plant. Jury would look at the typewriter and the rose and go *aha!* Macalvie and Jury were intuitionists.

But Macalvie (who was to meet them in Lamorna, towards which they were now hurtling on a narrow coastal road) also wanted to know everything – every rose petal, every bent blade of grass, the precise length of every bit of string; he was famous for this attention to detail. It wasn't easy to work with Macalvie if you believed (as most men surely do) that some little things are eminently forgettable.

Wiggins didn't believe in forgetting. To him, everything was memorable. His mind operated like the four-race accumulator; you left the bet on the table and, through the next three races, 'accumulated' winnings.

Right now, he was informing Melrose (who was doing the driving) that Kaposi's sarcoma wasn't a kind of cancer as originally supposed. 'It's caused by a herpes virus, HHV8, it's called. Though I doubt,' he added, sympathetically, 'it makes any difference to poor Tom Letts.'

Melrose marvelled: here was Wiggins, who often talked as if a walk through a field of dandelions could do him in, yet who could shake Tom's hand, sit beside him, breathe a common air – all without blinking an eye.

Wiggins went on, reporting in staggering detail the status of each guest at Bletchley Hall. He had met them all, talked to them all, listened to them all; this was Wiggins's great talent, even if he did not know what he was listening *for* (which was Jury's job, Macalvie's job).

There was Mr Clancy with inoperable pancreatic cancer, Mrs Noonan, who had come to Bletchley after a bone marrow transplant had failed ('Imagine going through all of that! You know how painful a transplant is'); Miss Timons-Browne, who had been a piano teacher before rheumatoid arthritis had taken away her livelihood; Mr Bleaney—

'That's a poem by Philip Larkin,' put in Melrose, to

show he was interested in the fates of these poor people. He recited:

> 'This was Mr Bleaney's room; he stayed
> The whole time he was at the Bodies, till
> They moved him'.

'Ah, that's as may be, Mr Plant, but I doubt *your* Mr Bleaney suffered from pancreatic cancer.'

'He's Philip *Larkin's* Mr Bleaney, and he suffered as much as anyone – well, go on.' He tried to concentrate on the waves (out there) crashing against the shoreline (in here), and it would have been a pleasant enough drive had the road not been potholed and had he not had the incarnation of Hippocrates or Sir Richard Burton sitting beside him. Every detail of every illness and, thrown in for good measure, a complete picture of every thankless, graceless relation.

'Poor Mrs Atkins, she's the one suffered three strokes and no one can see how she's holding on, and you'd think her daughter-in-law could do more by way of bringing the grandchildren—'

Et cetera, thought Melrose. Was Wiggins through? Had he run down the entire roster of twelve patients? Take away the three met in the sunroom – no, four, including Tom – that left eight; take away Bleaney, Timons-Browne, Clancy, Noonan, Atkins, Fry. Still two to go.

The Hoopers' long battle with Alzheimer's brought them into Lamorna and Melrose pulled up, spitting dirt and gravel, in front of the Wink.

'Bit tired-looking, innit?' said Wiggins, slamming shut the car door. His tone hinted at the superciliousness one might expect from a Londoner – in this case Wiggins, who ordinarily hadn't a shred of the city snob about him. But then he was ordinarily with Richard Jury, who was the least supercilious human being Melrose had ever known. Oh, that he were here!

Although the layout and the shape of the Wink were completely different from his pub in Long Piddleton, it reminded Melrose nonetheless of the Jack and Hammer. Perhaps it was the nucleus of regulars seated at a round table, three men and two women, the same as had been there three nights before, and he toyed with the notion that they were the actual models for several Dorian Grey-like portraits of the habitués (Melrose being habitué number one) of the Jack and Hammer. That old one with the pinched cigarette and the pocked face, surely that would be no other than the true soul of Marshall Trueblood; the woman with the long sad face wearing a dusty brown jumper, Vivian Rivington to a T; the other woman, stout and squat with shreds of grey hair boiling about her forehead – well, actually, she wasn't the inward self of Agatha, she was the outward incarnation.

Yes, as he and Wiggins stood at the bar waiting for their drinks, he thoroughly enjoyed his little sci-fi fantasy, his little ghostly dimension, and was also quite sure that everyone in here was delighted that he had something wonderful to chew over, something to get his teeth in. Murder! No longer would they have to pretend Lamorna was a village to excite the administration of tourists. Now, it really was! The clay pipe, the black patch, the wooden leg, the rheumy eye, the oil lantern – these were now things to be reckoned with.

'I don't know what I want,' said Wiggins, in a pedestrian way that jerked Melrose back from pirates' gold and *Jamaica Inn*.

'What do you mean? It's just another pub. Get what you usually do: horn of toad, eye of frog, whatever. Have a beer.'

Wiggins just gave him a look. *Have a beer* was not one of the Wiggins fallbacks in emergencies. He sighed. 'A lemonade, maybe.' He was already getting out a small tubular glass bottle.

Bromo Seltzer. It was by now one of Wiggins's staples. Melrose wondered how much of the damned stuff he'd consumed since that trip to Baltimore. Wiggins only remembered the city as the home of Bromo Seltzer. He'd taken a snapshot of the tall building with the logo.

'Finally got here,' said a voice at their backs. It was, of course, Brian Macalvie, for whom one can never arrive too early. He was always in a hurry, another reason for the coat's staying on. He gave Wiggins's shoulder an enthusiastic thump; he'd already seen him at police headquarters in Camborne.

The finally-got-here part of the greeting had been directed, apparently, at Melrose Plant, who – Melrose would like to remind him – was not on the payroll of either the Devon and Cornwall Constabulary or New Scotland Yard.

Macalvie looked at the optics and said, 'I don't know what to have.'

'Is this the biggest decision you two have had to make today?' said Melrose. 'Have what I'm having.' Melrose put down some coins that clinked together. 'Or what he's having. Whatever, with Bromo Seltzer.'

Macalvie ordered a Guinness, got it, and the three went to the same table that Melrose and Macalvie had shared before.

'Between me and my men and the local police, we've talked to everyone in this place' – he waved an arm to take in the Wink – 'and found out sod all, except a few who remembered Sadie May but don't remember anything more about her.' Macalvie shook his head. 'Can't be coincidence. Two little kids die in peculiar circumstances; a woman disappears; another woman is murdered; the mother of the children turns up now after not having been back here for four years . . .' He shook his head again, lit another cigarette, and said, 'Daniel Bletchley . . .' His voice trailed off with the smoke from his cigarette.

'He's still not given you the name of the woman?' said Wiggins.

'No,' said Macalvie.

Wiggins said nothing for a moment. Then he said, 'Bletchley could have left and then come back, but what about this housekeeper? Wouldn't he have been concerned that she would see him?'

'No reason to be. It *is* his house, after all,' Melrose said. 'Maybe it's simply because the idea is so repugnant. I just can't believe it: a parent doing this to his own children.'

'Tell that to Medea,' said Macalvie.

Melrose looked around the pub, at the smoke that lifted up to the ceiling like cirrus clouds. 'Morris Bletchley says you didn't believe Karen's story, the one she told about people in the woods.'

Macalvie brought out a crumpled pack of cigarettes. 'He's right, I didn't.'

'Neither do I. Seabourne is well stocked with wine and Henry James. Karen Bletchley's story sounds suspiciously like *The Turn of the Screw*: two children, Miles and Flora; the woman across the pond as the governess; the strange man who talked to them, Peter Quint; there's even the unimaginative and literal housekeeper, Mrs Grose. I'd say Mrs Hayter is the embodiment of that character.'

Macalvie was thoughtful. 'That's interesting.' He was silent, drinking his beer. 'Anyway, she could've concocted the story to get herself out of the frame.'

'Or to direct your attention away from her husband,' suggested Melrose.

'If she thought there was any possibility that Daniel Bletchley had something to do with her kiddies' death?' Wiggins suggested.

Melrose put his glass down. 'She wants the money. If the children pre-decease Daniel, he gets the whole Chick'nKing fortune. But if he's convicted of their murder, all that money goes elsewhere, *not* to the wife. Karen certainly couldn't look forward to Morris Bletchley's handing it over to her. He doesn't like her; he doesn't trust her. It's the reason he made the fortune over to the children – with, I'm sure, adequate provision for a trust – to keep Karen from getting her fair white hands on it.'

They were silent for a moment.

'And Chris Wells?' said Melrose. 'You think she's dead, don't you? Isn't it the rule that every hour she goes missing points in that direction?'

'It points to her being missing one more hour.'

'Very funny.'

'I'm not trying to be,' said Macalvie. 'I go on the assumption there are no rules.'

Someone had slotted money into the jukebox. 'When You and I Were Young, Maggie' is what came up. At the first baleful words of this old song, Melrose looked anxiously at Macalvie, but Macalvie was looking at nothing, the pint he had lifted frozen in the air as if he were toasting the three of them. He put the glass down, rose and went over to the jukebox, and with the line 'The sunshine has gone from the hill, Maggie' he yanked the plug from the socket. To the protestations of the few who had been listening and now even the ones who hadn't, he walked to the table where sat the man who had selected the three songs and slapped a ten-pound note on the table. The customers there looked up, surprised.

Years ago, in an old pub on Dartmoor, Macalvie had put his foot through the jukebox.

He was improving.

35

In the kitchen of the Woodbine Tearoom, Johnny sat at the small desk Brenda used for doing her accounts. He was shuffling his deck of cards, fanning them out, scooping them up, and reshuffling. The only thing that could keep his mind off Chris was going through his repertoire of tricks.

Brenda was taking baking trays out of the oven. Like Chris, she did most of her baking at night. 'I know it's hard, sweetheart, and gets harder to believe she'll be back, but she will, I know it. I know she will.'

He hadn't been able to keep the anxiety out of his face. He'd never make much of a hand-is-quicker-than-the-eye fellow. 'No, you don't. You're just trying to make me feel better.' When she turned from the oven to protest, he smiled and held up his hand. 'It's okay, Brenda; it's okay.' He went back to laying out cards and she went back to the gingerbread men she was decorating with currants.

'Pick one.' Johnny held out the fan of cards.

Brenda ran the back of a floured hand over her temple to get the hair out of her eyes. 'Is this that old trick?

Haven't I seen you do this a thousand times?'

'At least.'

She took a card; she put it back. He shuffled, picked out her card.

'Surprise, surprise,' she said, pressing a currant into dough.

'You needn't dismiss this trick, especially since you still don't know how I do it.' He put the cards aside and looked at the things that covered the desk, the big chequebook, the envelopes, and on its top surface the pictures, the snapshots of Brenda's dead daughter. He lowered his eyes; the daughter only made him think of Chris. How could she have disappeared so effectively when she'd done it so hurriedly, without time to really think? He asked Brenda.

She stopped and picked up her mug of coffee. 'Maybe it's not being able to see the forest for the trees, love.' She looked over at him. 'Maybe it's something really simple. What happened, I mean.'

'Come on, Brenda, the police aren't stupid. The one who's in charge is a commander. That's one of the highest-ranking officers in the whole Devon and Cornwall force.'

She sighed what sounded like a long and pent-up sigh. 'I expect you're right.'

Johnny went back to looking at the snapshots of Ramona. They showed her at different ages over the years, as if she had magically been whisked from childhood to adolescence. A toddler, a schoolgirl, a teenager. Chris had told him Brenda rarely talked about Ramona; the sadness was too overwhelming.

He could remember Ramona, beautiful as a young girl, who in the last months of her life had all but faded away, as if she were vanishing right before everyone's eyes, like the beautiful woman in a magician's act disappearing into the locked trunk, empty when it was open. *Now you see her, now you don't.* He crossed his arms and lowered his chin to rest on them, his eyes still on the pictures. 'She was really pretty, Ramona was.' His own voice startled him slightly, for he had not meant to say it aloud, reminding Brenda of her daughter.

As if – you arse – the poor woman could ever forget. He felt the weight of her silence. Then she came to stand behind him and put a hand on his shoulder. 'She was, wasn't she?'

Johnny heard such woe in her voice, he thought he might cry himself. Instead he reached his own hand round and covered hers. He thought he almost knew how she must feel. It probably wasn't possible to really know unless you had children and had lost them. It made him think of those poor little Bletchley kids. God. It hardly bore thinking about.

Brenda said, 'Remember she used to baby-sit for you when you were eight or nine?'

'Too old to need a sitter, that's for sure.'

'Oh, go on. You would have thought the same thing when you were two.'

'I did. I was.' What Johnny remembered about Ramona was how much of a golden girl she had seemed to him. Her hair was flaxen, her skin with a sheen like sunlight. She had had bright amber eyes and her mouth was naturally pink. She never needed anything to enhance those colours. She'd gone off to some public school and then to London. When she'd come back, how pale she'd looked. As time went on her eyes looked hardly darker than water, her lips silvery. Some kind of leukemia that leaches colour from you. The swinging door over there made a space she had walked through; the pavement outside sent up echoes of her footfall; the window reflected her image.

Brenda's hand still rested on his shoulder, though his own hand had slid away, for he thought of it as cold comfort for her. He tried to imagine what the world after Ramona must be like for Brenda. Here was this space, this chair, Ramona had inhabited. Ramona had filled this room, now empty. How could Brenda stand it, the lack of her? The unfilled space, the silent pavement, the unreflecting window, the empty door? He put his head in his hands and thought of the lack of Chris, and the Gilbert and Sullivan tune went through his mind:

> *If anyone anything lacks,*
> *He'll find it all ready in stacks . . .*

He got up; he had to go. He told Brenda he'd see her tomorrow and avoided looking into her eyes.

She called something after him, probably just *Good night, sweetheart.*

Passing the chestnut tree, Johnny stumbled over the big root he'd managed to avoid tripping over for years and went tumbling down, not hard, just in a stupid pratfall. Embarrassing had anyone been around to see. He fell on his face and just lay there for a while.

Finally, he turned over, brushing earth and grit from his face to look at the dead white moon casting its beautiful, useless light across the pavement.

After a bit, he got up, swept some dirt from his jeans, and trudged on home.

36

PC Evans, when he'd received the call at midnight, decided that the presence of the Devon and Cornwall higher-ups had its sunny side. *Let them handle it* had been his second thought; his first had been blind disbelief.

He'd been pulling up his trousers when Mrs E had half woken and mumbled a question as to where he was going. He'd answered by saying it was just a bloody cat up a tree. God knows he didn't want to say 'murder' and have her sit bolt upright in her curlers and start firing questions at him. He tugged on his blue jacket, shoved some boiled sweets into his pocket – blackcurrant, his favourite – and went out, climbed on his bike, and wheeled along at a good clip to the Drowned Man.

Getting that old bugger Pfinn out of bed by pounding on the front door of the pub had been a bonus. Making him trudge up the dark steps to yell awake that detective from New Scotland Yard had been bonus number two. Yes, this was when he felt like a copper.

Feeling he was in charge of the mills of the gods, PC Evans sucked on a blackcurrant sweet as he brought his palm down on the bell just to let everybody know he was down here waiting as the body grew colder by the minute. Evans had passed through his initial fright at the notion of having to take responsibility himself for the body at Bletchley Hall and was delighted he could pound on doors and ring bells and hurry people along who themselves would have to be the responsible parties.

Therefore it came as a sharp disappointment to him to discover, when he finally got up to the Hall, six police cars already there, blue lights turning. Also to find that scattered around the grounds, torches beaming light up and down, were at least a dozen policemen from Camborne headquarters. PC Evans recognized none of them. How had they got there so quickly?

The bullet had torn through the back of the wheelchair with enough momentum to make an entrance wound the size of a lemon and an exit wound in the front just below the rib cage the size of one of Evans's boiled sweets before embedding itself in a panel of dark red textured wallpaper on the far wall, next to the door in which Matron stood, swaying a little.

Brian Macalvie, for once, was speechless, not because of focusing all of his attention on the crime scene, but speechless with disbelief. He was not shocked that someone had murdered a man, only that someone had murdered *this* man.

Detective Sergeant Wiggins was white-faced, his mouth agape. He was the first to speak, however. '*Why*? The poor devil – I just saw him this afternoon. So did Mr Plant. Should I call him?'

Macalvie nodded. He turned to the stout woman in a

terry bathrobe who had called PC Evans. A long braid hung over her shoulder and she was hugging herself.

Constable Evans watched the police photographer set off flash after flash, making it look like a film shoot. Now, happy to take up his policeman's duties if it meant merely telling Commander Macalvie who's who and what's what, he motioned towards the elderly man whose face looked hot and tight as a blister and said, 'This is the man you want to talk to, sir. Mr Morris Bletchley.'

Macalvie nodded. 'We've met. In a minute.' In *this* minute, he was hunkered down before the wheelchair.

His diminished duties having been even more diminished, PC Evans thought, arrogant bastard, and dropped his hand.

Macalvie peered up into the downturned face, the head that had dropped forward as if the dead man were sleeping. He then rose and walked round behind the wheelchair and looked at the splintered band of wood, one of several across the back of the chair.

Wiggins was back from making the call to Seabourne and said Mr Plant would be right over. Ten minutes, tops.

Macalvie asked, then, 'Who was he, Mr Bletchley?'

'Tom Letts.'

Macalvie nodded. 'Sergeant Wiggins, come here.'

Not 'Constable Evans, come 'ere,' oh, no, just that emaciated boyo from Scotland Yard, come 'ere. Even though I'm the police presence in the village. No, no deference shown. Bastards! Evans stood straighter, just to let everyone know he wasn't affected at all by being ignored.

A car pulled up outside, a door slammed shut, and the police surgeon from Penzance came in. 'What've we got?' He looked neither to right nor left but headed towards the dead man and set about his preliminary examination.

Again, there was the sound of tyres on gravel, a car coming to a halt, and running feet, and Melrose Plant stood in the doorway of the red drawing room, his coat over his dressing gown, feet still in leather bedroom slippers.

'Ah, no.' Plant turned away.

Thus far she had said nothing, but for some reason, perhaps because it was such a sad little understatement, Matron began to sob. Another woman, smaller and older, patted her shoulder and started crying herself. Morris Bletchley said something to the small old woman about bringing in coffee for everybody.

Melrose looked around this room where he and Tom had been talking seven or eight hours ago. This poor boy, he thought, was talking about the miracles that had occurred at Bletchley Hall. Melrose had been astonished that Tom had actually looked happy. Maybe that was enough of a miracle right there.

Melrose looked across at Macalvie, who looked back. Melrose shook his head.

Macalvie asked how many cases they had here at the Hall at present and was told there were a dozen. 'That's all we can accommodate,' said Matron.

'Are they bedridden? That is, could any of them have been out of bed, moving about?'

Morris Bletchley said, 'Several *could* have. I mean, we

have some that are ambulatory, of course.'

'Then I want Sergeant Wiggins to go room to room; I imagine everyone's awake at this point with a dozen police tearing up the flower beds. You don't have to worry about his upsetting anyone unnecessarily. If you'd just show him where, Mr Bletchley?'

Moe Bletchley nodded and left with Wiggins and Matron. Macalvie dispatched PC Evans to the grounds.

'What's hard to understand,' said Dr Hoskins, putting away his instruments of life and death and getting up so the ambulance attendants could move the body to a stretcher, 'is why anyone would shoot to kill a man who was in the final stages of AIDS. Poor chap was going to die soon anyway; why would anyone try to kill him?'

Melrose said, his voice thick, 'I don't think anyone did.'

Both Hoskins and Macalvie turned to look at Melrose.

'It wasn't supposed to be Tom. He wasn't the intended victim. It was Morris Bletchley.'

Dr Hoskins shut his bag briskly. He was a man who dealt with the body in situ, not the body out of it.

Macalvie nodded. 'When can you—'

'Tomorrow morning. Early. I'll talk to you then.' Dr Hoskins bowed slightly to Melrose and left.

Macalvie looked at Melrose, waiting.

'It's the wheelchair. It's Morris Bletchley's.'

'Bletchley? He doesn't need a wheelchair.'

'No. But he uses it, he says, so as not to present a picture of too-perfect health to these terminally ill patients.'

A voice behind them said, 'He's right.' Morris

Bletchley took a step forward, as if they all stood for inspection. 'The bullet was meant for me. No end of suspects for *that*. Probably keep you busy for years, Commander Macalvie.'

Macalvie stared at him. 'Not this time, Mr Bletchley.'

37

They were sitting now, but not comfortably. Macalvie and Melrose were on one of the dark red velvet settees, Moe Bletchley on the other. PC Evans was still in the grounds, helping with the search for forensic evidence.

'Everybody's seen me in that wheelchair; they know it's mine.'

'Including visitors?'

Moe shrugged. 'What visitors had you in mind?'

With a thin smile, Macalvie answered, 'What visitors have *you* in mind?'

'No one. Few people come here, Commander; terminal illness isn't very tempting.'

'Nursing homes aren't popular with family and friends either, even if the illness isn't terminal.'

'No,' said Moe Bletchley, looking sad.

No sadder than Melrose felt. What they were talking about, the failure of people to come to cheer you just when you were really sinking, made him think of Tom and Tom's parents. On the other hand, there was his sister, Honey, a young lady Melrose would like to meet.

Probably would, too, at the funeral.

'Late at night, though, Mr Bletchley, would someone expect to see you sitting up?'

'Why not? I never go to bed before midnight anyway. I've been known to sit in just about any room at night, reading or just thinking. So, yes, there's a high probability of finding me sitting alone at night.'

Macalvie nodded. 'Okay. Anyone in particular you can think of who'd want you dead?'

Bletchley was silent for a few moments, then shook his head.

'Why not?'

'What?'

'Why can't you think of anyone, since you're convinced the bullet was meant for you?'

Morris Bletchley looked straight at Macalvie but offered nothing.

Macalvie's gaze was blue and unblinking. His hands, stuffed in the pockets of his coat, seemed to be pulling him forward on the settee. 'Come on, Mr Bletchley, you're a billionaire. Are you telling me you can't think of anyone in your will who might be eager for a hunk of your money?'

Bleakly, Moe smiled. 'A number of them. But I don't see the Sailors' Home killing me for it.'

'Who has the most to gain?'

'My son, Dan, naturally. Now that the grandchildren are gone.'

'And your daughter-in-law.'

Moe Bletchley said nothing.

'As I recall, you're no big fan of Karen Bletchley.'

'That's right. Nor is she fond of me. I don't think that means we'd shoot one another.'

'Oh, *you* might not shoot *her*. Why don't you like her?'

Moe shrugged, as if it should be obvious. 'I think I told you that night. She married Dan for his money. I know it.'

'How?'

'Commander Macalvie, if there's one thing I can sniff out at a thousand feet it's someone who's in love with money. She was here, incidentally.'

'When was that?'

'Three days ago. She stopped by to see me.'

'Is this something she often does?'

'No, never. It's the first time I've seen her in over a year, but that was in London. She doesn't come back to Bletchley. I've seen Dan a number of times, but without Karen. That's why I was surprised.'

'What was her reason?'

Moe looked over to the window through which the shot had come, but Melrose thought he was merely looking at blankness – the black sky, the blacker trees. 'She said she wanted to see Seabourne again. She said she was trying' – he rubbed his eyes as if to bring something into inner focus – 'to come to terms with Noah's and Esmé's deaths. Well, I don't have to remind you—'

'No, you don't. But why now? Especially since the house is leased to a stranger. Didn't she know it was taken by Mr Plant, here?'

'Yes. She'd been to see the agent, Esther Laburnum, who handles the property for me.'

Macalvie leaned forward. 'Mr Bletchley, doesn't it seem strange to you that she'd show up, first time in four years, just when all these other things are happening?'

Moe looked off towards the black glass of the high windows again. 'Yes, I guess it does.'

After a few seconds of silence during which nothing could be heard but the ticking of the grandfather clock, Macalvie asked, 'Who else might wish you harm? Given the way you've built up a business empire, there must be some toes you've stepped on; you must have made some enemies.'

'Sure. But not the shoot-'em-up kind.'

'Then what have you got that I don't know about that someone either wants or wants to get rid of?'

Moe frowned. 'What's that conundrum mean, exactly?'

'That you have something you don't know you have or, more likely, know something that you don't know might be lethal. To someone else. A secret shared with you that you might even have forgotten. That's merely an example. In other words, someone who thinks you're a danger to him.'

'That's just – too unlikely, Commander Macalvie.'

Macalvie sat back then and studied Morris Bletchley.

Macalvie, thought Melrose, didn't want to remind him that leading two little children down a stone stairway to frigid water was even more unlikely.

38

'I can't eat strawberries, can't touch 'em, me,' Sergeant Wiggins was saying, by way of sympathizing with Mrs Crudup. 'Minute I get a taste of one, like in some pud or trifle, I'm off.' Wiggins was sluicing the palm of one hand off the other to show how quickly 'off' a strawberry could send him.

Old Mrs Crudup looked tissue thin, someone whose every breath seemed proof that the air was unbreatheable, as if she might have been living at an extraordinarily high altitude and been brought down from it in a bubble. She was gossamer, as sheer as the gauze-like curtains at the window.

But she was not, apparently, so ephemeral that she couldn't dip into the public complaint bucket and give as good as she got. 'I know, I know, don't tell me.' Her reedy voice wavered. 'Strawberries is what's caused all this, and that's a fact. Sick as a dog, I am, sick as a dog. Could die before the night's out.'

'Don't say that, Mrs Crudup. I can sympathize, I can sympathize.'

Apparently, thought Melrose, Wiggins had quickly

picked up Mrs Crudup's habit of saying things twice. Melrose also noted that Mrs Crudup was one of those patients whom Wiggins had been told he need not question. She was hooked up to enough IVs and machinery to furnish Dr Frankenstein's laboratory.

At Macalvie's request, Melrose had gone to find out if Wiggins had discovered anything. Yes, he had apparently discovered that he, Wiggins, and the ghostly Mrs Crudup both had a strawberry allergy.

But Mrs Crudup, as Melrose learned from lounging in the doorway, suffered not from just an allergy but from a whole strawberry conspiracy.

'They disguise 'em in chocolate. They think I don't know! Take 'em away, Mr Wiggins! Take 'em away!'

Wiggins had the plate in hand. 'Certainly I will. And I'll just see Mr Bletchley about stopping people bringing them round.'

Melrose interrupted. 'Sergeant Wiggins?' Wiggins turned. 'Commander Macalvie needs you.'

Wiggins bade adieu to Mrs Crudup, who exacted a promise from him that he'd come back as soon as he'd dealt with the ones who were trying to kill her.

There had been three or four of the ambulatory old people standing in their own doorways when Melrose passed by. It was Mr Clancy who had directed Melrose to Mrs Crudup's room.

Now, on the way back, there were several more. There was the piano teacher, Miss Timons-Browne, Mr Bleaney, and Miss Livingston, who caught Wiggins's sleeve in her small talons and rattled on about the murder of poor Tom.

Wiggins managed to disengage himself, but all down the hall voices called to him and seemed to want to haul him this way and that. Mr Bleaney and Mrs Noonan (also on the not-to-question list) were two of the most vocal. How in God's name had he managed to visit, much less question, all of these people? Yet he waved to them or said hello, hello, as if he'd known them forever.

As he walked he was thumbing back the pages of his small notebook. 'You remember the Hoopers?'

'Who could forget them? Oh, excuse me, *they* could forget them.'

'They saw something.'

Melrose stopped, turned. 'What?'

'Someone or something, right round the corner.'

'Corner?'

'They were in the conservatory, playing chess.'

'At midnight? Good grief, are people permitted to wander around here at all hours?'

'Well, knowing how much Mr Bletchley believes in his patients' freedom, that doesn't surprise me, sir.'

Melrose supposed not. He started walking again. 'Someone or something. That just about suits them, given their memories.'

Macalvie sat on the same dark red settee, but across from him this time were the Hoopers. All three of them sat leaning forward, as if they were about to try out one-armed wrestling.

'Okay,' said Macalvie. 'Exactly what did you see?'

The Hoopers leaned even closer to Macalvie, looking puzzled.

'And you might be . . .?'

'Macalvie, Devon and Cornwall Constabulary.'

They all had, of course, been introduced, or at least the Hoopers had introduced each other. But that was all of fifteen seconds ago.

'A policeman?' said one of them, his squiggly eyebrows dancing.

Melrose expected Macalvie might be about to reach across the seductively reachable distance and knock their heads together. On the Hoopers' part – well, they appeared to be waiting for Macalvie to go on.

So he did. 'You told Sergeant Wiggins, there, you saw someone or something at the time we judge the shot was fired.'

The Hoopers sat; the clock ticked.

Then one said, of a sudden, 'It was . . .'

The other snapped his fingers. 'Yes, it was a . . .'

They looked at one another, urging one another forward. 'It was a . . .'

Macalvie shut his eyes, tightly. When he opened them he turned to Wiggins. 'Is it hoping for too much that you . . .?'

Wiggins, whose brow was furrowed as if in sympathy with the Hoopers' brows, blinked. 'Oh. Oh, of course. Sorry, sir.' And he started thumbing through his notebook, turning page after page after page.

Melrose wondered what in hell he could have in it. How many people up there in their bedrooms had he interviewed and for how long?

'Here it is.' Wiggins read. 'Hoopers: "We were just in the middle of our game, I mean, nobody knows just what the middle is, anyway it was just on midnight, for a moment later the clock chimed. We looked out – we saw this person, well, more a shape it was, going past the window." '

'And?' asked Macalvie.

'I'm afraid that's all I've written down, sir.'

Macalvie looked at the Hoopers. 'You saw this shape. Can you be a bit more precise there?'

'It was a . . .'

'He could've been – sort of small.'

'Or *she*, she could've been – well, small.'

Just at that moment one of the uniformed police outside raised the window round the corner from the one the shot had been fired through and called to Macalvie, asking if this was what he meant.

'Yes. That's what.'

'Just when the conversation was getting interesting.' Melrose walked over to the window.

Finally, the Hoopers were excused. The little woman who'd been sent to get the coffee came in with a tray of cups and saucers and biscuits. Matron followed her with an enormous coffeepot. Having observed the party atmosphere, Mr Bleaney, Mr Clancy, and Miss Livingston crowded in after them.

What Melrose liked about these people was their sporting nature, their smiling in the face of such adversity, and it set him to wondering about the chemistry among people for whom death was right round the corner. To use Tom's metaphor, it must have been like this in war, at least it always was in war's representations. As if at the front, he and Wiggins were passing amid battle-ravaged troops taking strength from one another. You depended, he thought, upon another man's spirit to pull you through. And it was all overseen – the battle plan, the deployment of troops, and, at the end, the demobbing, the mustering-out, all of the cliché-ridden, unashamed, canting patriotism – by Morris Bletchley.

39

'I heard what happened; I imagine everyone has. It's terrible. It's worse than terrible if Tom got shot – by mistake. He was going to die anyway, and soon; that's what people are saying. As if that made it all right. As far as I'm concerned, it makes it worse. It makes it ten times worse. Even the little he had to live, that's gone now.'

Johnny stood in the open doorway of Seabourne and said this to Melrose before he'd even stepped inside. He stood turning his cabby's cap in his hands and his eyes glazed with tears that didn't spill.

'Come on in, Johnny. You're right. It does make it worse. Come on back to the kitchen; I just made some coffee.' It was late morning and Melrose had just arisen, having had no sleep to speak of the night before.

Johnny followed him, talking about Tom all the while, talking nervously as if his licence to talk might be revoked at any moment, so he'd better get it out fast. 'I always talked to him when we went to the Hall. He was so – calming, somehow. You probably never noticed but I'm kind of tightly wound—'

Melrose smiled and nodded.

'—and it was actually relaxing to be around Tom. It seems strange it should be, with his problems. You'd think he'd be bitter, getting AIDS when he wasn't even gay, but he wasn't bitter, not at all—'

'Tom wasn't gay? But—'

Johnny was shaking his head. 'He told me when we were talking about the chances of getting Alzheimer's or oesophageal cancer, you know, the various things the people at the Hall have. We started discussing AIDS and he said the chance of getting it with only one – uh – you know, contact – ranged anywhere from one in a thousand to three in a hundred. This relationship he had happened a long time ago and was very short-lived. Anyway . . .' Johnny shrugged. 'But maybe a crisis is what shows you what you're made of.' He finished this looking at the cup of coffee Melrose had placed before him, looking as if what he himself was made of must not be much.

'Tom's crisis was in the past, Johnny; it was horribly painful but he'd lived with it for a long time. It was old. Yours is new.'

Johnny was quiet for a moment and then said, 'Police think Chris shot this Sada Colthorp and then took off, don't they?'

'No, that certainly hasn't been my impression. Commander Macalvie hasn't come to any conclusions about that murder.'

'Chris didn't like her, though. I think they had a couple of fights.'

'A long way from fighting to murder, Johnny.'

Johnny shook the hair fallen across his forehead out

of his face. 'What the bloody hell is going on around here? Why would anyone want to kill Mr Bletchley? He's done nothing but good for this village.'

'That's what I understand.'

He shoved his cup aside, slapped on his cap, adjusted it, and said, 'I'm on call. I've got a ride to pick up and take to Mousehole. Thanks for the coffee.'

'Is your uncle still stopping with you?'

'Charlie? He went back to Penzance yesterday morning.'

'I had dinner with him the night before last under Mr Pfinn's watchful eye. I thought him quite a good fellow.'

'He told me. He thought you were, too. 'Bye.'

The bell rang again and Melrose started to rise from the comfort of the fireplace and the book he was reading. He hesitated, thinking it might be Agatha already or, worse (since Agatha might have needed a ride), Agatha and her bosom buddy, Esther Laburnum.

He tiptoed. How ridiculous, he told himself, and straightened up as he walked the last twenty feet. Still, once there, he did not open the door immediately. Instead he took a furtive glance through one of the leaded-glass panels on both sides of the door to see a man standing there, a stranger in a lightweight wool suit. Good wool, too. At least the back was a stranger's. He was quite tall and seemed to stand at ease, not with the stiff uncertainty some backs can muster if they're on unfamiliar ground.

Then, disgusted with himself for keeping the poor fellow waiting, he yanked the door open.

The man turned. 'Mr Plant? Or Lord Ardry? Mrs Laburnum didn't seem sure what to call you.' He smiled. 'I'm Daniel Bletchley.'

The serviceable stereotypes of composers Melrose had trusted and trotted through his mind – effete, absent-eyed, cloud-ridden – would have to go. The man's sheer physical presence erased the stereotype. He was tall, though no taller than Melrose; yet he was more densely packed. He was not conventionally handsome, but then he didn't need to be. His sexuality was something like Richard Jury's only more so. (A lot of women would have been surprised that there *was* a 'more so'.) Nothing in the expression of his unconventionally handsome face seemed held back, restrained, or secret.

This went through Melrose's mind in the moment it took him to say, 'Come in.'

40

Daniel Bletchley was happy to come in and stood in the hall, shaking hands. His eyes, though, Melrose noticed, seemed to be following the sweep of the graceful staircase that he had once climbed so often to the upstairs rooms with which he was so familiar.

'You're the musician,' said Melrose.

Dan turned his eyes from the staircase and laughed. 'I don't know if I'm *the* musician, but, yes, I'm one of them.' His expression and his tone grew more sober. 'When I heard about what happened, I thought Dad could use some help. Tom.' Dan shook his head. 'He was with Dad for a long time. A long time.' He brought this out on an expiration of breath, as if Time had been profligate with Tom Letts's life, as if Tom should have been able to count on it for more. Then he added, 'I hope I'm not bothering you.'

'You're not bothering me in the least. My aunt is coming for tea at five, and you'll want to be gone before that event horizon. But as for now, join me in the library. I've got a fire and whisky going.'

'Sounds great.' As Melrose led the way, a way

267

with which Dan Bletchley was thoroughly – and sadly – familiar, Dan said, ' "Event horizon"? Sounds ominous.'

'It is. It's my aunt, who, knowing I wanted to get away from Long Piddleton – my village in Northamptonshire, that is – and all things Piddletonian, just for a change, a damned change, followed me and has taken up residence at that B and B in the village.'

Daniel laughed. 'Not to worry; she won't last. No one can stand that place for more than a night or two.'

'Wrong. Wrong on that score. She's been there for over a week.'

Melrose might not have recognized Daniel Bletchley with only the snapshots to go by. Sitting now in the wing chair beside them, and with a drink in his hand, he still might have escaped recognition. He was a man who was very alive, an aliveness not captured by a camera's lens. He was apparently one of those people subdued by them; cameras didn't 'catch' him. Certainly, he was one who wasn't tempted by them, for he was always looking away, or down, or in shadow. Melrose might have wondered if the two men were the same person.

They were. From the way Daniel picked up the photograph of the children and looked at it, carefully set it back, and looked in his whisky glass, there could be no mistaking who he was.

'Dad said you were a lot of help. He said you were at the Hall last night. With that detective.'

'Commander Macalvie.'

'Yes. I know him from . . . does he have any idea what's going on?'

'No, I don't think so. Not yet.'

'Dad sometimes gives the impression of being – uh, demanding and impervious to people's feelings.'

'I've seen no sign of that, none.'

Dan smiled, if a little uncertainly. 'He's very tough in business. Sometimes he appears to be steam-rollering right over people . . . I'm trying to explain it to myself. The police seem to think whoever it was was trying to kill *him* and not Tom. I know Dad can be headstrong, arbitrary, intractable, but . . .' He shrugged.

'If those qualities earn you a bullet in the back, I have a relation who'd be riddled.'

Dan laughed. 'Yes. You're probably right.'

Melrose thought for a moment. 'Could it be some old grudge? Some old damage your father caused?'

Dan was thoughtful, head down, the whisky glass, empty, swinging from the tips of his fingers. Melrose got up and took the glass from his hands. Dan thanked him absently. He put his elbows on his knees, made a bridge of his now empty fingers, and rested his mouth against them. He stared at the fire.

Except for the occasional spark and split of wood and the click of glass against bottle, the room was perfectly still. Beyond the window, the quiet day. He could easily check Karen Bletchley's account of what happened with that of her husband.

'Daniel,' Melrose said without thinking; he was not usually free with first names on short acquaintance. 'If you don't mind my calling you that?'

Of course he didn't mind. The long fingers, the

pianist's fingers, waved this away and took the whisky. 'Go on.'

'I met your wife. I met Karen.' He felt uncomfortable, as if he were telling a secret. Or would have done, had it not been for what he suspected was an artful story of hers.

Daniel was surprised. 'Really? Where did you meet?'

She hadn't mentioned it. Why not? 'She came here, actually. It was only a few days ago.'

Daniel set his drink on the table and again leaned forward, mouth against entwined fingers. Full attention.

'She wanted – she said – to see the house again. I imagine tragedy – well, pulls one back. Look, I'm terribly, terribly sorry about your children, what happened to them. It was . . .' He searched for words. 'I have none of my own.' Suddenly, Melrose felt the lack and was ashamed of it, as if he'd been considered for parenthood and been found wanting. Ridiculous, but there it was.

Dan said nothing, but his eyes, scarcely visible over his fingertips, were wet. It would take very little, thought Melrose, to bring this man's feelings to the surface. 'She told me . . .' He tried to sort out what Karen had told Macalvie four years ago and had since told him. Then he went on to report what Mrs Hayter had told him and, before that, Macalvie. And the rest of it. 'The thing is this: Commander Macalvie has never let this case, what happened to your children, go. He's never closed it. Now he wonders if the strange things that have been happening are related to what happened back then. That's the reason I bring it up.' He felt fuddled. 'I'm probably overstepping my bounds; Macalvie will talk to you about all of this. I certainly don't want to bring up something that you must find painful.'

'No. I don't mind. I don't *want* not to talk about it. It makes me ill not to be able to talk about it. So, please, go on.'

'Well.' Now Melrose sat forward too, hands circling his glass. 'Your wife went over that terrible night. She told me that earlier the children had come upon some people in the woods, more than once, a man and a woman. At first your wife thought nothing of it when they talked about it, but after a while she got to thinking it was peculiar. She didn't know who the man was or who the woman was. That is, she didn't actually see them. But . . . what do you make of all this?'

'I didn't know what to make of it. Mr Macalvie asked the same questions.'

'Did you think she was – they were real?'

'You mean did the kids make them up?'

'Not exactly. I wondered if . . .' What the hell was he doing? He knew nothing about Bletchley's present relationship with his wife. Why should he be putting himself in a policeman's place, in Macalvie's place, raising issues like this? 'I'm sorry.'

'Nothing for you to be sorry about. Through no fault of your own you've got involved with my family. I've no idea what Karen told you. Since Noah and Esmé died, we haven't talked much.' He turned his face towards the high window that faced the cliff and the bay. 'I'm not sure we did before.' He rested his head against the tall back of the chair and closed his eyes in the manner of a man who is tired to death. Life, however, would never let Daniel Bletchley go merely at his bidding. 'Sometimes I catch my own thoughts and wonder, how can I think of anything at all except what happened to those little children? Have you ever had something happen in your life, some event that washes over everything else and flattens it?'

Melrose couldn't answer. It was as if something were stuck in his throat.

There was a silence. Into it, Daniel said suddenly, 'Chris Wells has disappeared.'

Melrose was surprised by the seeming irrelevance of the remark. 'You knew her.'

'Yes. I knew her well.' He took a long drink of his whisky.

'There was a woman murdered in Lamorna Cove. Your father told you about this?' When Daniel nodded, Melrose went on, 'She once worked at the Woodbine.'

'I think I remember her slightly.' He leaned forward, rolling the glass between his hands. 'But I didn't know that this woman and Chris had had a falling out.'

'I think it was over Johnny.'

'Johnny? But, dear God, if it was four years ago, the boy couldn't have been more than – what? Thirteen?'

'He's probably always seemed older than he is. And he's a very handsome lad, very appealing to women, I'd think.'

Daniel shook his head. 'And now because this woman was murdered and Chris has disappeared, it's *post hoc, ergo propter hoc*, is that it? Ridiculous. Absolutely ridiculous.' He shook his head again, unable to come up with a word that would convey his disdain for such an idea.

'Chris could never, never do that.'

Dan Bletchley had known her well, clearly. 'Not even to protect Johnny?'

Dan looked at him with a surprised quickness. 'Protect Johnny? From what?'

'Sorry. I'm just playing devil's advocate. I had no reason for saying that. I don't know her, of course; I've never met her. But I've certainly got the impression she loves him a lot, and for his part – well, his feelings for her seem to stop just one step short of worship.'

'Yes. She certainly does love him. Still.' He ran his hand through his straight light-brown hair, which had a way of standing up in ridges when he did this. And this gesture, too, made him look young, like the boy he must have been. That was one more thing about him, a boyishness that would have appealed to women. His sexuality would simply bowl women over. He had a force and a heat about him a woman would feel like the siroccos that blow across the dunes.

'Let's have another,' said Melrose, heading for the drinks table again. When he was back in his seat, he turned the talk to something less volatile, telling Daniel how the house had affected him the first time he'd seen it.

Dan laughed. '*The Uninvited*. I thought I was the only one who remembered that film. It must have been a rerun on the telly. I have to confess one thing: I loved that background music.'

Melrose waved his glass and hummed the tune. Was he drunk?

Dan drained his glass, stood up, and said, 'Come on. And bring the decanter.'

'Where?'

Dan was already out of the room. 'Upstairs,' he called back over his shoulder. 'The piano's still there, isn't it?'

Following him up the stairs, Melrose said, 'I was trying to play it.'

Dan stood looking around the nearly empty room as if long absence might have altered things irrevocably. 'How I missed this room. I could stand where you are now for what seemed like the entire day watching the water, getting the rhythm of it, thinking music. God, what a cliché.' He set his glass on the corner of the piano and sat down on the bench.

Melrose recalled how Daniel's gaze had travelled the length of the rosewood banister the moment he'd set foot in the house. He was speaking the truth when he had said he'd come to console his father, but Melrose wondered if this house and this room hadn't been part of what pulled him back. As there must be for Daniel Bletchley many rooms and countless pianos, Melrose wondered about his attachment to this one. Or, rather, if the attachment were so strong, could anything have driven him away?

The music happened so suddenly and with such force that Melrose had to take a step backward. Waterfalls of music, cascading notes, a whole rich canvas of that song Melrose had tried to pick out with a finger. He stood looking out of the window as if the music might be rushing against the rocks, shaking the waves in some violent rapprochement with the elements.

And the thing about it was, the original composition, though vastly appealing, was not great music, not complex, not textured, but a sentimental song with rather predictable crescendos and diminuendos. Yet this was such *felt* music. The sheer volume made it seem as if all the air had been drained from the room and gone to swell the music. Were he truthful, he thought, there were only two responses to such a sound: to faint or to weep. He was not truthful and did neither.

' "Stella by Starlight",' said Daniel. 'Do you know what I did? I was eleven or twelve when I heard it. I wrote to the composer and told him how much I liked it. He sent me his original score. I never got over that.' He shook his head as he fingered the opening bars again.

'But that's wonderful. You must have been very persuasive as a lad. Not to say very talented. Play something of yours.'

'Of mine? I just did.'

'I thought you said—'

Daniel smiled. 'Sorry. I'm being enigmatic.' He sighed, thought for a moment, and began to play an étude.

Melrose thought it was technically very fine, yet it didn't have the weight of the Stella he'd just played. Although 'Stella by Starlight' was, no matter how beguiling the melody, sentimental stuff, whatever it lacked in complexity was more than made up for by the complex emotions of the man who played it.

Lost in these reflections and the water below, Melrose jumped when he heard the door knocker.

Dan stopped playing. 'Your aunt?'

Melrose looked at his watch and answered, ruefully, 'My aunt.'

Talk about the Uninvited.

41

Before she was even over the doorsill, Agatha was running on about the shooting at the Hall. 'It's not hard to see it, I've done a little – how d'you do?' she said, acknowledging Daniel Bletchley's presence, before herding herself into the living room on the right, talking a mile a minute as she went through, unaware that Melrose wasn't with her. Talk talk talk.

'Listen, thanks for the drinks,' said Daniel.

'Thanks, dear heavens, for the music!'

'My pleasure.' Daniel went out of the door and turned. 'You'll come to the funeral?'

'Yes, of course.'

'Ah. Good. You're really a part of all this. You knew him. Anyway, please come.' With that, he trudged across the gravel to his car.

Agatha was at the window, watching Daniel Bletchley drive away. 'Who is that man?'

'Daniel Bletchley. You just met him, remember?'

'That's the name of the person who runs that depressing home.'

'He's Morris Bletchley's son.'

Agatha hugged herself and made a shuddery sound. 'It's freezing in here. You could at least have laid a fire. You knew I was coming for tea.'

'True. We're not having it in here. Come along.'

Complaining all the way across the hall and down the short corridor about the temperature, the size of the place, the velvet hangings in the dining room she passed, the draughts, the prospect she glimpsed through a round window facing the bay, the bay itself, the coast of England, all of England, and the world – she finally came to rest on the small sofa by the fire. The air through which she'd passed hummed and vibrated with the tinny sound of a plucked banjo string.

Melrose said, 'I'm surprised you didn't recognize Bletchley. He's a pianist. He played that white piano in Betty's or Binkey's or whatever that tearoom was called.'

'What are you talking about?'

It was as good a story as any. 'Harrogate, dear aunt. Don't you recall staying at the Old Swan with your friend Theodore?'

'You mean *Teddy*.'

'Well, she looked like a Theodore.' Sighing with genuine pleasure, Melrose recalled that wonderful twenty minutes of conversation when he had set himself the challenge of not speaking a word, yet all the while giving the impression of a man with brilliant conversation. Wasn't it amazing how blind people could be to the world outside of their own egos?

'You mean *that man* was the afternoon-tea-hour pianist at Betty's?'

Betty's was a Harrogate landmark. Agatha was

impressed; she always was by the wrong things.

'Yes. I was trying to talk him into playing in the Woodbine. Well, excuse me while I put the kettle on.' Melrose turned to go.

'You mean the tea's not *ready*?' Her sigh was pained. 'Oh, honestly, men!'

She seemed to have forgotten that oh-honestly-men had been producing her tea daily at Ardry End without fail or error. He put the kettle on the hob and was back in the library quick as one of young Johnny's card tricks.

'I was telling you about my own little investigation. We cannot leave it to doltish police such as that Constable Evans!'

'There are some distinctly un-doltish police on the job. Mr Macalvie, mainly.'

She straightened the ruffle of her fussy flowered blouse. 'Of course, they're all barking up the wrong tree.'

'Which tree is that?'

Ignoring the tree, she leaned forward and whispered – whoever she thought might be overhearing, Melrose didn't know – 'What we need to search for is your local homophobic, and I think I've got him!'

The kettle screamed.

No wonder.

Melrose was out and back barely in time for the tea to steep. This announcement of his aunt's might prove to be entertaining. He told her that her homophobia was misplaced, since the killer hadn't even intended to kill Tom Letts. 'It was Morris Bletchley he or she was after.'

'That's patently absurd. That's the trouble with you so-called intellectuals, you can't see what's right under your noses. What I heard was' – again she leaned towards him and said in a whispery hiss – 'he has AIDS, full-blown AIDS! Can't have *that* in a village. And it wouldn't surprise me at all if that Pfinn person shot him. If ever there was a homophobic, it's that man!'

Melrose had a hard time of it not to pour scalding tea down her neck. He was never a proselytizer of gay rights or anything else; he didn't care much one way or the other. But for Tom, yes, he would proselytize. 'Your bigoted nature—'

'What?' Sheer amazement sat on her features at the realization that Melrose was overtly criticizing her.

'– precludes any possibility of your seeing a person's true worth. All you're doing is projecting your own fears on another person or situation. That's what homophobia is, isn't it? Projecting one's own fear of partaking of other men's needs and desires? That's what phobia in general is, a fear of being the Other. Anyway, you didn't know Tom Letts. I did, and I liked him very much.'

Agatha looked all around, as if the dread virus might have infiltrated Seabourne. The look made Melrose laugh; it was so much the look that would be called forth by the doors crashing open upon them. The Uninvited!

'I don't see it's anything to laugh about.'

Too bad. 'As for your chosen homophobic – Mr Pfinn, is it? – I don't know how you come to that remarkable conclusion, since Mr Pfinn engages in conversation only to be contradictory. He stays away from words.'

'Well, he didn't with Esther and me. Of course, people do tend to confide in me, you've noticed.'

Melrose felt his eyes open as wide as any cartoon character's. As did Mr Pfinn, Melrose stayed away from words.

Agatha leaned forward, balancing a biscuit on her knee. 'The man absolutely loathes homosexuals!'

'Mr Pfinn loathes everyone. Loathing is not a criterion by which to judge Mr Pfinn.'

42

Pfinn was living up to Melrose's assessment of him (splenetic, peevish, and unaccommodating) that night in the Drowned Man by refusing to allow Brian Macalvie another drink in the saloon bar.

'Just you order another at dinner,' commanded Pfinn. 'But get your skates on. Can't keep the cook around all night, can I?'

Dinnertime thus determined, they had gone into the dining room, where Melrose was now picking another bone out of his turbot. This had been served by a humourless middle-aged lady he had never seen before. Johnny was not around. 'You say the same gun killed both of them?'

'Yes, but we already knew that. Smith and Wesson twenty-two.' Macalvie had stopped eating five minutes before and was smoking a cigarette, having considerately asked Melrose's permission.

'*We* didn't know anything. *You* apparently did.'

'Did you really think there were two shooters involved?'

'I—'

'There are too many similarities between the shootings to believe that.' Macalvie pierced a piece of aubergine and held it on the tine of his fork as if it were a little green world he needed to decipher. He gave his fish a poke, put his fork down again, and looked around for the waitress. 'We're the only ones in here, for God's sake, so why can't we get service? I want another beer. Has it occurred to you, Plant, that everything significant in the background of these two cases – *three* if we count the little kids – happened four years ago, give a month, take a month? Listen: Sada Colthorp turns up here four years ago; the kids died in September four years ago; Ramona Friel died in January four years ago.'

Melrose drank his wine, a Meursault at some outlandish price, but he felt he deserved it. Why, he wasn't sure. 'That bothers you?'

Macalvie's head turned from the dining room search and cut Melrose a glance. 'Doesn't it disturb you? You don't think it's coincidence, do you?'

Actually, Melrose hadn't worked out that there *was* a list of events to consider. He watched the waitress trudge grimly towards their table, thinking not about Macalvie's list but about where Johnny was.

Macalvie told the woman what he wanted and she trudged grimly off again. 'The night the little kids died, the housekeeper thought she heard a car, woke up, but turned over to go back to sleep. Why did she do that?'

'I don't follow you.'

'You're an elderly woman of a nervous disposition, alone with two children in an isolated house—'

'*Turn of the Screw*, as I said.'

'Uh-huh. A car drives up or drives off. Wouldn't this keep you from going back to sleep? It would me, and I've got a gun. I'd be pumping adrenaline – unless, of course, the sound was familiar.'

'You mean one of the *family* cars?'

'There were three: Daniel's sporty Jaguar, Karen's BMW, Morris Bletchley's Volvo.'

Melrose recalled his visit to Rodney Colthorp. 'Or Simon Bolt's. If she heard a familiar car, it didn't have to be Dan Bletchley's. Bolt had the same make; Dennis Colthorp tried to buy it, remember? The car would have to have been leaving, not arriving, because Mrs Hayter did then go to investigate.'

'Right. That's possible. Too bad Bolt's not around to question. He died three years ago.' Macalvie paused. 'So Daniel and Karen were out on the razz. Don't give me that alibi look. Daniel's fell apart pretty quickly. Karen's lacks the essential watertightness we detectives hate; her dinner companions said they actually *hadn't* seen her every minute as they went on to a concert after dinner. Tickets were hard to get, so they had to sit apart. I only got this from them, mind you, when I questioned them again.'

'So they didn't really know where she was for some time.'

'An hour and twenty minutes. They were vague. I went back and checked up on that particular event.'

'What you're saying is that one of the Bletchleys came back?' Melrose's scalp prickled.

Macalvie shrugged. 'Not necessarily. I don't know.

Even so, it doesn't mean one of them was responsible for the children's deaths.'

'And Mrs Hayter only now mentions the car?'

Macalvie nodded. 'She said, "It could never be Mr Bletchley, as he was in Penzance with his business friend." '

'How could she leave this out before?'

'People are funny about what they see and hear. If you ask a witness to describe a man, he might say, "He looked a lot like that gentleman over there, green eyes, dark blond hair, tall, classic looks, yes, like Melrose Plant. Wore those little gold-rimmed glasses, just like 'im." Given the *possibility* that you, Plant, could actually have been there, then why not hit on the obvious? It wasn't a man who looked like you, it *was* you.'

Melrose said nothing; he was trying to think up reasons why it couldn't possibly have been Dan Bletchley. He didn't somehow think Macalvie would go for the nice-guy defence. He pushed his plate aside and took out his Zippo and cigarettes and listened.

'They must've been careful. I had someone on Dan Bletchley's tail for two months.' He nodded at Melrose's look of surprise. 'All we got was dinner with his wife once a week at the Ivy, then concerts, the theatre. It must have been someone living near enough for him to see her and get back in an evening.'

'How about here in Bletchley? That's near enough.' He lit a cigarette, rasping the flint. 'Chris Wells.'

Rarely had he ever surprised Macalvie, but her name in this context certainly did. 'Chris Wells? What makes you think that?'

'I'm inferring it from the way he talked about her. She was no passing acquaintance.'

Macalvie had forgotten his cigar. The coal end was dimming.

'And she's disappeared. Jesus.' He took the cigar from his mouth.

'Another woman. Chris Wells. I knew it'd be something simple.'

'If you call that simple,' said Melrose, ruefully.

43

Johnny had stayed in all day and was staying in all night, too. Rarely did he call any of his various jobs to say he wasn't coming in, but after last night, and falling over that stupid tree root, and the awful way he felt, he'd decided to stay in.

He was dividing his time between house-cleaning and practising magic. Up to then, he hadn't done anything, hadn't touched anything, as if, by some alchemical process, leaving things exactly the same meant she would come back, she would magically appear.

It had by now been nearly two weeks. Twelve days. It seemed months, years, since he had last seen his aunt. He dried the last plate and stacked it, snapped the tea towel, and flung it over his shoulder.

Johnny picked up his book, named *Sorcerer's Apprentice*, in which the 'Sorcerer' led the reader Apprentice through the tricks. He disliked the comic-book illustrations, but the actual text was all right. He leaned against the kitchen counter and continued reading what he'd interrupted to sweep the floor. He looked at the big table where Chris's baked goods still lay on trays, the meringues and the ginger biscuits, and told himself to put the meringues in plastic bags. Most of the biscuits he'd already eaten. He wasn't all that fond of meringues, although Chris's were better than Brenda's. Brenda liked things really sweet.

He looked back at the book and read the instructions for this particular trick.

> You will need: (1) three ashtrays, glass or metal, 3–4 inches diameter; and (2) three small objects – safety pin, button, penny.

They hadn't any ashtrays except for a heavy one of blue Murano glass. Chris was supposed to have stopped smoking. Charlie might have brought one of his tin ones; he'd started carrying them around because ashtrays weren't such a familiar sight any more. But Johnny didn't see any.

It had been nice having Charlie around, if only for twenty-four hours. He rarely visited.

He looked at the pudding plates he'd washed. Too big to stand in for ashtrays. He read on to see what the Apprentice (meaning himself) was supposed to do with them. Just put one of the small objects on top of each one. He looked around the kitchen and saw the lid from an empty jar; yes, that would work, except he had to have three of them. Then his eye fell on the meringues. He walked over to the table. Three, maybe four inches. Perfect. The centre was depressed so he could put the 'small objects' in them. He stacked up five – in case they broke easily – and took a big napkin from a drawer in the table, where he also saw a small picture hook that would do as a 'small object'.

This loot he carried into the living room and put down on the card table. Its smooth green baize made it an excellent surface. Then, with one of the meringues to munch, he went to a small sideboard and opened a drawer where Chris kept odds and ends – the 'junk drawer' she called it – into which she tossed things she couldn't think what to do with.

He found several safety pins and chose the smallest. An amber plastic tube of white pills rolled to the front of the drawer. The pills were just the size of small buttons. But what were they? Medicine for what? He could make nothing of the name. He took a bite of the meringue and let it melt in his mouth, turned the tube to read the date. That wouldn't tell him anything. Chris wasn't a pill popper; he hoped she wasn't sick and he didn't know it. He took one of the pills to use in place of the button.

He went back to the card table, where he polished off the meringue and wished he had some strawberries and some of that wonderful custard, sabayon. Chris made it for pudding sometimes, piling strawberries on a meringue and pouring the custard over it. You could get drunk off that custard, there was so much Madeira wine in it.

Telling himself to stop thinking about Chris, to concentrate on the book and the trick, he aligned the ashtray meringues as instructed and laid out the napkin. He read:

Stack ashtrays, cover with the handkerchief.

Johnny stacked the three meringues and dropped the napkin over them. This was going to be one of the Sorcerer's no-brainers, he thought. He picked up the last meringue – since he wouldn't need it for reinforcement – and bit into it while he read:

It is important that the viewer(s) believe that the button, coin, or pin will reappear if they have faith that this is the case.

Johnny's head snapped up. He stared at the wall opposite. *Wait*, he thought, and shook his head. *Just wait now*. It was as if to proceed, as if to take one small step, would have him rushing like an avalanche towards an answer he couldn't believe.

Fragments of remembered conversations jostled for his attention. *She would never go off without telling me . . . This time she did.*

Johnny knew he was right even while more and more adrenaline was pumping through his body.

This time she did.

No, she didn't!

He was out of the door in a flash and, virus excuse forgotten, went running towards the Woodbine. He stopped abruptly where the roots overlapped the pavement and thought, no. Not the way to do it.

He looked across at the Drowned Man and darted across the street and in through the door, again uncaring of the virus that was accounting for his day off from serving dinner.

Mr Pfinn, however, hadn't forgotten. He came into

the bar from the dining room carrying dirty linen. 'Well, Johnny? Ya better now t'meal's done and I had t'get Ursula in?'

Johnny didn't waste time making excuses or acknowledging the sanctimonious tone. 'Is Mr Plant here by any chance for dinner?'

'He were. Gone, now, him and that other'n, too.'

'Which other – you mean the detective? Mr Macalvie?'

Mr Pfinn, happy to add to Johnny's anxiety, merely said, 'Mebbe. Whoever.'

Johnny looked wildly around the room as if something might yet remain of the two men, some fragment he could address. But the only things here to commune with were Pfinn and the dogs in the doorway.

'Where'd they go? Do you know where they went?'

Mr Pfinn's white eyelashes blinked several times. 'No cain tell that. Listen, boy, I'd ought t'fire ya, I ought.'

'Stuff it, Mr Pfinn, and you can stuff your job too.'

He was on the point of tears; then he was at the doorway, jumping over the dogs, and out of the front door, where he ran straight into Megs who served along with him at the Woodbine.

Not that it mattered, but now Brenda would know his reason for not coming in was bogus. He decided to make it three out of three and walked as quickly as he could to the Cornwall Cabs office.

'Feeling better, love?' asked Shirley who, not waiting for an answer, continued with, 'Look kinda peaky to me. You sure you should be out of bed?'

For the first time that evening, Johnny smiled. 'I'm

better. But I want to ask a big favour. Can I have a car for a couple of hours?'

'You certainly could, love, except one's in the shop and the other two're both out on calls. Is something wrong?'

'No, no. I just have a little business that I need a ride for.'

'Sorry. One of them's gone to Mousehole and one to St Buryan. Bit of a distance. But you can wait if you like.'

Johnny was biting a thumbnail. He shook his head. 'Listen, could I just make a phone call?'

'Sure, love.' Shirley shoved the black telephone towards him.

He punched in the number and listened to the bleak *brr-brrs* sounding in Seabourne. He let it ring a dozen times before he turned off the transmit and handed the phone back to Shirley.

'No joy there either?'

'No joy, right.'

'Shouldn't be long before one of them gets back – speak of the devil, here comes Trev. You can take that one.'

Johnny tossed her a 'thanks' over his shoulder as he ran out of the door.

44

Melrose was sitting in his favourite chair, looking at the fire and entertaining himself with thoughts of a séance. Surely there had been a séance in *The Uninvited*; in films like that there was always a séance. He wondered if real séances (or was that an oxymoron?) were like those portrayed in films: the medium's voice turning deep and guttural, uttering the oracular words of one centuries dead; the candle flame flickering and dying; that clammy hand holding yours later discovered to be wearing a glove . . .

Melrose shuddered slightly. He was wracking his brain or, rather, un-wracking it, downloading his thoughts about the murder of Tom Letts and Daniel Bletchley's visit into his glass of whisky.

The doorbell rang.

Again? Who the devil . . .?

He sighed, got up from his chair, and carried his drink with him. He got to the door, glad that at least it wouldn't be Agatha, since it already had been, and, yanking it open, hoping it would be Stella making a magical appearance.

It was Richard Jury. Just standing there.

Melrose gaped. His mouth opened and closed, opened and closed. He'd like to appear to be just standing there too, with a drink in his hand and Jury's cool. Instead, he knew he must look like a fish. Mouth open, closed, open, closed.

He found his voice, finally. 'Is Ireland over?'

'It's still there. It didn't much want me around. I don't take it personally. But I do take it personally that I'm standing out here on your doorstep when I'd much rather be inside, sitting down, with one of whatever you're drinking.' Jury smiled.

It was one of those smiles that didn't end with the mouth. It seemed to radiate everywhere, as if his whole person were pitching in to help that smile along.

'Oh! Sorry.' Melrose threw the door wide.

Jury shrugged out of his coat and looked for an available coat rack or surface. Melrose took it and tossed it over the staircase banister. 'Come on into the study. There's a fire.'

Jury settled into the chair Daniel Bletchley had occupied earlier. With a strong sense of déjà vu, Melrose handed him a drink. It was true; Dan Bletchley did have something in him that reminded Melrose of Richard Jury. No wonder he and Daniel had hit it off.

'This fellow who was murdered last night, Tom Letts, over at the nursing home in Bletchley.'

Melrose felt Jury hadn't dropped a beat since the last time they'd seen each other. It was as if they'd been discussing this case all along. 'But how do you know about him?'

'Because I've been three hours in Exeter talking to Brian Macalvie. Why was I in Exeter? Because I was on this side of the country. Why was I on this side of the country? Because the ferry from Cork goes into Wales. Why was I in Cork instead of Belfast? Because I had to go to Dublin at the last moment. Why was I in—'

'Look, I'll leave, if you think the conversation would go better without me.'

Jury laughed. 'Sorry. I was just saving you the trouble of asking a lot of inane questions.'

'Inane? Thanks. So Brian Macalvie filled you in.'

'At length. He seems to have taken this case pretty much to heart. But I don't know why that should surprise me. He usually does take cases to heart.'

'Remember Dartmoor? That pub named Help the Poor Struggler? He put his foot through the jukebox when someone played a song – what was that song?'

'Molly something.' And Jury started to sing: '*Oh, mahn dear, did'ja niver hear, o'pretty Molly da da da.*'

'Brannigan! That's it, that's it!' Then Melrose sang: '*She's gone away and* – and what?'

'*And left me, and . . .*'

Then they sang together or, rather, apart: '*And left me, and I'll niver be a mahn again!*'

They laughed, but then Jury said, 'Christ, why does love have to be so sad?' He rolled the cool glass across his forehead. 'I'm lightheaded; I haven't had any sleep in a couple of days.'

'You can sleep here, of course.'

'Thanks. That pub in the village didn't much tempt me.'

'The Drowned Man. Sergeant Wiggins is staying there.'

Jury smiled. 'When this case is closed, or even if it's not, may I have him back?'

'Don't blame *me*. It's Macalvie who insisted on getting him down from London.'

'He's always liked having Wiggins about. Funny.' Jury looked around the softly lit room. 'Nice room, this. Nice house.'

'I've got it for three months. Look, since you're here, give some thought to this business, will you? The only thing I have in common with Hamlet is that I've been thinking "too much on the event".'

'I don't believe it's thinking too much; that's just a symptom. What's causing it? I know what's causing it for Macalvie: the murder of those two children. For four years he's been a little obsessed. Really, it reminds me of the whole Molly Brannigan thing. Molly Singer, I mean.'

But Melrose remembered that it hadn't been Macalvie alone who'd been interested in Molly.

Jury had been looking over the silver-framed snapshots and now picked one up. 'These are the children? What a tragedy. And what a puzzle. If Macalvie hasn't solved it, who could? He can cut away everything extraneous to a situation. He's like a laser.' Jury drank the last of his whisky. 'I can't do that. I get too muddied up by stuff. Anyway, he's sent you a message.'

Melrose did not tell him that Macalvie could get muddied up and overinvolved himself.

Jury reached into the pocket of his shirt, under a heavy Aran sweater, and pulled out a folded paper. He spread this on the coffee table between them and smoothed it out. 'It's about Morris Bletchley and Tom Letts.' It was a diagram of the red drawing room. 'Does this look accurate to you?'

Melrose put on his glasses. 'Yes, absolutely.'

'What Macalvie says is that if he wanted a cleaner view of the target, he'd have picked windows two or three' – Jury pointed – 'and not window number one.' Jury tapped the representation of the window through which the bullet had been fired. 'There's a lot of thick shrubbery around windows two and three; besides that, the ground is lower on that side. It's possible for nearly anyone to *see* through one of those windows, but you'd have to be taller than we are to *shoot* through them.'

Melrose frowned. 'So the shooter picked that window.' Melrose indicated the same window Jury had. 'Window number one.'

'Right. But Macalvie's point is this: how would you know this unless you reconnoitred? You can't tell the ground's lower unless you actually stand there, and if you do look through the other windows on this side, either one of them—'

Melrose finished the sentence for him. 'You'd see who was in the wheelchair.' He stared at the diagram. 'Tom Letts really was the target.'

'Looks that way,' said Jury.

45

On a heavy Empire table between the two chairs sat a Murano ashtray of deep blue and green, colours that shifted with the shifting firelight. In the bowl were small polished stones that Jury had used to mark the tragic events that had taken place in Bletchley and Lamorna. At the moment there were four stones forming the beginnings of a circle: the deaths of the two Bletchley children, the death of Ramona Friel, the murders of Sada Colthorp and Tom Letts.

'Sada Colthorp.' Jury started to say something, then paused, searching his pocket for some item.

Melrose said, 'Ah, Sadie May, right. Both the ex-Mrs Rodney Colthorp and Viscountess Mead. Viscountess Mead, redoubtable star of blue movies. Funny old world. This Bolt fellow, producer of said films, turned up at the manor when she was still married to Colthorp. Dennis, the viscount's son, threw him out. Not until after he'd valued Bolt's Jaguar.'

'Macalvie told me about Simon Bolt.'

'In her younger days, Sada worked at the Woodbine, that's the local tearoom owned by Chris Wells and

Brenda Friel. They're partners. Sada Colthorp reappeared four years ago in Bletchley for a visit.'

Jury had found the item, a brown envelope, and sat tapping it against his thumb, thinking.

Melrose wished he'd stop thinking and let him see whatever it was.

'There it is again.' Jury leaned forward to look at the table, at the little semicircle of stones he'd made.

'There what is again? And what's in that envelope, the winning lottery ticket?'

'Four years ago. When, four years ago?'

'I'm not sure. Brenda Friel could tell you. She was the one who identified her. The people in Lamorna didn't recognize the police photo.'

'Perhaps her appearance had altered, having lived the life of a viscountess for all those years.' Jury put another little stone near the one representing the deaths of the children.

'Some of those years, you mean. She was Viscountess Mead for less than two. Rodney Colthorp was clearly embarrassed about having married her. I put it down to the usual midlife crisis.'

Jury had opened the packet and drawn a photo out – two photos, one being the familiar scene-of-crime picture of Sada Colthorp. He handed them to Melrose.

'I see what you mean.' One photo was of Sada, or Sadie back then, during her years in Lamorna and Bletchley. The young woman in this earlier photo had quite pale hair, as opposed to the hard yellow of the more recent photo, the crime scene photo of her dead on the public footpath. The eyes were quite different too, but that would be owing to the generous application of cosmetics: eyeliner, shadow, mascara. But the most telling difference was that the rather plump face of the earlier photo had changed to one gaunt and angular, though not unattractive. The changes seemed to have been caused by something other than time.

'They look different, don't they? If you know it's the same person, you can see the resemblance even with the change of hairstyle and colour, even with the meltdown from drugs. Clubs and Vice picked her up a couple of times in Shepherd Market for soliciting. Then again she was picked up in Soho for dealing drugs, charge later dropped.'

Melrose was shocked, not by Sada's habits but by Jury's knowing them. He'd been on this case for less than eight hours and he seemed to know more than Melrose himself. And now he was reading Melrose's mind.

'Macalvie only just got this report, which is why you haven't heard about it.'

Melrose decided to carp at police reporting. 'It took all of this time? It took over a week for the police to send this?'

Jury nodded. 'Sometimes it happens. Bureaucratic slowdown or maybe it was hard to get stuff on her. Who knows? Anyway, Sada had a big drug habit she couldn't support on her negligible salary as hostess in a club in Shepherd's Bush, so she had to supplement it, and prostitution and dealing were the most profitable means. Her habit meant big money. My guess is that was what she was here for. Just a guess, mind.'

'Blackmail?'

'That, or to sell something.'

'Same thing, isn't it?' Melrose got up and took their glasses to the dry sink. 'The only person I know of around here with what you call big money is Morris Bletchley.'

'What about Daniel Bletchley, his son? Or his daughter-in-law – who would have access to it, even if she didn't have a fortune of her own?'

Karen. Melrose thought about this. 'She was here in the area at the time of the shooting. She came to see me. Or see the house.'

'Does she come back to Bletchley often? It must be painful.'

'Often? Oh, no. This was the first time in—'

Jury smiled. 'Four years.'

'True.' Melrose took another look at the stone circle. There was something he was overlooking.

'Why Lamorna?'

'What?' asked Melrose absently.

'Why was she found in Lamorna?'

Melrose shrugged. 'You've got me.' He said this a trifle testily, since it probably *hadn't* got Jury.

'There's a pub there?'

'The Lamorna Wink is what it's called.'

'Come on.' Jury got up quickly.

'Damn it! People are always going somewhere and wanting me to go with 'em.' But he was not displeased. 'To Lamorna? At *this* hour?'

' "This hour" is only nine fifty. Come on.'

'Can't we solve the damned puzzle sitting here? Must we take *steps*?'

'Well, I don't have your little grey cells; all I can do is plod plod plod plod plod.' Jury reached down and pulled Melrose from the sofa.

'You sound like Lear. I wonder how it would have sat with the audience if Cordelia's death had him saying, "And she will come again, plod plod plod plod plod" instead of "Never never never never never?" '

Johnny brought the cab to a stop, saw several lights in the downstairs windows, and Melrose Plant's car. He ran up the steps and banged the brass knocker as hard as he could and waited. In another thirty seconds, he banged it again. And waited again. *If his car is here . . .*

Johnny found a pack of Trevor's cigarettes in the glove compartment and sat in the car and smoked, something he very rarely did. Smoking helped to calm him, made his head clearer. He could understand why it was such a hard habit to kick.

By a little after ten o'clock he'd stubbed out three cigarettes. He slid down in the front seat and tried to think, tried to work it out. But it was like hitting a brick wall.

The trouble was, he was afraid. He was afraid to try anything alone. Backup, that's what police called it. He needed backup. He thought about Charlie, but Charlie was in Penzance.

For a few more minutes he sat in the car before he gave up on Plant's coming home. He was probably somewhere with that policeman, Commander Macalvie.

One more cigarette and then he started the car, let out the clutch, backed up, and, venting some of his frustration and fear, jammed his foot on the accelerator and nearly ricocheted down the drive.

Why were the police always somewhere else when you needed them?

46

'You'll find them a close-mouthed crew,' said Melrose, crawling out of Jury's hired Honda. 'If you're thinking of questioning them, that is.'

There was a sea fret covering the path, encasing their lower legs in mist so that they appeared to be walking footless to the door of the Lamorna Wink.

Melrose continued, 'Macalvie says it's blood out of stones.' He sighed. 'I wish they had a takeaway window.'

It looked to Melrose, once they were inside, as if these were exactly the same people he and Macalvie had encountered. And why not? Where else was there to go? They pulled up to the bar and sat down between an old man in an oilskin and a heavy woman drinking pale beer. Sediment at the bottom of her glass suggested it was one of the local brews.

Perhaps it wasn't fat that had her bulging over into Melrose's allotted space; it might have been the layers of clothes she wore. Beneath a mustard-coloured sweater was a plaid woollen shirt, its arms rolled up to show a grimy biscuit-coloured flannel that might have been underclothing, but Melrose doubted it, for he saw something lumpy jut above the elbow, suggesting yet another garment beneath it.

Melrose was deciding on what conversational approach to take – she hadn't turned to give him so much as a glance – and found he was listening to the old man on Jury's left, apparently in fulsome answer to some question of Jury's, mapping out the watery course through Mounts Bay into the Atlantic that he apparently had once travelled as a fisherman.

Or a smuggler, thought Melrose, though it was more likely that role would have fallen to his grandfather. Now, upon seeing the woman's glass was empty, he asked the barmaid to refill it and to bring him an Old Peculier. This done, he turned to his drinking companion, asking, 'Are you a resident of Lamorna or just visiting?' This he decided was not the most brilliant conversational gambit.

The woman, whom the barkeeper had called something that sounded like 'pig trot', obviously agreed with him as to the appropriateness of his question. 'Me? No. I just got off one of them Princess cruise ships, me. Docked out there, it is.' She had turned to him a face that obviously did not know on which side its bread was buttered.

Melrose pushed forward. 'I'm Melrose Plant. Glad to meet you.' He thrust out his hand, but she ignored it.

'Peg Trott, that's me in a nutshell.'

'Have you lived here long?' Another brilliant question.

'Aye.' She pulled a vile-looking cigarette from a pack on the bar. It was a brand Melrose hadn't seen before and enough to induce anyone to quit smoking.

Melrose hastened to light it. 'Lamorna's quite charming.'

Peg Trott shrugged and inspected the coal end to see if he knew how to do it. Satisfied, she put the cigarette back in her mouth.

'You must be pretty excited about what happened here last week. The shooting, I mean.'

'Aye.'

Apparently, the aforementioned nutshell was to be taken literally. There was no more here for him than her name. Except her glass, empty once more. She picked it up and looked at it as if appraising the glassblower's skill.

Melrose gestured once more to the woman behind the bar, who then came to fill the glass. Having no luck himself on the conversational front, Melrose turned to his right, where the old man in the oilskin was still going on in answer to Jury's single question. And Jury wasn't even buying beers. Someone out there yelled, 'Shut it, Jimmy!' the diktat lost in the Greek chorus of conversational waves.

While Melrose was girding up for another go at Peg Trott, he felt a hand on his shoulder, glanced in the mirror, and saw an artist named Mark Weist, one of several that lived here, looking less handsome than Weist was sure he was.

'Getting any further along with your investigation?' He laughed at this, seeming to think the question was droll.

'I'm not, but he is.' Melrose nodded towards Jury, who turned and was introduced to the painter.

'New Scotland Yard!' crowed Weist. 'Bringing out the big guns, are we?'

Jury smiled patiently. 'You've already met the big gun. Commander Macalvie.'

'Ah, yes. Smart chap.' It was all so unbearably condescending. 'As I told him – Commander Macalvie – we didn't know the woman.'

Melrose marvelled at Weist's range of the banal. He also seemed adept at making himself spokesman for Lamorna.

'Some-a' us did.' It was Peg Trott speaking. 'Nasty bairn, nasty woman, ah don't wonder.'

'How so?' asked Jury.

'Bairn used to show herself in public.'

Thinking of the Cripps children, Melrose thought, don't they all?

'Ya know what ah mean? You, Tim.' She was leaning across Melrose to speak to the wiry little man beside Jury.

'Oversexed, she were,' said Tim.

'Whatever,' said Peg. 'Found out t'ings, people's private business, then used it against them.'

'Blackmail, you mean?' said Jury.

'Call it what ya will. One poor soul name of McPhee – dead now, McPhee – she found out he was up at Dartmoor for fifteen years, put there fer takin' a breadknife t' his wife. Sadie tells it all over. So ah dunno did she try to blackmail him or not. He must not of paid; he hung himself.' She fell silent, holding up her empty glass yet again.

If a few drinks were all it took to get her going,

Melrose was willing to buy her the pub. The barmaid was near them, listening. Indeed, a little crowd must have picked up on the ghoulish story and half a dozen had come to join them. The people within earshot were listening hard. A youngish couple, very London-looking, standing talking further along the bar, became interested in this small drinking circle and came to join them. The woman had a spun-glass beauty, complexion fine to the point of transparency, eyes pewter-grey and clear as seawater, hair a limpid sort of white gold. She was wearing white silk. The man, equally good-looking, was dressed in tweeds and a black silk turtleneck sweater.

It was hard to tell who lived in Lamorna and who didn't. Melrose imagined it attracted people of high sophistication, the sort Mark Weist thought he was numbered among.

Peg Trott picked up her narrative. 'When Sadie were only ten she were makin' indecent advances to men, puttin' her hand in their pants pockets, feelin' 'em up – you know what's what, you bein' a copper. She'd go creepin' up to windows after dark an' watch. Out at all hours, Sadie was. Turrible. Her mum was never no better'n she should be. Mum left, no one knew where to, and Sadie stayed on with her da. Raised a few eyebrows, know what I mean?'

Although she was addressing her remarks to the ingratiating Jury (even though it was the uningratiating Plant who was paying for her drinks), the clutch of people gathered round all nodded sagely.

Peg drank off her urine-coloured beer and wiped her mouth with the back of her hand. 'Then she gets t'be fourteen, fifteen, and t'trouble *really* starts.'

Weist, who felt he was being crowded out by recent comers, said, 'The Lolita of Lamorna!' When Peg ignored this explication of her story, he said, '*Lolita*, Nabokov's *Lolita*.'

She glared at him. 'I know who bleeding Lolita is.' She waited for Melrose to light her fresh cigarette and ploughed on. 'There come a man t'Lamorna, a London man name of Simon Bolt. Well, if our Sadie was bad news, this Bolt fella, he was worse. Ain't surprising them two found each other real quick. He said he was a "fil-um producer".' Here she drew squiggles in the air to show her suspicion of Bolt.

The woman in white silk raised her satiny eyebrows and asked, 'Pornography?'

Abruptly, Peg Trott nodded. 'An' worse.' She seemed a trifle annoyed that some good-looking city woman was getting a march on her story. 'There's some said devil chased 'em across Bodmin Moor.'

Some always do say the devil in these parts, thought Melrose.

'That's hardly surprising in good old haunted Cornwall,' said Weist, not one to get out while the getting's good. He tamped tobacco down in his briar pipe.

'Tim here,' Tim nodded eagerly, though he didn't know how he would feature in this tale, 'Tim said he seen the piskies over in the bluebell woods, and Lydi Ruche – over there,' she pointed to a table where sat three men and one rather hard-looking dark-haired woman, 'says she be drivin' by the Merry Maidens an' seen this spectre – this spectre.' Peg enunciated clearly here, seeming to like the sound of the word.

'The Merry Maidens, that's the stone circle,' said Weist, offering an explanation no one had asked for.

Muscling Weist out with her voice, which she raised a decibel or two, Peg Trott went on, 'Anyway, that ain't my point. This Bolt fella made fil-ums, like I said. He was livin' in the old Leary house that sits atop that cliff out there, and we heard from a woman used to char for him there was a room he kept just for runnin' these fil-ums. Oh, she never fooled with 'em; she was takin' her chances just to go in the room. But she said there was a projector and a stack of these tapes beside it.

'Simon Bolt and Sadie May – those two just had t'git together. Simon liked 'em young, is what people said, the younger the better. Sadie'd say t'me, "I'm goin' t'be in the pictures, me. I'm goin' to be a star." '

'He was shooting pornographic films, is that it?'

Peg Trott nodded. 'Worse'n that. T'was bairns. T'was Sadie helped 'em find the poor tikes.' Peg shook her head. 'Why'd anyone want t'see bairns die?'

Melrose frowned. 'Die?'

'Well, that's what I heard.'

In the awful silence that befell them, they all stared at Peg Trott.

'Snuff films,' said the man in the black turtleneck.

47

The idea was so repugnant that several of them turned away just on hearing it. Yet the subject was too seductive to make them leave the little circle at the bar, and they turned back again.

'How is it that the Devon and Cornwall police didn't know this?' asked Jury.

Peg shrugged. 'Prob'ly did and couldna catch him at it, like.' She accepted a light from Melrose. 'He was in London lots when he warn't livin' up atop 'ere.'

Jury frowned. 'Atop where, Peg?'

With her glass, she pointed off in some northerly direction and upwards towards the moon. 'There's a road I kin show ya.'

'We'd appreciate it.' Jury tossed money on the bar and rose.

They did as Peg Trott directed – parked the car on the paved area and walked the rest of the way, about an eighth of a mile, on the public footpath.

The house had a beautiful prospect, finer than the view from Seabourne. It was a stark building unrelieved by any sort of architectural embellishment that might have softened its facade. There was at least none that Plant and Jury could see by the light of their torches. Jury kept a spare in the car, which he had given to Melrose.

He also kept a small box of lock-picking equipment. 'Remind me to get a warrant next time I'm in Exeter.' The lock was old and easy.

'I could've done it with my finger,' Jury said, as he pushed the door open.

The inside was bleaker than the outside. In the room facing seaward, there was a sofa and two overstuffed and ugly chairs. There was a small fireplace with a tiled surround and ugly Art Deco wall sconces.

They roamed from room to room, upstairs and down, then further down into a basement that seemed to be doing service as a wine cellar.

'Good stuff,' said Melrose, blowing dust from a bottle of Meursault, a Premier Cru (straight from the abbé, doubtless. Or was he mixing it up with Lindisfarne?). 'God, what a waste. Isn't anyone going to collect this wine?'

Jury was adding a skin of light to the walls as he shone his torch carefully round. But he saw nothing that might have served as a hiding place for the videos he was sure must be here and said so.

'Why do you think they'd be here instead of in London? According to Peg Trott he spent most of his time in London.'

'I don't think "instead"; rather, I think "in addition to"; he would have at least a small collection here.'

Melrose was studying a simple appellation of Puligny when Jury started up the cellar stairs and asked, 'You going to have a wine tasting or are you coming along?'

Regretfully, Melrose returned the bottle to its shelf.

Upstairs, Jury made another torch circuit of the room. Melrose said, 'We've already done that. What do you expect to find?' He switched off his torch and sat down on one of the chairs and lit a cigarette.

'I don't know. I'm working on the assumption that this house might have been the meeting place chosen.'

'Meeting place?'

'She obviously had a meeting arranged; I doubt she just ran into her killer on the public footpath.'

'They could have arranged to meet at the point where her body was found.'

'Yes, they could have. It's just that it's difficult to know a point in advance, unless there's a very clear marker. Sada Colthorp might have chosen to meet here because she was familiar with the house and because the house was out of the way; no one would see them.' Jury switched the torch off and sat down too, on a sofa across from the chair.

It was the darkest dark Melrose had ever experienced. He could barely distinguish Jury's outline.

'I imagine they left the house to walk along the public footpath. Whose idea was that? The killer's, most likely. He – or she – wouldn't have wanted the body found too close to the house, so he put some distance between the house and the spot where he killed her.'

'Why?'

'Why what?'

'Why not have the body found in the house?'

'Because it would raise the possibility of a connection between Bolt and the Bletchley children's deaths.'

'You think that's what happened?'

'I do. Lured by God only knows what reward or reason, they stumbled down those stone steps while Simon Bolt recorded it on film. He watched them drown.'

'How could a man do that?'

'Because there's a market for it. A big one.'

Melrose switched his torch on and off, on and off. 'One thing I fail to understand is why a man would trust a young girl with knowing what he was up to, the way he did with young Sadie.'

'Ever read *Lolita*?'

'Yes, both Peg Trott and I are familiar with Lolita.'

'It's not a question of trust, anyway. People in Bolt's line of work probably don't trust anybody.' Jury flicked his own flashlight on, then off, and asked, 'Did you ever take food and stuff up to a tree house at night and a torch to read by?'

Melrose's cigarette glowed in the pitch blackness. 'No, I can't remember ever having a tree house. Did you?'

'No, but I imagine some children must have. You hear about that sort of childhood. Idyllic.' He swept the torch in Melrose's direction.

Melrose ducked, but not soon enough. 'I suppose no one ever did. An idyllic childhood is probably illusion.' He aimed his torchlight at the sofa and Jury moved quickly out of its way.

'Maybe,' said Melrose. Then, 'It's hard being an only

child. You were one. It's as if there's something missing, like a hole in the world that someone fell through. Of course, my childhood wasn't as obviously bad as yours was. A person can empathize with yours, but probably not with mine.'

'You mean yours was only superficially better? Yet you had your mother, your father.'

Melrose was quiet, flicking the torch on and off, aimed at the floor. 'My mother, yes; my father . . .' He changed the subject. 'You know, there's something I've always wondered about.' Lights out, cigarette snuffed, they were plunged into darkness again. 'You and Vivian.'

There was an engulfing stillness. Neither of them moved. Until Melrose flashed the light on Jury.

'Cheat! You knew that question would distract me!'

'Oh, come on, sport.' Melrose laughed. 'So, there's something in it, eh? You and Vivian?'

'That Christmas dinner years ago. Remember?'

'Yes.' Melrose wanted another cigarette, but it would give his position away.

'I walked Vivian home and we had a drink and a talk. You see, what I couldn't understand was this business of her marrying Simon Matchett. He wasn't at all her type. It was pretty clear that she wasn't in love with Matchett from the passionless way she talked about him. You know Vivian. Though at times she can be very straightforward, when it comes to her feelings she's – well, indirect. So in the course of our talking about various people, I inferred that Vivian loved *somebody*, but who was the somebody?' Jury flashed his torch and caught Melrose full in the face.

'Hey! Not in the middle of something *important*.'

'That's what you just did to me, isn't it?'

They sat in darkness again.

'You want a cigarette?' asked Melrose.

'No. You know I haven't smoked for over a year.'

'Okay, then we've got to have a break while I light one. Because obviously you'd see the match flare.'

'I can also see the coal end as you smoke it, so what's the big deal? I could get you anytime you inhale.' Jury leaned his head against the back of the sofa. 'Simon Bolt,' he said, exploring the name.

'Yes. Simon Bolt was taking a hell of a chance,' Melrose said, 'appearing at Seabourne, even if it was at night. He could so easily have been seen.'

'If the Bletchleys had been there, but they were out. The only possible witness would be the ageing housekeeper. Didn't you say her room was on the other side of the house?'

'How would Bolt have known that?' asked Melrose.

'From the person who put Simon Bolt onto the children in the first place.'

'You mean Sada Colthorp.'

'No. Sada was probably the middleman, is my guess. Whoever wanted these children killed and thought of this way of doing it knows the habits of people in Bletchley. Possibly Bolt and Colthorp were the people in the woods. At any rate, the children saw somebody.'

'Correction: their mother *said* they saw somebody.'

Jury said, 'You think her story was fabricated.'

'I think Henry James wrote it.'

There was a long silence.

'You sure you don't want a cigarette?'

'What? Jesus, some friend you are, encouraging me to go back to that foul habit.'

'Oh, don't sound so much like a missionary selling Christianity to the natives. I just thought if we both had one we'd be at the same disadvantage.'

'Ye gods! I'm supposed to smoke just so you can shine that bloody light in my face?'

'Go on with what you were saying about Vivian, about her being – good lord!' Melrose dropped his torch but quickly recovered it. 'Vivian! I forgot to tell you. Vivian claims she's going to marry Giopinno in a few weeks.'

'You're lying.'

'No, I'm not.'

'You're just trying to catch me off guard.'

'Oh, don't be ridiculous. I've completely forgotten about the torch.'

Jury moved on the sofa, sitting forward. 'Are you telling me she's really going to marry this creep?'

Melrose shook his head. 'Who knows? With that weird relationship, anything could happen. Maybe Viv's going to ditch him.'

'Ditch him? How can you ditch anyone after all these years? Kill him, maybe, but ditch him, no.'

'Well, anyway.' Melrose's torch went on suddenly.

Jury switched his own on. 'Oh, for God's sake, you can't put the torch somewhere else on the sofa. How childish!'

Melrose sniggered.

'*What the bloody hell is going on?*'

As if choreographed, both torches swung towards the

living room door and caught Brian Macalvie in twin circles of light.

'This is how you carry out an assignment?'

'You didn't give me one,' said Jury.

'How'd you know we were here?'

'I was in the Wink at closing time. A large woman in there told me you'd come up here. She didn't want to tell me how to find you.'

'So you broke her jaw.'

'Obviously, I got the information, but you don't need to know my methods. And I sure as hell don't want to know yours. Get that damned light out of my face. Come on, let's get our cars.'

The night deepened around them as they stood between Macalvie's Ford and Jury's Honda, dark green, dark blue, both cars looking black in the unlit clearing.

They were talking about Simon Bolt.

'Simon Bolt? We tried to nail him for possessing and distributing pornography. When I say we I mean the Vice Squad. I wasn't on the case myself. He took photos, films too, I heard. But *snuff* flicks of kids? Christ, no, I heard nothing of that; they must not have found anything like that or I'd've heard.' Macalvie turned in a half circle, mouthing epithets.

It did not sound at all like a wounded ego; the self-abrading tone sounded more like dereliction of duty.

'You weren't on that case years ago. How could you possibly have connected it with this one?'

'You got it out of a witness, Jury. I should have too.'

'Macalvie, it was luck. I happened to ask a question that provoked Peg Trott to give up the information.'

Melrose said, 'Let's go back to Seabourne. We can at least have a fire and a drink. I can even do us an early breakfast.'

Climbing behind the Honda's wheel, Jury said, 'Just not soft-boiled eggs and soldiers. I refuse to eat toast cut into soldiers.'

Melrose eased into the passenger seat. 'It was the bright spot in a ruined childhood, soldiers.'

'How heartrending.' Jury gunned the engine and they sped away, as much as one could speed down such a narrow and rutted road, eating Macalvie's dust.

48

Johnny parked the cab in front of his house and wondered if he was letting his imagination, overworked in the best of circumstances, run away with him. There might be another explanation.

Might be, but he doubted it, because what he believed had happened explained too much for him to be wrong. But it didn't explain everything. It didn't explain *why*.

He got out of the car, didn't bother locking it – which was part of the point, wasn't it? Who bothered locking up cars and houses around here – and walked the short distance to the Woodbine. Brenda was always up, usually baking till all hours, which had been a real comfort to him these days, in case he couldn't sleep and wanted to talk.

The bell made its discordant little clatter when he opened the door to the tearoom, a room that always gave the impression of warmth, even in the dead of night with the heat turned down.

From the kitchen came the sounds and smells of baking. The rattle and click of pans, the swish of the big beater, the whir of the blender – it always sounded as if

Brenda had an army of undercooks back there. He smelled ginger.

He could understand why customers came here, morning and afternoon, to be lulled into a sense of well-being, an illusion of ease, even if that was far away. He could see by moonlight or memory the heather design on the polished cotton curtains, the faded roses on the chair cushions, the burned wood and the bay windows' mullioned panes through which the moonlight spilled silver. Everything in the place – the faded roses, the smell of ginger – blended like spices and milk and honey into a satiny dough of contentment. It was all over-whelmingly sensuous.

Like sex, Johnny thought.

He stood in the open door to the kitchen.

Brenda was pulling a baking tray full of gingerbread men from the oven and when she stood and turned, she smiled. 'Sweetheart! Couldn't you sleep?'

'No. Where is she, Brenda?'

49

Wiggins's bleary-eyed greeting at the door of his room
in the Drowned Man was only marginally more welcoming than Mr Pfinn's had been. At least Wiggins was
aware that a police investigation knew neither time nor
tide. Mr Pfinn, on the other hand, didn't care if the
three of them were pod people come to borrow his
body. He needed his sleep, he said.

But Wiggins's mood improved immensely when he
saw Richard Jury was one of the three. He was all ready
to have a long talk about Jury's travels while standing at
the door in his pyjamas.

'Ireland, nil; Scotland Yard, one,' said Macalvie,
cutting into this reunion. 'Get dressed.'

They were now in Seabourne. Melrose and Wiggins
repaired to the kitchen to prepare some sort of meal;
Jury and Macalvie stayed in the library.

'What are these stones? Avebury? Stonehenge? The
Merry Maidens?' Macalvie inspected Jury's little stone
circle, or semicircle.

'Very funny. I was trying to get the sequence of what's
happened to whom in the last four years. In most cases,

death has happened. I was trying to get straight in my mind the events of four years ago. Then the events of today – that is, recently.' Jury picked up another stone. 'We can now add Simon Bolt to the four-year-old section of the circle, setting him beside Sada Calthorp, who came back four years ago and who'd kept in touch with Bolt – well, she must have done, since she was in his films.'

Macalvie said, 'And, according to Rodney Colthorp, Bolt visited the manor. Yes, they kept in touch.'

Jury set the two stones side by side.

'So what have you got here?'

'Beginning with the Bletchley children, with Simon Bolt and most likely Sada Colthorp involved in that, then the death of Brenda Friel's girl, Ramona; that's the four-year-old part. More recently, the disappearance of Chris Wells, the death of Sada Colthorp, and the death of Tom Letts.'

Macalvie slid a stick of chewing gum into his mouth and was silent, looking at the stone diagram. He hadn't sat down, and he hadn't taken off his coat.

'Why don't you take your coat off?' Jury didn't expect him to; he just couldn't resist mentioning the coat.

Instead of taking it off, Macalvie shoved the sides back and put his hands in his trouser pockets. He chewed the gum, thinking. 'Bastard was making snuff films.'

'That tape's somewhere in or around that house.'

Macalvie was still gazing at the stone circle. 'It's with whoever murdered Sada Colthorp. I found part of it.'

Jury gave him an inquiring look. 'Where?'

'Just a fragment of the black casing. It was lying near

her body. At least, I expect it's a safe assumption. The piece was definitely part of a videotape casing. Of course, that's not the only copy. Four years ago, whoever got Bolt to do this, that person would have the original. Then of course Bolt would have kept a copy, at the same time claiming there wasn't one. I'd say there are at least three copies. We went over his house with tweezers. Sada Colthorp had another copy. Or the same one Bolt had stashed; maybe she knew where it was. How else was she going to blackmail the person who wanted those children dead if she couldn't produce a copy?'

'The video wouldn't prove who this person was.'

'No,' said Macalvie. 'But it would certainly show how it was done.' Macalvie walked over to the fireplace and leaned his forearm across its green marble mantel. 'Bad enough the children died, but *that way?*'

Macalvie was always intense, thought Jury, but he didn't think he'd ever seen him this emotionally involved. Not since the serial killings of children on Dartmoor and in Lyme Regis. Jury waited for him to go on.

He did. 'I'd say Colthorp knew the motive, but even if she didn't, whoever wanted that video made would not want a fresh investigation into the Bletchley business. Anyway, the video is the best theory we have; it's a working hypothesis that explains a hell of a lot.'

Melrose and Wiggins came through the door, bearing coffee, fresh bread, and cheese and cold ham. 'Couldn't find any eggs, so I didn't make toast,' said Melrose, setting down the tray. Wiggins put down the coffeepot.

Jury set about making a sandwich. 'Wouldn't have any pickled onions around, would you?'

'No.'

Wiggins was turning over the coat he'd draped across the back of a chair and drawing something from an inside pocket that looked much like a soft leather jewellery case, the sort that folds and ties. He untied it, revealing several zippered compartments. From one of these he took a dung-coloured pill and from another a couple of large white tablets. The tablets he dropped into a glass of water and watched it fizz with almost religious application.

So did the other three, chewing and watching the fizz until a fine scum of white powder showed on top.

Apparently waiting to catch it at the height of the fizz, Wiggins drank it down, leaving a little in the bottom to swallow with the brown pill. Jury wondered about the pill; it seemed new to the Wiggins pharmacopoeia. But he refused to ask what it was. He did not want to know about any new ailment or allergy.

'Chris Wells,' said Macalvie, holding his mug of coffee between both hands to warm them. 'Look in your notes and tell me what you've got about Chris Wells,' he said to Wiggins.

Wiggins thumbed through the notebook; it looked as if he'd written reams of notes (which was why Macalvie had wanted to stop at the Drowned Man and drag him out of bed). He mouthed a few words to himself, then read: 'According to young Johnny, his Aunt Chris took over the care of him when he was seven. He thinks his mother was going to the States, but he doesn't know. The maiden name was Wells, the father's name Esterhazey, but Johnny changed his to Wells, same name as his aunt. The mother just took off and that's the last he heard of her.'

Macalvie uttered a low imprecation, and Wiggins looked up. 'Sir?'

'Nothing. Go on.'

'Chris is Johnny's only family, except for the uncle who lives in Penzance, Charlie Esterhazey. Unmarried, keeps a magic shop. You know,' Wiggins said to Jury, 'sort of place that sells trick decks of cards and magic metal rings that look like they couldn't fit together but do.' Wiggins stopped reading, seemed to be pondering.

'Don't worry, Wiggins. We're coppers. We'll make him tell us.'

Wiggins shot Jury a grazing look and went on. 'Getting down to the night in question, when young Johnny got in touch with the police. Chris Wells disappeared sometime between eleven a.m., which is when she left the Woodbine and is the last time anyone saw her in Bletchley, and nine p.m., when John Wells actively started looking for her.'

'It could have been later,' said Jury. 'I mean, she could have been in Bletchley, only Johnny didn't see her.'

'Just wait a minute,' said Wiggins. 'The biscuits she was baking could have been done some time earlier. But meringues – well, that's a different story. They were still in the oven. That's what you do with them, you know. You leave them in to cool. Very slow cooling period. The oven was still slightly warm. Since it takes an hour to bake them at four hundred degrees, that would mean they went into the oven about seven thirty. There are two different kinds of meringues served in the Woodbine, quite tasty too.'

'Thank you, Wiggins,' said Jury. 'We'd like the recipes when we finish this case. If we do.'

Macalvie said, 'Sada Colthorp, Wiggins.'

Wiggins read: 'Murdered the night of September twelfth, pathologist says between seven p.m. and eleven p.m.'

'In other words, murdered during the time Chris Wells did her vanishing act,' said Melrose.

Macalvie had moved away from the fireplace and sat down on a narrow, uncomfortable-looking side chair. 'The connection between Chris Wells and Sada Colthorp?'

Wiggins moved forward a few pages. 'The person who knew about that was Brenda Friel. She said Sada was trying to get her hands on young Johnny, who'd have been no more than thirteen at the time. Apparently, Sada and Chris really had it out.'

Melrose said, 'Johnny Wells looks older than he is, probably did when he was thirteen, too.'

Macalvie asked, 'How did Brenda know this?'

'Chris Wells told her,' said Wiggins.

'Still, trying to seduce a child is hardly a motive for murder, is it?' said Jury.

'People don't often behave as you'd expect them to, sir,' said Wiggins sententiously. Looking at his notes, he added, 'And Brenda Friel told me Chris Wells threatened Sada Colthorp, said if she ever showed her face in the village again, she'd wish she hadn't.'

'Chris Wells,' said Jury, 'appears to be the chief

suspect, doesn't she, by virtue of her sudden disappearance just at the time the Colthorp woman was murdered?'

'Hold on a minute, Richard. She doesn't sound at all like a person who runs away. She's too responsible.' Melrose cited her work at the Hall, her care for her nephew. 'Not only that, you'd surely have to be looking for two killers, not just one. I see no reason on earth you could say she was the one who planned the Bletchley children's deaths or murdered Tom Letts.'

'But you don't know her,' said Jury. 'You've never met her.'

'No, you're right. I've never met her.'

Macalvie broke the silence. 'There's another way to look at this woman's suddenly taking off.' He turned from the window. 'Maybe it was made to look that way. Maybe it was staged.'

Wiggins raised his head from the little stone circle and gave Macalvie a questioning look.

'To make it look like Chris Wells murdered Sada Colthorp.'

'Then where . . .' Melrose began. He didn't finish the question. He thought it was almost too much to bear. And made worse because he hadn't been given it to bear: the children, Tom Letts, the sadness of Daniel Bletchley and his father, and Chris Wells. He was a stranger to it all; he had no business feeling desolate; the actors in this tragedy, they were none of his business. And it wasn't his tragedy. 'You think she's dead, don't you?'

Wiggins had put his small notebook back in his pocket

and was bending over Jury's improvised calendar of events, his small circle of stones. 'Sir, go over this again, for me.'

Jury rose and walked over to stand beside him, pointing clockwise round the stones. 'These first two here: the Bletchley children died on the rocks; next, we've got Sada Colthorp and Simon Bolt, most probably arranging the death of the children. But to keep the sequence right, Bolt and Colthorp should be up here.' Jury moved the two stones to first place. 'Next, Brenda Friel's daughter, Ramona, dies. Moving on four years, Sada Colthorp is murdered; Chris Wells disappears; Tom Letts is murdered.' He looked at Wiggins, who had retrieved his notebook from an inside pocket. 'Okay?' Jury turned away.

Wiggins shook his head. 'No, that's not right.'

Jury turned back.

Wiggins was reading from his notes and putting another stone down.

'What's that for?'

'You're forgetting the baby, the unborn baby.' He had put the second stone beside Ramona's. 'It's actually *two* people who died here. And you've got the order wrong.' Wiggins moved the Friel stones up to first place. 'The Bletchley children died *after* these two, not before.'

Both Macalvie and Melrose had joined Jury at the table, and all three were looking at Wiggins's new arrangement of the stones.

Macalvie turned to stare through the window, looking out through the black glass as if he should be able to see through the dark. 'Jesus,' he said, and turned back again.

'Jesus, how could I have missed—'

'How could *we* have missed it, Macalvie?'

Wiggins hadn't, and he was wreathed in smiles. 'It's easy to overlook, sir. They all died in the same year, but Ramona Friel and her baby, they died early, in January. The Bletchley children's deaths, that came months later, round about now, in September.'

Macalvie appeared to be looking around the room for something to throw. He picked up the blue Murano ashtray holding the other stones and stared down at them. Then, almost delicately, he returned the bowl to the table.

'Am I just slow here?' said Melrose, irritated that he hadn't thought of whatever they'd thought of.

50

'Where is who, sweetheart? I don't know what you're talking about.' Brenda wiped her forearm across her temple, shoving back strands of hair.

'Chris *didn't* leave suddenly. And I was right. She would never have left that way.'

Brenda looked up from the baking trays, annoyed with this nonsense. She stubbed out the cigarette she'd smoked down to the butt end. 'Of course she did. What are you saying?'

He shook his head. 'You went to the house and made it look not only as if she'd gone but as if she'd *run*. A few hours ago I ate a couple of those meringues she supposedly left in the middle of baking. They weren't hers; they were yours.' He pulled over the stool at the end of the pastry table. 'Meringues, yours and hers. That's always been a kind of good-natured competition. It doesn't look good-natured now, though.'

Brenda stood looking at him as he sat down on the high stool. She didn't answer.

'I asked myself: why would Brenda want to make it look as if Chris had run out?'

'This is so silly, darling.' Brenda sighed. 'And what did you answer yourself?'

'I couldn't. Not until I remembered the police were asking about Sada Colthorp. According to you, she and Chris had some kind of falling out four years ago. And you made it look worse by bringing it up with that detective and then refusing to talk about it. So what the police are supposed to think is that Chris kills her in a rage. Chris goes to Lamorna and shoots her. With this?' Johnny had pulled Charlie's small gun from his pocket. It lay cold on his palm.

Brenda looked at the gun for a long moment, then up at Johnny for yet a longer one. Then she pulled open the knife drawer behind her. 'No.' The gun came out of the drawer as if she was the one used to pulling silk scarves from sleeves and doves out of the air. 'With this.'

The gun was twice as big, twice as black, twice as evil looking as the one Johnny held. He had never fired a gun in his life; he had never even *handled* a gun until tonight. But he was as deft with his fingers as a sharpshooter was, and he had the gun from the palm of his hand and between his thumb and forefinger in less than the blink of an eye.

'If you shoot that,' she said, 'you'd probably hit me, but you would miss any vital spot. You're not used to guns.'

'But you are.'

'If I fire this, Johnny, it would kill you.'

Looking at the barrel of that gun seemed to wake him out of a trance, as if up to that point this had all been a fantasy. His hand felt numb; he laid the small gun on the butcher's block.

'She's dead, isn't she?' That she must be was a fact that outweighed even the danger of the gun pointed at him.

'Chris?' Brenda snorted. 'Of course not. She *did* go away. To Newcastle.'

The relief of what he felt as an almost comic turn in all of this made him laugh. 'Newcastle? She doesn't know anybody in Newcastle.'

'Really, sweetheart, you can be so arrogant. You think Chris had no life apart from you? Children, children.' It was an admonishment, her tone merely exasperated, as if they might have been chatting about the rearing of them. 'They think they know everything about their parents. And their aunts.' Her smile was almost indulgent. 'She has an old friend up there who needed someone right away to take care of her because her home help died suddenly. It was for two weeks, until this woman could go into one of those homes they advertise for "retired gentlefolk". That always amuses me, that phrase; doesn't it you? But you're right. I did want to make it look as if Chris had run off and there wasn't much time to improvise because Sadie May – the *Viscountess*, I should say – was in Lamorna.'

Johnny looked down at his empty hands. It didn't come clearer; it just got deeper. Like a ladder to the sea you go down and down. Like the stone stairs in the rocks where the little Bletchley kids had wound up. Then he raised his head. 'You killed Sada Colthorp.'

Brenda said nothing.

'Why?'

She still said nothing.

'And if Chris left right then, it would look like she did it. That was the idea, wasn't it? But if you're telling the truth, she'll be back. What then?'

'Newcastle police will pick her up. When I finally tell them where she is. She could call at any time.' With her free hand, Brenda reached for the pack of cigarettes, found it empty, balled it up, and swore softly.

Got to get out of here, thought Johnny. *Get out of this kitchen. Get back to where I'd have, if not a sporting chance, maybe a fighting one.* Just knowing that Chris was alive had cleared his mind utterly, even of fear. He could think now. 'If I worked it out about those meringues, I'm sure somebody else could too.'

'That was very clever of you, sweetheart. I knew you were smart, but not that smart. I honestly don't see how anyone else would, but' – she moved in a sideways walk, over to a coat rack, and unhooked her coat – 'I'll just get rid of what's left. Get up.' She struggled into the coat. 'Come on. And remember something. I *will* shoot you if you try to run. So walk beside me when we get outside.'

The sporting chance was now on offer. At least, in his own living room he might be able to find a way out of this. Johnny turned slowly, as if reluctantly, and waited while she switched off the lights. Then he moved towards the swinging door, wondering if he could slam it back in her face when she followed behind him, knowing he couldn't. She *would* shoot him. The total folly of so doing did not occur to her; how would she ever explain *that* to the police? It hadn't occurred to her because her thoughts were pointed like an arrow to one thing and one thing only, and he still didn't know what it was. He had no doubt of that at all. He walked through the tearoom where the moonlight still flooded the window embrasure as if nothing had happened. It was almost consoling to think that rooms you walk through still hold fast to their identity.

'If you did anything to Chris, I'll kill you, Brenda. I will. She's all I have.' He opened the door. The bell sounded its tiny discordant chorus of welcome.

'Like Ramona,' said Brenda, 'was all *I* had.'

51

It was after midnight by now, and Macalvie decided there wasn't a hell of a lot they could do until they had some hard evidence. 'What,' asked Macalvie, 'did she have against the Bletchleys?' No matter what their theories, they had nothing to link her to the murder of Sada Colthorp or to Simon Bolt's film.

As Macalvie and Wiggins were leaving, Melrose beat a little tattoo on Wiggins's shoulder, saying, 'Well done, Sergeant. Well done. We none of us saw it except for you.'

Wiggins tried to be casual about it; he held up his notebook and said, 'It's just good note-taking, Mr Plant. The Bletchley kids' deaths – well, that was so dramatic it's easy enough to forget poor Ramona Friel.' He added generously, thereby depreciating his own role in any solution, 'And we don't really know, do we? We've still got Tom Letts's murder to deal with. Assuming, of course, that Mr Macalvie is right and it's not Morris Bletchley we should be thinking about. That's just theory too.'

Jury stood there, listening to Wiggins. He smiled. It

was probably the most the sergeant had ever said about a case without a meditation on his or someone's illness. It was certainly the first time Wiggins had ever called into question a theory of Macalvie's.

They said good night.

Back in the library with whisky in hand, Melrose said, 'Noah and Esmé, poor benighted children. You wouldn't think a mother, *any* mother, could be part of such an arrangement.'

Jury raised his glass and watched the dying fire through half an inch of whisky that turned the hearth into a liquid amber sea. 'Daniel Bletchley. What if it wasn't Chris Wells but Ramona Friel he was having an affair with?'

'It was Chris Wells. Anyway, the night his children died – that couldn't have been Ramona Friel. The poor girl was dead.'

Jury lowered his glass. 'What I meant was earlier. If he'd had an affair with Ramona Friel and the child was his and she died of complications in childbirth, I would imagine a mother would lust for revenge.'

Melrose frowned. 'What complications?'

Jury looked at him.

'Leukemia isn't a complication of childbirth. I have no idea how pregnancy could affect such a disease.'

'It wouldn't, as far as I know. But it might have made no difference to her mother. She died, and so did the baby. Brenda Friel would make that add up to murder,' said Jury.

'Then why the hell not grab a gun and kill Dan Bletchley if she thought he was the father? No, you're wrong. Bletchley isn't, I think, a profligate man. It would take a most unusual woman – woman, not a twenty-odd-year-old child – to move Daniel Bletchley.'

'Perhaps. You've met him, I haven't. I feel sorry for that boy, Johnny. How old is he? Sixteen? Seventeen?'

'Seventeen. He's a magician. Amateur, but pretty good, I think.'

'Really?'

Plant nodded. 'You know what he wants to do? Go to Las Vegas. That's what he wants. I suppose for somebody like that, Las Vegas is the Promised Land. He wants to go to the Mirage and see Siegfried and Roy.'

'Don't think I know the lads.'

'No. Well, you don't know much about the States.'

'Does not knowing Siegfried and Roy constitute not knowing much about the States?'

'Everybody knows them. They're the magicians with the white tigers. They can make an elephant disappear. They can make anything disappear.' Melrose looked up at the ceiling. 'Except Agatha.'

'An elephant? Jesus. How do they do that?'

'Well, they don't, do they? Charlie told me you obviously begin with the premise that they *don't* do it. If you accept that premise – and it's amazing how often people really don't – you go on with that in mind. It's mirrors, or something. I didn't really understand—' Melrose stopped abruptly, thinking.

'What's wrong?'

'Why didn't we do that with Johnny?'

'What?'

'Accept the premise that his aunt wouldn't go off

without a word to him? And if we accept it – well, it means she *did* leave word, a note, or she told somebody else.'

Jury sat up. 'The disappearance was all staging.' He shut his eyes and leaned his head back. 'Siegfried and Roy.' He sighed. 'We could use a little magic.'

52

He wished he'd got some exploding cigarettes from Charlie. But with his luck one would go off in Brenda's face and she'd shoot him.

A cigarette was what she wanted, and he found a pack in the pocket of Chris's blue wraparound apron, the gardening one. Chris wasn't supposed to be smoking, but the apron pocket was safe enough. He never did any gardening. 'A putter about' was the way Chris referred to digging on her hands and knees.

Brenda had stood in the kitchen with the gun in her hand, watching him crush all the meringues and toss the crumbs in the sink and wash them down the drain.

Now they were seated in the living room. Instead of the green baize-covered table for performing card tricks, he'd chosen the trunk in the alcove, with Brenda across the room in Chris's favourite chair. Johnny motioned towards the gun Brenda had placed on the gateleg table by the chair and which, he knew, she could retrieve in far less time than it would take him to lunge for it. 'What're you going to do?' he asked.

She did not so much exhale smoke as let it slowly

escape through her slightly open mouth. It made Johnny think of ectoplasm. 'I don't know, do I, sweetheart? I may have to leave Bletchley, and that might mean taking you with me.'

He tried to hide his anxiety and was grateful for the time he'd spent in perfecting a poker face and the attention he'd paid to body language, his own and that of others. His own he had under control. And he had trained himself to notice the tiny signs that give people away. Others didn't have themselves under control unless they were also in the business of not-giving-away – police, for instance. That detective, Macalvie, would have made a good magician.

'What are you thinking about?' Brenda frowned.

He didn't answer immediately. Silence, Johnny had found, could be a formidable weapon. After a few more beats of it he said, simply, 'Nothing.'

She smoked and watched him. 'You've very cool, sweetheart. You know that, I suppose. Quite amazing for someone your age. Quite stunning.'

He didn't comment. She wanted him to ask questions. He could tell that in order for her to maintain her belief in her control over this little tableau, she needed him to appear the one without the answers. Thus, if he did ask a question, it would be innocuous. He would not ask her again about Chris. Whatever had happened to Chris, that was Brenda's ace in the hole with him. It could be dangerous to thwart her, but he had to try every trick in the book to get himself out of this. He picked up the deck of cards he'd left on the table hours ago – a lifetime ago, a childhood ago. He held the deck up. 'Mind?'

'Yes.' She picked up the gun.

He set the cards down. 'Why?'

'Because you want to. I don't trust you, sweetheart. You're up to something.' Her smile seemed to snag on an unhappy memory.

Briefly, he laughed. 'A pack of cards wouldn't stop a gun.'

Surprisingly, she found that amusing and laughed too.

Johnny wondered what she really thought of him right now. He knew how much she had always liked him, and he felt sad. Even now, and her over there with a gun she just might use, even now it saddened him. But this feeling he could box off until it was safe. That she did like him so much was in his favour because it left her more vulnerable.

She said, 'Oh, go ahead,' and sighed as if he was an obstreperous child. 'Show us a trick, why don't you?'

He took up the deck, feeling for the slick card, shuffled it, fanned the cards out in a half-moon, swept them up again, shuffled again. None of that made the slightest bit of difference to a trick, but it gave him a few seconds to think. That was what he needed, time to think while appearing to be concentrating on the cards. He could do one slick card trick after another without thinking about the tricks themselves. He saw the pack of cigarettes she'd put down on the coffee table and looked around the room and spotted an ashtray. He said, 'Mind if I get a cigarette?'

'I'll get it.'

'And that ashtray over there?'

Holding the gun, she brought the ashtray and picked the cigarettes up with the same hand. The gun never faltered. 'Just when did you start smoking?'

His answer was a smile. 'Thanks.' Her eyes were on his movements as he took out a cigarette. 'Match? Or there's a lighter in that desk drawer. Charlie left it.'

Her smile was rueful. 'Now why would you want me to go and get the lighter when there's a book of matches right inside this.' She turned over the pack of cigarettes to show the matches nestled inside the cellophane.

It was a wonderful fact of human behaviour and the mainstay of magic: distraction. Make them look at what is completely irrelevant and they'll miss what's right under their noses. It worked every time. Brenda thought she was being so careful – the cigarettes, the ashtray, the drawer, the 'don't-moves' – but she was missing the whole thing.

Johnny lit a cigarette, pulled the ashtray closer. It was quite heavy, he knew. 'While you're here, pick a card.' He held out the cards, the slick card as usual in the middle. He didn't think she'd reach for one, not that it mattered, but she did. Then withdrew her hand before she'd taken one.

'I don't think so.' She backed away and found the chair she'd been sitting in.

He squared the deck, tapped it a couple of times, and fanned out the cards again. His movements were so smooth you could have skated on them. That, of course, was what did it. The card, except to be turned over, had never really moved. It was dexterity, all dexterity.

Brenda had lit one cigarette from another and stubbed

out the first. 'I've seen you do that a dozen times and still don't see how.'

With the cards he took a few steps towards her. She snatched up the gun. 'Uh-uh. Stay back. I told you. I don't trust you.'

Back was where he wanted to be, which is why he'd moved forward. 'Okay, something more elaborate. But I'll have to get the props out of a drawer in that sideboard.' He started towards it.

'Johnny. I'm not stupid.' The gun gestured him back.

He stepped back into the alcove, this time a bit further to the right. 'Another card trick then. But I don't know if you can see this from that distance.'

'I've got good eyes.'

'Watch.'

53

Sleep, he knew, would elude him, so he sat in the study and read one of Polly Praed's thrillers. He didn't like it at all but felt compelled to read a book written by a friend. The trouble was, Polly had published so many of them he could spend all his reading life trying to beat the detective to the denouement, which he never did because he couldn't sort out the puzzle, much less the solution. The one now in his hands had a plot that had lost him somewhere in a Welsh wilderness, the *mise-en-scène* (one of Polly's favourite phrases) having shifted from Aruba to Wales. Melrose imagined the only thing that could move one from Aruba to Swansea would be a gun at one's back, as was the case here. He hoped the hero would be riddled, he was so boring. The hero should have sent him straight into the arms of Morpheus. But the hero didn't, nor did the chase scene. Melrose set it aside and picked up his drink, hoping brandy and soda would have a more salubrious effect. It didn't either.

So Melrose left the study and climbed the stairs to the music room, where he could plunge himself into sadness, the sadness that had overcome him last night and whose source seemed to be the history of this house.

It was not difficult to plunge, given the black sky beyond the long windows and the implacable, repetitious drone of the waves. He thought of Daniel Bletchley's wonderful, unselfconscious playing and how it had filled the room. His mind on this music, he was looking down, expecting, surely, Nature would indulge him and let the wind whip up a storm of water . . .

Something moved down there.

Because of the angle of the windows, part of the path was cut from his view. But someone, he was certain, was standing or walking down below.

When the figure came into partial view, he assumed it must be Karen Bletchley. It was a woman, but the hair was not light, not Karen's; it was dark, the colour of mahogany. And suddenly, she looked straight up and straight at him. It was the middle of the night, but the moon glowed like white fire.

The glass dropped from his hand, splashing brandy down the leg of the immaculate flannel and drowning the top of his shoe.

He would have known her anywhere.

Stella.

Part IV

Stella by Starlight

54

Dan.

Standing down here and looking up at the dimly lit window, seeing a tall man with light hair in the room that held Daniel's piano and where he wrote his music, of course she thought it was Dan.

It was easy enough to make the mistake, wasn't it? No, not really, if there was no music. That alone should have told her. She would have heard the piano. God, if only she *had* heard it!

It had seduced her before she'd ever seen him, that music, even though she'd never thought of herself as a music lover. She listened to it, of course, and liked it. (She was afraid her taste might be somewhat banal.) But music had never affected her like that, never.

That day she had brought boxes of pastries for a children's party – the little boy's birthday – and while she'd been standing in that huge marble and granite hall, the piano, from somewhere at the top of that magnificent staircase, had started. Thundered, really thundered, making her sway where she stood. The rolls, the flourishes, the arpeggios were so beautiful she had to keep her eyes on the marble floor to keep from doing something really stupid – weeping or something.

'My husband,' said Karen Bletchley in uninflected tones, by way of explanation, as she tore off the cheque she'd been writing for the pastries.

Chris's mouth went dry as she took it. She knew that Karen Bletchley was looking at her as if she was used to women swooning on her doorstep.

And was she, Karen, so used to that music, to hearing it, she could define it simply with 'my husband'?

Chris could think of no excuse to linger; she wasn't much good at the kind of conversation that would allow her to do so, especially with this woman who was so smooth and so cool. Ash-blonde hair architecturally cut, as if the face had been born with this hair framing it. But the grey eyes were opaque. They had no depth.

So Chris had left quickly and got into her car, parked thankfully out of range of the front door but not out of range of hearing. With the window rolled down, the music came as vividly as the sound of the waves. How could a person do that? How could a mere man split you open, rearrange everything, heart lungs flesh bone?

She had rested her forehead on her hands, crossed over the steering wheel. So she was (and it amused her to think this) a goner even before she'd met him. If he'd been the Red Dwarf she'd have followed him to hell. And Dan Bletchley was anything but the Red Dwarf. Was it because she'd romanticized him so completely that she was bound to find him physically beautiful? No. He simply was.

When she finally met him – by accident, thank God,

and alone, thank God again – the same feeling came over her as when she'd heard him playing. She'd come apart again, everything got rearranged again.

A goner. Then, a double goner.

Heart lungs flesh bone.

The face disappeared from the window – had he seen her? – and Chris looked down at the ground, crunching some gravel around with the toe of her shoe, one of the several habits she had that had made Dan smile and put his arms round her. *Chrissie.* No one had ever called her that but Charlie. *Chrissie.*

'*Hey, Chris,*' Johnny had said, '*hey, Chris, you look weird, you look enthralled, you look like you're in the kingdom of thralldom.*'

Johnny. She should have gone directly to the village, but she had felt compelled to stop here at this house that no one had lived in since the Decorators, an appellation that always made her smile. The house had been standing vacant, but Morris Bletchley didn't have to sell it and, she suspected, really he couldn't. He couldn't turn over the place where his grandchildren had died. Keeping it might mean keeping hold of some part of them. It was the worst thing that had ever happened to Morris Bletchley.

It was what had ended them, of course, ended Chris and Dan. He'd been with her that night and she knew – though he'd never said it because it might seem he was blaming her for being there – that he believed, somehow, it had been his fault.

Up to then, they had been so buoyant; for that year

they had known one another she had felt untethered, not bound to earth. They had been weightless and guiltless. Until the children.

A door opened and slammed shut in the wind.

Well, he *had* seen her.

Trespasser, she tried on a smile. After midnight; no wonder this man thought it odd somebody was out here, on his property (even if rented), staring at the sea, staring up at the music room.

Who was he? He, too, was handsome, another reason she might have confused him with Dan. But he was slightly taller, slightly thinner, and looked furious.

55

He was downstairs and out the back door like a shot.

She was still standing there; the face that had been turned towards the sea (as if it had comforts to offer beyond the scope of what humans had to offer) was now turned towards him.

The wind blew her black hair across her pale skin, and he saw how much she looked like her nephew, the colouring a genetic trait, like the straight nose and narrow, squared chin.

He wondered as he came through the door why that look of happiness had flashed across her face as if light had struck warmth into marble; he wondered now, walking up to her, why the look was just as suddenly withdrawn and she stopped and took root where she stood.

His feelings were a total muddle. He was genuinely – even rapturously – glad that she was alive, but at the same time was only too aware that he had been, all along, daydreaming about this woman, or about some woman, from the moment he'd set foot in this house. And now it was as if a dream had thickened to flesh and blood, only to mock him.

His mounting anger surprised him, but he let it mount. Melrose was not a rash person, nor did he make rash judgements, but he was growing angrier by the second over this woman's nonchalant reappearance and her failure to see she wreaked havoc in people's lives. How could she simply turn up like this and stand gazing seaward?

He knew the anger showed in his clumsy attempt to grab her arm. That she was genuinely shocked and bewildered by his movement was plain. That she had not carelessly mislaid herself was equally plain. He knew that and knew at the same time that when she had seen him so briefly before he turned from the window above, the moonlight on his light hair, she had thought he was Daniel Bletchley. And this was intolerable, but why? It had been clear three days ago when Bletchley spoke of her where his sympathies lay – his heart, his music, his past, but not (the music said) his future. Chris Wells had been the woman Daniel had been with but had never named (despite the fact she would have provided him with an alibi).

If she was anywhere, *anywhere* as charming as her young nephew – and she was certainly as handsome – Melrose could easily understand why Bletchley had wanted her, and just as easily understood why she had wanted him. All of this went through his mind in the seconds it took him to walk up to her and grab her arm.

'Where the hell have you been?'

Her astonishment robbed her, for a moment, of

speech. Then she laughed uncertainly and said, 'Who are you?'

Melrose dropped her arm and felt the spread of a furious, adolescent blush. He smiled and answered, 'The Uninvited.'

The first thing he did was lead her to a telephone so she could call her house. No one answered.

'Could he be out in his cab? There's a dispatcher, isn't there? Try calling there.'

'Shirley. Yes. But it's after midnight.'

'Try anyway.' He stood over her as she placed the call, as if fearing she might disappear again.

Chris still did not know what was going on, but she took him at his word and made the call to Cornwall Cabs. Shirley was speechless for a few moments, so that Chris had to keep saying *hello, hello*.

Finally, Shirley found her voice and told Chris, yes, she would make every effort to get hold of Johnny. He'd borrowed one of the cars to go to Seabourne, but that was nearly three hours ago. 'But where've you been, love? Are you all right? Johnny's frantic.'

'He is? But – I'm fine, Shirley. There's just some kind of misunderstanding. Try and find the cab, will you?' She hung up and said to Melrose, 'I'll call the Woodbine. Brenda—'

'No. Leave that.'

Melrose had been sincere in his apologies for his abrupt treatment of her when she had no idea who he was or why he was here. And why he was surprised that *she* was here.

They were sitting down in the study, still the only really warm room downstairs, when he finally asked her, 'Look, why did you disappear like that? Your nephew has been worried sick.'

She frowned. 'Disappear? Well, I didn't exactly do *that*. Didn't he get the note?' She sat back. 'Obviously he didn't. I should have called from Newcastle.'

'Newcastle? You've been in *Newcastle* all this time? We thought you might be dead. Same thing, I imagine.' He did not add *or guilty as hell*.

She was still frowning, and deeply. 'I have a friend there who's very ill – but that's hardly important. What's happened?'

'Haven't you been reading the papers? There was a murder in Lamorna Cove. A woman you apparently knew: Sada Colthorp.'

Her face went even paler. 'Sadie? Murdered?'

'Her body was found on the path between Lamorna and Mousehole.'

Chris seemed to be having a hard time taking this in. 'Well . . . but she came back four or five years ago . . .'

'Does this suggest anything to you?'

'What? No. What should it suggest? Please stop talking in riddles.'

'I'm sorry. But it is one. Someone murdered her, and the police have you down as a suspect.'

She was open-mouthed with astonishment.

'The point is, what happened to that note? Who did you give it to?'

Chris shook her head. 'To nobody. I left it on top of the card table where I knew he'd be sure to see it.' She made a dismissive gesture. 'Anyway, Johnny knows I'd never go off without telling him where I'd gone. How could he doubt?'

'Ah, but he didn't. He kept insisting you wouldn't. And we should have paid attention. If we'd paid more attention to his insisting you would have left word, rather than coming to the conclusion you didn't and he must be wrong, God knows how much would have been saved. So, who took it?'

'I don't know. I can't imagine. Brenda was supposed to make sure he knew why I'd left—'

Her face went white. Then she was suddenly out of her chair and the white was replaced by heat. She was angry. 'In thirty seconds or less. Tell me. Because I'm leaving. In thirty seconds.'

Melrose stood up too. He managed it in under that.

But it didn't keep her from leaving. She ran. She ran through the hall, out of the door, and to her car.

Melrose followed, running too. By the time he'd got his own engine going, she was down the drive and out of sight.

56

It was called 'the card under glass trick'; Charlie had taught it to him. He still hadn't got it quite right, but that made no difference to his purpose. Instead of a glass, he would extemporize with the gun, as she'd just set it down again. All he needed was to get her eyes off him in such a way they'd stay off for that bit of time, long enough for him to unwind the cord, which he hoped wasn't wrapped round the cleat more than once.

He fanned the cards out across the top of the trunk and asked, 'You want to pick a card?'

'Do you think I'm getting that close to you?'

'Probably not. I'll have to do it for you again, then.' With his index finger he flipped the entire half-moon of cards face up. 'Full deck, just wanted you to see.' Then he shuffled, cut the deck twice, fanned the cards again, and, in spite of the fix he was in, enjoyed the irony of doing all of this on top of the trunk. It was like that Hitchcock film, *Rope*. But that was the point about knowing what you wanted to do in life and being able to do it. It blotted out everything else when you were doing it.

He picked the Ace of Spades from the half-moon, held it up, flicked it with his finger before returning it to the fanned-out cards. He swept the cards together, shuffled, cut several times quickly, fanned the cards out again.

'Ace of Spades? Gone.'

'I'll take your word for it, sweetheart. Where is it?'

'Look under the gun, Brenda.'

That made her flinch and focus.

He could have told her anywhere, to look at the floor, or the chair itself, or the door. But, he reasoned, only the gun would do it, would distract her long enough. She would have (as did most people) the primitive fear, some half-formed belief – it was this that magic played on – that he could make the gun disappear. And in the split second she looked away to the gun on the table beside her, he unhooked the cord that held the curtain taut and jerked the heavy material across the embrasure.

The first shot went through the curtain just as he threw the ashtray through the glass and kicked open the French windows. To confuse her was what he wanted. The second shot followed as he raised the lid of the trunk, and the third as he jumped in, closed the lid, and pulled down the false bottom. He knew she'd look in the trunk, but not before she'd got to the open French windows, through which she'd think he'd left the house.

Her bafflement was almost palpable. The lid of the trunk opened upon a second of silence when she saw nothing. There was no explanation for her except to assume he'd gone by way of the French windows.

But she'd be back; she'd have had time to realize that

he was, after all, a magician and this trunk was big enough to hold a body.

Lying in the dark, he listened to the rain blowing in through the French windows. He'd been too focused before to realize it was raining. But he heard it now as if it was riveting the lid of the trunk closed. Much as he would have liked to stay in it (for it created even for him the illusion of invisibility), he would have to move before she came back, and he knew that would be soon.

Yet might it work, staying here? He finally scotched that idea; it was too uncertain. Much better to be able to move about the house. He was afraid to leave until she came back inside; she could be making a circuit of it, and this time he might not be lucky and run right into her. Better to wait and see which way she came in – probably the front – and he could slip out the back.

He was out of the trunk now and had never realized before how bright ordinary lamplight could be. To avoid being seen through the windows, he crouched and, in this position, made his way as quickly as he could across the living room. He went to the kitchen. He opened the little grey metal door of the panel box, pulled the main circuit breaker, and plunged the house into darkness.

He stood listening. The hard rain was letting up. Somewhere, a car door slammed.

57

First, she walked swiftly from her car down the street, wondering what instinct told her that it would be dangerous to park in her usual space, that she should park some distance from the house. She walked quickly past the Woodbine, momentarily tempted to go in and shout for Brenda to explain, to fix things. But Chris knew it was inexplicable. The note she'd left on the card table for Johnny, the word she'd left with Brenda . . . It was incomprehensible.

Why Brenda would have failed to tell him was beyond her, utterly beyond her. What her, Chris's, supposed running away was meant to accomplish was just as mysterious. She didn't care about the mystery at this moment; she cared only about letting Johnny know she was back and she was all right.

Lights shone through the windows of their house and then, suddenly, they didn't. Suddenly, and all at once, both downstairs and upstairs went dark. That the lights were not being turned off one at a time, that the house was abruptly thrust into darkness really frightened her. She stopped. In the diminished light along the street she heard a car in the distance, getting closer, perhaps Plant's, for she knew he had made for his car when she was leaving. Perhaps she should wait . . . oh, but this was ridiculous, holding back this way.

She shoved her fisted hands down into her pockets. Fear fuelled her anger. How dare Brenda do this? Chris walked, but slowly, towards her house, which had grown unfamiliar to her without even the porch light on to guide her.

Chris saw that someone was standing in front of the Drowned Man, hands cupping a cigarette, sheltering the match against the wind and what was left of the rain-mist mostly. Someone. Was she seeing him every-where now, having seen him nowhere for so long?

Dan. She shrank back into a doorway. How could he possibly be here now? Then she remembered what Melrose Plant had said about Tom Letts and his funeral. Dan would of course come to help his dad. No matter how painful or what memories the place stirred, Dan would do that. He really loved Morris Bletchley.

Another figure, stocky and wearing a dark robe, had come out to join Dan. It must be Mr Pfinn. She heard their voices, drowsy through the mist, floating towards her. She could make out nothing they said as they looked off down the street, in the direction of her house.

Chris stared at the fragment of Dan's face the cigarette illuminated when he drew on it. She needed help; she was sure she needed help. She should not have come by herself; she should have brought Mr Plant with her.

But she turned away from help and started walking

again towards the house, now little more than fifty feet away. Only a few doors down the street. What had they been looking at, Dan and Pfinn? Why had they come out onto the pavement? She had left her own sheltering doorway only when the two of them had turned to go back into the pub.

Not sure why she wanted to avoid the front door of this house that lay in a total, unnatural darkness and silence, she made for the French windows round the right-hand side and soon found her feet crunching gravel, and something else. Glass. The cloudy moon showed her a window was broken. She moved through the French windows and found an even darker darkness than outside. When she reached out she felt the heavy curtain, loosened from the fixture that usually held it back.

She heard a noise, at once far away and shatteringly close, felt something like a heavy and violent hand shoved against her chest, jerking her back, and then tripped over the heavy curtain that was in front of her. No, she hadn't tripped. Pain only flickered at first and then gathered a hideous strength.

'*Johnny!*' Chris thought she screamed it, but heard little more than a whisper, less than the hiss of the sea against rocks which she could almost hear, even at this distance, less even than the lovely voice of Dan over across the road. *Johnny!* She knew she hadn't said it aloud, not this time. He was in her mind with the blinding, searing light, as if the whole house had suddenly and completely been lit with the sun.

That was all.

58

Melrose saw Wiggins coming out the door of the Drowned Man just after what sounded like a shot was fired. He ran towards him.

'Sergeant! Was that—?'

Wiggins stopped. 'It came from the Wells house.'

Light flooded the house before they reached the end of the path to the Wellses' front door, which was open.

'I'm going round the back,' said Wiggins. 'You'd best stay out of sight.'

He didn't. Melrose waited for a moment, then moved towards the door.

Brenda Friel was backed up against the doorjamb between kitchen and living room, her rigid arms extended, hands holding a gun as steady as a cross beam. It was aimed at Johnny.

Melrose urged himself on. *Do something, do something, damn it!* But what? He was paralyzed when he saw Chris Wells lying in the little alcove at the back of the room.

'I'll kill you, I swear to God.'

Johnny hadn't shouted this, but the intensity with

which he'd uttered the words left no doubt that he would.

Brenda said nothing. Her face was wiped clean of expression.

Then Melrose saw Wiggins approaching silently, coming through the kitchen and up behind her. He brought the side of his hand down on her arm. The gun discharged, and simultaneously a knife flew across the room and lodged in the wood of the doorway at exactly the spot where Brenda's heart had been.

Johnny moved to his aunt's body and did not so much kneel as drop down. He put an arm beneath her shoulders and lifted her. Then he wept.

Wiggins held on to Brenda Friel, who struggled to get out of his grasp.

And, frozen in the doorway, stood Daniel Bletchley, staring at Johnny and his awful burden. He was cradling his aunt's body, rocking it back and forth. Dan was wide-eyed, unable to move.

Hoping she's only fainted, Melrose thought.

For one could see no damage to Chris. The blood that had seeped into the dark carpet had now collected beneath the dark curtain at her back. Her equally dark clothes showed no wound. It was as if Johnny, in passing his hand above Chris's body, had rendered the damage invisible.

The blood was on Johnny. When he sat back Melrose could see his T-shirt was covered, from where he had pulled her close.

Daniel Bletchley walked over to Johnny and knelt

down, putting an arm round the boy and saying nothing.

For anything said, any word of comfort or false cheer, would have been a lie.

59

The service was held in the little Bletchley church, conducted by a rector of about the same age Tom had been. All youth, to Melrose, now looked sad, this age that old people so much envied but through which, he thought now, it would have been better not to pass. Standing with this little group of mourners, he watched the casket being lowered into the ground and bowed his head, thinking he had seen enough of death in the past twenty-four hours to last his lifetime.

Whichever occupants of Bletchley Hall were able to leave their beds were there, along with staff. The Hoopers, black-suited, stood next to Morris Bletchley, on whose other side stood Daniel and Karen. Little Miss Livingston, her acorn face obscured by a small black veil, seemed more bent than even before. Beside her stood Mrs Atkins; Mr Bleaney and Mr Clancy were on the other side of the grave.

Melrose stood beside Johnny, who had insisted on coming, despite his having to endure, in the following days, his aunt's own funeral. Her body now lay in the police morgue in Penzance. It would be released to 'the family' (the pathologist speaking here) when the autopsy was complete.

The first person to step forward and let fall a handful of earth onto the coffin must have been Tom's sister, Honey; she was a slight, very blonde, and pretty girl. She stood back, and Morris Bletchley stepped forward, repeating the sad ritual. Then the rector of Bletchley's single church finished the ceremony.

It would probably have been no compliment to tell Honey Letts that black became her, as if she'd been designed for sad occasions such as this. It made her fragile blondeness more intense, deepened the blue of her eyes to black.

She was only seventeen, but she had the composure of a woman decades older. He wondered how it had been bred in her, certainly not by her mother and father, given what Tom had told him.

The mother and father were not even with her today. Melrose found it difficult to believe that parents could be so hard and unforgiving.

'Honey,' said Melrose, looking down at her, 'I didn't know Tom for long, but I still felt I knew him.'

She nodded and looked up at him out of those bottomless dark blue eyes.

'You have no idea how much you did for him,' Melrose said.

'No, people don't, usually. But it certainly wasn't any sacrifice on my part. I don't know many people and certainly no one as interesting as Tommy.' She looked off towards the bottom of the garden and Tom's grave.

For some moments she held that silent pose, a young person who could bear silence.

'Your parents didn't come.' It was as close to accusation as he could get; that they hadn't come made him furious.

With her eyes still on the grave, she shook her head. 'They couldn't get over that Tommy had AIDS. They couldn't get past it. It's the way some people are; they get stuck and can't go on. The really tragic thing is that Tommy wasn't gay.' Honey turned to look up at Melrose. 'He didn't bother telling people because they wouldn't believe it; besides that, he didn't think it should make a difference. He told Mum and Dad, finally, but they didn't believe him either. After all, he had the mark, so what difference did it make if he was or wasn't gay?'

Melrose remembered what Johnny had told him. He said, 'I'd have believed him, Honey. I think I'd have believed anything he told me. He was that kind of person; you believed him, that's all.'

A tear ran straight down Honey's cheek. 'Thanks. Thanks. It was only this one fellow – would you like to hear about this?'

She asked this as a real question, not a rhetorical one. Honey, apparently, took things seriously.

'Of course I would, Honey. Of course.'

'It was a long time ago – it must have been fifteen or sixteen years ago. It was with a friend of his who'd got really sick. This was his best friend since childhood. They'd been through school together, dated together; he's always been popular with girls – they'd been through just about everything together. After Bobby got the virus it was hardly any time, less than two years, before he had full-blown AIDS. He was dying and Tom went to visit him. He stayed for less than two weeks. He told me about it when he got sick himself; he'd wanted to comfort Bobby, Tom said. That's all, just comfort. It was only a few times. He told me he'd been tested afterwards, more than once after Bobby died, but there wasn't any sign Tom had it. Not until three years ago.' Honey had to look away. 'It's awful this should happen to Tom because of that, and yet I wonder if Tom's being that sort of person, if it didn't make all of us better somehow. If you know what I mean.'

The little eulogy was so heartfelt that Melrose could say nothing; he simply nodded.

There was another silence, shared. Then Melrose said, 'You see that boy over there?' He nodded in Johnny's direction.

'Yes. He looks really sad.'

'He is. His aunt was murdered last night.' Melrose would have thought it impossible for Honey's face to grow even paler, but it did.

'*What?*'

'The police think the same person's responsible.' But that's hardly a consolation to Honey.

'Poor boy. How awful for him. Do you think I should go and talk to him?'

Melrose smiled. If anyone could infer human need well enough to answer that question, it was Honey herself.

'I think that's a good idea.'

And she did. Melrose watched. He saw Johnny turn

to face her and watched as Johnny listened. Honey talked for a little while, leaving her hand on his arm as she looked up at him.

Melrose watched as Johnny's expression changed. It was as if the lid of a coffin had opened and the person who lay there, mistaken for dead, at last could breathe again.

Honey had the touch.

60

Murder or no murder, funeral or no funeral, Agatha could not be avoided forever. Melrose was to have tea with her that afternoon and he talked Richard Jury into coming along.

It surprised him that the Woodbine Tearoom was open and full, as it usually was, at four o'clock. That it was open for business at all was in part owing to the efforts of Mrs Hayter, whom Melrose recalled saying that she often baked her popular berry pies for the Woodbine, and that when Brenda was called away she would come in and help out.

Brenda had certainly been 'called away'. And, Mrs Hayter declared, 'Enough said on *that* subject, I'm sure.'

Melrose could see tears forming on her lower lids, but her mouth was pinched with barely contained rage. But it wasn't 'enough said', judging from the whispers flying from behind hands at the other tables.

And God knows it would never be 'enough said' for Agatha. She was so eager to get down to it she could barely spare a hello for Richard Jury, whom she was usually all over like a fishnet. 'I knew the first time I had dealings with that woman Brenda that something was wrong.'

'What dealings, Lady Ardry?' asked Jury, as he sipped his tea. There were still things that didn't add up, that made no sense – most important, the murder of Tom Letts.

'No dealings,' said Melrose. 'Unless you count your vain attempt to pry her recipe for Sweet Ladies out of her.' Melrose watched as Johnny came through the swinging door, a boy who shouldered his responsibilities as if they were the heavy tray he carried. It was piled high with cups, pastries, and buns.

'Don't be absurd,' said Agatha. That being the brunt of her rebuttal, she changed the subject. Lowering her voice to a whisper, she said, 'With his aunt shot just last night, I'm surprised to see that boy working.'

Melrose watched him. His movements were heavy and his smile a mere remnant of what it had been. '*I'm* not surprised. Do you think he'd be better off lying about in bed, thinking of her and how she died?'

'Work,' said Jury, 'is the best antidote for what ails you, at least according to my boss, who has little experience to back him up. I'm sure Sergeant Wiggins would disagree about the best antidote, he having a great deal of experience to back *him* up.'

Johnny came over to their table. He was introduced to Jury, who stood up to shake his hand. 'Johnny, I'm very sorry for your loss.'

He looked at Jury and seemed in danger of crumpling. Jury who had that effect on people; he could project an empathy that breached their defences and frequently had them turning away, weeping. This was one thing that made him so good with witnesses.

'Thanks,' said Johnny. Then, as if this response might be too perfunctory, he said it again: 'Thank you.' He blinked several times 'Chris was great, wasn't she?' he asked Melrose.

Melrose had told Johnny about Chris's visit to Seabourne. 'The greatest, Johnny.' He had only been with her for a very short time, but he felt that he spoke the truth. 'The greatest,' he repeated.

Even Agatha managed to mumble a few words meant to console. 'Sorry . . . great pity . . . awful for you.'

Melrose asked, 'Where's Honey? Did she go back to Dartmouth?'

Johnny looked over his shoulder. 'No, actually. She's in the kitchen.'

And to Melrose's surprise and as if she had been waiting for her cue, Honey came through the door, butting it with her hip; she was carrying both a pot of tea and a tiered cake plate. Both of these she set on Melrose's table.

'This is for you, compliments of the house,' said Honey, as if she'd worked here for years. Her smile was brilliant.

Agatha's was hardly less so when she saw the selection of cakes and meringues. 'My goodness, thank you.'

Johnny said, 'It's for all your help.'

'We do what we can,' said Agatha, taking credit.

'What help?' asked Melrose, quite sincerely. 'I don't feel I was much help.'

'You certainly were, Mr Plant,' said Johnny. 'For

starters, it was you who got the police here by knowing Mr Macalvie.'

'I don't think he'd claim to have been much help either.'

'Okay,' said Jury. 'I'll make the claim for Sergeant Wiggins and give you his recipe for herbal tea so it'll be ready for him when he comes in.'

Seeing that Johnny was distinctly brighter when Honey was around, Melrose asked her how long she was staying.

Honey sighed. 'I'd like to stay longer, but I've got to go back to school. I got excused for three days and tomorrow's the third day, so that's when I have to leave.'

'I want her to come and work here during the summer.' As if he needed a reason for this, Johnny said, 'There's only Mrs Hayter and me to run this place, and I'd like to keep it going. It was Chris's life, after all.'

Honey said, 'I'd really like to but I promised this family that's going to the South of France I'd go along to watch the children. You know, as an au pair. But I might be able to get out of it if I can find someone to take my place. I hope so, at least. I always did like Bletchley, and maybe I can take Mr Bletchley's mind off things by being around.'

Melrose had stopped listening. He was staring off across the room, his mind elsewhere; he was trying to remember. Something Tom had said. Or Moe Bletchley. Had they been talking about the South of France? He frowned. No, that wasn't it. His look at Honey must have been so probing, she asked if something was wrong.

And then he had it.

The au pair!

He stood up, setting the teacups to rattling. 'Come on,' he said to Jury.

'Come on where? I'm not finished.'

'Now! Agatha can take care of the bill.'

Jury rose. There's a first time for everything, he thought.

61

'Mr Bletchley,' Jury said, 'I'm Richard Jury, New Scotland Yard.'

Morris Bletchley shook the proffered hand. 'You're a little late, aren't you, sir?' He could not keep his face from clouding over. 'A little late.'

'I'm sorry,' Jury said, with all the earnestness of one who felt he really should have appeared earlier.

'He's been in Northern Ireland,' said Melrose, as if he had to justify Jury's dereliction of duty, and that a stint in Northern Ireland would justify anything.

'Of course,' said Moe Bletchley. 'Just a little black humour and not very funny at that. Let's sit down.'

They'd been standing in the wide hall between the blue and red rooms. Moe led them into the blue room and asked if they'd like something. Tea? Whisky? Both declined.

'There's something I want to ask you,' said Melrose. 'Tom described your house in Putney, said it wasn't very big, three bedrooms, one of them for the au pair. You had one for when the children came to visit.'

Moe's gaze was puzzled. 'That's right.'

'Who was she?'

Morris Bletchley looked very unhappy. 'Mona Freeman was the name she gave me. She was actually Ramona Friel.' Moe looked at them and gave a helpless little shrug. 'I wouldn't have known if she hadn't told me, much later, just before she came back to Bletchley.' His frown deepened. 'I was completely surprised. I didn't know Ramona by sight because she'd been away at school for years, and hardly ever went into the village the times I was at the house. Wouldn't have seen her anyway because she'd been away, like I said. She never told her mother she was working for me – well obviously, since she'd changed her name to hide the fact. Brenda didn't want her in London, working.

'All Ramona wanted from me was to help her – not an abortion, mind you, but just to sustain her until the baby was born. I told her she really should tell her mother, but she didn't want to. Finally, though, she did. I guess Mona just had to have her mother's support. And that's the last I ever saw of her until I heard the poor girl had died. I could certainly feel for Brenda, I'll tell you.'

'Did she tell you who the father was?'

Sadly, Moe shook his head. 'No. I knew it was Tom. But that, I'm sure, Ramona didn't tell her mother; she swore me to secrecy on that score. I'd have known anyway, wouldn't I? She refused to tell him, adamantly refused. If she had, Tom would have done something; he'd have married her. But she didn't want to marry anyone. Very stubborn girl.' He smiled slightly but then looked from Plant to Jury, as if he feared what was coming. 'I was told she died of that non-Hodgkins leukemia.'

'That's what Brenda Friel told people. But I'll bet you any amount of money that Ramona Friel died from some complication of AIDS. If not AIDS directly, then indirectly. Whatever was wrong with Ramona was exacerbated by this virus. Didn't Brenda know Tom Letts? Didn't he drive you here from London?'

Moe shook his head. 'Maybe once or twice. It's a hell of a drive from London. No, Brenda didn't know Tom; she certainly didn't know he'd worked for me in London.'

'Brenda Friel didn't know who the father was and found out only recently about this Putney arrangement. Then she knew the father must have been Tom Letts.'

Morris Bletchley looked away then sharply back again. 'Brenda Friel's the one who shot him? Jesus.' Moe leaned over, his head in his hands.

'She had a motive, certainly,' said Jury. 'She found out somehow.'

His head still in his hands, Moe shook it back and forth, back and forth. 'A couple of weeks ago – feels like years – Tom was talking to her about Putney. She said she had family – some cousins, whatever – in Fulham. You know, right next door. Brenda's not stupid. Ramona had worked in Putney and Ramona had died of AIDS.'

Melrose and Jury were silent, watching him.

Finally Moe asked, 'And Chris Wells? What did she have to do with all this?'

'I'm guessing again, but I'd say Chris Wells presented a danger after Tom was murdered. Chris would have been the *only* person who knew Ramona had the virus. So it was not what Chris knew then, it's what she *would* know if Tom Letts were suddenly murdered.'

Morris Bletchley set his head in his hands again, shaking it. 'Poor Ramona, that poor girl. Ramona was so good with Noah and Esmé.' He stood up. 'It's too much. You know whom I suspected: my daughter-in-law. I've never really liked Karen. She's just so *plausible*.'

Melrose knew exactly what he meant. Plausible. He remembered that enjoyable evening at Seabourne, marred by a moment of discomfort, when she'd shown her resentment of Morris Bletchley and a certain banal turn of mind. Small things, and perhaps he'd been small-minded, but he supposed a person should attend to his intuitive responses to small things.

'And I've always known she married Danny for his money. Danny' – he looked at them sadly – 'never wanted to leave here. Karen was the one who was always agitating to go back to London.'

'She told me,' said Melrose, 'just the opposite. She told me a story that was half fact and half fantasy. I think she wanted to make sure the police understood there were other people on the scene because she was afraid your son would come under suspicion.'

'You mean that *she* would.' Moe sighed. 'She'd want to convince the world she's the inconsolable mother. It's Danny who's inconsolable.' He looked around the beautiful room as if the blue had fled from it, as if it had drained of colour. 'Will we ever know what really happened?'

Melrose had gone to call the Penzance police station, where Jury now imagined Macalvie questioning Brenda Friel. He said, 'Don't worry, Mr Bletchley. We'll know.'

62

He'd been here in one of the interrogation rooms of the
Penzance police station for half an hour, waiting for her
to say something.

Brenda Friel hadn't got beyond hello and asking for a
cigarette.

'Where are the video tapes, Brenda?'

Macalvie assumed she wasn't going to answer that
question either. She surprised him, even though the
answer was a question.

'What tapes?'

'The film Simon Bolt took for you and for himself,
presumably to peddle over the Internet. A good cross-
over between snuff film and kiddy porn. The one Sada
Colthorp had when you shot her.'

Her smile was all for herself. Hemmed in, parsimon-
ious, nothing left over, not even bad humour, for anyone
else. God knows not for him.

Despite her relentless silence, Macalvie was getting
to her; he could feel it. It was an odd chemistry; he'd felt
it before with suspects. It wasn't his experience as a
policeman or his cleverness that was getting through. It

was something else, some quality in himself that the person under question seemed to think they shared. Macalvie hated the feeling. Not that he empathized, not that he understood. Some killers he did come to understand. Brenda wasn't one of them. It made him uncomfortable to sense she didn't believe this. *That's your problem, boyo.*

'Yeah, a real classic,' he went on, 'that film. I can see the paedophiles slobbering all the way from Bournemouth to John o'Groats.'

Her eyes were sparking now, live wires touched to some electrical source. Anger? Good.

'But it didn't start out that way, Brenda.' He got up and walked over to a little window, his hands thrust into his trouser pockets, holding back his raincoat. 'Before Ramona died you wouldn't in a million years have thought of having a sociopath like Bolt follow those kids to their deaths. I can see it, I can just see it. Noah and Esmé . . .' He looked round at her, sitting there, not looking at him. The children's names touched off nothing in her – no sympathy, no remorse. At least, these emotions weren't present on her face.

He went on. 'You know what I've been wondering? How it is you didn't send the tape to Morris Bletchley. Wasn't that the idea? Make him suffer as much as you had?'

'No.'

Macalvie kept himself from turning round, from registering surprise. He was surprised the film hadn't served the double purpose as instrument of death and sadistic revenge.

'Not knowing is worse. Now, though, I would. I'd like to rub his face in it,' said Brenda. 'By taking Ramona into that house, he killed her as surely as if he'd held a gun to her head.'

Fucking melodrama, thought Macalvie. 'Seems to me Mr Bletchley provided your daughter with safe harbour. Would you rather have had her wandering all over London? You never wanted her to go, and she didn't communicate with you.' That Bletchley could be seen as a saviour, Macalvie knew, would fuel her rage.

'Safe harbour? Throwing Ramona into bed with a bloody gay chauffeur who'd got AIDS?' She made a noise in her throat of disgust, dismissal.

Macalvie did turn round then. 'Morris Bletchley—' No. Don't defend him any more, even though God knows the man deserves someone's defending him. 'I guess that wasn't very smart of him.'

Her sour laugh was more a snarl.

'He paid a heavy price, Brenda. His grandchildren.'

'No price could have been too heavy.'

She was not crying, but tears were clotting her throat. It was thick with them. Wait. Wait for a moment. Macalvie leaned wearily against the cold wall, as if sick of death. The weariness was not an act. He was drowning in it.

Her only child. He could sympathize with that part of it, certainly. Then it occurred to him, and he was surprised by the conviction. 'You didn't see it. The film. You didn't watch it.' Now he was leaning on the table, arms rod straight. She looked up at him, disclosing nothing. He said, 'You weren't there when Simon Bolt shot that film. You didn't see it.' He could have hit her. *You bitch!*

And then he realized she'd finally admitted her tie to Simon Bolt. She'd forgotten herself enough to do this, just as he'd forgotten himself enough to want to kill her. 'Tell me how he did it.'

She actually shrugged, as if it was really no affair of hers, since she hadn't been there. 'He had what I suppose you'd say was an assistant. I imagine Simon Bolt had a string of assistants, including Sadie May. They met up with the Bletchley children in the woods just beyond their house, several times. He took pictures, Polaroid shots, which he showed me. Nothing nasty, of course. They might have reported that to the grown-ups back at the house. He merely took pictures of them playing. Told them he was a filmmaker and showed them one. He had this little telly, you know, screen hardly as big as your hand. Anyway, he told them he could do one of them, if they fancied it. He found out a lot about the Bletchleys, about the boat down at the bottom of the stone steps. I expect he just made up a story to get them to go down there, or the girl did. Or the girl led them down there just when the tide was coming in. I don't know. I didn't ask for details.' Her voice took on a colourless, hollow quality, as if she were forever removed from what she was describing.

She was, thought Macalvie. She had arranged this but hadn't had the courage to look at it. That way, perhaps in her own mind, it had happened without her. 'He would have given you a tape. A copy. He'd keep a couple for himself.'

'Oh, he did. Said it was for proof. Well, I didn't need proof, did I? They were drowned. Proof enough there. The Bletchleys left Seabourne. End of that marriage to all intents and purposes.'

'Yet Morris Bletchley didn't leave. He stayed. He would have stayed through hell rather than desert his grandchildren. He must have looked at it that way.'

She didn't comment.

'Sada Colthorp put you in touch with Bolt.'

'She told me about him. I'd never have used her as a go-between. She couldn't be trusted. Obviously.'

'Sada came back a couple of weeks ago and tried to blackmail you. She had a copy of that tape, or maybe it was Bolt's copy that she found in the house. Only there was nothing on that tape to link you to the children. You'd been very careful. It was only her word against yours. You thought she'd be believed instead of you?'

'Her word was what she intended to whisper in Morris Bletchley's ear. Along with giving him that tape. Him seeing that tape? Why, he'd have turned heaven and earth upside down to discover who was responsible, and if she told him it was my idea, he'd concentrate on me. He'd have had me investigated in a way police don't have time for – they've got a hundred other people, a hundred other murders to deal with. Morris Bletchley would only have me. Even if he couldn't prove it, even if he couldn't satisfy himself, Moe Bletchley would've hounded me the rest of my life.'

'But Chris Wells?' Macalvie didn't have to frame a question or a conclusion. She had reached that point where it was in for a penny, in for a pound. She was even more tired than he was; she thought she might as well tell the rest of it. Finally, suspects wanted to. They wanted someone else to know either how clever they'd been or how much they'd suffered. Finally, Brenda Friel wanted him to know.

She said, 'If Chris were all of a sudden to leave the village at the same time there was a murder in Lamorna Cove, and if it was someone Chris had been known to hate – well, how else could the police look at it except the way you did? The minute she set foot back in Bletchley, you'd have arrested her. My word against hers. Right?'

Her smile was like something engraved in acid. He wanted to slap it off her face. He asked, 'But why? Why did you want Chris Wells out of the way?

'She knew, didn't she? About the AIDS. She was the only one I told. She was no danger to me until I killed Tom Letts. I had to get her out of the way because she would have worked it out. It wouldn't have taken long for Chris to do that, not her; she's as clever as her nephew.'

'Why did you wait so long to kill Tom Letts? Four years.'

'Why? Because I didn't *know* it was him. I only just discovered it a few weeks ago. Ramona never told me who the father was.'

They sat in silence for a few moments.

Then Macalvie said, 'The Bletchleys had children, Chris had Johnny. Not only did she have Johnny, he was always there, in your face, the kind of boy every parent hopes his son will be like.'

She didn't reply to this, only looked off at the wall as if she could see through it.

For a couple of minutes they sat that way, Macalvie staring at her, she staring off into nothing.

'Where's the fucking tape, Brenda?'

Part V

The Uninvited

63

Jury and Plant were standing on the pavement in front of the Drowned Man when a white Rolls hove into view and continued its glide down Bletchley's main street. The late sun lapped about its bonnet and boot, dazzling pedestrians who, like Plant and Jury, stopped to watch.

'What the hell's that?' asked Jury.

'Moby Dick. What are *they* doing here?'

Jury squinted as the car got closer. 'Doesn't look like a whale. I think it's Marshall Trueblood driving.'

'Same thing. Ye gods.'

The car drew abreast of them and the passenger window whispered down. A white silk-sleeved arm was thrust out and a hand waved. The car glided to a stop. 'Richard Jury! Oh, what a treat!' called out Diane Demorney. Melrose, the non-treat, got only a perfunctory 'Hello'.

Like a cork from a champagne bottle, Marshall Trueblood popped from behind the wheel. Champagne was the colour of his Armani suit; his shirt, pocket handkerchief, and tie were all done in watery Monet-garden pastels – pinks, blues, lemons – bringing to mind more a box of Turkish delight than the gardens at Giverny. Still, he was, as usual, sartorial perfection.

Trueblood could barely contain himself. After opening the passenger door he extended a hand towards Diane, who took about the same amount of time as Cleopatra did getting off her barge.

Diane was dressed to match the Rolls: white, slick, and moneyed. But she made tracks from car to kerb when it looked as if Trueblood was about to steal all the storytelling thunder. He said, 'Wait until you hear about Viv!'

'Marshall!' Diane could really crack the whip when she wanted to. Indeed, this was Diane at her energetic best, talking without a martini to hand, but that lack was about to be filled.

Jury said, 'There's a nice little tearoom right behind you on the other side of the street.'

If a look could shrug, hers did. 'There's a nice little bar right in front of me on this side.' When it came to bars, Diane was a radar gun; she could pick them out faster than traffic police could target speeding cars.

As they filed into the Drowned Man, Jury asked, 'But what about Vivian? What's going on?'

'Viv-Viv's going to—' Trueblood's answer was cut short by the heel of Diane's shoe grinding down on his Hugo Boss one.

'Can we get a room here?' asked Diane. 'Or is there a boarding house?'

'You can join Agatha in Lemming Cottage. It's a B and B.'

Diane shuddered.

'Listen,' said Melrose, annoyed. 'Is this related to all

that stuff you were gibbering about a couple of nights ago when you woke me up at two a.m.?'

'Never mind,' said Diane, homing to the bar.

When they were seated round a table and had been served by the unenthusiastic and underemployed Pfinn, Melrose said, 'You should have taken the train from Paddington station instead of doing all that driving.'

Diane actually stopped the first martini on its way to her blood-red lips. 'Taken *what*?' She had never been one to explore alternative modes of travel.

'You made good time if you left Long Pidd this morning.'

'We didn't. We left on Tuesday.'

'Tuesday? But that's three days ago!'

Trueblood smiled stingily at Diane. 'Despite the need for haste, Diane insisted on stopping at Le Manoir aux Quat' Saisons. You know, that restaurant where Raymond Blanc is the chef.'

Jury frowned. 'But isn't that place near Oxford? I was on a case once very near it.'

Trueblood pounded his drink on the table. 'Here, here! A Scotland Yard man who's a bon vivant. Yes, it is near Oxford.'

'Oxford's north, Diane. Cornwall's south,' said Melrose.

'Don't I know it,' said Trueblood. 'We stayed there two nights. Food's a rave, I'll give it that.'

This time it was Jury who pounded his pint on the table, uncharacteristically for him. 'So, give. What's this prodigious news you haven't been telling us?'

Plugging a cigarette into her long ebony holder, Diane said, 'Our Vivian's going to marry the count.'

'Count Dracula,' offered Trueblood, in case Jury had forgotten.

Which he hadn't. 'Oh, for God's sake. That's news? She's been going to marry him for – what? Eight years? Nine?' Complacent now, he drank his beer.

'No, old sweat, you don't understand. Dracula's *here*. The ship's landed, the coffin's ashore, and all over Northamptonshire there's a shortage of crosses and garlic.'

'Oh, do bloody *shut* it,' said Diane, who occasionally reverted to her Manchester upbringing. She turned to Jury and Melrose. 'He's in Long Pidd. The wedding's in two weeks' time, and she's in the process of sending out invitations. So we've come to collect you,' she said to Melrose. To Jury, she added, 'You too, except you're not so easily collected.' She sighed. 'You work for a living.' She said this as if it had a strange and alien ring to it. 'Naturally, I've been doing what I can, writing warnings into her horoscope. Things like "Beware any venture requiring new clothes".'

'Oscar Wilde said that,' Melrose informed her.

'Oh, hell, I thought I did. Then "You are about to embark on the darkest journey of your life" and "You will escalate fatuousness into a fatal fall".'

'Sounds good,' said Melrose. 'What does it mean?'

'Who cares as long as it sounds good? Anyway, none of this has had any effect, as far as I can tell.' Diane crooked a finger at Pfinn, who paid the table even less attention than Dick Scroggs would have done. Melrose got up and went to the bar, first enjoining Diane to say nothing more until he got back. He didn't want to miss a word.

As if taking Melrose literally, there wasn't a word spoken until Trueblood nodded towards the dimly lit doorway and asked, 'Whose dogs?'

They were out in full force, all five of them lined up and solidly together, staring at the newcomers' table. 'Pfinn's,' said Jury. 'They line up like that.'

'Okay, go on,' said Melrose, depositing the round of drinks and salt-and-vinegar crisps in the middle of the table.

'As I was saying, our Vivian didn't appear to be paying much attention to the horoscopes.'

'The only thing we could think of was sabotaging something or other,' said Trueblood, as he tore open one of the crisp packets.

'Sabotage?' Melrose forgot his fresh pint of Old Peculier and leaned forward, all ears.

Trueblood was searching his pockets and found what he wanted in an inside coat pocket. He unfolded a small square of white cardboard and laid it in front of Jury and Plant. 'Of course, all she has to do is hand in fresh copy. Still, I see it as delaying things for a while. One has to give the person ample time to respond.'

They both looked at it, Jury and Plant. It said:

> *The pleasure of your company*
> *is requested at*
> *the marriage of Miss Vivian Rivington*
> *and Count Dracula on*
> *the fifteenth of October at two o'clock*
> *at the church of St Rules*

Melrose sniggered. 'Did she get them?'

'Of course. The shop delivered.'

Melrose sniggered again.

Jury looked from one to the other of them. 'Of course, she would have absolutely *no* idea who did this, you simpletons.'

Trueblood raised his Campari and lime. 'Oh, I expect she'll sort that out. I've been avoiding her lately.'

'I don't wonder,' said Jury.

Diane said, languidly, 'As Marshall says, it only delays things for a while, for her to get fresh invitations printed up. I've been wracking my brain—'

Which didn't put up much of a fight, thought Melrose.

'—for some solution, but I can't come up with anything short of killing him. That is of course a possibility for us, but it would be much better were Vivian to call a halt to this thing of her own accord, which I'm sure she wants to do anyway.'

'What makes you so sure?' asked Melrose.

'*Mel*-rose, try to engage your mind, will you? Because she's having the wedding here, of course, I mean in Long Pidd instead of Venice. She's counting on us stopping it.'

Jury said, 'Come on, Diane, Vivian's not that spineless.'

'Yes, she is,' said Trueblood, though not unkindly. 'Spineless is too harsh a word, perhaps, but by now the poor girl's totally intimidated by the fact she's let this engagement go on for donkey's years.'

'What's he like, then, Dracula?' Melrose asked.

But when Trueblood opened his mouth to speak, Melrose said, 'I mean, really. I saw him once, so don't try telling me he looks like a toad.' To Jury he said, 'You remember him, don't you? We were in Stratford-upon-Avon, in the Dirty Duck.'

'Vaguely,' Jury said.

'In addition to being fairly tall, fairly dark, and fairly handsome, he's politeness on a platter and usually seems to be lost in contemplation of a world beyond the Jack and Hammer.'

'Is there one?' asked Diane, tapping ash from her cigarette. 'And am I in it?' She looked vaguely, dreamily around the room.

Trueblood went on, 'I think he's intelligent, but since he doesn't talk much, it's hard to say. It's all so – irregular.'

'What does that mean?' asked Jury.

'Vivian shouldn't marry a foreigner. She shouldn't even marry a person we don't know. He won't fit, you know, our little routines.'

Said Diane, 'He won't be *around* for our little routines, Marshall. I expect they'll want to live in Venice instead of Long Pidd.'

'Good lord!' said Jury. 'Prefer Venice to Long Piddleton? What philistines!'

Trueblood took him seriously. 'It's the truth, though. We don't like it at all.'

'Tell me, who's *we*?'

'Who? Why, the Long Piddletonians. Ada Crisp is dead against it, as is Miss Twinney. Jurvis the Butcher is all out of sorts. Dick Scroggs doesn't think this foreigner has any business just marching in here and carrying off Vivian. Trevor Sly's beside himself—'

'No,' said Jury. 'Richard *Jury*'s beside himself listening to this twaddle. Trevor Sly? Since when did any of you ever give a bloody damn what he thinks? And how did you collect these opinions anyway? Do a door-to-door canvas?'

'Well, no, not exactly . . .'

'Not exactly. What you did was buttonhole anybody you could and talk about Franco Giopinno in most unflattering terms. The point being,' Jury went on, just as testily, 'how do you know she isn't in love with him?'

Three pairs of eyes looked at him as if he'd taken leave of his senses.

Love?

Love was quickly jettisoned. 'I hope you're intending to come back with us, old sweat,' said Trueblood to Plant. 'We've got to fix up – you know – something, some way to get Viv-Viv out of this.'

Jury's tone was sarcastic, something he rarely reverted to. 'I hope it's as successful as your trip to Venice to announce my impending wedding.'

They had done this but preferred not to be reminded.

Trueblood said, 'It did *work*, Superintendent, remember? It got her back to Northamptonshire, didn't it? C'mon, Melrose, think, will you?' He tented his hand over his brow as if his brain wattage was about to blow.

Melrose sighed. 'Why bother? Look who's here to do it for us.' He nodded in the direction of the doorway.

Lady Ardry, accompanied by her doppelgänger, Esther Laburnum, filled the spot recently vacated by the five dogs. It wasn't, Melrose decided, much of a trade-off. They stood, arm in arm, then moved forward towards the table, still arm in arm, as smoothly as a couple in a ballroom dancing contest.

Said Agatha, 'Well! Here's half of Long Piddleton come like the mountain to Mohammed. I'd like to introduce my good friend Esther Laburnum.' She did so, coming round to Jury. 'And this is my great friend Superintendent Richard Jury, who's solved more cases than you could shake a stick at, but like your typical policeman is never around when you need him.' Agatha laughed at her little joke. 'Thank you,' she said to Jury, who had politely risen to pull two chairs up to the table.

Esther Laburnum, who could talk a blue streak selling property, was silent; but then, Agatha would make up for it, as she was always worth two people talking. They sat down and she ordered large sherries for both of them.

'Superintendent, this is a bad thing, isn't it? I was astounded when I heard it was that Friel woman—'

Melrose interrupted. 'I thought you said you suspected her right along, Agatha.'

'More or less. Yes, my heart does go out to that boy, having his aunt killed in that way.'

Was she, Melrose wondered, delivering a message to *this* boy, Melrose?

'What will happen to him?'

Esther Laburnum drank off her sherry in one go and,

thus lubricated, found her faculty of speech had not deserted her. 'The Woodbine is heavily in debt. Of course, it belongs to young John now, or the controlling interest does. Brenda Friel's interest in it – well, who knows who that'll go to.' She looked round the table as if she expected someone there to cough up an answer. 'She has no family I know of, except some distant relations in London; her life revolved around that girl of hers, Ramona. Oh, such a tragedy, such a tragedy. I expect John'll have to sell up to pay off the debts, but property such as that tearoom is not in demand.'

While Esther handed down this litany of woe, Agatha sat there smiling approval as if Esther was a wind-up doll set to present the opinions of its mistress.

'The dear boy,' Esther continued, 'seemed not to want to heed my advice, but then I expect he's too upset to think of practical matters. I told him that perhaps he could induce Mrs Hayter to help run the place as long as her sympathy was involved—'

Even Marshall Trueblood was taken aback, listening to such blatant cynicism.

'—to do the baking and so forth, but I couldn't imagine her doing all of it, and advised him again, quite firmly, to sell up.'

'Who's the buyer?' asked Diane Demorney, narrowly regarding Esther through a scrim of cigarette smoke.

Esther sat up straight, her hands fluttering about her throat – her pearls, her neckline. 'What? What are you suggesting?'

Diane shrugged. 'I'm not suggesting anything. I'm merely saying you must have a buyer. You seem to be so anxiously advising this boy to sell his property. Sounds like there's scarcely a moment to lose, I mean, seeing how you intrude upon his grief this way.'

There was dead silence, as there so often is if one speaks a hugely embarrassing truth. Diane looked at Melrose and then away again with a tart little smile. A speech like this from Diane came around as often as a chorus of carolling goldfish at Christmas.

Esther Laburnum looked to Agatha for something – support, Melrose imagined. And pigs might fly. Esther then took the only course open to her: she changed the subject. In a simpering manner, she said to Melrose, 'Lord Ardry, I don't imagine you had any idea what you were in for when you took Seabourne House.'

This innocuous observation called forth nothing from Melrose but, 'No, I didn't.'

'It was so dreadful, what happened to those poor Bletchley children. Unimaginable.'

'Not, unfortunately, unimaginable. Someone was very able to imagine it.'

'But it's still a mystery. Had she – you know – anything to do with it?'

She-you-know meaning Brenda Friel. Hers was now a name one best not speak, as if it carried in it some black enchantment that might lead other innocents down to the sea.

Melrose answered, 'Not that I know of.'

Esther kept going. 'And that poor young man at Bletchley Hall. I heard she was the one who shot him. Good heavens! Her mind was obviously disturbed, wasn't it?'

Jury said, 'There was a great deal of disturbance.' He rose. 'I'm going to collect my things. Got to head back to London.'

'Now? Oh, surely not!' said Esther Laburnum, as if she was fully conversant with Jury's job.

'I'm afraid so. As soon as I can find Sergeant Wiggins.'

'But . . .' Diane paused. 'You can at least stop in Long Piddleton. It's right on your way.'

'For anyone who thinks Oxford is on the way to Cornwall, yes, I suppose it is.' Jury smiled.

'But we've been absolutely *counting* on you.'

Jury laughed. 'Not too much, Miss Demorney. You only saw me an hour ago.'

Diane wasn't giving up. 'But that's the effect you have on people, don't you know? The minute one *sees* you, one begins to count on you. One begins to undertake all sorts of supposedly *impossible* schemes because you can pull one *through*.'

Jury laughed harder. 'You can certainly take a compliment and run with it.'

Melrose said, 'I'll be cutting my visit short, Miss Laburnum; I'll be returning to Northamptonshire with my friends.'

'I myself,' said Agatha, 'will be staying on in Bletchley a bit longer.'

Was that a collective sigh of relief Melrose heard?

'Esther here is giving me a crash course in property selling. She seems to think I've a natural aptitude for it.'

Melrose felt like resting his head in the peanut bowl. Agatha couldn't sell anyone a winning lottery ticket.

Imagine her trying to sell a house. He felt weak with held-back laughter.

'Well, I don't see what's so amusing about that! I've nothing more to say to you, Melrose, nothing at all.'

'Oh, I don't know. You could say you've been to Bletchley, but you've never been to you.' Melrose tossed a handful of peanuts into his mouth and smiled.

Jury was upstairs packing ('my meagre belongings'); Trueblood was valuing the furniture ('A George the First bureau, by God; do you think this Bletchley fellow would let it go?'); and Diane and Melrose were standing in the hall as she gazed round and round and finally landed on the staircase.

'Melrose, did you ever see an old film . . . what was its name? It was before my time of course – most things are – but it's on video. It's about this old house . . .'

Diane recounted the entire story of *The Uninvited* as Melrose stood rooted, mouth agape, absolutely flummoxed by the idea that he and Diane shared a common memory.

'It always made me feel—'

Diane *feeling*?

'– rather queer, rather off.'

Even if the feelings hardly reached beyond the murky depths of 'queer' and 'off'.

'As a matter of fact, Diane, yes, I do know it. *The Uninvited*, it's called. I thought of it the first time I saw this house.' He was prepared to explore this strange coincidence of his and Diane's being, possibly, the only two people in the world besides Dan Bletchley, who had seen and remembered *The Uninvited*. 'Now, the music, if you recall—'

'But the *girl*, Melrose. That dreadful white dress!'

So much for exploration; they were back safely in Demorney territory of paper tigers and cardboard alligators and designer wardrobes. She was plugging a cigarette into her foot-long holder, which he then lit.

'What are you going to do about Vivian, Melrose?'

'Do?'

'Yes, do.'

'Oh . . . Trueblood and I will think of something.'

Diane heaved a great sigh. 'I'm not *talking* about one of your daffy *schemes*. Good God, I still remember that black notebook business.'

Melrose preferred to forget it. To pay her back, he smirked and said, 'You wouldn't be interested in Count Dracula yourself, would you?'

Diane looked pained. 'Don't be absurd. I don't want to live in Venice. All that wine and water.'

'You make it sound like quite a religious experience.'

Looking round, as if she expected the doors of a drinks cabinet to fly open on seeing her, Diane asked, 'You wouldn't have any vodka about, would you?'

'Oh, I'm sure we can find some.'

Martini in hand – or, rather, vodka in hand, vermouth having eluded their search, 'as if it mattered' – Diane trailed after Trueblood, making unschooled comments about the carpets and sideboards and silver and never shutting up, no matter how many times he told her to.

Jury had come down with his duffel bag.

'Three weeks in Ireland and that's all you took?'

'Since one might not survive three days, I didn't see the sense in packing for a long and happy life, right?'

'Did you call Macalvie? You said you were going to.'

'No. I thought we'd stop in Exeter. Unlike Oxford, it *is* on the way.'

Melrose pulled him aside (as from an unseen audience) and said, 'Listen, you really should stop off in Long Piddleton.'

'And *like* Oxford, that is not on the way.'

'Come on. Vivian would listen to you.'

Jury laughed. 'No, she wouldn't. And who the hell are we to tell her what to do? It's her life.'

'Oh, *please*. You're not going to resort to that old cliché, made up for people who want to abnegate responsibility?'

'She's my responsibility? *Moi?*' Jury clapped his hands to his chest.

'Certainly. It's not "her" life.'

'It isn't? Then whose?'

'All of ours. You've got to do something, Richard. She'd listen to *you*.'

Jury just gazed at him.

'Don't give me that look. It's your *what a chump* look.'

'It is indeed.'

64

Brian Macalvie did the search himself.

He'd been permitted a 'limited' warrant to search only for this tape, and for this tape only. Anything else found in the course of the search could be appropriated. *Her rights*, thought Macalvie. He was only glad there wasn't anything else he wanted, at least not at the moment.

The tape was in a kitchen cupboard that Brenda reserved for over three dozen prettily wrapped packages of ginger biscuits waiting to be apportioned half to Bletchley Hall and half to a home for abused wives and children in Truro.

How fucking thoughtful, Macalvie thought.

The two packages were the same size as all the others and wrapped in identical colourful paper, the only difference being that these two did not wear one of the WOODBINE TEAROOM silver stickers. That was to tell Brenda which packages held the tapes. Damned funny if someone was expecting biscuits and found that film instead.

Damned funny, thought Macalvie.

⋆ ⋆ ⋆

Brenda had sat three hours longer in that scarred and straight-backed wooden chair. She was not going to give up the tapes. She looked at him and exhaled smoke from the last cigarette in her packet into the already smoke-filled room.

'What's the difference?' she said. 'Why would you want to know anything more than the fact Simon Bolt did film it. It's what I already told you. I shouldn't think the details of their deaths would be very pleasant to watch.'

'I'm sure.' Macalvie had risen and was pacing in the room's semi-darkness. The only available light was that coming from the shaded bulb hanging above the table, casting a pool of bleached light over her hands. Shadows played tricks with her face.

Macalvie stopped pacing. 'The thing is, Brenda, it's not past. It'll never be past for the Bletchleys. It will never be past for Morris Bletchley.'

'May I have a cup of tea?'

Macalvie ignored this as he had every request she'd made, except going to the loo. A WPC had escorted her. She had also been given water. The police code no doubt dictated a certain amount of consideration should be given the witness, but Macalvie didn't give a damn.

He continued, 'Morris Bletchley has been living in a sort of limbo – you yourself predicted that – not knowing exactly what happened: how they got down there, what made them stay. Not knowing is a kind of hell. You must have experienced something like it, though hardly to the extent Bletchley did.' He stopped and waited.

'You're not going to show that tape to *Morris Bletchley*, for God's sake!'

It was the only time in this interrogation she had actually shown some emotion. And what she apparently felt was shock and gratification. And hunger, a hunger to enlarge upon the old man's suffering. It showed in her face, which appeared to lose some of its pliant smoothness and take on a bony, chiselled gauntness, as if a death's head were showing through. The tricks of shadows.

Macalvie said, 'Don't you think Bletchley deserves to know what happened? Now, you've got nothing to lose if he knows.'

She actually tilted that skeletal face back and laughed, the laughter like some residue of a saner time, even a carefree time, when her daughter was alive. But it was just that: a residue, quickly used up. Nothing to laugh about now, except . . .

'Morris Bletchley.' She sighed. 'How I wanted to send it to him! But that wasn't the purpose of the film; that would have been icing on the cake.'

Icing on the cake. Macalvie turned away.

'I knew I wasn't clever enough to outwit the army of investigators he'd hire.'

Macalvie interrupted. 'You told me all that.' He splayed his arms on the table and leaned close to her. 'So you can make this your dying wish, can't you? Poor old Bletchley watching that tape.'

Brenda smiled that thin death's-head smile.

She told him.

★　★　★

Macalvie sat in Brenda Friel's little sitting room watching a hand-held camera panning the dark cliff and the shiny-wet stair down to the water behind Seabourne. That little oblong from the top of the plastic casing was missing, but it still worked in the VCR.

Some sort of light arrangement had been set up near the stone steps, which would have revealed this little drama had anyone else been there to see it. But there was only Mrs Hayter, whose room was on the other side of the house.

Moonlight augmented the artificial, making the latter almost superfluous. The camera followed a pretty girl – how old? Teens, most likely – wearing a dress made diaphanous by the moon, and Macalvie wondered at what uses beauty could be put to. The whole scheme needed a woman, any woman, to go down the steps with them, to make them feel at all safe. Macalvie could only speculate on the little kids' feelings; he imagined daring was outweighed by the adventure of it all.

The stone steps, after all, were utterly familiar. It certainly wasn't the first time they'd gone down them. Of course, they'd been told never to go down them without an adult. Well, here was an adult to make it safe.

They stood either side of the older girl. She was holding their hands as they stood, posing for the camera, at the top of the stairs. The little girl Esmé's sharp giggle startled Macalvie. He had expected the sound of the sea but not of the children.

The three of them started down the steps in a sort of

awkward single file, the girl in between, holding both of the children's hands. Esmé, the older, was in front; Noah was behind.

The camera followed close behind. There was only a bit of wind and Mounts Bay was almost calm, water insinuating itself under the boat and gently washing over the steps at the bottom. The Bletchleys' boat rocked peacefully in the slurred waves, tethered by a long rope anchored by a ring in the cliffside.

Even as Macalvie watched, he could swear another step, further up, was now sluiced by water. It was as if the tide were obliging Bolt's camerawork, a fake sea against fake rocks. But there was no denying the power of this terrible film as Macalvie watched the children go further and further down the steps and the camera move further and further back, as if it did not want to chance going down to those bottom steps.

But the camera could make out what was happening at the bottom. The children were now into water that covered their feet but still delighting in this game, one part of which seemed to be something the young girl had taken from her shoulder bag, but whatever it was, was hidden by her back.

Macalvie leaned closer, squinting as she turned and the viewer could see what she was doing. A bracelet winked in the light. No. A choke chain, something a dog owner would put on an unruly pet. His mouth went completely dry. How could he have missed it, for God's sake? Looking at what she was doing: two chains, one for Noah, one for Esmé, gone around their wrists and then hooked to the ring that kept the boat moored.

Esmé's right wrist, Noah's left, their other two hands free.

The water was up their legs now. They had stopped laughing. Bolt now dared the slippery steps (fucking coward, afraid he'd get wet?) and the camera honed in on their faces. The faces were beginning to crumple. Both of them wanted to stop the game, to go back up the cliff.

But it was the young woman who went back up, and then of course they knew. They were trapped at the bottom in water now waist high and they couldn't move more than a few feet. They wept; they began to howl with fear. The girl kept walking up the steps.

And then Esmé became aware of the boat, shoved a little closer to the cliff by the waves. She grabbed Noah's hand and lunged for it. If they could reach the boat, it would buoy them up.

Macalvie was standing now. He was watching the children manoeuvring towards the boat (and the boat, as if in silent assent, rocking towards them); he was watching as if this was a story whose ending was as yet unknown. As if the little kids really were actors and the scene was counterfeit.

She made it. Esmé was close enough to haul herself into the boat and then to drag Noah in after her, once she—

But the girl went back down the steps as quickly as the slippery surface permitted. She went into the waist-deep water and pulled Esmé and Noah out and shoved at the boat, which then turned and floated out of reach.

The children screamed. Macalvie shook his head at

this visceral image. They'd been so close to saving themselves. He looked, then, to see their faces, the last view he'd get of their faces before the waves washed over them, and then their two free hands, holding onto each other, raised above the water—

And that was all.

That was the end.

Macalvie crossed his arms on the table, lowered his head to them, and wept.

65

Melrose might have said that Count Franco Giopinno pretty much lived up to expectations, except for his ability to cast a reflection in a mirror and appear without apparent difficulty during the daylight hours and in public at the Jack and Hammer.

That was where Melrose had first seen him, entering with bright daylight at his back, dramatically silhouetted in the doorway through which Vivian Rivington had just preceded him.

Franco Giopinno paused there to light a cigarette he'd extracted from a gold case. If he was posing, it was effective. The contours of his face looked sculpted, chiselled, hardly flesh.

'At least,' said Diane, seated at their favourite table in the window, 'he smokes.'

'But what,' asked Joanna Lewes, their local writer of romance stories, 'does he drink?'

Trueblood immediately whisked out his money clip, clapped down a note, and said, 'Fiver says Campari and lime.'

Melrose pulled out a ten-pound note and slapped

that down, saying, 'Dry dry dry dry dry sherry. A glass of dust.'

Joanna put down a twenty. 'Gin and tonic.'

Diane covered those two bills with a ten-pound note of her own. 'Definitely dry dry dry dry, but a martini' – she pondered – 'olive, ice. Though God only knows why anyone would want to water down vodka.'

Even Theo Wrenn Browne, not ordinarily at their table and certainly not ordinarily a betting man (as it cost money), carefully extracted two pound coins from his purse and put them down.

'Red wine, probably burgundy.'

'Theo,' said Diane, 'that's only two pounds.'

'It's only red wine, too.'

'We're not *buying*, we're *betting*,' said Joanna.

Diane said, voice low, 'He knows how to dress, that's certain.'

The count had now met two of the Demorney criteria for 'amusing'. It was true; he did know how to dress. His suit was of such a fine material that it aroused one's tactile sense, as if one simply had to touch it. It was a fine soft grey, the colour of the ash hanging from the end of Diane's cigarette.

'Um-*um*, um-um, um-*um*,' murmured Diane.

'Armani, Armani, Ar-*man*-i,' murmured Trueblood.

'He's coming,' whispered Browne. 'Don't stare!'

Theo then looked everywhere else, as if not seeing this Armani-in-the-flesh bearing down on them, an ashen angel whose presence Vivian didn't seem to register, for she walked straight to the table.

She did remember to introduce him, and quite

graciously. One could hardly blame poor Vivian's nervousness and reticence; she'd taken so much over the years on this man's account.

The table needed one more chair, so the count wheeled one round and placed it beside Vivian's. Small talk about Italy, about Venice, occupied them for the few moments it took Dick Scroggs to make his way over to the table for orders.

'Just a sherry,' said Vivian.

And the count? 'Pellegrino.'

Scroggs asked, 'You mean the fizzy stuff? That mineral water, like?'

Giopinno nodded.

Scroggs started to move away when Diane said, 'And what?'

'Pardon?' The count's smile was a trifle supercilious.

'Pellegrino and *what*?'

'Nothing. I always drink water *minerale*. Good for you.'

Looking at Diane Demorney's expression, one might challenge that last statement. Melrose hoped she had not gone into a coma, and that hers was merely like that look of wild surmise that Keats attributed to Cortez, or perhaps that seaward look on the face of Hardy's heroine, 'prospect impressed'.

For that of course was what 'water' meant to Diane – the sea, a river, something to swim in, to boat on, to idle by. One might wash in it, dip one's pedicured toes in it, give one's flowers another measure of it. It even had its uses in tea or coffee, whereupon it ceased to be 'water'.

The only thing one didn't do was drink it. The count contravened that rule, airily pouring the bubbly stuff into the tall glass Dick Scroggs had brought him, and drank it down.

They all looked at the money on the table.

You could have heard a pin drop.

Today was Melrose's second encounter with Vivian's intended.

'Where's our Viv?' asked Trueblood of Franco Giopinno as they sat round the table in the window of the Jack and Hammer.

Giopinno's smile was knowing and proprietorial. 'Gone to London.' He exhaled a stream of smoke, thin as his smile. 'To see about her dress.'

'Ah,' said Diane. 'Then she isn't going to wear her mother's?'

Not only did Giopinno raise a questioning eyebrow, Trueblood and Plant did as well.

Diane also blew out a dragonlike puff of smoke. 'Mad Maud's.'

The eyebrows went higher all around the table.

'Well, surely she told you about her mum.'

'No. No, she didn't,' said Giopinno.

When both Trueblood and Plant seconded this 'no', Diane gave them a blistering look as if she'd seen quicker uptakes. 'Don't tell me *you two* don't know about Vivian's mother.' This was said in such a slow, lesson-for-idiots way that both of them wiped the confusion from their countenances and said, oh, yes, of course. Sad little story, that.

'And what might that sad little story be?' asked Giopinno.

'Oh, it's just the family, you know, with this strain of madness which only turns up in the women, for some reason,' said Diane, who then quickly, falsely, took Vivian off the hook of this crazy streak in the Rivington ladies. 'I don't mean that Vivian—'

Pompously, Trueblood put in, 'Of course not, no, not Viv-Viv. I certainly wouldn't say that little episode last year had anything to do with the mother and so forth.'

'Episode?'

'Oh, never mind,' said Diane. 'It was nothing.'

'Nothing at all. Hardly worth the mention. I wonder you even bring it up, Diane. I mean, after all, it's Vivian's business—'

'Let's just drop it,' said Melrose. 'It's nothing, anyway.'

Franco Giopinno looked from one to the other, chillingly. 'There is probably some level of madness in every family. Certainly, there is in mine.' He excused himself and walked over to the bar where Scroggs apparently gave him directions to the gents'.

'Oh, bloody great,' said Trueblood. 'Certainly-there-is-in-mine! How condescending, how fatuous.'

'They both can sit around going crazy together. What a lark.' Melrose watched Giopinno's elegantly suited figure disappear into the dark environs of Scroggs's back rooms.

Diane looked at Melrose. 'Vivian, darling, is not crazy. God, you two.'

'A brilliant idea, though, Diane.'

Trueblood had plucked a stub of pencil and an old

envelope from one of his pockets. 'We must make a list.' Trueblood loved lists. 'A list of anything that might provoke some anxiety in old Drac. Now' – he scrunched down over the bit of paper – 'money is notorious for provoking it. I'll just put that down.' He wrote. Then, 'Okay, what else?'

'Property,' said Melrose.

Trueblood paused for a beat. 'But wouldn't that be covered by money? It's part of the estate, after all.'

'Yes, but it's not liquid. There's her house, probably bring in a million quid on today's market, but there's no cash flow there.'

Trueblood grunted, nodded. 'Okay, I have "Property" down under "Money" as a kind of subheading.'

Diane screwed another cigarette into her ivory holder and said, 'Cohorts. Friends and cohorts.'

Trueblood frowned. 'But that's us.'

'Don't be ridiculous, Marshall. I'm talking about anyone around who might be considered unsavoury. Tonight, the two of you could begin by taking him to dinner. Somewhere rather awful; that should be easy around here.'

'You mean the three of us. You too.'

'Melrose, I have no intention of eating anywhere awful. No, you two must do it. Three of us would be too threatening. Anyway . . .' She sat tapping her fingernail on her glass. Ordinarily, she only did this when she wanted her glass refilled, so she must have been thinking hard. 'We'll divide it up. You two take "friends and cohorts" and I'll take "money and property".' She sat up straighter. 'Hush. Here he comes.' She whispered,

'Remember, dinner tonight, somewhere awful.'

'Awful' was probably the first word that came to mind in describing the Blue Parrot, Trevor Sly's one or two acres of Mojave or Sahara. The gaudy sign on the main Northampton road pictured a smoky room, a belly dancer, dark-featured and festooned gentlemen in turbans and golden chains in a scene meant to depict a place such as Tangier. The sign pointed the thirsty traveller down a rutted, narrow road, at the end of which was what one might have taken for a mirage: a bright blue building sitting in a waste of stubble and sandy gravel.

Leaving behind him the scorching Arabian sun (or so it must have made the count feel) and entering the cooler environs of the pub, Franco Giopinno stood for a while staring at the camel.

Trueblood gave him a little dig in the ribs. 'Clever, that. Sly has so much imagination.'

'Sly? You confuse me, dear man.'

'Trevor Sly's the owner.'

'And is the owner a foreigner, then?'

'Only if you consider Todcaster foreign.'

Said Melrose, 'Many do, I'm sure.' He was scanning the menu on the black board set into the papier-mâché camel's middle. It was the same as always. Half a dozen unpronounceable Middle Eastern or Lithuanian dishes. He was familiar with only one, one being enough.

Trueblood said, 'The Blue Parrot is way off the beaten track—'

The count choked up a derisive laugh. 'I can well imagine.'

'– but it's Vivian's favourite place to dine.'

'That I *can't* imagine.'

Melrose, who had left the camel to make its own way, was standing now at the bar. 'Hey! You two!' He waved them forward. 'We want to order before he closes the kitchen.'

Joining Melrose, the count looked at his watch in astonishment, pointing out that it was but six thirty.

'Sly is eccentric; he shuts down the food by seven.'

Again, astonishment from the count. 'But that is very early to dine. Does this Sly have to feed the camels?'

Melrose and Trueblood whooped with laughter. Only 'whooping' could describe the breathy, braying noises that came from their throats. It was such staged laughter that Melrose was amazed the man could be taken in.

Trevor Sly made his angular entrance, his sharp shoulder blades separating the beaded curtain, which tinkled behind him, his thin gnarled hands washing each other in the insincere supplication Melrose was used to. This tendency towards deference greased all the joints of his tall body. He was a study in seeming submission.

'Gentlemen, gentlemen, so honoured.' His hands kept washing away. 'Mr Trueblood, Mr Plant, and . . .?' Sly raised a quirky eyebrow as he looked at the count, who bowed slightly and tendered his name.

He pronounced it, thought Melrose, almost as well as Diane, hitting those first two syllables with a hammer so that they came out Gee-yp-*peen*-o, almost with the unfractured sound of *gyp*.

And now, as if the gods looked down for a good

laugh, Sly asked, 'And how is Miss Rivington? Always enjoy seeing Miss Rivington.'

For once, Trevor Sly's trying to convince his listener that everybody in the English-Arabic-speaking world loved nothing more than a drink and a meal at the Blue Parrot ('Tony Blair only just missed the turnoff; I'll have to do something about the placement of my sign')—for once Melrose welcomed Sly's name-dropping. They might have dragged Vivian here once, but certainly once had been enough for her. Melrose had never been able to sort out just how Sly managed to keep the place running, for in all the times he'd been here he'd never seen more than one or two other people.

'You've not run out of the Kibbi Bi-Saniyyi, now?' said Melrose, turning to the count. 'You must have that,' he said, clamping his hand on Giopinno's shoulder. He and Trueblood had been doing a lot of clamping, punching, and shaking of the count.

Trevor Sly had drawn their beer – a Cairo Flame for the count – despite the man's preference for Pellegrino. Trueblood insisted. 'Good lord, you don't expect our old drinking buddy Vivian to quaff mineral water!'

Sly had helped himself to a tot of cognac after Melrose told him to have a drink on them and was sitting on his high stool, legs wound round its legs like ivy. Now he said, 'There's been a real run on that today, Mr Plant.' To the count, he said, 'You see, it's my specialty of the house—'

If no one was ever *in* the house, how could the kitchen have had a run on anything?

'– but I'm sure I can eke out one order of Kibbi Bi-

Saniyyi, seeing it's you, Mr Giopinno.' Sly had it rhyming with Geronimo.

'Eke-ing out' was about all the Kibbi Bi-Saniyyi could do.

Mr Giopinno said he would gladly give up the order to Mr Plant or Mr Trueblood; Mr Plant and Mr Trueblood waved away his most generous offer.

'No, no,' said Trueblood. 'You must have it; that dish is Vivian's favourite and she makes it herself now, having got the recipe from Trevor here.'

Trevor looked about to interrupt, and Trueblood hurried on.

'Miss Rivington is soon to be married, Mr Sly, and *this* is the lucky man!' He punched Giopinno's shoulder.

Sly was all astonishment. 'Well, I never . . . well, that's good news, isn't it, gentlemen? And when's the happy event to be?'

'Next month,' said Trueblood. 'October . . . tenth? Is that it?'

Giopinno seemed a bit reluctant to confirm this. 'We were thinking of the fifteenth. There has been some little problem with the invitations.' His smile was a trifle weak.

Sly said, 'You'll be living in Italy, I expect? How romantic.' Back on his stool after pouring himself – at Melrose's suggestion – another slug of cognac, he said, 'And where is the reception to be?'

Melrose said, 'Why not here, Mr Sly? They could come by camel.'

Before the count could clarify their intention to live in Italy, Melrose said, 'Not in Italy altogether, no. Much of the time they'll be living right here!' He pounded the bar as if 'right here' really did mean 'right here'.

Unfortunately for him, the count had just taken a mouthful of Sly's Cairo Flame and choked on it. The beer was hellish all by itself; coupled with the announcement that he would always have access to it by living 'here' – that was hell indeed.

'So they'll be in Italy only part of the year,' Melrose said. This was, actually, what Vivian had told them. The truth was so relaxing, he reflected. One didn't have constantly to be keeping track; one could always revert to it with confidence and a clear conscience. Melrose raised his glass and Trueblood followed suit. 'So drink up! Mr Sly, bring on the Kibbi Bi-Saniyyi.'

'And another Cairo Flame for Franco, here!' Melrose clapped him again on the shoulder.

66

To her credit, Diane Demorney was not, for once, looking out for number one. She had no designs on Franco Giopinno. Had she at first been a little smitten, that went out the window with San Pellegrino. He was certainly handsome but not really awfully amusing. Indeed he seemed a bit dry, a bit too literal, and (Diane was certain) a bit too poor.

It was plain as the nose on his well-chiselled face that the man was a fortune hunter, a type of which Diane could hardly disapprove, having been one herself for so long and having been amply rewarded for her troubles by her three wealthy ex-husbands.

Yes, she knew the signs because she knew herself: cool reserve, an excessive desire to please, masked by a certain hauteur (for one couldn't be seen as a pushover, could one?), but more than anything else – tenacity. And God only knew, Giopinno was tenacious. No man could put up with the ambivalence of Vivian Rivington (who definitely needed to be *taken in hand*) unless he knew he would be rewarded handsomely.

It was the following morning and the two – Diane

Demorney and Franco Giopinno – sat in the little café annexed to the library. Marshall Trueblood's idea of introducing 'Latte at the Library' had been a howling success and had saved the librarian's goose. Otherwise, the place might just have been closed down for lack of custom, whereas now it was quite abuzz with the stuff.

Two tables away sat Plant and Trueblood; Diane had insisted (out of the count's hearing, of course), 'Leave, or sit by yourselves! Too many of us would look like harassment!' They sat at the corner table, pretending to read a couple of library books.

Diane had made small arrangements herself. One of these had just walked in: Theo Wrenn Browne, the owner of the local bookshop (who'd been behind trying to get rid of the library). When Diane had first settled in Long Piddleton, she'd found Theo Wrenn Browne rather amusing, with his conniving, acerbic temper and relentless attacks on other Piddletonians. But he had fast become rather a bore, for there was no acerbic wit to match the acerbic temperament.

Now, Theo stood in the doorway of the café, looking around in that self-important way of his, as if he couldn't make out where Diane and Giopinno were sitting (although there were only six tables). Theo was waiting for *her* to see *him*. It helped his flailing ego to have her raise her hand and motion him over. She did, he went.

Theo had been told that the count was looking for a solid business investment and was especially interested in books. 'A bookshop such as – oh, what is it – Waterstone's? One of those discount places.' The count had said this, he had said *precisely* this, with no further augmentation of the subject by way of his wanting to own a bookshop. They had been talking about reading. Diane avoided it and so (she thought) did he. That was because he talked about it so much. To quiet him, she brought up Henry James. She brought up *The Portrait of a Lady*. 'You remember' – of course he didn't – 'that awful clash of cultures? How the sweet young heiress falls into the clutches of the corrupt Europeans?' Diane truly warmed to this subject. 'And that absolutely dreadful husband of hers? They lived in Venice, coincidentally.'

This was the sum and substance of Diane's knowledge of the Henry James novel. And of the entire James oeuvre. It was simply one of the bits of knowledge she gleaned from reading just a little so she'd never have to read a lot.

Oh! But Franco Giopinno had gone more than a little white when she'd brought that up! Indeed, she considered reading more of this author's work; James just might be amusing if he could call up such a look of trepidation on Giopinno's face.

Theo was at the counter getting himself a latte, and Diane called to him to get Count Giopinno another espresso. Looking disgruntled, Theo gave the order. Espresso (she thought) was probably the only thing the count had enjoyed in the last twelve or sixteen hours.

Theo set the little cup before the count; Diane performed the introductions, the count gave his little seated bow and a *grazzi*, and Theo started in immediately talking about his bookshop. Theo was about as soigné as a skunk, Diane thought, which was the reason for choosing him.

'So, Mr Giopinno, excuse me, *Signore Giopinno*, you're interested in books? I have, you know, the local bookshop called the Wrenn's Nest – bit of a pun there, you know? Anyway, it's done extremely well, had a gross of – oh, one hundred and fifty thousand pounds this past year, looking to do even better by the end of this year . . .'

And on and on, with Giopinno looking – well, bemused, at best. He did, however, have silky manners and would never in the world have presented a bored countenance.

Diane, turning Theo out, glanced at Melrose and Marshall, who had given up all pretence of reading and were leaning as far as they could towards her table, trying to hear. She made a lightning-quick run with her finger across her neck. Immediately they went back to their books. Marshall, she noticed, was reading his upside down. God.

'. . . that the area could easily support one of your chain bookshops – not that I'm suggesting we get a Dillons, God, no; an independently-run big bookshop, that's the ticket!'

While Theo droned on, Diane waited for Agatha to appear. Diane had told Agatha that the count was interested in investing in property; she had suggested using Vivian's house as an example.

'Why? Vivian's living in it.'

'Oh, but of course she'll want to sell it when she moves to Venice.'

Agatha now stood in the café's doorway, and that woman was with her, that estate agent from Cornwall. All the better. Diane waved and smiled.

Theo Wrenn Browne excused himself and took his empty cup up for a refill. He detested Agatha except on the occasions she was useful to his cause. His biggest cause was getting rid of Miss Ada Crisp so he could expand his quaint little bookshop.

The two women hurried over to the table as if property deals were falling from the ceiling and were introduced to Franco Giopinno. Graciously, he rose and made a brief hand-kissing movement and sat down again, looking extremely unhappy.

'Well, now, Franco,' said Agatha, never one to stand on ceremony or good manners. 'You've got a marvellous property turnover here, and it's wise to consider an investment. Vivian's house, for instance, is better got rid of than kept. It's high-end, not practical with all that thatch, which clearly needs rethatching; in a little place like this – well, there's not much call for such properties, and if one needs the money—'

A look at the count's face made it clear one did.

'– the wise thing to do is sell up and put the money in other properties.'

'God!' exclaimed Theo Wrenn Browne, who'd returned with his fresh cup of cappuccino. 'Property's a hell of an investment these days. You don't want property, Count, you want—'

'I beg your pardon – Mr Browne, is it? You own that sweet little bookshop?'

Theo fumed. 'Sweet' and 'little' was not the picture

he was trying to get across. 'I'm expanding, got to, what with all the custom—'

'To where?' asked Agatha, shaking with manufactured laughter. 'You lost out on Ada Crisp's place next door. Shouldn't have started that lawsuit, it only made you look bad.'

Considering it was Agatha's lawsuit, Diane reflected on the shortness of the memories and the division of the loyalties of some of these people.

Esther Laburnum picked up with what she'd been about to say to Theo. 'You're quite wrong to think property a poor investment; it never is. You just have to know what you're doing.'

As with anything, thought Diane. Blowing a curl of smoke into the air, she saw the awful Withersby woman leaning up against the counter and talking the ear off little Alice Broadstairs. Mrs Withersby charred here occasionally. She fitted the cohort *and* property category to a T. Now if she could only work the woman in.

Mrs Withersby, doughty advocate of positioning herself wherever drink and smokes were being consumed, worked herself in. There was, after all, a new person sitting at that table who might be good for a glass or two.

As she approached, Agatha was saying, 'What Vivian could do, once she sells up, is buy one or two of the almshouses where those Withersby people live.'

'Someone callin' fer me?'

Yes, thought Diane. *God is*. She closed her eyes briefly and gave thanks to Saint Coincidence. She hadn't set foot in a church in decades. The closest she'd got was that wine-tasting in the vestry of St Rules. Now she wondered if her judgement about the faith had been too hasty. 'Mrs Withersby!' She'd never said more than two words to the woman in her life. Now she was offering her cigarette case. 'I'd like you to meet Count Franco Giopinno.'

Having helped herself to four of Diane's cigarettes, she looked the count up and down. 'Don't know as you'd fancy me as a neighbour.'

Giopinno, his colour having gone from white to whiter, rose and, bowing to the three women said, 'If you will be so kind as to excuse me, I have an urgent call to make – my mother.' He mumbled something about his mother's illness as he put on his coat; then he slipped away like smoke.

Diane excused herself and went to sit with Plant and Trueblood.

'Where's he going? Is he *gone*?'

'I'd certainly imagine so. He went to call his *mother*, for God's sake, mumbling something about her being ill. That, I suspect, is the prelude to his having to leave suddenly.' She sighed and said, 'Well, that's sorted, then.'

She felt something akin to sadness, such as children feel when their favourite game is over and they have to go in to tea.

67

Brian Macalvie rose when Morris Bletchley – without his wheelchair – came into the blue room, which Macalvie had been sharing with an old lady dressed in dark blue, as if she meant her dress to match the silk upholstery of the chair she sat in. She had spoken to him only once, and that to ask him to turn her chair so that it faced the window. He had done so, and since then she had sat and stared out. Occasionally, her lips moved and she smiled.

'Commander Macalvie,' said Bletchley. They shook hands.

Macalvie said, 'I wanted you to know what's happened. We've got the person who shot Sada Colthorp and Tom Letts *and* Chris Wells in custody.'

'Constable Evans told me. I'm not much given to surprises, Mr Macalvie, but that damned well did it. Brenda Friel.' He shook his head and motioned to a Queen Anne wing chair covered in heavy blue velvet. 'Sit down, please.'

Seated across from Bletchley, Macalvie told him, not all but enough, about the three shootings.

Moe Bletchley said, 'But the Friel woman apparently has no qualms about killing. Why not just kill Chris to begin with? Why go to the trouble of making it look as if she'd run off?'

'For one thing, when Chris Wells came back here, Brenda thought we'd finally take her in for the murder of Sada Colthorp. And for another, she didn't want to have to. Chris Wells was her best friend. I know it sounds implausible that the woman could still think in those terms, but that's how I see it.

'Still, Brenda couldn't be sure Chris was a real danger to her. Chris knew Ramona died of an AIDS-related problem. But Chris didn't know who the father was because Brenda herself didn't know until Tom Letts mentioned Putney. Brenda knew Ramona had been working in London but didn't know she'd been working for *you*. Brenda thought Chris would work it out if Tom Letts was murdered.

'But what I think is that Chris wouldn't have done anything. I think she was too good a friend to take her suspicions to the police. I think she was like that.'

Moe sat unhappily, looking down at the carpet at his feet. 'Poor Johnny. The poor lad.'

'Yes.'

They sat in silence for a moment, and then Macalvie said, 'There's another thing, Mr Bletchley, that I think you need to know.'

Tentatively, Moe raised his eyes to look into Macalvie's. 'You're going to tell me something about Noah and Esmé. You found something else.' He said this as if new knowledge about the deaths of his grandchildren would fall on his head like an axe. He stiffened. 'Go ahead.'

Macalvie, who had never thought of himself as a comforting person, searched for words. 'That's always been a mystery. It's stuck with me. I never closed the case. I'm afraid that we'll never be sure; still, I went over the file again and wondered if the pathologists report was absolutely clear to you.'

Moe Bletchley looked at Macalvie, his eyebrows raised in question.

'It's the drowning. There were deep abrasions to Noah's skull. What must have happened was Noah slipped and was knocked unconscious and Esmé tried to pull him back and got pulled in herself. What I'm saying is that Noah wouldn't have known anything and Esmé would have drowned very fast. And drowning definitely isn't – if you have to die – the worst way to go.' *What a lie, what a bloody lie*, thought Macalvie, moving his eyes away from Bletchley's, for he was sure the old man could read the lie in them.

Moe was perceptive, but he was being told something he wanted to believe, and no matter how sharp his mind, perception went out the window. 'What you're telling me is that they didn't suffer much, that it was quick.'

'Yes, sir. I don't know if that helps at all; I just think the worst of remembering is imagining the terror a little kid would go through.'

Moe had his face in his hands now and tears leaked through his fingers. All he could do by way of answer was to nod his head.

'And probably you – you and your son – have always

felt responsible.' Macalvie leaned towards him and put his hand on the old man's shoulder. 'Mr Bletchley, you weren't responsible. Neither of you. It was a hideous accident.' Macalvie said it again. 'You weren't responsible.'

Macalvie had never had any intention of letting Morris Bletchley see the tape; saying that he did was the only way to get Brenda Friel to give it up.

He stood on the cliff above the stone steps and looked out over water like steel and a sky the colour of lead. He imagined how a visitor knowing nothing of its history would consider it an impressive, even a beautiful prospect. The bay, the sea beyond it, the ragged, precipitous cliffs had an almost calming effect on his mind. Whatever perilous events had taken place here, they had left no footprints.

Macalvie had never destroyed evidence before. He reasoned – yes, rationalized – that the tape would do little if anything for the prosecution's case against Brenda Friel; the tape wouldn't even work against Simon Bolt, had he been living, or Sada Colthorp. The only person who would be convicted on the basis of this film was the young woman who'd led the children down the steps, and Macalvie marvelled at her utter disregard for the danger this film would put her in. If she were found and charged, she might possibly enter into a plea bargain and give up the other three, but two of them were dead and the case against Brenda Friel in the deaths of Tom Letts and Chris Wells was so strong that adding conspiracy to commit other murders would merely add one more life sentence to her time.

His concern was for the Bletchleys. Why should they suffer more than they already had just to see Brenda Friel get a third life sentence? This video was what the tabloids lived for. Some unwritten law should protect innocent survivors such as the Bletchleys. Such as Maggie.

He held one of the tapes as if weighting it, reached back, and flung it as far out as he could; then he did the same with the other, watching it flip and then hang there, defying gravity for a moment and then falling.

Time ticked by as he stood there, doing nothing but looking. Grey sky, grey sea, grey cliffs. It was a relief to look out on a scene that met the eye with such utter indifference, that was blanker than the blank faces of strangers. It was one of those Indian summer days, August in September, that comes along so seldom. It was late and he should have been at Camborne headquarters an hour ago. Still, he stood there, prospect impressed.

It was getting hot. Macalvie took off his coat.

The Case Has Altered

Martha Grimes

The Lincolnshire fens are the setting for Superintendent Richard Jury's latest case. This landscape is one that can easily deceive, volunteering nothing – much like the locals of the only pub for miles around, The Case Has Altered.

There's been a double murder. The body of one woman is found on the Wash; another woman lies floating in a canal in Windy Fen. Both are connected with the manor house, Fengate: Dorcas Reese worked there; Verna Dunn was the louche ex-wife of the owner, Max Owen – a man with a passion for antiques. So when the principal suspect turns out to be Jenny Kennington, a woman Jury has long loved, he decides he needs someone inside Fengate. Someone who can impersonate an antiques expert. Who better than aristocratic Melrose Plant, detective *manqué*?

'One of the finest voices of our time. Martha Grimes is poetry' Patricia Cornwell

'Entertaining . . . intriguing . . . thoroughly researched' *Sunday Express*

0 7472 5695 0

HEADLINE

The Stargazey

Martha Grimes

Saturday night was not a night to be spending alone, riding a bus through southwest London. But had he been anywhere else, he wouldn't have seen her. She came out of The Stargazey on the Fulham Road, pulling up the collar of her fur coat against the cold November evening. He was drawn to her; he couldn't help but follow her.

Twelve hours later the body of a young woman is found in the grounds of Fulham Palace and Superintendent Richard Jury is faced with the embarrassing task of explaining his rather detailed knowledge of her last movements. But when a visit to the morgue reveals that the fur coat in question seems to have come into the possession of an entirely different woman, Jury has some questions of his own.

'Entertaining . . . intriguing . . . thoroughly researched'
Sunday Express

0 7472 5696 9

HEADLINE